T̶H̶E̶ ̶D̶U̶B̶I̶O̶U̶S̶ ̶G̶I̶F̶T̶

OF DRAGON BLOOD

Visit us at www.boldstrokesbooks.com

THE DUBIOUS GIFT
OF DRAGON BLOOD

by

J. Marshall Freeman

2020

THE DUBIOUS GIFT OF DRAGON BLOOD

ISBN 13: 978-1-63555-725-1

This Trade Paperback Original Is Published By
Bold Strokes Books, Inc.
P.O. Box 249
Valley Falls, NY 12185

First Edition: December 2020

CREDITS
Editors: Jerry L. Wheeler and Stacia Seaman
Production Design: Stacia Seaman
Cover concept by J. Marshall Freeman
Cover Design by Tammy Seidick

Acknowledgments

This book has had many loving hands helping me raise it from infancy. First and foremost, I would like to thank the other two vertices of my reading triangle, Matt W. Cook and A. M. Matte. They read every chapter as it emerged and let me know that a character had died while I sputtered, "Maybe he's just wounded!" Matt continued on as the book's godfather through all its drafts.

Thank you to beta readers, Béla Hegedus, Laura Kuhlmann, Stephen DeGrace, Matt Gordon, Stanley Freeman, Martin Cohen, Jojo Carreon, Steve Hutton, and members of the Toronto Writers' Co-operative.

Much appreciation to Stephanie Fysh for her insightful review of the second draft, and to Jerry Wheeler, my editor at Bold Strokes Books, for his keen eye and deep understanding of my book.

Two wonderful authors acted as mentors: Michael Thomas Ford, who offered kindness, advice, and encouragement; and David Demchuk, who gave generously of his time, experience, and knowledge of the publishing world.

Thanks also to author Michael Lyons of the Glad Day Bookshop for his help with market analysis.

The writing of this book was supported by the Toronto Arts Council with funding from the City of Toronto.

To Béla. You are the realm I fled to, and where I found my true home.

PROLOGUE: *Davix, the Realm of Fire*

Davix told himself it wasn't a scream; it was only the wind howling outside the Atmospherics Tower. But the windy season was not yet upon them, and the seasonal fog was thick and still. Shaking off his worries, Davix lowered his head and continued filling the rows and columns of the workbook with meticulous notations. All the other apprentices had headed home for the night, but Davix had been busy with the Prime Magistrate for the past four days, helping to prepare for the upcoming festival of *Sarensikar*. Now he had almost a week's worth of weather data to enter in the log before he could go to sleep.

"Why is the sheep fog so heavy this cycle?" he had asked the Atmospherics Master. "Could it be spinward wind off the lava pools?"

The old man had grunted sourly in response. "These days, nothing is as it should be."

It couldn't have been a scream, could it? Davix rose to his feet, listening, every muscle taut. He tried to tune out the noises around him: the rattle of the spinning wheels that recorded wind velocity; the trickle and drip of graduated cylinders filling with rain water; the flaps and coos of the kingsolvers in their cages. Davix knew his ears had not fooled him; there was no wind. It *had* been a scream.

He stepped from the measurements room into the stairwell, closing the heavy door behind him to preserve the stove's warmth. Descending one level, he stood on the landing outside the charting room. The sturdy chair where Lraga, the chaperone, had been sitting all evening was empty. Odd.

He leaned against the door of the charting room and called. "Rinby?" The Lead Apprentice did not answer. "Rinby! I'm coming in, all right?" Looking around to make sure he wasn't observed, he pushed open the door. Notebooks like the one he had been filling were open on her desk. Drawing tools lay scattered around a half-finished chart.

Rinby's cloak was hung on a wall peg, and her pack lay by her chair. But she was gone.

Davix peered down into the stairwell. The younger apprentices had forgotten to carry their lanterns with them when they left, so while it was bright on the landing, the steps spiralled down into shadow. A finger of dread rose with the cold from below. He took a lantern off the wall, the large torchstone within glowing bright, and made the circular descent in superstitious silence.

Halfway down, his light illuminated four parallel scratches in the stone wall, dark spots at their leading edges. He touched a finger to one of the spots and brought it back with a drop of blood on the tip. A terrible certainty grew in his chest. He ran down the stairs two at a time, as if Rinby was still arcing through the air in mid-fall and a swift enough boy might still catch her.

She lay twisted at the bottom of the stairwell, legs sprawled on the last steps, blood pooled beneath her head, soaking into her braids. Davix kneeled beside the body and listened. No breath, no pulse.

He knew what he had to do. He had to speak her full name aloud so her spirit would know who it was as it crossed into the Vale of Memory. But Davix wasn't ready to accept the finality of the act. Not yet. Not like this.

"Rinby," he coaxed, touching her shoulder as if she had just fallen asleep at her desk, running formulas on wind speeds and temperature differentials. He had been jealous of her being chosen Lead Apprentice instead of him. But she never acted superior. Davix had hoped someday the Arbiter of Blood would allow her to pair with G'sander. Anyone could see how tangled they were. That would never happen now.

He was shivering. Just below him was the tower's vestibule, and he saw the main door was open, cold fog pouring in. At that moment, Lraga stepped inside, shoulders hunched against the damp. The chaperone screamed when she saw Rinby's broken body.

"What happened?" moaned Lraga. "Poor girl, poor thing!"

"She fell..." Davix heard himself saying as the chaperone began to sob. It was time to speak Rinby's full name and let her go. "T'lexdar-inby-thon," he said, his voice choking on the last syllable, her discipline name, the same as his. The tears he had been holding back began to fall.

Through the pull of emotion, Davix tried to rein in his mind. Twisting around to peer up the stairwell, he could clearly imagine Rinby slipping on the steps, braids flying, fingers scratching at the stone as she scrambled for a handhold. But Rinby was a nail biter, chewing them ever shorter when concentrating on her work. And even if they had been long, he thought, how could they have made those scratches in the ancient stone? He examined her hands and found no blood on the fingertips.

The chaperone was babbling through her sobs. "I was only gone a moment. I had to relieve myself! Please, Davix, you are close to the Prime Magistrate. Tell him I'm not to blame!"

He ignored her. In his head, Davix heard the voice of the Atmospherics Master. "These days, nothing is as it should be."

PART I

HERITAGE

CHAPTER 1: *The Monster Inside*

"Criiispiiiin?" Sylvia mewed like a cat in the rain as we contemplated the blank canvas of our poster board. "What colour should the headline be? Something confident."

"Teal?" I suggested, swallowing a phlegm ball of annoyance. *Hi! I'm the gay. Ask me style questions!*

It was eleven fifteen a.m. of that most depressing day (Wednesday) of that most depressing month (November), and we were in grade eleven history class, divided into workgroups to draw War of the Roses recruiting posters. The members of my group—Karen Parkenter, Liza Chen, and me, Crispin Haugen, the only boy—were orbiting the social centre of gravity that was Sylvia Dubrowski. How I ended up with this group of popular girls as my friends still confused me. I spent most of middle school in social isolation, not that I can really blame anyone but myself; I'm mostly too shy to put two words together. I mean with actual humans, not in my head. There, as you will soon realize, I never shut up.

"Teal, yes!" she said. "Someday, and I mean this, you're going to colour-coordinate my whole wedding."

I had accidentally shown up on my high school's gossip radar the previous March because of a disastrous breakup. Dražen was my first boyfriend, the first guy I kissed, the first guy whose name I wrote on my notebook over and over, surrounded by fireworks and coded banana doodles.

Everything was going fine until the day his parents went away and he asked me to come over to his house so he could "put it in me." When I said, "Ugh, no!" we had a major fight, and the very next day he decided to come out in a simultaneous detonation across all social media. His status changed to "in a relationship," and since I was known to be his only friend, it didn't take a genius to solve the mystery.

Dražen, I should point out, didn't take any of the shrapnel in said detonation. He was two days away from moving with his family to Vancouver. That's why he had been so eager to accelerate our sex agenda. But I wasn't lucky enough to be flying three thousand kilometres away, and for the rest of the school year, I woke up with a stomachache about the day to come.

Have you noticed how in any TV show where the gay kid is immediately and unconditionally accepted, he is also outgoing, white, and possessed of some extraordinary talent? He's a piano virtuoso or the star quarterback or the tragic victim of some enviable cancer. Well, dorks like me—half-Asian introverts with postures like question marks—don't fare as well. I didn't get thrown into lockers or anything. I wasn't really bullied, but the homophobic f-bomb was scrawled on my locker along with random racial slurs, because why not?

Contemplating my hollow eyes and full array of facial tics, my mom had asked with probing insight, "Is everything okay, Crispin?"

"Couldn't be better," I said, nibbling at my bleeding cuticles.

Then suddenly in the first week of school this year, after a summer of isolation and dread, Sylvia Dubrowski had swooped down like an eagle, and I was the little queer mouse borne lovingly aloft in her razor-sharp talons. Apparently, her social circle had acquired a hole in the shape of "gay friend." I was lucky. Liza Chen was already occupying the Asian hole, but I'm only half-Filipino, so Sylvia bent the rules. Get it? Bent?

Out in the hall after class, Sylvia did her signature Euro air-kisses with Karen and Liza and then hugged me like I was the big, pink teddy bear that lives on her bed.

"You're my best friend, Crispin!" she shouted for all to hear, and I could only think she probably knew more of the pink bear's inner life than mine. Anyway, I was too distracted to care, because Altman Shendorf, captain of the hockey team, was moving in our direction. He rolled down the hall in his big, shiny shoes like a celebrity who can't be bothered to wear a disguise, his green eyes lighting up the school's drab interior, the bulge of his crotch shining like the star in the middle of the Christmas tree.

I tried to keep my breathing even as he and Sylvia kissed sloppily. He adjusted his hair and seemed to notice me for the first time.

"Oh, hey, Crispin. You ready?"

"Unh-hnn," I grunted, swinging my knapsack around to the front to hide my hard-on, which had come on so fast, I was amazed I didn't black out.

Sylvia turned to me, her face full of concern. "You take good care of him, Crispin. He has to get at least a B minus on his English paper, or they won't let him play hockey next term."

Altman was already hiking away down the hall, and I had to scramble to catch up. By the time we were crossing the parking lot, I had matched his confident pace, bouncing along beside him, my grin splitting my face in two.

When I bumped against him, he muttered, "Don't touch me, man. Not while they can see us."

The jock clique was hanging out, hip-hop pounding from one of their cars, trying to impress the assembled girls with impromptu and frankly homoerotic wrestling moves. They greeted Altman with a howl. Him and one of his teammates traded coded monkey gestures and suggested vulgar things they would do to each other's mothers. As usual, I was not included in this male bonding. Yes, I was protected by Altman's status and not to be messed with, but I was also definitely not one of the gang.

While I waited for them to finish their boy rituals, I noticed a woman peering in through the chain link fence that marks the edge of school property. Her coppery curls were cut short, and her tailored silk suit billowed in the wind, too light for the damp chill of this November morning. The suit jacket's shoulders were wide enough for fighter planes to land on, as if she had just stepped out of some 80s music video.

Even at this distance, I felt totally x-rayed by her gaze. Did I know her? Clearly not. And yet she looked familiar, like an aunt you meet at a wedding, and she tells you how you stayed at her house for a week when you were five. But how could she be looking at me? I was the great nonentity of the universe. It was obviously Altman's grace and beauty that had her attention.

As we left the parking lot, I told him, "Some perv's perving on you."

He looked over at the woman and frowned, not doubting for a second that he was indeed the object of her attention. "What're you staring at, creeper?" he shouted, and the woman turned and hurried away down the sidewalk, disappearing around the corner.

"My hero," I said.

"What?"

"Nothing, sorry."

We walked the single block to Altman's house, buzzing with our growing excitement, and bounded up the front steps in perfect unison.

Inside, he called his mother's name, then the names of his four siblings. As usual, no one was home at lunch time. We headed straight for his bedroom on the second floor of the chaotic house, hopping over piles of clothes, schoolbooks, and sports equipment that littered the floor like landmines.

Under the dull, watchful eyes of his hockey-hero posters, Altman pushed off his shoes, threw his jacket over a chair, and began unbuckling his belt and tugging at his fly. In a flash, he was naked except for his T-shirt, dropping back onto the bed, feet on the floor, eyes focused on the ceiling. Meanwhile, I was busy opening my own pants, tearing back the curtain on the little Wizard of Oz who called the shots in my brain. We began, my mouth on Altman, my hand on myself—fast, wordless, well-practiced.

Sometimes I think there's a monster inside me. Maybe I've always known. I can clearly remember that jarring, molten feeling that flowed through me at six years old when I saw Kevin Singh's wiener at YMCA camp. How did I already know I should look away quick, only contemplate this picture in the privacy of memory? It wasn't like I understood the ramifications of my curiosity yet. I didn't know what I *was.* "Gay" was just a magic word kids intoned to cast a spell of shame on each other. But if I didn't understand that this word described me, why didn't I block the spell like the other boys? Why didn't I just respond, "Shut up! You bite farts in the bathtub" like they did? No, I was the one who blushed crimson and asked for a bathroom pass, running out before anyone saw me crying.

You know how it goes from there. You deny and deny and grow weird hair and deny some more. But eventually you have to admit that maybe you are…*different.* Eventually, the truth rises like the tide around your ankles, or else it crashes down on your head like a mighty wave. Either way, there is no unknowing. Either way, you get soaked.

Damn, I interrupted a sex scene with a bunch of journaling shit, didn't I? Sorry, where was I? Right! Crispin is on his knees, um, what's the word? *Servicing* Altman, who swears with gusto, though little imagination, when he ejaculates. This splat-tastic event is followed by Crispin's own orgasm, which can only be called poetic. He arches his back like a dancer, hand reaching into the air to thank God, nature, the cosmos. Altman lies on the bed, spent and panting, and Crispin slides up beside him, devastated and grateful. He drops his thick, two-tone hair on Altman's pretty pecs and twists around to kiss Altman's jaw. Altman lifts his head from the mattress to bring their lips together. They laugh conspiratorially at the genius of their illicit love. For it is love.

They exchange those magic words that are the simplest and richest of poetry. "I love you." "No, I love *you*," and everything is perfect. Except that last part didn't happen. Ever.

No, after the splatty bit, I dropped to the floor, thrashing in post-orgasmic spasms, graceful as a trout on a dock, while Altman sprang to his feet and climbed over me on his way to the bathroom. The speed with which Altman could be in the shower after he finished was as impressive as it was depressing. His clean-up usually lasted long enough for me to get chilled and thoroughly marinated in self-hatred.

I reached up to touch the silver chain around my neck and the silver wolf's head that hung from it. It had been a gift from my parents—well, really from my mom—on my last birthday. Before Sylvia. Before Altman.

"You're my lone wolf," she had said, trying to act like my isolation was cool and not pathetic. "But don't worry; you'll find your pack." I wondered what she'd think if she saw me like this, covered in sex mess in another boy's bedroom and still all alone. I felt a stupid tear start in the corner of my eye and shook my head violently to stop it. The little wolf's head banged against my chin.

By the time Altman returned, I had my emotional shit on a tight leash. He stood at the mirror, towel around his waist, applying product and gentle caresses to his hair pouf, which I had secretly named Norman. I put on a face of unabashed confidence, as if to say, "This is exactly how I want it. No strings, no worries."

"Here, clean up," Altman said, pulling a dirty T-shirt from the hamper and throwing it at me. "We need to look at my Hemingway essay and then get to class."

As I settled in for thirty surreal minutes of English tutoring, tasting essence-of-Altman on my breath as I fixed his sentence fragments, I found myself wondering for the hundredth time why he'd chosen me. Was I wrong to feel special? I thought of that first time behind the equipment locker, when he grabbed my hand and pushed it down his pants. I was shocked, but I wasn't going to say no; I'd been crushing on Altman since we were twelve. As we neared our first orgasms that day, I already knew it was just a matter of time before the grunting jock found the words to express his love. Three months later, my faith was getting a bit ragged around the edges, but I still believed if I loved him hard enough, he would realize he felt the same. Besides, I really, really wanted the sex.

With Altman's essay at least resembling an earnest attempt, we headed back to school. Walking with the wind in our faces, we passed leafless bushes full of squabbling sparrows, and I pulled up my collar against the cold. Altman—one hand keeping Norman the hair pouf in place—was reading a text from Sylvia, snorting in amusement.

"Hey!" I said, trying to wrench his attention back my way. "Your family's driving down to Florida for Christmas holidays, right?"

"Yeah." *Text, text, snort, chortle.*

"Why don't you tell your parents you want to stay here? Then I can come over every day and, you know, maybe even spend the night."

"I don't think so," he said, without betraying much regret.

That was the end of the discussion, and I knew better than to push it. There were rules to our relationship. Lots of them. Mostly for me. In lieu of conversation, I recited a poem in my head, one I had written for Altman:

> *O, Captain of the hockey team*
> *Offence is your game*
> *But you will bend to my sweet charms*
> *When I call out your name*

> *O, Captain of the ice men*
> *Your bulging pants so tight*
> *I'll make you mine, I'll make you cum*
> *I'll make you love me right*

Hardly T. S. Elliot, I know. But as my English teacher liked to say, "Always write your truth." Not that she or Altman even knew about the poem. It had been folded up in my back pocket for the past month. Sometimes I reached back and touched the top crease to reassure myself. At those times, maybe I imagined it was Altman touching my ass.

When we got back to school, Sylvia was waiting by our lockers. She gave my shoulder a quick squeeze before turning her boyfriend around to face her and throwing back her head like a swooning diva. Altman pulled her tight and brought their mouths together, tongues tangling like wrestling ferrets. I turned abruptly away, my eyes filling with tears, and hurried down the hall toward the bathroom, same as when I was six.

CHAPTER 2: *Visit from an Octona*

So, shocking but true, just having access to some kind of regular sex is not enough to satisfy a teenage boy! The old people on Facebook must be right about our generation being ungrateful. The rest of the day went by in a depressed blur. I kept my eyes resolutely on the floor and did my best to remain the kind of student whose reports read, "Crispin consistently fails to live up to his potential."

When I emerged through the school's front doors at three thirty, my dad honked twice from across the road. This was a pleasant surprise, as taking crowded public transit home is one of my least favourite things. I tossed my knapsack on the back seat and slouched into the front beside him.

"Why aren't you at the office?" I asked. "Fired again?"

He ignored my blistering wit. "Working from home today. How was school?"

"Terrorist attack. Sarin gas in the ventilation system. Seven students with permanent nerve damage, and they *still* gave us a pop quiz in math."

"Well, you can't let standards slip. Do you want to practice driving?"

"No."

"How about a few rounds of parallel parking?"

"*God*, no."

"His Majesty is in a mood." Dad sighed and handed me a bag of chocolate croissants from Estelle's. I all but shoved one down my throat, the buttery, chocolaty pastry immediately melting away the sharp edges of my misery. The truth is, my dad's okay. He never really loses his cool, which I admire. Still, if I give him a hard time, it's because of how freaking superior and *Yoda* he sounds when he lectures me about stuff. That and his ridiculous habit of whistling early 90s grunge songs.

I watched him as he pulled into traffic, checking his mirrors and blind spots, which I always forgot to do. He looked good driving—competent, masculine. When I'm behind the wheel, I'm more like a frantic chicken, lurching an erratic course down the street as if some farmer is chasing me with a hatchet.

Dad was whistling "Jeremy" by Pearl Jam, and I watched the scenery go by for a while before venturing, "There's a party this weekend."

Dad nodded. "At whose house?"

"Karen Parkenter. She's a friend of Sylvia's."

"Listen, I'm glad you're finally making friends. Your mother and I were frankly concerned about you last year. But, Crispin, the last time you were at a party, you came home not exactly sober."

I felt something unclench in my chest. Maybe I actually wanted Dad to say no. Sure, being Sylvia's friend got me invited to parties, but what fun was it to sit alone in a broken IKEA chair in the corner of some tacky family room while everyone else got drunk and stupid and asked me, "What *are* you, anyway? More white or more Chinese?" and then watch Sylvia lead Altman up the stairs to some deserted bedroom with that glow of pink-frosted triumph on her face? Given those circumstances, getting a little wasted was really the sanest option. Still, I felt obliged to show some outrage.

"I wasn't anything like drunk! There was beer, okay? People drink beer at parties. God!"

"I know, Crispin. But you need to take responsibility for your own actions. Just because your friends are drinking—"

"Fine, I won't go."

Dad laughed. "Clever ploy. Okay, you wore me down…go. But be home by midnight and promise you'll call if there's no one sober to drive you."

We turned off the main road into our neighbourhood, and I was already looking forward to just being in my room with my headphones on, blasting glitchy alt-dance and puzzling my way through a text-adventure game. But then Dad *had* to ruin the mood. "How's your buddy Altman? You two hanging out a lot? I hear the hockey team's having a good season."

Instant panic! Visions of oral sex so vivid, I figured they had to be projecting onto my eyeballs like a dirty multiplex. I said, "I-I'm just helping him out…with English…because Sylvia asked me to."

"That's nice of you."

"No, it's not!" I shouted, blushing and looking away out the window again. Congratulations. Another awkward conversation courtesy of my cowardice. Here's the thing: Despite everyone at school knowing I was gay, I had never officially come out to my parents. I was pretty sure they knew and were just waiting for me to get up the courage to tell them, but that communication gap was only making me feel more pathetic. I almost wished they'd corner me one night in the family room. "Admit it! You're a little rainbow refugee! You're the glittertastic leather grand marshal of the Pride parade!"

But my dad just said, "Being rude is not a job requirement, Crispin." Even without looking, I could feel his eyes burning into me.

"Sorry," I mumbled. "Just watch the road."

"You know you can talk to me about anything, right? Anything."

"Watch the road, Dad. Seriously, oh my God, watch *out*!" Because I had looked up at that moment, just as the woman stepped into the street, right in our path. The same woman that was spying on me and Altman. Short copper hair, silk suit, and shoulder pads that, while formidable, were not going to be much help if we ran her down.

Dad stomped hard on the brakes, and the car stuttered angrily to a halt maybe three feet from where she stood. Dad was gasping, I nearly crapped my pants, but the woman didn't seem the least bit concerned. She just walked to Dad's window and tapped on it twice with one of the many rings she wore.

"Dad…?" I said, confused, because he was just sitting there, white-knuckle grip on the wheel, eyes closed, mouth moving like he was reciting a prayer.

"Should I call 9-1-1?" I squeaked in a stupidly high voice. "Or… Wait, do you *know* her?"

Without turning to look at the woman, Dad lowered his window and asked in a husky whisper, "Are you here for me? Or for him?" Which is some creepy shit right there.

The woman's voice was calm and authoritative. "Let us go to your home, Elliot," she said. "I will explain the details there."

"Me or *him*?" Dad said, angry now, still not meeting her gaze.

"I am here for Crispin. May I get in the vehicle, please?"

She was here for *me*? What? I considered calling 9-1-1 anyway.

"Crispin, get in the back and give the Consul your seat."

But the woman was already opening the back door and pushing my knapsack out of her way. "I will be fine here. Let us proceed to your home. We have much to discuss." She climbed in, stowing her big cloth bag at her feet, and fastened her seat belt.

It was intensely bizarre having this *Consul* person follow us into the house. Something about her didn't fit the mundane reality of our suburban inner sanctum, with its piles of unsorted mail and the worn carpet with the stains of long-dead pets. Dad led her into the living room and offered her the best armchair. Much as she freaked me out, I had a million questions and wanted to interrogate her immediately. But Dad ordered me to the kitchen to help him prepare snacks, and I had the distinct feeling he didn't want to leave me alone with the woman. His phone rang, and he looked at the display nervously before switching off the ringer.

"Was that Mom?" I asked and got no answer.

Soon, we were sitting in silence, sipping our drinks. I hadn't even been introduced. She drank with her eyes closed, and I took the chance to observe her. She didn't wear any makeup other than a bit of lipstick. The silky fabric of her suit was like waves of woven colour—sea tones shot through with strands of scarlet and gold. I hadn't noticed before, but she was wearing long, sea-green opera gloves. Her rings, with their big green stones, were pushed up over the gloved fingers.

Suddenly, she opened her eyes and stared right at me. I felt my breath catch. Her eyes were the strangest colour I'd ever seen, bright copper, flecked with crimson and green. They almost glowed.

I felt a blush rise in my cheeks.

"Crispin," said the woman. "I've waited a long time to meet you properly. How would you like to take a trip with me?"

A paranoid chill went through me. Was this one of those deals where your parents have you kidnapped and taken off to a camp with a barbed wire fence and crosses on the wall, where they try and make you forget your love of hairy legs and prominent collarbones? I pulled myself deeper into the corner of the sofa.

My dad raised a reassuring hand and said to the woman, "Consul Krasik-dahé, we have a lot to explain to Crispin before we get to, uh, travel arrangements." He stared at me, and I knew he was about to say something that, once heard, could never be unheard.

"The thing is," Dad said and cleared his throat elaborately like he'd accidentally swallowed a slug, "I've never really told you the whole story of your…ancestry." His phone vibrated noisily, and he gritted his teeth until it stopped. I had never seen him so uncomfortable.

"My ancestry? Your dad's Norwegian, right?" I said, grabbing cracker after cracker from the tray and munching manically. "And Grandma was Irish. And then on Mom's side, it's all Filipino. Maybe some Spanish."

The Consul spoke then, her eyes widening, and I swear the reds and greens seemed to pulse in them, like lava seeping from the rim of a volcano. "Your father is not referring to your terrestrial origins, Crispin. You were born with the copper in your blood. You are of the cloud beasts, the inscrutable rulers of the Elemental Realms. You are *dragon!*"

And I laughed. The sound that came out of me was an awful "whoop" like a howler monkey, and cracker crumbs shot from my mouth in a geyser of gluten. But everything was going a little wonky inside me because a single tear was rolling down my dad's face, and I was thinking, *This is screwed, this is utterly...*

Dad picked up one of the napkins from the snack tray and dabbed at his eyes. He said, "I know, Crispin, it doesn't make a lot of sense at first, and—and maybe I should have told you before—"

I leaned back in the sofa and stuck my legs out, like I was born casual, like lounge music followed me around. At the same time, I was hugging myself so hard, my arms ached. "I am *dragon?* What does that even mean? Is this some ridiculous frat you pledged in university or what?"

Dad looked at the Consul, and she rose to her feet imperiously and crossed to the window. The last of the bleak November afternoon light was snuffed out as she closed the drapes, leaving only the swag lamp in the corner to illuminate us. The woman returned to her seat and undid the ornate gold clasp on her big cloth bag. She rummaged inside, probably for something else to shock me with—a severed baby's head? An enormous sex toy with Satanic symbols on the shaft?

My mouth was dry from all the crackers, and I slurped my milk as the woman pulled five stones from her bag and laid them on the coffee table. They were nothing special, just rough, porous grey rock—lava rock, maybe—the smallest the size of a chicken egg, the biggest more like a grapefruit.

In the darkness, my impression her eyes were glowing was even stronger. "There are many ways off your planet, Crispin. Humans recently learned to harness fire to escape into the cold of outer space."

"Not so recently," I shot back, sounding pissy and superior, like I do when I'm freaking out.

"Oh yes, in the grand scheme of things, *very* recently. But that show of brute force is only one way to leave the Realm of Earth. I want to take you somewhere through subtler means, somewhere rich in wonder and terrible in its primordial beauty. It will be your first time there, and yet it is your home. I am speaking of the Realm of Fire, the land where the fire dragons rule." She began to remove the rings from her right hand, dropping them into the pocket of her jacket.

I desperately wanted to make some brilliant sarcastic reply or retreat to my room and blast my music loud enough to erase everything in my brain. But I kept listening to her.

"Humans live there, too, and they serve the Dragon Lords. And not just humans. Beings such as myself also serve the Five Dragons."

"Aren't you human?" I heard myself ask. I looked at Dad, who was looking at the floor. Great.

The Consul woman was now peeling off a glove like a moulting lizard. I was relieved to see it was just normal skin underneath.

"I am of the mixed beings," she said. "I am an *octona*."

It sounded like a skin product, or an exercise machine from a late-night infomercial.

"It means one-eighth of my genome is derived from the great dragons. Watch!" She reached down and put a bare finger on one of the rocks. From inside the porous stone, light glowed, sending a cascade of little beams out through every hole. Her face, lit by this effect, looked a lot less human.

"Cool trick," I said, a quaver in my voice.

She removed her finger, and the light vanished. "Elliot," she said, and Dad's chin snapped up. "Touch the stone."

He looked at me apologetically and then reached out a hand to touch the same stone she had. This time, three of the stones lit up, a different coloured light radiating from each one. Where the beams intersected, more lights were born. Each corner of the room was touched by this weird, pulsing display, and I could hear a faint humming sound. Dad removed his finger, and the light and the humming both stopped.

My spinning brain was trying to make some sense of the craziness. "Dad? You're a-a…octona, too?"

The woman answered for him, and I almost told her to shut up, because suddenly I really needed to hear my dad's voice, which, I should explain, is a very rare desire on my part.

"Your father carries the copper blood. He is one of twenty on this planet. The copper is passed from generation to generation, and there are always twenty."

"Generation…?" I breathed. "Are you trying to tell me that I'm also…whatever Dad is?"

"Touch the stone," she said, and her voice was stern.

Again, I almost got up and left, because what good outcome could there possibly be here? But, no, I got up from the far reaches of the sofa and kneeled by the coffee table. I could feel her eyes and Dad's eyes on me, but I just stared at the little family grouping of lava rocks. The biggest act of defiance I could muster was to touch a different rock than they had. It didn't matter, because as soon as finger connected with stone, the light show was on, but bigger and better, because when I touched one of the rocks, *all five lit up.*

I pulled my hand away like I was touching a hot stove. I touched a different stone, and again, five glowing rocks. I looked up then, and the whole room was bathed in swaying, converging light beams which ricocheted from the walls and ceiling like this was some big EDM concert. And the humming was back, but deeper, richer, like walking by the stadium and hearing the rumble of the concert inside.

And it was pretty impressive, I have to admit. Convincing, I mean. 'Cause, you know, who would go to this much trouble to con me? If this was some kind of elaborate shakedown, the octona lady and whoever she was working for were barking up the wrong tree. I wasn't anyone, my family didn't have any money. So, yeah, the only conclusion I could come to was that me and Dad were—too weird to say it—actually somehow, some kind of fire-breathing…

"What the hell is this?" The overhead lights flipped on, and I was so startled I fell back on my ass, losing contact with the stones and killing the light show. Dad and I both turned to look at my mom, who was standing in the entrance of the living room, still in her lab coat from work, holding her briefcase in one hand and two shopping bags in the other. I felt like I'd been caught committing a crime, but that's how everyone feels when my mom has that volcanic pissed-off look in her eye.

"Isabel!" Dad said. "I wasn't expecting you so early. We—"

She dropped the bags to the floor with a clunk, and I hoped she didn't have eggs in there. "No! You said this couldn't happen until he was twenty-five!"

"What I actually said was—"

"And that even then it was probably *not* going to be Crispin!" Under all her anger, I could see the fear. I looked back at the woman in the chair—Consul Crabstick or whatever—but she hadn't even turned to look at Mom. She was just calmly pulling her glove and rings back on, waiting for this minor interruption to end.

"Crispin, get over here!" Mom said, and I scrambled to my feet and crossed to her. She grabbed me in a protective hug. "He is only sixteen, Elliot. You lied to me!"

"I did not plan this, Isabel!"

"No, but when she showed up, you conveniently forgot how to use your phone."

"And what would you have done if I told you?"

"We could have faced her together, nipped this crap in the bud before it got out of control. But, no, you let this *monster* into our house. You let her do a number on your only child."

"There is no need to be rude to Consul Krasik-dahé, Isabel! She is our guest and we owe her—"

"Come with me, Crispin!" Mom said, digging her fingers into my shoulders and steering me through the dining room and out the glass door to the patio, which she slammed closed behind us.

"I'm not wearing a coat, Mom!" I said and she pulled me down on the rickety love seat and wrapped an arm over me. I dropped my head on the shoulder of her lab coat, which is kind of a baby thing to do, I know, but I was having a weird day, okay? At times like this, I didn't think of my mother as head pharmacist at the drug store. She was just my mom, the one who made amazing pork adobo and rolled her eyes when I dyed my hair or used eyeliner. And it was tempting to just stay like that, all quiet and peaceful, but it's kind of my life's mission to ruin beautiful moments.

"So," I said. "The plan is, we sit out here and hope she goes away before we freeze to death?"

"I don't want to talk to her. I don't want *you* to talk to her."

"This dragon stuff can't be true, right? It's just bullshit."

"Language, Crispin," was all she said in reply. Anyway, there wasn't any reason for her to answer my stupid question. I saw how I made the stones glow. And even more importantly, I knew my mom saw. I knew she believed the whole thing.

"God damn your father!" she said, and I watched anger and tears fighting for supremacy in on her face. "I should have left him when he told me. Dragons!" She exhaled loudly. "And I never should have given him a son to suck up into this madness."

"So, you're saying if only I hadn't been born, I'd be safe? Thanks for that, Mom." She slapped the top of my head and then wrapped her arms tighter around me. I asked, "Did you meet this woman—Consul Crossfit—before?"

"When you were three, yes. It was the same as today. I came home from the store with you and found them together. Your father was so nervous, I thought they were having an affair."

"Ugh. Don't."

She laughed. "It would have been easier to deal with. You were asleep in your stroller, and I wouldn't let her even look at you." Mom sighed. "I wanted to give you a little sister, you know. But I couldn't after that. I didn't dare." Suddenly, her cozy hug felt like a cage, and I didn't want to hear any more.

As if on cue, the patio door scraped open. Dad kept a steadying hand on the doorframe, wary of setting Mom off again.

"Isabel, please come inside. We can't hide from this. Crispin has a right to hear the whole story. It's his future we're talking about."

"I'm his mother. I have some say in the matter!"

"Wait a minute!" I said, extricating myself from Mom's chokehold. I stood and stared at my parents. "Why didn't anyone tell *me* about this? If you both knew all these years about my copper blood or whatever, didn't you think the information might, I dunno, interest me? Amuse me on snow days or something?"

Dad looked away. "We thought we had time. But then Consul Krasik-dahé appeared out of nowhere, and it all just…happened!" There was a gleam of excitement in his eyes. "It's a tremendous honour, Crispin."

Mom shouted, "Then *you* go, Elliot. You have the blood. *You* fulfill this wonderful destiny." She spat out the word like she was naming an STI. "Instead of sending your son into God-knows-what kind of danger!"

Desperate to get away, I pushed past Dad, back into the house. The Consul was still sitting there in the comfy seat, maddeningly calm.

My parents followed me inside, and she said, "It is your son who has been chosen. After calculations and measurements too arcane for you to comprehend, it has been determined that Crispin alone of the twenty must take on this duty. It is Crispin's fate, and it is Crispin who will accompany me to the Realm of Fire and do what he was born to do."

Mom's voice was strained now. "He was born to be whoever he chooses to be! You can't just swoop in here on your broomstick and read him some fortune-cookie future!"

Mixed metaphors aside, she had a point. On the other hand, it was kind of nice to be a chosen *something*. It made the needle on my vanity meter swing over a bit. And what about this copper blood? Would Altman be impressed? They were all looking my way, apparently waiting for me to say something.

"I–I'm not sure. Tell me more about this Realm of Fire. Is it dangerous? Is this a swordfighting and death spells situation?"

"I'm sure it's very dangerous," Mom said, glaring at the Consul. "Do you hear that, lady? He doesn't want to go." She tried to grab me again, but I dodged to the side.

"I didn't say that. This is all happening too fast. I have to think about it." I looked at the octona, and for the first time I actually believed she wasn't completely human. "Are you staying here with us tonight?"

"No," said the woman. "I have a room downtown at the Ambassador Hotel."

I barked out another hysterical laugh, because it was too…what? *Normal.*

"Okay," I said. Dizzy and overwhelmed, I walked to the front door.

"Crispin, don't you go anywhere!" Dad ordered, but there was an edge of hysteria in his voice, and I knew I could disobey. This situation made him weaker than me, and I kind of hated him for that.

"I'm fine. I've just got to get out of here and think. I'll go for a walk. Or maybe over to Altman's." I pulled on my coat and grabbed my knapsack. I checked inside for my phone and my wallet. I was attentive and methodical. As I adjusted the hem of my coat, I touched the edge of the folded-up love poem in my back pocket. *Yes*, I thought, *I'll go to Altman's.* I turned back for one more look at the strange tableau in the living room.

"One question," I said to the woman with the glowy eyes. "What am I chosen *for*, exactly?"

"To mate with her most potent excellence, the Dragon Queen."

We all blinked at each other for a millennium or two before I broke the silence. "Exit Crispin…with noodle thoroughly cooked," and I fucking ran out of the house. I didn't stop running for three blocks.

CHAPTER 3: *Sick*

Forty minutes later, I was sitting around the dining room table with Altman's complicated, blended family. His thirteen-year-old twin sisters, Ida and Dorothy, kept giving me cryptic, amused looks. Ida would then text something to Dorothy, who would nod and say "Totes" as she received her sister's no doubt mixed review.

"More kale fritters, Crispin?" Altman's mother asked for the third time in less than five minutes, her wide grin oddly brittle.

"That's right, champ, you need some meat on your bones," said Altman's greasy stepdad, king of the table in his purple sweats. "You should be working out with Altman. He's going for that athletic scholarship. And he better get it!" He laughed, though he was the only one at the table who seemed amused.

"You're so quiet tonight, Altman dear," his mom said with concern before her attention moved elsewhere.

Altman had somehow arranged not to sit beside me. He didn't say one word through the whole dinner, just kept shovelling chicken and rice into his mouth without looking up. To my right, his eight-year-old half brother, Jonah, gave a barking cough, sending bits of fritter batter sailing through the air like confetti.

The youngest child, a seemingly nameless six-year-old who drifted around the edges of the family like a ghost, put a crayon drawing in front of his dad and looked up from under long sweaty bangs for the man's opinion.

"What's this, buddy? Are they playing hockey? Is that supposed to be your big brother?" The boy stood frozen for a minute, brow creased, before pulling the picture back against his chest and retreating into the shadows.

"Everything's delicious," I said winningly, perched on the edge of my chair, unable to relax. Dorothy snorted in amusement and texted more commentary to Ida.

"Thank you, Crispin," Altman's mom said. "I had to throw it together in a hurry. I was volunteering with *unfortunates* again today. Such sad, sad stories." She sighed and Jonah coughed, spattering my hand with damp debris.

Suddenly, the six-year-old squeezed in between me and Ida, handing me his drawing for inspection. This weighty responsibility made me panic for a second, but then the swirls of colour on the page began to make sense.

"It's a horse, right? With crimson and gold wings. Oh, he's flying over the mountain to that...that princess." The little face nodded gravely. "She's very pretty," I said. The sudden absence of background noise made me look up. The whole family was staring at me except Altman, whose head had notched down another ten degrees.

I finally got up the nerve to call home after dinner and all I said was, "I'm fine. I'm staying the night at Altman's." Then I hung up quickly and turned off my phone.

I watched some boring action movie with Altman, and he didn't once look me in the eye. Even though I was staying in his bedroom, we never got off that night, which was too damn bad because it would have taken my mind off everything. *Mate with the dragon queen* was a phrase that had lodged itself front and centre in my brain. "Would you like some hot milk before bed, Crispin?" "No thanks, I have to *matewiththedragonqueen!*"

Something did happen in the middle of the night, but it was so weird, and I was so groggy, that by the next morning, I wasn't sure it hadn't been a dream. I was fast asleep on a camping mattress beside Altman's bed when he shook me awake. I opened my eyes and found his shadowed face hanging down close to mine; Norman the hair pouf, absent hair product, was dangling free from his forehead like a fat tentacle.

"Sylvia doesn't know me, man. No one knows me. You..." He hesitated, and I held my breath, willing him to continue. "I just can't, okay? I have to go to Florida." He made a weird little choking gasp. "Even if I'd rather..."

Time stretched out. The moon glinted off my wolf's head necklace. Somewhere in the house, Jonah coughed. Then Altman's face retreated into the darkness again, like it had been some incursion into our universe by a hell beast, writhing in eternal agony, begging for release.

Nothing was said about this incident the next morning, but Altman wasn't ignoring me so hard either. He loaned me one of his T-shirts, which made me feel like the cheerleader in some teen drama who got to wear the quarterback's letter jacket.

As we walked to school, he finally thought to ask, "Hey, man, is something bothering you? Why'd you come over, anyway?" Even though I obviously couldn't tell him, it meant a lot to me that he noticed.

Things started snowboarding into a tree as soon as we entered the parking lot and met two of Altman's teammates.

"Your girlfriend's going nuclear in there, man, watch out," said one.

The other snorted. "You two-timing her again, Shendorf? What chick you banging now?" which made me want to take a swing at him. Or at Altman. Or at Sylvia. I looked up at Altman, asking the obvious question with my eyes, and he just shrugged. As we headed for our lockers, we were both on the lookout for Sylvia, Altman with mere curiosity, me like an antelope, drinking twitchily from the watering hole where crocodiles are known to hide.

And crocodile-like, she struck suddenly and fatally from behind, just as I was hanging up my jacket. "You!" Sylvia growled, with nerve-shredding menace. And, yeah, she meant me.

"Hey?" I asked, with a little appeasing smile as I closed my locker.

"In there." She was holding open the door of one of the little music practice booths on the other side of the hall. I watched her face flow from fury to wounded misery, and she turned to Altman. "You, too, baby."

Down the hall, Karen Parkenter caught my eye and shook her head sadly. I knew something horrible had happened, like maybe I had gone through the last three months of school with my fly down. No, whatever this was, it was definitely worse.

With a full drum kit inside, the practice room was a bit of a squeeze for three. But I guess you don't need much room when your act is detonating a grenade. Tears in her eyes, Sylvia pulled a note from the side pocket of her schoolbag. A core of ice shot through me. It was my love poem.

Eyes wide, unable to speak, I slid my hand behind me and pulled the paper out of my back pocket that I had spent the last twenty-four hours thinking was the poem. It was a receipt for batteries from Hector's Electro-Mart. My legs went weak. As I stumbled backward into a crash cymbal, it occurred to me Sylvia could have made use of some percussion for her big reveal.

"Where…where did you…?" I asked, as if understanding all the facts would undo this horror.

"What's happening?" Altman asked, annoyed by all the drama.

"I found it on the floor in the back seat of my car, Crispin. I guess you lost it when I drove you home Monday." She paused, her shining eyes drilling into me. I was searching for some perfect excuse, but she didn't give me the chance. "You're sick. What an idiot I was not to realize this before." Sylvia started crying. Hard. I had never seen her lose her shit like this, and I felt awful for her. But at the same time, I was thinking, *She doesn't know! She doesn't know I've actually been sucking off her boyfriend for two months.* Of course, that only got Altman off the hook, not me.

"I just can't believe this," she hissed. "You were literally no one at this school before I found you, and this is how you show your gratitude? Did your deluded little fag mind think that you could steal Altman from me?"

For once, that epithet shook me, because now it was synonymous with the worst things in the world, universal revulsion and isolation, loss of status. Loss of Altman.

With a humiliating little quaver in my voice, I whimpered, "No one was supposed to see that."

She was angry now. Ignoring my lame excuse, she pushed the poem into Altman's hand. "Here! Crispin's only pretending to be your friend. This is what he really thinks about when he's tutoring you!"

I could see Altman's lips silently forming the words. *I'll make you cum / I'll make you love me right.* It was awful how cute he looked, grappling with my words like they were advanced math. When full comprehension finally settled on his face, I could see he was in as much shock as I was, and that's when I turned fully pathetic.

"It's just a joke, dude," I whimpered. "Just…a literary experiment I was trying…" I didn't care about Sylvia anymore, I didn't care about her friendship or my position in her social circle. All I wanted was Altman to wink and say, "Don't worry about it, man." Or "buddy," or even "champ."

But instead he turned red as a tomato and stormed out of the practice booth, pushing through the crowd that had gathered outside. I ran after him and tripped on someone's foot. I stumbled forward, ending up on my hands and knees. Above me, some guy was making kissy noises, and a girl said, "They're all like that. No self-control." They weren't individuals anymore. They were a mob, speaking in the voice of a mob, promising hatred and cruelty, every day, all day, forever.

I looked back and saw Sylvia in the arms of her girlfriends, who held her as she sobbed. I spun around and stared up into Altman's face.

He stood at the edge of the crowd, surrounded by boys who were darkly, maniacally amused. Altman was staring back at me, full of disgust. And I didn't know if he was just putting on an act to assert his hetero bona fides, or if his disgust was real. Either way, it was unbearable.

You knew the rule, Crispin, I could hear him thinking. *Don't ever let anyone know.*

So, in order to show I was in complete control of the situation, that I didn't give a shit what anyone thought about me, that I was a proud, self-determining gay man, I climbed to my feet, turned on my heel… and ran. I blasted through the exit doors, across the parking lot, and out into the street, legs pumping until the school was around a corner and four blocks away. I finally stopped, gasping for breath in front of the sad little excuse for a parkette off Snowrose Avenue, charmingly decorated with used condoms and a syringe or two. I sat down on one of the benches and cried and cried and cried until my guts hurt so bad that I cried from the pain.

Where the hell do I go now? In ten minutes, my whole life had spun apart like jars of spice flying off a lazy Susan. I couldn't go back to school, maybe not ever. I couldn't just walk the streets, because for one thing I had run off without my jacket. Go home? You must be kidding. After all the dragon stuff—and wow, I had actually forgotten all about the dragon stuff for an hour—my parents had probably both called in sick and were waiting at home so we could have a *good talk.* No, the last place I wanted to go was our house. If I showed up a blubbering mess like this, I'd end up coming out to them in the worst possible way. I'd confirm every fear they had about what a stupid homo whore their son was, getting with his friends' boyfriends.

The truth was, I wanted to be nowhere. How could there ever be a place where I was accepted? Where could I ever find love? A devouring darkness was closing over my head, dragging me down into a place where light couldn't reach me. I had never felt like this before, and it was terrifying. But I'd had enough. I wanted out of this world altogether.

I was starting to really feel the cold, and I thought, *Good, let it kill me.* But that's when my brain kicked over, like that first blip on the cardiac monitor after everyone's given up on the fallen hero and quit the CPR. I suddenly realized there *was* somewhere I could go, somewhere literally out this world.

Surfing the wave of renewed determination, I opened up the map on my phone and looked up directions to the Ambassador Hotel.

Chapter 4: *Small Talk with a Quadrana*

Luckily, my transit card was in my back pocket, and I caught a bus to the subway station. As I stood on the platform, waiting for the subway downtown, I felt marked, as if everyone could see I was skipping school. Or maybe they could see I was gay. Was I more effeminate than I thought? Did the fact that I dyed just the top of my head blond and left the back and sides my natural dark brown give it away? Maybe they could even see that I had been preying on a poor defenceless straight guy. The train arrived, and I stumbled on board and sat down in the corner.

The mid-morning subway was half-empty, especially out here at the end of the line. With no signal for my phone underground, I had nothing to do but turn everything over in my head again and again. For instance, was Altman really straight? I mean, I'm a guy, and he, um, enjoyed what I did for him. But was I just a convenient orifice? Did he think of me when we did that, or was he running clips of porn girls behind his closed eyes? It didn't matter. It was over. He hated me forever.

I started to cry again and realized that someone really was watching me—a middle-aged lady in a purple duffle coat. I hoped she wouldn't offer me a tissue or free advice, though I wouldn't have minded one of the doughnuts in her paper takeout bag. She exited at the next stop.

I got off the train twenty minutes later and walked down Jarvis Street in the direction of the Ambassador. The farther south I walked, the sketchier the area got. In the park north of the hotel, homeless people were cocooned in sleeping bags, and I'm pretty sure the women leaning against the metal fence were already open for business despite the early hour. But the hotel, disconcertingly opulent, didn't seem to care what a crappy neighbourhood it was in. As I climbed the marble steps, a doorman in impeccable grey livery pulled open the doors for me, complete with a "good morning, sir."

My shoes tap-tapped on marble and shuff-shuffed across thick carpets until I came to the front desk. A soft lounge arrangement of Nirvana's "Heart-Shaped Box" was leaking through the speakers as a clerk approached and fired his professional smile at me.

"Can I help you?"

"Uh, there's this woman staying here. Consul Crazy-Ducky or something." The clerk's smile didn't falter, though his eyes widened. "Short copper hair?" I suggested. "Shoulder pads?"

The clerk made a show of squinting at his monitor and typing. Probably he was just humouring me, or maybe playing solitaire.

"Nothing that I can…" He paused, and I leaned forward hopefully. "No, nothing. Is she expecting you?"

"Um, yeah, maybe. Can I sit and wait for her?"

"Certainly!" And he was gone so fast, he might have dropped through a trap door.

I collapsed into an enormous wing-back chair, exhausted by the futility of my life. All around me, people were coming and going purposefully: business professionals talking loudly into their phones; well-heeled tourists corralling their confident, French-speaking children and heading out for a day of sightseeing; a man and woman throwing each other covert looks across the lobby, the man mouthing "five minutes" before walking to the elevators and disappearing. Life was going on for all these people while I had no next move. Maybe I'd just make my new home in this chair. How long would I be able to sit here in the opulent warmth of the lobby before they threw me out? Maybe I could charge meals to random rooms until I got caught.

Someone tapped me on the shoulder, and I spun around in panic to find the front desk clerk crouching beside my chair.

"Are you Crispin?" he asked, and I nodded. "And it was…" He consulted a scrap of paper. "Consul Krasik-dahé you were looking for?"

I jumped to my feet and began babbling. "Yes, that's it! I forgot her name because, see, she's my aunt, but she used to have another name before she married this guy from, uh, Iceland and she was going to hyphenate it, but her lawyer said…" I realized the guy didn't give a crap, so I just repeated, "Yes."

"She phoned down to the front desk. They're waiting for you in room 1412. The elevators are there beside the bar." He pointed and then vanished again, leaving me thanking the empty air. How had the Consul known I was down here? Who was this "they"? My heart started beating faster as I stepped into the elevator, because it had just occurred to me this plan of mine might be the equivalent of escaping a bear by jumping off a mountain. I was sharing the elevator with the woman who had been told to wait five minutes by, presumably, her illicit lover. She seemed just as nervous as me.

Ms. Hotel Quickie got off on the fifth floor, and I travelled alone to the fourteenth. As I walked down the empty hall, my footfalls muffled by thick carpet, I wondered what was going on behind all the closed doors. Were people watching me through the peepholes? Were the rooms filled with the bloody aftermaths of mob hits? Were there dragon eggs inside, ready to hatch?

I turned a corner, and at the end of the corridor stood a strange, skinny figure in a long trench coat, so tall the fedora on his head brushed the sprinkler nozzle on the ceiling. He lifted his long arm and motioned me closer with a bony finger. This did nothing to slow the pounding of my heart, but still I approached, like the next victim in a horror movie.

His face was shadowed by the brim of his hat, but I could have sworn his eyes were glowing.

"*Strrrzzkral*," he said, and "*khalkhh.*" I moved forward like I was sleepwalking as he intoned, "*Thoc. Thoc, thoc!* Bound you are by *ekdahi. Thoc!* Welcome, Dragon Groom.*"

And now I was standing in front of him, looking up into his long, bony face, with its high cheekbones and what might have been the scar from a harelip under his nose. The pupils in his big eye sockets weren't round—more like vertical ovals.

"*Khhif*," I heard myself say and cleared my throat. I tried again, and my voice, though unsteady, seemed to be working this time. "Thanks."

To my left, the door of room 1412 was slightly ajar, and now it swung open to reveal Consul Krasik-dahé. I was impressed I could remember her name now. Her outfit today was a silky dress in shades of blood and earth, the matching jacket again equipped with mega-shoulders. She was padding around in her stocking feet.

"Come in, Crispin," she said, not sounding the least bit surprised I had shown up. Something about her voice was…wrong.

In no uncertain terms, I told her, "*Wekhtrrz.*" Now something was wrong with how *I* was speaking. "Why did I say that?" I asked uneasily as I entered the room. It was actually a full suite, with decor that was trying too hard. We were in the living room, and through the door to our left was a bedroom.

"Linguists call it code switching," she answered unhelpfully and invited me to sit. The door clicked closed behind me.

"I don't know if I can stay long," I said, noticing the tall guy was standing between me and the door.

The Consul smiled, the first time I'd seen her do that. "Well, you're here now. Tiqokh, you're making Crispin nervous. Tiqokh is a quadrana, another of the mixed beings. He has more dragon in him than I, and is therefore less attuned to human social conventions. We'll all sit down and have a pleasant talk in a minute, but I'm just in the middle of a conference call, if you'll excuse me."

She disappeared into the bedroom, closing the door behind her. I sat on the couch. The quadrana, Tiqokh, had removed his hat and coat. He folded himself into the desk chair opposite me and stared, unmoving. I could see why he needed to cover his body when he was out of the room. Bony protuberances tented his shirt and pants at the elbows, knees, and shoulders, and two lines of bumps ran across the top of his hairless head. The skin stretched over this frame was grey and cracked, almost like scales. Unlike the Consul, he couldn't pass for human.

I tried the small talk thing. "So, you're, um, one-quarter dragon?"

"I am," he answered. Did he ever blink? I didn't want to stare back long enough to find out. Something about him seemed always on alert, poised to pounce.

"Uh, do you live around here?"

"I have spent seven of your years here on Earth," he replied. "I manipulate the strands. I facilitate the crossing."

"Good to know," I said. "Tiqokh. Your name sounds…familiar." My brain was reaching for something, like when you're writing a history quiz, and the name of the guy who defeated Napoleon is *just* on the tip of…

Sitting up straighter, I asked, "Does it mean, like, 'crimson,' or 'tower'?" How did I know that? Other than twenty-five words in Tagalog and enough forgotten French to earn me a B minus on last year's finals, I didn't speak any languages other than English.

Consul Krasik-dahé had slid back into the room, silent as a breeze. "Yes, both meanings are correct. Together, they can be understood as bonfire or a signal light."

I stared at her. "In what language?" I asked, but you know what? I already had a guess and I didn't like it.

"In the Tongue of Fire, the language of our Dragon Lords."

The surreal, heart-slipping feeling I'd had at my house yesterday was back. "But I don't speak the Tongue of Fire," I said. Helpfully.

"You are speaking it now. Can I get you some tea?" She disappeared back into the bedroom.

"*Rakhdin*," said Tiqokh, and I realized I was hearing both that strange word and simultaneously, *heritage*. "The copper in your blood allows you to speak the ancient tongue."

It felt like some alien embryo had started moving in my chest. Who was I? What was hiding inside me that I could make rocks glow, speak languages from another world, *impregnate lady dragons*? Whatever it was, I suddenly didn't want it.

I jumped to my feet. "Coming here was a mistake," I said, in English probably, though I had no proof of that.

"Not a mistake," Tiqokh said. "You came here because of the copper. I smelled it as soon as you entered the building. You came because of your *duty*." The equivalent word in the Tongue of Fire—*ekdahi*—rolled on my tongue like a bitter lozenge. Then the quadrana leaned forward stiffly, seeming to pivot only at the hips and the neck. His upper lip pulled back, and he began sniffing. "Or are you here for more earthly reasons?"

He stood and crossed to me, sniffing, sniffing, bringing his face close to my chest, my armpits, my crotch. I pulled back against the cushions, frozen in terror. I could smell him, too—stone, smoke, something earthy.

"Yes," he was murmuring. "I sense pain, rejection. You come here stinking of misery. Someone has hurt you." He pulled back and stared at me with eyes that looked more lizard-like now that I knew what he was. "*Ekdahi* is more important than your human concerns. The Realm of Fire has need of you! What more reason do you need to respond?"

I jumped up and escaped sideways over the arm of the couch, knocking down a lamp on the side table. I ran for the door, waiting to feel a clawed hand raking across my back. The door was locked, and I spun back in panic just as Consul Krasik-dahé—which I now understood meant "honourable flying frog"—entered, carrying a tray with my tea in a fine china cup, little roses on the side, matching milk and sugar.

"Please sit and have your tea, Crispin," the Consul said. "I understand how unusual this must all seem." And damned if I didn't obey.

Back on the couch, I tried to keep my cool, to think my way through this madness. "Why now?" I asked. "Why didn't you come to find me next year, or the year after? Or when I was twenty-five, like my mom thought?"

"There has been a prophecy," said Tiqokh, as undramatically as you might say, "I got an offer code in my email."

But my imagination grabbed hold of this word. "Prophecy? You mean, like the coming of...*the One?*"

Krasik-dahé shook her head. "No, not like that."

But I wasn't giving up so easily. "Am I...I don't know, the lost heir to the ancient throne? Gondor, or...or Narnia!"

"Crispin..."

"Am I *the boy who didn't die*? Is that why you chose me?"

"If you had died," Tiqokh said, "you would obviously not have been chosen." Deflated, I glared at him. He was like some dead-eyed school guidance counsellor, who wouldn't even laugh at a knock-knock joke.

Krasik-dahé said, "A dragon will die. One of the five. We don't know which, and we pray it is not the Queen, but this tragedy has been recently foretold."

The gravity of her words hit me, maybe because I was now talking in Dragon. "I'm sorry," I said.

The quadrana touched his forehead and his heart. "The Realm of Fire cannot exist without its celestial lords. The Five must be maintained. That is why you are needed, Dragon Groom."

"Okay, could you maybe *not* call me that?" I slurped my tea to buy some time to think, although frankly I had been trying *not* to think about the details. Did a dragon look like I thought it did? Four-legged, big as a bus? Because I couldn't quite picture the...uh, act. My mind flashed images of a giant squatting lizard with its tail raised while I climbed up a step-ladder with my shorts around my ankles. I shuddered.

I decided to focus on some simpler questions. "If I do choose to go with you to this realm place, how do we get there? Where's the magic chariot or the portal, or how does it work?"

Consul Krasik-dahé stood. "Come, we will show you." At the door of the suite, she pulled on a pair of chunky brown pumps, and I followed her into the corridor, Tiqokh bringing up the rear, again in his trench coat and fedora disguise. We took the elevator up to the seventeenth floor, then opened the fire exit and climbed up one more flight to the flat gravel roof. Tiqokh propped the door open with a lava rock pulled from his deep coat pocket.

"Are we allowed out here?" I took a circuit around the roof, checking out the views of the city. The dragony folks didn't seem interested in the question. The clouds had parted, and the pale November sun was offering at least the idea of warmth. Looking east, I could see the Don River and the bridges that crossed it. To the west was the Eaton Centre's glass roof. In the south, the lake was a brooding slab of slate patterned with triangular white caps. My circuit of the roof ended on the north side, where I looked down on some guy in the park peeing against a dumpster. So much for sightseeing.

I wandered back to Consul Krasik-dahé and Tiqokh, who were closed into a tight huddle in the middle of the roof. Tiqokh had removed not only his trench coat but his shirt, revealing a gaunt torso that seemed to have too many ribs and vertebrae. As I approached, I could hear a familiar humming coming from another lava rock in Tiqokh's hands. It glowed like the Consul's disco rocks had. The quadrana was chanting softly, almost a cooing sound. *Come on, pretty little rock, do your thing.* That's a really rough translation. Not taking their eyes off the rock, they shifted apart, offering me a place in the circle.

"Ready yourselves," said Tiqokh, and Krasik-dahé took a step back. I was so intent on the glow and the unearthly hum, it took a moment for me to realize the world around us had grown dark. Looking up, expecting to see a storm cloud overhead, I was greeted with a sight that made me cry out and stagger backward. I would have fallen on my ass if the Consul hadn't grabbed my arm.

"Behold," she said. It was the kind of bogus, overblown word a magician uses to impress you because he's made some smelly pigeon pop out of a shoebox, but she had every right to use it. Though the rooftop of the Ambassador Hotel hadn't changed, I couldn't see any city beyond its limits. Instead, we were surrounded and surmounted by a new sky of blue-black, shot through with fractures of crimson and yellow. And hanging in this primal expanse were three planets— massive and way too close.

CHAPTER 5: *Out*

Every few seconds, great world-rending thunder reverberated through the terrifying new sky. It was like ice sheets shifting, or a giant cracking its neck. A harsh, hot wind that tasted like chalk and ozone blew around us. I wasn't cold anymore, but I was shaking.

The quadrana, Tiqokh, held the rock up over his head, mouth moving, eyes bulging. Veins stood out all over his body as if he was a weightlifter who had just clean-and-jerked the three planets into the sky. I was kind of hoping Krasik-dahé would announce this was all a big hologram trick they'd concocted to freak me out. In fact, she was smiling broadly, but with awe, not, you know, comedy.

"These are the Elemental Realms, Crispin," she shouted over the wind and thunder, "made visible through the summoning stone and Tiqokh's virtuosity. Above us, the Realm of Water."

It was a blue sphere, close enough that I could see the shimmering glints of cresting waves. Were those whales breaking the surface, or were they dragons? Fluffy white mountains of cloud gathered at the horizon.

"It's beautiful," I said. "Can we go there?" In my imagination, I could see myself travelling that boundless sea in a great sailing ship. Altman was with me, of course, and we were doing the *Titanic* pose at the front of the boat, though I'm not sure who was Jack and who was Rose.

The Consul shook her head. "The strands that connect the Earth to the Realm of Water have been badly degraded. If Tiqokh had a stronger stone, and if he were powerful enough to control the link—"

The quadrana spoke, gasping a little. "The Realm of Water is not our destination."

The sky itself was rotating, carrying its celestial bodies with it. The Realm of Water began to sink behind the horizon, and Krasik-dahé pointed to the next world passing overhead.

"That is the Realm of Air," she said into my ear. "The dragons of that realm are the most warlike and secretive. We have heard no news from behind its storm clouds for hundreds of cycles."

Clouds girdled this globe in wide bands of green, white, and mocha. A big spot like the eye of Jupiter swirled in one hemisphere, but deep blue and spitting out lightning bolts. Streamers of coloured gas leaked off the world into the void, giving the Realm of Air a fuzzy outline. Was there a core of rock below or just clouds on top of clouds?

Before I could ask, Tiqokh said, "Nor is that our destination."

Then a more peculiar celestial object was rising—not a sphere, but a rough football shape. Like over the Realm of Air, fog banks danced across this world. But between them were patches of colour: the green of fields and forests, the white of snow-covered mountains, small vibrant patches of blue water, and at either end, geysering jets of lava that shot high into the air—red-orange at one end of the world, electric green at the other. My breath caught as the Realm of Fire rose into the sky like a phoenix. And yes, I knew this strange planet was the Realm of Fire. I'd never been there, but part of me felt homesick for it.

"You see, Dragon Groom?" Tiqokh wheezed, his breath even more laboured than before. "The strands are strong." He pointed at what looked like shimmering shoelaces of thick, shifting copper that hung between the Earth and this new planet. "When the Realm of Fire is in position, I will transport us there as if climbing a sturdy ladder."

I panicked. "Wait, I'm not ready!" I shouted. "This is too soon!"

As if my words had broken a spell, the quadrana fell to his knees, the stone dropping heavily on the roof of the hotel. The realms vanished from the sky, and the city flickered back into existence around us. Thunder was replaced by the roar of traffic and the wailing of sirens. The sky was just normally dark, dotted with the few stars you could usually see through the light pollution.

Tiqokh's prominent ribs rose and fell as he struggled to get his breath back, and I dropped to the ground beside him, overwhelmed.

"Sorry," I said. "I didn't mean to break it." Tiqokh didn't look at me, and I thought he was pissed off, but then Consul Krasik-dahé offered a hand and pulled me to my feet.

"No, Crispin, Tiqokh could not hold the connection any longer. And in any case, we must wait until the Realm of Fire is directly overhead. I think that will not happen for more than an hour." Without looking up, Tiqokh nodded at her estimate.

"Okay. Great. I was worried that—" I froze. "Wait a second! Why is it dark? When we came up here, it wasn't even noon." With a sinking feeling, I started digging in my pocket for my phone.

"Yes," the Consul said calmly. "Time passes very differently when the connection to the realms is established."

"Oh no, oh no," I moaned, staring at the screen in dumb horror. Six fifteen p.m.

"What is troubling you?" Krasik-dahé asked.

I gave her a look that my father called Generic Adolescent Wordless Disgust, or *GAWD*. "It's after dinnertime, and I didn't come home. *That's* what's troubling me. After everything that went down yesterday, what do you think they're thinking now? Oh crap, look at that. I have fifteen messages."

The consul was frustratingly calm. "They will come to the hotel? Is that your guess?"

"Yeah, with the cops and the army and dogs and a big net."

She laid a hand on my shoulder, and I wasn't at all sure I liked this new touchy version of the octona. "Come, we will return to the room and await their arrival. Tiqokh, are you sufficiently recovered to join us?"

Without a word, he stood up and put on his clothes. As we returned to the hotel room, my stomach made an audible rumble. I hadn't eaten since breakfast at the Shendorfs' house, either four or ten hours ago, depending how these things worked. Krasik-dahé let me phone down for a bacon cheeseburger on ciabatta with sweet potato fries and a peach smoothie. The Consul added a small Cobb salad to the order. I was relieved when the meal arrived before my parents, but even so, the suspense wasn't good for digestion.

"Shouldn't I call them?" I asked.

Krasik-dahé headed for the bedroom with her salad. "Just wait for events to unfold," she said, closing the door behind her, apparently unperturbed by the coming apocalypse.

I looked at Tiqokh. "Don't you eat?"

He turned his strange eyes to me. "Once a week. A very large meal."

I didn't feel like imagining that, so I took the conversation in another direction. "The prophecy was, uh, forecast or whatever up in the Realm of Fire?"

"Yes. Eight days ago."

"And what? They sent you a text or something?"

Tiqokh reached out his long arm and took a fancy leather-bound book off a side table, handing it to me.

"Correct," he said. "A text."

I opened the book and began flipping through pages of weird, undecipherable calligraphy. "Is this the Tongue of Fire? If I can speak it, why can't I read it?"

"The written language is relatively new, but the blood you carry is ancient." It took me a second, but I got what he meant. I kept turning pages, and every one was crammed full of the swirling black text. The writing ended about halfway through the book, and the rest of the pages were blank. The last and, I guess, most recent entry was not in black ink, but in deep blue. The letters seemed to pulse. I put my fingers on the page, and the text was warm to the touch.

"Is that the prophecy?" I asked, lowering my voice, taking a slow sip of my smoothie.

Tiqokh recited it from memory. "The balance has been disturbed. The Great One flies from Farad'hil, magnificent in blazing fury. And there, where the ground is wounded with light, the dragon dies, coloured tears falling on frozen ground."

I couldn't breathe. The plastic straw sat unmoving on my lip. The words were beautiful. Beautiful and awful. Maybe this was what our English teacher always hoped we'd feel when he read us his favourite poems. The phone on the coffee table rang, so unexpected and loud, I accidentally inhaled some of my smoothie, sending me into a coughing fit. The Consul swept back into the room and picked up the receiver.

"Yes," she said. "He is here. I understand. We are in room 1412." She hung up. "That was—"

"Yeah, I got it." No time to worry about prophecies, this was a *real* emergency. "What are we going to do?"

Tiqokh stood, flexing his arms. "I will help you escape. Just say the word *'ekdahi'* and we're off. I will smite any that stand in our way."

My mouth dropped open, but Krasik-dahé said simply, "There will be no smiting, Tiqokh. Go into the bedroom so you don't alarm Crispin's parents." As he closed the bedroom door, he gave me what I took to be a conspiratorial nod. A minute later, there was a sharp knock on the suite's front door.

The Consul opened it, and there was my father, a sweating monolith of injured pride. My mom stood behind his right shoulder, sighing with relief when she saw me.

Consul Krasik-dahé said, "Please, come in." Mom started forward, but Dad stood his ground and didn't let her past.

He ignored the octona. "Crispin, I'm very disappointed in you.

How could you just vanish like that? Didn't you realize how worried we'd be?"

"It wasn't my fault. We were viewing another dimension; the time got away from us." This didn't sound as good out loud as it did in my head. Dad just glared, and I asked Krasik-dahé, "Did I say that in English or Dragon?"

The Consul gestured toward the living room. "Come sit down. Let's discuss this calmly."

Dad shook his head. "I trusted you. I vouched for you to my wife, but you were planning to steal him away without our permission from the start. How could you?" He sounded genuinely hurt.

The Consul's expression did not change. "Crispin came here of his own free will. This is bigger than any of us, Elliot. He is the Dragon Groom."

Dad raised his hands in the air, apparently done with the discussion. "Crispin, get your things and come with us!" His temper was shorter than a garden gnome, and I would have obeyed if Krasik-dahé hadn't spoken up.

"The choice is Crispin's," she answered, as cool as ever.

Dad would not be placated. "Anytime you want, you appear and turn our lives upside down! I didn't ask for the blood. Neither did Crispin." He pulled out his phone and waved it at her like some magical amulet, only to be used in times of peril. "If my son isn't allowed to leave right now, I'm calling the police and having you charged with abduction."

Mom broke the standoff by pushing past him into the suite. "Elliot, just ignore her. We're here to talk to Crispin."

Mom joined me on the couch but sat at the far end, giving me space. Dad, the wind blown out of his sails, entered quietly and dropped into Tiqokh's chair. I hoped he hadn't left any dragony residue behind. Krasik-dahé, to her credit, stood quietly in the corner and let the family drama happen.

Mom folded her hands in her lap and gave me little encouraging smiles that made me even more wary. "Crispin, honey—" she began, but I cut her off.

"Mom, honestly, I didn't mean to worry you. Everything's just been…" I let out a shaky breath. I was more emotional than I had admitted to myself. "It's been a weird twenty-four hours, okay?"

She nodded, a spooky marvel of serenity. "I know, Crispin. Adolescence can be a very tough time of life, and that's why you don't want to make any rash decisions about your future. Honey, I think there's more going on here than just this"—she waved a hand vaguely in Krasik-dahé's direction—"this dragon business. Lately, you've been so moody. You use sarcasm to cover it, but I can see you're in pain."

Even though all her amateur psychology was super obvious, I felt tears stinging my eyes. "Honest, Mom, I'm fine."

She nodded, but not like I'd said anything particularly interesting. "I want to ask you something, Crispin, and whatever the answer, your father and I love and support you."

I looked from her to Dad, but he was very busy picking dirt from under a fingernail. "What?" I asked, dread cramping my stomach.

"Are you and Altman in some kind of relationship? I mean, a romantic relationship?"

I jumped to my feet. "What? No! Why would you *say* that?" My heart started pounding, and my vision telescoped until her big, accusing eyes were the only things in the room.

Mom raised a hand like she was calming a startled horse. "It's okay, it's okay. If he is your boyfriend, that's…well, that's something we'll sit down and discuss. With his family, with you…Because we're all in this together and—"

I was backing up, putting as much overwrought furniture and faux-royal carpeting between us as possible. "No! No, we're not in this together. You have no idea what you're even *talking* about."

"Say something, Elliot!" my mother snapped at my father, and everything was just a freaking disaster. This was *my* thing, *my* coming out. And it was being taken from me in a hotel room full of octonas and quadranas and freaking huge realms floating over our heads. My *boyfriend*! I was nothing to Altman, and nothing but a slut to the rest of the school.

My head hurt. I couldn't catch my breath. "No, you don't get it," I gasped out. "You don't get any part of this."

Everyone was on their feet now, turned my way. Mom said, "Just come home and we'll work it out. I promise."

"No!" I screamed. "I don't want to go home with you. Why did you have to come here in the first place? Dragons only, Mom. Get out."

Dad tried the authority thing again. "Crispin, these people aren't your friends. The sooner we all go home, the sooner you'll be able to think straight."

Everyone looked blurry now, and I realized I was crying. "I *don't* think straight, Dad. I don't *anything* straight. Isn't that the *point*?" And then, without planning it at all, without considering the consequences, I shouted, "*Ekdahi!*"

The bedroom door burst open, and Tiqokh exploded out of it, an indistinct blur in a long trench coat. I was swept off my feet and thrown over his back like a sack of beans. I watched my parents' shocked faces retreating as the quadrana ran us out onto the suite's balcony. The world turned upside down, and it took a second to realize he was climbing the outside wall of the hotel. I screamed, and he tightened his grip around my waist.

In no time, we reached the roof, and Tiqokh dropped me on the tar and pebbles. The night was windless and calm, the city around us pulsing with the play of light and sound. I felt dizzy, barely able to comprehend what was happening as Tiqokh raised the summoning stone over his head, this time chanting out loud in the dragon tongue.

"Children of the Realms, lost ones from the belonging time, I reach for you. I declare our unity." A rumbling shook the building, the universe, my terrified guts. With an ear-splitting crack, the Realm of Fire appeared overhead.

The great, rough world of rock was so close now, I could see animals grazing in pastures dotted with fog and riders on horseback moving among them. Up on a range of hills was some kind of city, buildings rising on the rocky peaks, streets twisting around the landscape, everything hanging upside down. As if in celebration or warning, the polar volcanoes spewed geysers of green and red into the sky. And somewhere I could hear a song…a poetry that made a weird kind of sense to me. In fact, the more I listened, the more its meanings seemed to multiply, connection on connection, a history older than any I knew. There was sorrow and longing and loss in the song, but within that sorrow, a promise of reconciliation.

The noise was incredible, and I only barely heard Tiqokh call me. "Dragon Groom!" He stretched out his hand, and I hurried toward the blinding light of the summoning stone. The quadrana wrapped his bony arm around my waist, and together we lifted off the roof of the Ambassador Hotel, swept along like we were whitewater rafting on the copper strands connecting my home on Earth with a home I had never seen before. Together, we flew headlong toward the Realm of Fire.

PART II

THE COPPER GUEST

CHAPTER 6: *Deliberations*

"Please keep your attention focussed on me, D'gada-vixtet-thon, not on the gallery, beautiful as the inlaid panels may be. What does the DragonLaw say on the matter?"

D'gada-vixtet-thon—D'gada of the house of the dragon Vixtet, apprentice of Thon, the Atmospherics discipline, known to his friends as Davix—was seated in an ancient, uncomfortable chair. He lowered his eyes to Grav'nan-dahé's thin, pinched face. "Teacher, when serious matters are discussed, the eye must search for unassailable clarity, not whimsical delight. So it is written in the Collected Wisdom of Tarn."

Davix could tell Grav'nan-dahé, Prime Magistrate, the most revered human in the Realm of Fire and most learned in the ways of the DragonLaw, was pleased with the answer. The Prime Magistrate intimidated most of the People, but after more than a cycle studying at his side, Davix knew his teacher valued him, even if words of praise rarely left his lips.

"You can be forgiven your awe," Grav'nan-dahé said. "I have never before invited you to the Council chambers. It is a mark of my trust in you, a trust you have earned through dedication and obedience."

Davix tried to appear calm and focussed, even though his thoughts were swirling. He had received the urgent summons while at lunch, and his thighs still burned from running up the steep, winding streets to Etnep House. He would finally hear the results of the inquest, fifteen days after Rinby's death. While it could be explained as an accident, Davix had carefully noted to the investigators from Defence of Realm all his troubling observations.

Davix kept his eyes on his teacher, though he wanted to look up again at the panels. He was wondering if one or more of the bidahénas was hiding behind their latticework. Stakrat had told him sometimes these most inscrutable of the mixed beings listened unseen when the

Council of Masters met. Even the masters didn't know when they were being observed.

Grav'nan-dahé rose from his chair and crossed the room in his shimmering robes to stand at the window. Old as he was, his voice was strong and clear. "I have brought you here, D'gada-vixtet-thon, to give you news I hope will bring your heart a measure of peace. T'lexdar-inby-thon's death, though unusual, was simply ill luck."

Davix should have felt relieved. The matter was closed, and their lives could now go on. Still, the niggling grains of doubt could not be dislodged so easily from his mind. He squirmed in his uncomfortable chair.

"Teacher, the marks on the wall, the blood—"

"Child! The bidahénas have investigated all the circumstances and found nothing suspicious. It is not our place to question the wisdom of beings so exalted."

Davix shot a brief glance up. "I meant no disrespect," he said. "But, Teacher, let us examine the details once again." This was their way, the kind of open debate that Grav'nan-dahé encouraged when they considered problematic passages of the DragonLaw.

But the Prime Magistrate did not enter into the game. Instead, he snapped, "Do you dare question? You should be glad that the blame was not placed at your feet."

Davix felt like he'd been slapped. *I am not a child*, he wanted to shout. But then a cold chill passed through his body. It had never occurred to him he could be blamed for Rinby's death. He lowered his head in humility. "We are sustained by the love of the Dragon Lords."

This tenet was central to the People's beliefs; it was anchor and comfort. But for the first time in his life, the words felt strange on his tongue. His suspicions were reasonable. And yet the bidahénas, the closest any of the People came to standing in the presence of a real dragon, had made their determination. If their version of events wasn't already written in the DragonLaw, it soon would be. Any contradicting theories were now blasphemies, and he must abandon them. It was a blessing, he knew, to submit to the perfection of the DragonLaw. But try as he might, this submission rankled.

He was startled when the Prime Magistrate came up behind him and placed a hand on his shoulder.

"Davix," he said, suddenly gentle. "We all mourn Rinby's loss, and I understand the two of you were especially close. Be strong."

Davix felt tears come to his eyes. Grav'nan-dahé, whom so many regarded as remote and cold, was calling him by his familiar name, had brought him to the Council Chambers just to offer him comfort. Davix felt ashamed of his rebellious thoughts. From now on, he would take control of his heart and prove himself worthy of his Teacher's trust.

"Thank you, Teacher. I am grateful for your support. Many of Rinby's duties have fallen to me, and I have had to redouble my Atmospherics studies in order to perform these tasks. The Atmospherics Master believes I will have to step back from my lessons with you, at least for a time."

Grav'nan-dahé's took his hand from Davix's shoulder, and his voice again grew cold. "Does he? And does Tix-etnep-thon-dahé understand how I have come to depend on you?"

Davix looked nervously up at the man. The sky outside had darkened, and Grav'nan-dahé's face was in shadow.

"Teacher, my pledge to my discipline—"

"Have you not also made pledges to me?" The wind was rising, and Davix felt the tiny hairs on his neck stand up. "We make choices in life, Acolyte, and they affect our future in ways we can hardly imagine. Think carefully before you—"

As a crack shattered the air, the straining daylight was extinguished altogether and the wind began to howl. Davix ran to the window to see what the sky was doing, automatically making a reckoning. *Wind from redward, level four, gusting to six.*

"Krar's claws!" Grav'nan-dahé cursed as he joined him at the window.

Davix could hardly believe what he was witnessing. "Has someone energized the strands? Are they crossing over?"

Grav'nan-dahé's eyes were hard, black coals. "Come! We must put a stop to this." The Prime Magistrate hurried for the door, and Davix ran after him.

They left Etnep House and ran across the Retreat of Tarn. The great square was filling with the citizens of Cliffside, excited and a little fearful. All eyes were turned skyward, and though he was hurrying to keep up with the Prime Magistrate, Davix stopped to look up, too. Above them, the realm sky had appeared, turning day to night, and hanging in it was the Realm of Earth. The great globe, whose weather systems could be read in its cloud patterns, floated blue, green, and brown overhead, serene and majestic. The twisted strands that connected the two realms glowed with potency, a comforting connection to the ancient home world.

"It is the Dragon Groom," Davix said. "He comes because of the prophecy."

Grav'nan-dahé spun around to face his acolyte. "Where have you heard of this prophecy?"

"There have been rumours circulating through Cliffside for days."

"Exactly! Rumour and heresy. The followers of the Fire Revealed test my tolerance. Hear my unequivocal words, D'gada-vixtet-thon. The DragonLaw has no room for the fictions of false seers." The man was sweating, face red and breathing laboured.

"But, Teacher," Davix said. "What about the Prophecies in the Badlands? The agonies of N'rayaf are a cherished chapter in the—"

"That was in the Days of Wonder, when the Realm stood closer to the heart of creation." Thunder shook their chests. The glowing forks of the strands reached down from the sky to touch the Message Aerie, a tall building on an adjacent street.

"There is little time." Grav'nan-dahé took hold of Davix's shoulders and brought his face close. Davix could smell the fermented bean of the man's lunch. "You and I must stand as bulwark against the rising tide of superstition. Remember, prophecy is *heresy*!" The Prime Magistrate, breathing hard, took another moment to gather his strength, then turned and ran toward the Message Aerie, shouting, "Hurry!"

Davix worried for the old man's stubborn, ancient heart.

CHAPTER 7: *Another World, Another Rooftop*

Travelling between worlds, it turns out, doesn't feel like bungee jumping, which would have been my first guess. It's not flying, but it's not falling. Maybe it's like being an attachment in an instant message. You have no body. You're nothing but random impulses, then DING! BUZZ! you arrive as a full-fledged dick pic on someone's screen.

I was on my hands and knees, forehead drenched in sweat, staring down at rows of red-brown tiles. The air smelled of evergreens and baking bread, with a faint undertone of rotten eggs.

In my peripheral vision, Tiqokh stood up. "Rise, Dragon Groom. We are home!" His voice was more excited than I had heard in all the hours since we'd become BDFFs.

I tried to stand, but I only got halfway up before stretching forward and vomiting epically across the neatly laid tiles. My knees went weak, and I might have done a face plant right into my own puke puddle, but Tiqokh grabbed me and led me over to a low wall. I took in just enough of the surroundings to see we were standing on the roof of a tall, narrow building, but I was dizzy and needed to sit down before I did any more sightseeing. I closed my eyes and let the fresh breeze cool my face.

Somewhere above me, Tiqokh said, "I hope I'm in time for the colloquy."

"What's that?"

"The mixed beings meet twice a cycle to discuss pertinent issues. The discussions are most stimulating. I have missed them during my time on Earth."

The dizziness was passing, and the thought hit me like lightning. *I'm in another world!* My eyes snapped open.

The first thing I noticed—and it was hard to miss—was the Earth hanging above us in 3D IMAX with surround sound. It was just like the scene from the Ambassador rooftop, except with my home planet in the sky.

But before I could wrap my brain around this thought, the sky lightened, and the Earth faded and vanished. The obnoxious, interdimensional thunder receded into the distance, until the only sound was a flock of freaked-out birds circling the building and screaming the alarm. We were halfway up a big hill, above a green valley mostly covered in thick fog. Between the patches of flowing white mist, I could spot unplanted farmland, the earth tilled in long neat lines like a corduroy blazer.

Tiqokh handed me a mint with "Ambassador Hotel" printed on the wrapper and said, "Travelling the strands can be disorienting to mind and body. Are you feeling better?"

"Yeah," I muttered, popping the mint and stuffing the wrapper in my pocket. Polluting another world with Earth-branded garbage would have been downright obscene. The building we were standing on was one of many, built above and below us on the side of a hill, forming a small city. Up the hill to one side was a castle, its tall spires half hidden in the fog. To the other side was a stone-walled fort with its own towers, blockier and less graceful than the castle. If the city was the head of a bull, these two big structures were the horns.

"Who lives here? The Five Dragons? I was expecting more of a cave thing. Maybe with a big pile of gold coins."

"No, this is Cliffside, the habitation of the People, the humans who serve the Five."

The way he said "the People," I could tell it was capitalized. And right on cue, a trap door opened, and five or six humans climbed up from a stairwell onto the roof. Their jaws were hanging open at the sight of me, so I figured tourists weren't exactly common. But the People weren't there to gawk at me. They were trying to catch the dozen or so scared birds who were still circling the building, cawing noisily. The birds reminded me of crows, except that their heads were red and their beaks were longer. The humans stood at the edge of the building, making cooing noises, convincing the birds to land on their outstretched hands.

Now more of the People were climbing onto the roof. Unlike the bird herders, they were definitely there to see what the cat had dragged in across the strands. There were men and women of different ages, dressed in loose-fitting clothes in earth tones, reds, and greens. All were brown-skinned, and except for those going grey, they all had straight, jet black hair.

The group had grown to more than twenty when this dramatic-looking guy climbed up from below and pushed through their ranks. He was a tall, older man in a long, shiny robe, his steel gray hair pulled back in a ponytail. He looked pissed off.

"No!" he shouted in a big confident voice, holding a hand up like a traffic cop. "You do not belong here!" I stepped closer to Tiqokh, and you can tell how freaked I was if Tiqokh was my new standard for security.

A kid my age had climbed up with the old guy and was staring at me, arms crossed on his chest. His long black hair was tied in a little bun on top of his head, but stray bits leaked out, falling across his neck and over his forehead. Skinny waist, wide shoulders. His bare arms were lightly muscled—not like he lifted. More like he had a weekend job loading boxes in his uncle's warehouse.

"Greetings, Grav'nan-dahé," Tiqokh said as the old guy crossed to our side of the roof. "This lad of Earth, one of the twenty who carry the blood, has been chosen Dragon Groom. I was instructed to bring him to the Realm of Fire, following the recent prophecy of the death of a dragon."

"Prophecy is heresy!" shouted the kid with him, like some angry street corner preacher. His face, built around a big curved nose, was clenched in a hard mask of determination, but the warm dark eyes, gentle and intelligent, and his full silky lips suggested a softer side. If he and the old guy weren't making me feel so unwelcome, I'd be hoping for a chance to kiss him.

"Prophecy is heresy," Grav'nan-dahé agreed with a nod. "The Council of Earth, it pains me to say, has been poisoned by superstition. Rest assured, Tiqokh, the Five Dragons are strong and healthy. While we appreciate your hard work so far from home, you were wrong to bring this boy here. You will return him immediately to the Realm of Earth."

My heart sank. Was that it? We were being turned back by border services? In twenty-four hours, I'd found out I was part of this whole crazy world of fire dragons and had flown to another universe or dimension or postal code or whatever, and now I was supposed to head home without even a T-shirt from the duty-free shop? I gave Tiqokh a desperate look, but his face, as usual, betrayed nothing.

"That is not possible, Prime Magistrate. My strength is depleted from the journey, and the realms are no longer in alignment."

"How long until you are able to cross back?"

Tiqokh held up the summoning stone and examined the sky through it. "We have entered a retrograde slippage. Three days, I would guess."

Grav'nan-dahé licked his lips and wiped sweat from his brow with the sleeve of his robe. "I am not sure I believe you, quadrana."

"As you know, the quadranas are incapable of telling lies."

"Who knows what habits you have learned on Earth."

Tiqokh pushed me forward unexpectedly, and I almost tripped. "This boy, whatever you believe about the timing of his visit, is the chosen Dragon Groom. He deserves your deepest respect, not to be shooed out like a frog that has hopped into the dining hall."

Everyone on the roof grew very still, like they didn't dare take sides. The fog that had been drifting around rolled onto the rooftop. Noises carried strangely in the new humidity, and everything grew blurry. I started sweating like a spelling bee contestant.

Angry wrinkles had formed around the old guy's eyes. "Do not presume to school me in manners, Tiqokh," he said. "Very well, I concede your point. You and the youth have travelled far, and the copper in his blood means he is part of this realm. But as the time of his service is not now—may the Five long outlive us—he cannot be called the Dragon Groom." The man took my chin and tilted my head around, like he was a judge at the kennel show and I was in the running for pug of the year. "You will be known as the Copper Guest." He let go of me, which was good, because I was about to slap his hand away. "Welcome to the Realm of Fire," he said, touching his forehead and then his chest, like Tiqokh had back at the hotel.

"Uh, thanks."

Grav'nan-dahé turned to the people on the roof. "Peace and balance to the Copper Guest!"

"Peace and balance!" they echoed. Bells began ringing across the city. Were they for me or was it a coincidence?

The crowd went down the stairwell, with a lot of backward glances at this strange new animal that had fallen from the sky. Soon only six of us were left: Grav'nan-dahé, me, Tiqokh, and three kids around my age—the guy with the kissable lips and strong opinions about prophecy, a tough-looking girl, and another guy who was all buff and stuff, but not quite as cute as the first guy.

The old guy said, "Copper Guest, I am Grav'nan-dahé, Prime Magistrate of the Realm of Fire. We bid you welcome to our realm and to our city, Cliffside. Tonight, there will be a dinner in your honour with the masters of the ten disciplines." He indicated the three teens. "These young people are some of our lead apprentices, and they will help you prepare for that meeting. Apprentices, he needs to be properly attired and taught some etiquette."

I almost answered, *I'm not Eliza Doolittle, buddy*, but the girl said, "It will be done, Honoured One."

"And that needs to be cleaned up," Grav'nan-dahé said, waving through the thickening fog in the general direction of my vomit puddle. Ladies and gentlemen, Crispin Haugen knows how to make an entrance.

CHAPTER 8: *The Intruder*

ponder and strategize: the strands ignited, an unwelcome intrusion. the demi-dragons fail again. infuriating. The Intruder watched with keen eyes the gathering on the roof, the immature human who smelled of copper at its centre. *should he die, or might he play a useful part?* The Intruder watched and waited. *soon soon.*

CHAPTER 9: *Fog, Frog, and Fabric*

I followed Grav'nan-dahé into the stairwell, with Tiqokh behind me and the three apprentice kids bringing up the rear. As we descended, I peeked into one of the side rooms and saw rows of wooden cages filled with the redheaded crows. The bird herders from the roof were still cooing at their frightened flock, feeding them treats by hand. I stepped aside to let a woman with a sloshing bucket of water past, on her way up to clean my little offering. Should I have apologized? Maybe I did need etiquette lessons.

When we got outside, I was surprised to see Grav'nan-dahé already far down the street, gone without saying goodbye. Tiqokh, still dressed in his fedora and long coat, looked oddly at home in the thick, rolling fog, like he was doing private eye cosplay. He bent over and placed a hand on my shoulder.

"Do not fear, Dragon Groom," he said quietly in my ear. "Your arrival is of great significance to the People. They will not let you come to harm. Now, I must leave you for a time."

"Wait, who wants to harm me?" He just gave my shoulder a squeeze and walked up the street in the opposite direction from High Priest Creepy. I almost yelled after him, "Can we forget all this and go back to Earth?" But then the three apprentice kids were walking my way. The girl had her arm wrapped cosily around the waist of the preacher boy with the topknot. Not that he was really a dating option, but I was still disappointed to find out he was straight. A man in black walked past me, shooting the couple a crabby look, and they hastily disengaged, lowering their eyes.

"Are you in need of a chaperone?" the man in black asked.

The girl shook her head. "Thank you, Gan'sul. We will not be leaving the public sphere."

Laughing, the ripped boy added, "And there's four of us. It's not that kind of party. Especially not with the Copper Guest!"

Gan'sul didn't look convinced, but he walked on.

During this exchange, the preacher boy had moved away to stand alone in the shade of a building, brooding sexily. The girl and the ripped boy walked up to me.

"Welcome! Peace and balance!" said the girl. "I'm Stakrat, Lead Apprentice in Defence of Realm."

"Uh, hi."

Stakrat was about my height—not big and butch, but I could see by the sinewy muscles in her arms and calves how formidable she was. I guess that made sense if you were defending realms. She also wore a big nasty knife on her leather belt, so clearly she was a good person to have on my side.

The ripped guy was actually less intimidating than Stakrat, friendly like a pet ox with a big goofy smile. "Grentz," he introduced himself. "Lead Apprentice in Stonework." He reached out a hand to me, and I didn't know whether I was expected to shake, fist bump, or try a full-on gang sign tap dance. What we were supposed to do, it turned out, was grab each other's same-side forearm. We were both laughing by the time I had it right.

He said, "We are blessed to meet a real Dragon Groom. You must have been preparing your whole life for this honour."

"Well, I guess I did other stuff, too," I said, coughing in embarrassment. Grentz handed me his waterskin, and I drank a big, thirsty swallow.

He pointed at a half-finished building higher up the slope. "See that rotunda on the side? I designed that."

"Yeah," Stakrat snorted, grabbing Grentz in a headlock. "He designed a niche in the shade so he could sleep during his work shift." I jumped away as the two began wrestling each other in the middle of the street. Even though Grentz outweighed her by an elephant to an antelope, Stakrat was scoring most of the points. I could tell they were just having fun, but still I backed away like I did when a fight broke out at school. I found myself standing at the wall beside the preacher boy.

Our awkward silence lasted so long, I had to break it. "Hey, I know you don't think I should be here, but I'm kind of excited to see the realm."

"Grav'nan-dahé has declared you an honoured visitor, Copper Guest, and I will show you every courtesy." He then went on to contradict this by shutting up and looking away.

Well, thanks, I thought, nice to meet you, too. Stakrat and Grentz, having finished this week's episode of *Battle of the Dragon World All-*

Stars, joined us in the shade by the wall, grinning and sweating. I gave Grentz his waterskin back, and they both drank.

"He didn't introduce himself, right?" asked Stakrat, tucking a lock of her hair back in place. "This is Davix. Lead Apprentice in Atmospherics."

Davix snapped his head up. "I'm not lead." He looked angry, which almost made him less handsome, but he also looked like a sad Labrador puppy, which made me want to pat him.

"You're performing Rinby's duties, aren't you?" she said. "Do a good job, and Tix-etnep-thon-dahé will make it official. She would have wanted that."

Davix made a barely perceptible nod, and she smiled. Did they have that psychic connection I had with Altman sometimes? Well, if Davix was this brawling babe's boyfriend, I bet he had bruises to show for it.

"Let's go," he said. "We have to get the Copper Guest dressed for tonight."

The narrow, cobblestone streets of Cliffside were trenches of unbroken architecture, the buildings on either side made of neatly laid, rough-hewn stones in red and brown. It was hard to tell if they were twenty years old or two centuries. Over and over, I was thinking, I'm in another world! But it was hard to actually convince my brain of this.

We passed a low wall overlooking the valley, which was mostly lost in fog. Three frogs sat peacefully on the wall.

"*Krasik!*" I announced happily, and Grentz and Stakrat looked confused. Davix tilted his head, as if seeing me for the first time.

"You know the ancient word," he said.

Was he impressed? I shrugged as nonchalantly as I could. "Yeah, I guess I'm pretty fluent."

A sleek orange cat was sliding along the base of the wall and, without warning, sprang up to grab a snack of fresh frog. But before she could sink her claws into one, the amphibian trio jumped off into space. Webbing between their arms and legs spread taut as they caught a thermal and flew away into the fog.

"You'll have to be faster than that, kitty," I told the cat sympathetically, but she snarled at me and ran when I tried to pet her. "Hey! Aren't the cats here friendly?"

"They're predators," Davix said, like I was born yesterday.

I thought about Consul Krasik-dahé, who shared a name with the little frogs. What was happening back at the hotel? Maybe my dad had already called the cops on her. *I'm in another world, I'm in another world...*

As we continued our journey, descending through switchback streets, I noticed we were being followed by the same crabby man in black.

I whispered to Stakrat, "What does that chaperone guy want with us?"

She rolled her eyes. "Some of the elders are less trusting of the young than others."

"What doesn't he trust you about?"

"He's making sure we don't have reproductive sex."

Do toes get startled? Because mine managed to find a gap in the otherwise perfectly laid cobbles, and I stumbled. Grentz caught me by the arm and stood me back up.

"Okay," I mumbled through my embarrassment. "We'll take reproductive sex off the to-do list." The fog cleared above us for a second, and I looked up.

"You keep checking the sky," Davix said. "What are you looking for?"

"Um, dragons?" Had he been watching me the whole time? "I mean, assuming they fly. Do they?"

Grentz looked at me in bewilderment. "How do you not *know* that? You're the Dragon Groom."

"The Copper Guest," Davix said.

Stakrat explained, "Of course they do, Copper Guest. But we almost never see the Five."

Davix was looking up, too, and I could see the swirling clouds reflected in his dark eyes. "On the second day of *Sarensikar*," he said, "just before the sun sets, the Five Dragons will fly high above Cliffside, and we will sing to them." I wanted to ask what *Sarensikar* was and what kind of songs they would sing, but I also didn't want to say something dumb that would make him stop talking, because his voice was deep and dreamy.

Grentz, massaging my shoulders from behind, said, "You'll see for yourself in a few days, Copper Guest. But now you're getting special garments made by the Master of Textiles, Lok'lok-sur-nep-dahé himself. I'm sure he's already working on it."

"How is that even possible? I've only been here for an hour." As I said that last word, I could feel its strange taste on my tongue. I realized there was no translation for "hour" in the Tongue of Fire. Still, Grentz seemed to get the idea.

"Word travels quickly in Cliffside."

As if to prove his point, when we rounded the next corner, a tight cluster of six people stood outside a little building of red stone, their faces flushed and dusted with flour.

"We would be honoured if you ate our pastries, Copper Guest," one said, holding out a plate of bite-sized cakes, each decorated with a raspberry. Her nerve-choked voice reminded me of how I sound any time I have to speak in class.

"You shouldn't have," I said, polite like my mom taught me. But the bakers looked at each other in shock.

"We shouldn't?" said the one with plate, withdrawing it in humiliation. "Oh, forgive our thoughtless offence, Copper Guest. Is this one of your fast days?"

"Well, yeah, things are moving pretty fast, but…Oh! No, not what I meant."

Unable to explain without a lot of meaningless babbling, I took the plate from her, gobbling down one of the pastries with a big googly-eyed show of appreciation. It tasted of honey and nuts, like baklava but less syrupy. The berry added a tart, juicy explosion to the experience.

"Wow, so good!" I said. I passed the plate around to the apprentices, who each took one—well, Grentz took two—and then offered it to the chaperone. He acted surprised to be noticed, like he was a three-year-old pretending to be invisible. I thanked the bakers again as I returned the empty plate.

"*Ekdahi*, Copper Guest," one replied. "Duty enriches life."

They went back inside their bakery, and I found out we were just a few doors away from our destination. Up to this point, Cliffside had been all about stone, but inside the textiles building, everything was drapes, bolts of cloth, hanging sashes, and furniture luxurious with soft upholstery. We walked through the noisy weaving rooms and past the dye vats, where pools of crimson and blue burped up vapours that made our eyes water. Everyone looked up and stared at me, and it was hard not to feel self-conscious.

Finally, we walked down a corridor lined on all sides with fabrics of pure, unpatterned pigment. The colours swirled around us like a vortex, sweeping us toward a wooden door. Stakrat knocked.

The door was opened by a giant grin haphazardly attached to another girl around our age. She was tall and skinny, long wavy hair spilling out of a red silk kerchief. She was dressed in a simple shirt and trousers with a subtle brown-on-black geometric pattern, multiple rings on her fingers, and a jangling bundle of bracelets.

She looked at me over Stakrat's shoulder and whispered, "You must be the Copper Guest. I'm Kriz'mig, Lead Apprentice in Textiles." She reached out to do the forearm shake, and this time I was ready for her. Her grin was infectious, and me, Stakrat, and Grentz all caught it. What about Davix, you ask? Yeah, no grin.

"Come in," Kriz'mig said, "but be quiet, he's concentrating."

Inside was chaos—like a fabric art installation titled "Morning after the Hurricane." Big bolts of material threatened to topple on us, and scraps patterned with tiny flowers drifted through the air on the breeze created by the circling arms of the Master of Textiles. He was the first of the People I'd seen with curly hair, long strands held back from his sweating face by hair clips. His eyes were wide as saucers, but he didn't look away from the fabric he was twisting in his hands with graceful violence, like some sort of fashion kung fu.

The apprentice, Kriz'mig, caught a few of the flying scraps and stuffed them into a sack tied to the back of a chair. "My master will have your garment ready in time for the dinner, don't worry."

And at that very moment, Lok'lok-sur-nep-dahé shouted, "Yes! Yes, I see the design." Suddenly, he saw me, too. "Copper Guest, welcome. Take off your clothes."

All in all, I thought our relationship was moving too fast, and when Kriz'mig came forward and started tugging at my T-shirt, I said, "Hold it, wait! How much of my clothes? Don't you have a changing room or something?"

Lok'lok-sur-nep-dahé pushed a curly strand out of his eyes and regarded me sadly, lips pursed. "He has body shyness." He turned to his apprentice. "You see, Kriz'mig? It is sad, but you will occasionally meet members of the People so afflicted. They must be treated firmly but with compassion."

I was allowed to strip under a big piece of mauve fabric. If you've ever changed in the middle of a crowded beach under a towel, you'll know everyone gets to see your butt or worse at some point. And the humiliation didn't end there, because I was being dressed in what was apparently traditional formal wear. The outfit didn't even include the loose-fitting, calf-length pants I'd seen on most of the People. No, this was some complicated affair made of a single long piece of fabric tied elaborately around my waist, between my legs, over my shoulder, and God knows where. The elaborate gift-wrapping session concluded with a detailed demonstration of which piece to push aside when I needed to "make water."

My ears still red from blushing, I examined myself in the mirror.

The fabric was pretty incredible, repeating shapes in copper, like birds flying across a navy background shot through with red lines. It reminded me of the realm sky. The elaborate wrapping gave me wider shoulders and a slim waist, my legs showing from the knees down. I was a strange creature to my own eyes, the Dragon Groom, or at least the Copper Guest, special VIP at an invitation-only dinner. But did I look good?

I caught Davix's eyes in the mirror. Was I imagining it, or did he give me an approving head-to-toe once-over? I looked back at my image and decided that if I squinted, I might, for the first time in living memory, pass for kinda hot.

Lok'lok-sur-nep-dahé adjusted the fall of the material one more time. "That will do," he said before turning on his heel and hurrying from the room in a cloud of coloured scraps.

Kriz'mig assessed her master's work. "You look wonderful, Copper Guest!"

"Totally loop-worthy," Stakrat agreed, eyeing every part of me without embarrassment.

I caught sight of my orange and blue sneaks. "Don't you have any, uh, local shoes for me?"

Kriz'mig shook her head vigorously. "Never! Those are the best shoes I've ever seen. Do *not* take them off. Lok'lok-sur-dahé was jealous of them, I could tell." Then she surveyed the floor and sighed. "Always so much to clean up and document when he's done." She began sweeping up and bagging scraps, making notations in a small notebook.

She picked up a long strip of black fabric with blue feathers sewn into it. "Hey, Davix," she said. "You should wear this for *Sarensikar*. Unless you already have your outfit."

"I'm not dancing," he said quietly.

Stakrat grabbed him by the arm. "Did you really just say that?"

"I'm not in the mood. And it wouldn't be respectful to Rinby's memory."

Stakrat's glare grew more probing. "Why did Grav'nan-dahé call for you at lunch? Was it about Rinby?"

Davix wouldn't meet her eye. "Good news. The bidahénas have determined her death was accidental."

"But didn't you say—?"

He waved her words away. "There are more important matters than my useless theories, Stakrat." He looked at me like I was to blame for his troubles, and his look made me feel naked again.

"Too bad, brother," Grentz said, posing in front of the mirror with an improvised scarf of fuzzy orange fabric around his neck. "Everyone's been waiting for *Sarensikar* to see you dance again. Copper Guest, you should have seen him last year. He didn't win the laurel, but he looped a dozen at least." He adjusted the orange scarf some more. "Kriz'mig, I'm going to take this."

"It's late," Davix snapped. "We'll go to my house to get the Copper Guest ready for his evening." He stormed out of the room, leaving me and the other three apprentices to hurry after him.

When we got back out to the street, we waited for Kriz'mig, who appeared after a couple of minutes holding one of the redheaded crows, stroking its head as it looked at us with clear suspicion.

"Oh, I saw those when I arrived."

Kriz'mig smiled. "This is a kingsolver. Textiles keeps four of them for sending messages. I'm letting Convenor Zishun know you have been properly attired." She tossed the kingsolver into the air, and I could see it had a paper scroll tied to one leg as it flew off.

As we walked, Kriz'mig kept making adjustments to my outfit, tugging at me until I stopped saying thank you and she backed off. It was strange being out in public in my fancy gift wrapping, but everyone we passed seemed pretty impressed. More and more faces looked down from the upper floors of buildings that lined our route, and I thought I could get used to being a celebrity. We had again picked up our cheerless little chaperone, following twenty steps behind. I gave him a friendly wave, which seemed to pain him.

We were climbing again, following a curving path back up the hillside. "Why did the cobblestones just change colour from green to red?"

Grentz, playing with his new scarf, said, "We just left Sur House and now we're entering Vixtet."

"When you and the quadrana arrived," Stakrat added, "You were up on the message aerie in Renrit House."

Davix was the one who noticed my utter confusion. "At birth, each of the People is assigned to one of the five houses, named for the Five Dragons: Renrit, Vixtet, Inby, Sur, and Queen Etnep."

"Oh, she's the one I'm supposed to..." Not a sentence I could bring myself to finish.

"Prophecy..." Davix began.

"Is heresy, right. Forget I said anything."

"Each of us grows up in one of the houses, and we live our whole lives dedicated to our dragon patron."

"Kind of like homerooms at school," I said, being no less obscure. "But you're in the same house as your parents, right?"

Kriz'mig said, "You mean our genetic forebears? No, not necessarily."

"My genetic mother is in my house," Stakrat said. "We have tea together sometimes, but we don't have a lot in common. She works in Agriculture on bean varieties or something."

I was trying to comprehend this. "So, your parents don't raise you?" This idea appealed to me for a second, but then I thought of my mom watching reality shows with me while we ate spiced popcorn and cracked each other up. A little elevator of guilt and loneliness ran up my chest.

"No," Davix said. "You're raised and schooled by the caretakers and teachers, with the other kids in your house." He gestured at the buildings around us. "This is Vixtet, my house. I'm going to get a common room so we can do the etiquette lessons."

Davix led us up a narrow staircase off the main road and through an arched doorway. A man sat at a desk there, making careful notes in a large, leather-bound book. Every time he made an entry, a little yellow jewel in the corner of the cover winked. Davix waited patiently for him to finish, and when the man finally turned his odd, sparkling eyes our way, I could tell he was an octona, like Krasik-dahé. It was more than just the eyes or the smooth, pale skin. I could feel it in my special blood.

"Peace and balance, Cars'tat," Davix said. "I need a common room for the Copper Guest, just until fifth bell."

The octona examined my red carpet couture with cool but precise attention. "Sign in for your friends and for the Copper Guest, D'gada-vixtet-thon."

As we walked away from the desk, I turned back, intending to say, "Thanks for the help," but it came out as "*S'zista farad dr'kaden.*" Cars'tat nodded, so I guessed it was the right thing to say.

Davix seemed amused, looking down his big hawk nose at me. "That's a courtly form not heard in hundreds of cycles. You're a very formal fellow, Copper Guest."

I blushed, which seemed like an excessive reaction. "Yeah, that's what my friends back home say about me."

Sad little Davix was clearly perking up. Maybe he liked being tour guide. He showed us dorms and dining halls, telling us stories about his childhood, the significance of which mostly left me going, *huh, what?*, but the others thought they were pretty funny. He led us up a stairway, gesturing for us to be quiet.

"Class is in session, but if Teacher S'arnen doesn't mind, we can introduce you, Copper Guest. The kids will be excited."

We crept down the hall conspiratorially, smiling. Then there was this weird swishing sound, and the others hesitated and started to fall back. But I was curious and continued. The swishing sound again, this time followed by a little choked cry. I arrived at the door of the classroom alone and looked in. First I saw a circle of maybe ten kids, ranging from maybe six to thirteen years old, seated on cushions on the floor. They looked pretty upset, and a couple of the younger ones were crying. All eyes were turned to the front of the classroom, so I stuck my head farther inside and followed their gaze. A severe man in black and green, his head shaved, was holding a boy, around eight years old, firmly by one arm while he whacked a thin stick down on the poor kid's butt and leg. This time, the kid cried out sharply, and tears began washing down his face. He tried to pull away, but the teacher was too strong.

Without stopping to consider my actions, I barged right into the classroom, running straight toward this ugly Oliver Twist scene, shouting, "What the hell do you think you're doing, you freaking animal?"

Chapter 10: *Eliza Doolittle*

My mom likes to remind me of the time I brought home a litter of seven puppies from a sketchy neighbour that lived at the bottom of our street.

"He said he was going to drown them in his bathtub!" I screamed in outrage. "In the *bathtub!*" I was horrified such a sacred place of bubbles and boats could be transformed into a slaughterhouse.

"But what are we supposed to do with them all, Crispin?" my mother asked.

"I-I could start a circus!"

"You act without thinking," my dad said. Or maybe that was last week when I accidentally made a burrito explode in the microwave. The point is, I might be impulsive, but screw you, I always have a good reason.

I was down on my knees with my arms around the sobbing kid's heaving shoulders, keeping my body between him and the teacher's stick.

"You okay?" I asked him, but he looked more startled than grateful for my timely arrival.

"Children," said the teacher in a voice like a scratchy flute. "Do you know who this is? It is the Copper Guest, come to us from the Realm of Earth. Say, 'Welcome, Copper Guest.'"

The class mumbled an out-of-sync greeting. They looked like they were in shock, either from watching their classmate being whipped or from my defiance of their teacher.

"Children?" the teacher repeated, with an edge of menace.

"Welcome, Copper Guest," they repeated in loud, unison sing-song, and I just stared back in horror at their obedience. That level of kiss-ass would have rendered you utterly friendless in the schools where I grew up.

The kid pulled himself out of my hug and ran to a corner of the small room, wincing as he sat. Red-faced with both anger and embarrassment, I stared at the teacher. His nasty little stick still hung in his hand, and he was rocking it back and forth like a little orchestra on the floor needed conducting.

I stuck out my chin. "What do you think you were doing to that kid?"

The man stared into my eyes, trying to intimidate me with teacher hypnosis mojo, and I have to say, in my world or this one, it was a powerful force.

He called out to one of his students. "Glarndarn, what have we been doing this morning?"

She jumped to her feet. "Learning the order of crop rotation, S'arnen-da," she said, dropping right back down into her cross-legged position.

"That's right. And what was the miscreant child doing while we were studying this lesson from the sacred DragonLaw? Quirdin?"

Another boy scrambled to his feet. "Fexil...I mean *the miscreant child* was flying his frog around, S'arnen-da."

All eyes turned to a paper frog, a little kite by the look of it, that lay on the ground near the teacher's desk. Fexil, the punished boy, was hanging his head in shame, banished from the circle of his peers, apparently even without the privilege of a name.

"Come on!" I protested. "I used to spend whole math classes making rosters of boy bands in my notebook!"

I turned around, maybe with the intention of grabbing Fexil and walking out, only to collide with Davix, who had entered the room behind me. The other apprentices peered at me nervously from the door.

"Copper Guest," Davix said stiffly. "We have taken up enough of Teacher S'arnen's valuable time. And you'll recall we have our own responsibilities. Perhaps we should apologize for our rudeness and go."

I was full to the eyebrows with anger, and it was all too easy to tip it over onto Davix. I got up in his face, matching his glare with my sneer, and hissed under my breath, "I'm not apologizing to that horse-face dictator."

Davix didn't flinch. He just looked me deep in the eye and whispered, "And if you don't apologize, who do you think S'arnen will take it out on after we leave?"

That brought me down in a hurry. I looked again at little Fexil, who looked back at me with a sullen pout. I realized I couldn't really do much, so I said to the teacher, "Um, yeah, I'm sure Fexil—the miscreant, whatever—didn't mean to be disrespectful. Just, um, go easy on him this time. Please?"

The creep shot me a look of smug triumph that made me want to shove the paper frog down his throat, but then he nodded. "As the Copper Guest requests. *Ekdahi*. Your presence does us honour."

I was so mad as I stormed away from the classroom that I just started speed-walking wherever, inadvertently leading the apprentices on a pointless, erratic tour through the halls of Vixtet House. Davix came up beside me, matching my furious pace. I wanted to tell him to get unborn, to jump into a lava crater, but then I caught a whiff of his smell. Peaches and woodsmoke and rain. My anger became something more complex and confusing, and I fell back to let Davix steer us to the common room he had reserved. Not that I was in the mood to learn etiquette just so I could play nice with creeps like the teacher and Grav'nan-dahé.

"Pretend this is the dining hall in Etnep House," Davix told me as the others set cushions around a low table. "That's where you'll be eating tonight. Pretend I'm one of the masters, for instance my master, Tix-etnep-thon-dahé. You come in and greet me—"

"Oh, I know," I said, leaning in to do the forearm shake, but Davix kept his arms crossed on his chest. "What?"

"That is an informal greeting among equals. You should touch your forehead and your heart and bow." I tried it. "Not that deep, otherwise it looks like you expect them to bow back." I tried again. "Good. Now, let me show you some of the rules when you're eating."

We all sat down on cushions, except Stakrat, who pretended to be serving. I learned I was supposed to refuse the food once, let one of my fellow diners insist, then accept politely. There was some complex thing about when I was supposed to reply with certain pithy slogans, but I couldn't get the rules straight.

Kriz'mig simplified it for me. "Anytime someone says, 'The gracious Dragon Lords,' just reply, 'And gracious is the world they have built us.' That will get you through ninety percent of the interactions."

"And I guess I can throw in the odd '*Ekdahi*,'" I said, "and everyone will be impressed."

Davix said, "Just try your famous *S'zista farad dr'kaden*, and they'll all faint in their soups." The look on his face confused me. Was he being an asshole or was it meant as a joke? Could he actually— emoji of shock—have a sense of humour?

A low bell rang somewhere outside, and several more followed from distant corners of Cliffside.

"Fifth bell," Stakrat said. "We'd better go, or the Copper Guest will be late for dinner."

I was suddenly sick of being called that. "Listen, guys, is it, you know, legal for you to use my real name?"

"Sure. What is it?" Grentz asked.

"I'm Crispin." Davix's eyebrows shot skyward. Grentz's mouth dropped open. Stakrat was clearly on the verge of cracking up. "What?"

"Nothing," Kriz'mig said. "It's a nice name. Cute. And, of course, we can use it when we're not in public."

I was about to ask them to explain what was so funny, but Davix took me by the hand and said, "Come on, we have to go." And we left the building and climbed upward through Cliffside's winding streets with my skinny hand in Davix's big warm one. I told myself it didn't mean anything. They touched a lot, these kids in the Realm of Fire. Kriz'mig, for instance, was trudging along with her arm around Stakrat's shoulders, Grentz playfully pushing their asses uphill when the road grew steeper. The chaperone wasn't far behind, making sure this touch didn't become, you know, full-on intercourse.

Davix's eyes were focussed ahead and upward, like he was climbing Everest instead of just the streets of his city. Despite all the ways he was trying to annoy me, he wasn't a bad guy. Dr. Crispin's diagnosis was a case of acute taking-everything-too-seriously. But maybe serious was better than what Altman had to offer. Altman let life drift over him like fog, as if no one and nothing really mattered. And I couldn't deny it felt pretty amazing walking hand in hand up the hill, until I remembered he was probably Stakrat's boyfriend. That made me think of Sylvia and the whole scene at school. Altman had drifted through that, too, gawping like a fish instead of defending me. My stomach knotted, and I vowed not to make the same mistake again. Maybe I would just avoid the love thing altogether.

CHAPTER 11: *The Bidahénas*

Etnep House turned out to be the big, pretty castle I'd seen when I arrived. By the time we'd climbed all the way, I was out of breath. But at least we were above the damp fog now, and a fresh wind was blowing through my clothes, drying the lightweight material. I raised my arms to air out my pits.

"The days get so sticky, I know," Stakrat said. "But when *Sarensikar* comes, the season of fog will end, and it won't be so hot and humid."

Kriz'mig added, "Then it will be planting time, the nicest weather of the year."

"And Davix usually dances then?" I asked. I imagined him in a beautiful tuxedo with his long hair all blown out nice, waltzing around the dance floor with Stakrat in his arms, like in a BBC historical drama. *Dragons and Dragability.*

"Yes. Usually," Stakrat muttered, and I amended my casting. She would be more believable in some dinosaur action movie.

I looked around. "I see we lost our chaperone. What's with that? Don't kids, you know, ditch the adults and hook up behind the 7-Eleven or whatever?"

"The DragonLaw is clear on the matter," Stakrat said. "Only the Arbiter of Blood chooses which couples may reproduce."

Kriz'mig nodded. "Our friend Din'don was banished for three cycles because he and a girl he was looped with conceived a child. I miss him." She pulled off her kerchief and let her long hair fly in the wind. The sun was setting behind her, and I would have taken a pic, but my phone was back on Earth.

"Harsh," I said. Was it all arranged marriages here? And wasn't there any birth control? But before I could figure out how to ask any of this politely, I heard Davix call.

"Copper Guest," he said, and we looked up to see him and Grentz standing on a higher balcony. "They're ready for you."

We climbed a stone stairway and stood in front of a big open gate in the castle wall. A quadrana—the first one I'd seen other than Tiqokh—stood there, dressed in a gold and green toga, apparently waiting for me.

"I am Zishun, Convenor of Special Events. Come with me, Copper Guest. Many wish to meet you." His voice was kind of hissy, like someone voicing an animated snake.

Only Davix was allowed in with me, and I was glad for his company. We followed Zishun into an entrance hall, crossing an intricate mosaic of a copper-coloured dragon. The huge hall was lit by glowing stones on tall, cast-iron stands.

There were fifteen or twenty people way at the back of the hall, as well as two more quadranas, one of whom I was pretty sure was Tiqokh wearing a kilt. But between that group and me stood Grav'nan-dahé, flanked by two terrifying creatures.

"The bidahénas," Davix whispered, and I could tell they made him nervous.

They were maybe three metres tall, and other than the fact that they stood on two legs and were dressed in long, priestly robes, they looked more lizard than human. As we approached, the little leather umbrellas I figured were their ears stretched open and rotated like radar dishes, triangulating on my position. Their clawed feet scratched the stone floor as they shifted from foot to foot, like they had to pee. But who could tell what it really meant? Their eyes, unblinking globes with pinprick irises, betrayed nothing human.

Run away from the monsters! my instincts screamed, but Davix was holding his ground, so I nutted up and stayed. Grav'nan-dahé came forward to greet me, and I tried to look pleased to see him.

"Peace and balance, Copper Guest."

"Hi," I said in reply.

"Peace and balance," Davix prompted under his breath.

"Right! Peace and balance. Thanks for inviting me." Then I remembered to touch my forehead and heart, accompanying the gesture with a spasmodic bow. I straightened right up again, not wanting to take my eyes off the bidahénas in case they pounced. Just behind them was a short, balding middle-aged man dressed in orange jammies. He was up on a step-ladder, whispering into the umbrella ear of one of the bidahénas.

"The Council of Earth invited you to the Realm of Fire, not I.

But here you are." Grav'nan-dahé sure knew how to make a guy feel welcome. "Behind me," he went on, "are Kror and Throd."

I did a head and heart at each of them, but the only reaction they made was to randomly click the long claws on their hands like castanets. Then came a horrible, endless silence, during which those awful eyes just stared at me. Had Davix forgotten to mention something I was supposed to do at this point? Jumping jacks, recite dirty limericks? Then one of them leaned down and started sniffing me, which at least I recognized from Tiqokh as normal behaviour for the mixed beings. Still, it took all my willpower not to bolt.

In a sibilant rasp, as if it was speaking on an inhaled breath, the bidahéna said, "Strong copper. Traits and traces. What will be written in the DragonLaw when this story is sent and sealed?"

The little guy dressed like a cheese doodle scuttled over to me. "I am the Interpreter. Kror says he detects the strong presence of your copper blood. Further, he declares—"

"Yeah, I heard. I mean, I understand. Thanks."

Kror and Throd suddenly snapped open their wings—I hadn't noticed they even *had* freaking wings—in a terrifying exclamation mark to our one-sided conversation. I gave a little shriek and covered my head, as if they were going to drop a bomb as they flew off. I straightened with embarrassment in time to watch them disappear through a big arched window three stories up.

As if I hadn't acted like a complete loon, Grav'nan-dahé said, "Come, Copper Guest, the masters of Cliffside are anxious to make your acquaintance."

I turned to Davix, who seemed as unnerved by the bidahénas as me.

"Did you really understand the words of Kror?"

"Sure, why not?" He was clearly blown away by this, which I liked.

"D'gada-vixtet-thon," Grav'nan-dahé snapped. "You are dismissed. I hope you find time in your busy schedule to help with preparations for *Sarensikar*!"

His words sounded nasty, and I wondered what was up between them. Davix bowed and left, and I walked with Grav'nan-dahé to the back of the hall where the Realm of Fire version of a cocktail party was happening. The masters were in little clusters, having a half dozen animated conversations. They were holding ceramic cups filled with a bubbling drink that sometimes got too enthusiastic and sloshed itself on the floor. Two or three other guests were wrapped up in formal wear like me, but most were dressed in the same simple style as the people on the street.

In addition to the humans, several mixed beings were at the gathering, including Tiqokh and another quadrana. And yes, Tiqokh was wearing a leather kilt that fell just below his knees and nothing else.

A waiter passed me a cup of bubbly, and I stuck my nose in for a sniff, immediately snorting up a bubble and sneezing extravagantly.

Grav'nan-dahé started to introduce me around. "Copper Guest, this is Tiren-renrit-gav-dahé, Master of Agriculture."

I did the head and heart bow. "You must be really busy, with *Sarensikar* coming up."

She smiled. "We are ready, Copper Guest. The seeds are separated and waiting."

Score! Good small talk, Crispin!

"Please meet Krenlin-etnep-bor-dahé, Master of Health and Healing."

I bowed with a bit more elegance this time. "Hope I won't need *your* services."

I only gave myself a B minus for that one. Still, I got a smile out of him.

"That is down to the will of the gracious Dragon Lords," he answered.

"And gracious is the world they have built us," I responded like the etiquette champion.

But then, as if every dimension has to make sure Crispin doesn't feel too good about himself, Lok'lok-sur-nep-dahé strode up to me, clucking and shaking his head in disgust. He spent a good thirty seconds painfully tugging at places where my outfit was sagging, muttering "No respect, no respect."

Blushing, I turned away and found myself facing a woman whose deeply lined face and tightly bound grey hair were a total contrast to her ripped body.

"Copper Guest, how exciting to meet you," she said. Over her simple brown dress, she wore a leather apron and chest piece. Her boots looked like they could safely cross a field of razor-sharp lava rock or kick open a thick oaken door. I started to do the bow at her, but she grabbed my forearm for a shake. Clearly not the formal type. "I'm Koras-inby-kir-dahé, Master of Defence of Realm, but most people call me Korda. You know my lead apprentice, I think."

"Stakrat? Yeah, she's awesome," I exclaimed, happy to cut the formality, too. "Hey, can I ask you a question?"

Grav'nan-dahé, standing behind her, knit his brow and leaned a little closer to listen in. Maybe he didn't like me asking questions. But Korda didn't seem to have a problem with it.

"Certainly," she said.

"What do you defend the realm *from*? Are there terrorists? Or swamp monsters? Or what?"

"Monsters? Well, we do sometimes venture into the mountains to cull the population of accidentals—bears mostly. But our main duty is protecting the Realm of Fire from invaders that cross from other realms. From Air, from Water. Potentially from Earth, though that's never happened."

I looked down at the heavy sword on her wide leather belt. "Are there a lot of invasions?"

"Hasn't been one in more than four hundred cycles," she answered. "The strands connecting us to both Air and Water were damaged in battles long ago."

"He probably doesn't know what a cycle is," said an old man, as grey as Korda but much more frail, leaning on a walking stick as he made his way to us. The old man beat me to the bow, but I bowed right back, which I then vaguely remembered might be an insult.

He said, "There are approximately 2.3 Earth years to each of our cycles. For instance, my apprentice Davix, whom I believe you've met, is just over seven cycles old. Around sixteen and half Earth years."

"Oh," I said. "Same as me."

He ignored this and continued. "But what confuses matters is that time passes differently and unpredictably between the realms, making historical comparisons highly complex." He leaned on his cane and studied the ceiling as if running the calculation. "I would say the last war—it was between ourselves and the Realm of Air—happened around the time of the founding of the Delhi Sultanate on Earth." I gave him a blank look. He tried again. "The crowning of the first Swedish King?"

"Sorry, not sure…"

He grabbed hold of my sleeve, giving me a disbelieving look. "It was just before the Children's Crusade set off for Jerusalem. For heaven's sake, do they teach you nothing in your schools?"

Grav'nan-dahé interrupted the old man. "As you can see, Copper Guest, Tix-etnep-thon-dahé is a devoted student of your realm's history."

"Oh, right," I said, recognizing the name. "Davix mentioned you. You should tell him to dance at *Sarensikar*. Everybody wants him to, but he says..."

I trailed off. Tix-etnep-thon-dahé, still holding my sleeve, was obviously not listening. He was staring me in the face, looking deep into my eyes like he might find a clue to some buried treasure. He gave a quick sideways glance at Grav'nan-dahé and then said, "Yes, well, tell Davix to bring you to the Atmospherics Tower tomorrow morning. There are many instruments and formulae that might interest you. Our estimates for the dispersal of the fog, for instance. Yes..." And now he was the one who trailed off, turning and wandering away, tapping his cane against the stone floor.

"How old is he?" I asked, and then hoped I hadn't said it too loud.

An octona who had been following the conversation said, "He has amassed sixty-five cycles."

"Oh," I said and then did the math. "Wait! Isn't that like a hundred and fifty years old?"

"A great age, indeed, and the knowledge and wisdom he has accumulated is vast."

We were soon herded toward the dining room. Tiqokh ruffled the feathers of the Convenor guy, Zishun, by insisting he be seated next to me at the end of the table. I was glad to have someone familiar beside me, but Zishun looked put out. The blue jewel in the corner of his leather book blinked furiously as he redrew the seating plan.

"Are you going to that dragon convention thing?" I asked him as we lowered ourselves onto our cushions in front of the low table, which was decked out with glass dishes and little glowing stones in fancy metal holders.

"The colloquy of mixed beings, you mean? Sadly, I missed it. I have the impression it was a significant gathering."

"Too bad."

Servers were coming around, bending over us to refill our cups with more of the sparkly drink. I wasn't sure whether I was supposed to do the refusing thing yet, but no one else was, so I shut up. To the left of the table, a woman was standing behind a lectern. I thought she was there to make a speech, but in fact, she was writing in yet another big leather book. Next to us, Davix's master, Tix-etnep-thon-dahé, sat examining his utensils like he was the quality control manager.

Grav'nan-dahé rose and touched a hanging mobile of tiny bells above his head, producing a cascade of new age music. Everyone shut up and closed their eyes, listening intently until the sound faded.

With a big public speaking voice, he said, "In harmony, in peace and balance, we gather tonight to welcome the Copper Guest to the Realm of Fire. This is a page in the DragonLaw that generations to come will visit time and time again."

The woman at the lectern was clearly writing all of this down. The yellow jewel in the corner of her book blinked enthusiastically as she transcribed his words. He started into some long sermon about the "Courtly Days" when the strands were strong and visits from Earth frequent. I lost the thread of his talk and leaned over to whisper a question to Tiqokh.

"What's this DragonLaw he keeps talking about?"

Tiqokh's version of a whisper was more like a low vibration that rumbled somewhere deep in your ear. "It is the book of laws and history by which we live our lives."

"You mean, like the Bible or the Quran on Earth?"

Old Tix-etnep-thon-dahé leaned toward us, tipping over his cup, which his neighbour caught just in time. "Yes, lad, like the Bible, but still in progress."

I looked at the woman scribbling away behind the lectern and realized what he meant. "So this is all going into the Bible? I mean, the DragonLaw? I'm going to be mentioned in the DragonLaw?"

A loud noise made us look up. Grav'nan-dahé banged his cup again on the table, leaving a cloud of fizzy spray hanging in the air, and gave us a dirty look. I blushed, but Tix-etnep-thon-dahé went back to examining his cutlery with a mischievous smile on his face.

Grav'nan-dahé kept his gaze focussed on me as he continued, as if I might cause more trouble. I shifted uneasily on my cushion.

"And so, we trust the days the Copper Guest spends here will be enriching for him and a pleasant diversion in our lives of service—a reminder of the time when the realms were one. Soon, though, he will return home, and we will be left with only the memories. Pleasant memories."

I looked around the table for reactions. Did no one believe in the prophecy, or my groom mission? I mean, he made it sound like the Greyhound broke down at the local gas station, and I was just stranded here until the mechanic showed up.

My thighs were starting to complain from sitting cross-legged so long, and I was just wondering if I could maybe stretch them out when Grav'nan-dahé abruptly said, "If you would please address the masters, Copper Guest."

"Me?" I replied, in a stunning show of basic comprehension. "Oh, um…Peace and balance, everyone. Thanks for…uh, this drink. It's really growing on me." I took a sip and gave a thumbs-up.

"You should stand when you address the company, Copper Guest," Grav'nan-dahé said with a cold smile.

"Oh, right." I almost fell backward off the fat cushion before managing to scramble to my feet, worried my junk might fall out of the crotch of my toga.

"Sorry," I mumbled. Everyone was staring, and I had no clue what they expected me to say. Why hadn't stupid Davix prepared me for this? "Um, I like your castle. Especially that mosaic when you walk in. It reminds me of the logo of this metal band my friend Edwin used to make me listen to. He said they were—"

The woman at the lectern was writing furiously, and I realized every lame word I said was going into the freaking DragonLaw! I tried to up my game.

"I'm grateful for your, uh, *thy* hospitality, and if…if thou canst, uh, give me a clue how I can…*may*…be of service while I'm here…" Like banging a dragon for instance, I thought. "I hope thou wonst hesitate to—"

"For a start," Grav'nan-dahé interrupted me, "I would suggest that while you are with us, you respect our customs." His voice had hardened without warning.

"Of course," I replied carefully, my danger radar suddenly pinging. I began to lower myself back to my cushion. "I want to learn all about the realm and how—"

"Remain on your feet," he demanded, and I got back up. "Copper Guest, during your brief stay, you will be introduced to many situations you may not be familiar with, as you were in the classroom in Vixtet House today."

"The classroom…?"

"Teacher S'arnen is a highly respected member of that house, and knows his work well."

I realized I'd been set up. This old idiot was trying to humiliate me in front of everyone, like I'd been caught texting during an exam. I tried to explain. "Look, I didn't mean to cause any harm. He and I worked it out."

"It is not a matter of what you *worked out*. It is a matter of respect." Every word stung. "S'arnen has spent many decades shaping young minds—"

"Yeah, shaping them with a stick," I muttered, but loud enough to be heard. I forced myself to look him in the eye, even though I could feel my face burning.

If anything, my attitude made Grav'nan-dahé grow calmer and more confident. "We are all subject to the words of the DragonLaw, Copper Guest. The teacher, the child, the apprentice, the master…even I myself. When the obedience of the least of us slackens, the whole world suffers." His words were a slow, steady kick in the head. "We presume, Copper Guest, you have not come to our realm to disrupt the peace and balance." He smiled at me. *Smiled!* Like we were all good friends and he hadn't just ripped me a new one in front everyone.

The whole table was looking at me, waiting to see whether I'd grovel or tell the asshole where he could stick his speeches, or maybe run out of the room crying like a dumb kid. But I was frozen and might have stayed that way if Tiqokh hadn't saved me.

"Sit down, Crispin," he said, in his low-rumble voice.

Hearing my name shook me out of my paralysis. As I sat, Tiqokh unfolded his legs and rose smoothly to his full and considerable height.

"Prime Magistrate," he said, addressing Grav'nan-dahé with what sounded like high formality. "I would like to ask you now, in front of the masters of Cliffside, why you have stripped the Dragon Groom of his title?" I heard a couple of gasps, and otherwise dead silence. A small blue bird flew in one of the tall windows, chasing an insect around one of the glowing rocks, and then exited back into the night.

Grav'nan-dahé stood straight and still as a stone monolith. "Because, Tiqokh, prophecy is heresy."

"Prophecy has a long and revered history in the lives of the gracious Dragon Lords."

"And gracious is the world they have built us," muttered several of the masters.

"And yet it is not DragonLaw," the Prime Magistrate replied.

Tiqokh didn't look intimidated, although I'm not sure what an intimidated quadrana would look like. "The Council of Earth trusts the prophetic acumen of Glei'hak and Arjee. And with the prophecy delivered, they deemed it essential to seek out and send the Dragon Groom. Surely, even you see the wisdom of such action."

And suddenly, Grav'nan-dahé wasn't quiet anymore. His voice rose, like a TV minister getting to the part about evil gay people and upping your monthly donations. "Superstitions!" he shouted. "Lies!" He banged the table. "The Fire Revealed, with its heresies and idolatries, infects the spirit of the People. On market days, more and more fetishes are quietly sold, more false talismans slipped under garments. Farmer and stonecutter alike stand before their secret kitchen shrines and whisper profane prayers that insult and enrage the Dragon Lords."

The old guy was practically hyperventilating. He pulled away from the table and began circling the dining room with his hands in the air. "Oh, great Etnep! Oh, Vixtet and Inby! You granted us salvation when you brought us to your bountiful realm! Renrit, Sur, do not forsake us, though we spit in your faces with our childish profanities!"

Returning to the table, eyes red, he stared into the faces of the dinner guests one by one. "Mark my words, masters of Cliffside, I have long been patient with the People's private heretical worship, but my patience grows thin. I began my rule with the banishment of the so-called seers, Glei'hak and Arjee. But I also did away with exile to the Badlands and the offering of the flesh. Heed me! If called to, I will again pull taut the reins and forego my many cycles of leniency."

The masters' reactions ran the gamut. Some nodded, some looked down at the table embarrassed, and some shook their heads at Grav'nan-dahé like they didn't think much of this speech. Korda's back was straight, her face neutral—a soldier awaiting orders.

I glanced sideways and noticed the woman transcribing the speech had stopped writing. Did she get a signal to cease and desist? Or maybe fights didn't make it into the pages of the DragonLaw, like the way a family edits out the nasty parts of its history. I looked at Tiqokh, wondering if he would respond, or maybe challenge the Prime Magistrate to a sword fight right in front of us.

In fact, they both just sat down, as if by unspoken mutual agreement. To go with my family metaphor, it was like a Thanksgiving dinner where the daughter announces during the salad course that she's pregnant by her heroin dealer, but Grandma still trundles out of the kitchen with the mashed potatoes, right on schedule.

CHAPTER 12: *An Unexpected Visit*

After my public humiliation and the Prime Douchebag's epic meltdown, I didn't think I would have any appetite, but it's actually pretty hard to make my stomach go on strike, and the food was surprisingly good. Beef with pickled vegetables, crusty bread, tiny boiled eggs, peeled and served in a dark, tangy sauce. I remembered to refuse each course once before accepting. Tiqokh and the other quadrana didn't eat.

Maybe the fight did have an effect on the assembled masters, because everyone got all polite and fake with me. Were they giving me space to lick my wounds, or did they agree with Grav'nan-dahé that I was some rude little foreigner who wouldn't be missed when he was gone? In any case, I felt like I had shit the bed in the Realm of Fire.

By the end of dinner, I was tired and cranky, and I hoped there weren't any more surprises in store for me. Like, "Hey, Crispin, every guest of honour has to fight the noxious pit monster. Naked!" But, in fact, I was dismissed early while the masters stuck around for some meeting. Much as I wanted to get away from Grav'nan-dahé, I resented being treated like a kid—sent to bed before the grown-ups got out the joints and cranked the 80s music.

"Please follow, Copper Guest," said a guy not much older than me. "I will show you to your quarters." He was dressed in the usual brown shirt and pants, but with a kind of silky cape around his shoulders. I figured him for the bellboy of the guest quarters. There actually *were* little bells dangling off the end of his cape, making faint tinkling sounds as we headed for the exit.

Just before I left the hall, I turned around and hissed, "Tiqokh!" and gestured for him to follow us into the corridor. The bellboy stood discreetly to the side, pretending not to listen. He was holding a lantern like some old-fashioned sailor, but one of those glowing rocks was inside instead of a candle. It was the only light in the corridor.

"Dragon Groom?" Tiqokh asked.

"Don't call me that! I'm supposed to be the Copper Guest. Are you trying to get me in more trouble?"

"You are not in trouble, Crispin. The argument between myself and Grav'nan-dahé is purely a point of religious interpretation."

"Easy for you to say. That guy's got it in for me. If looks could breathe fire…"

"You would be wise not to do anything else to disrupt the normal proceedings of the Realm."

"That wasn't my fault," I insisted. "Look, I'm just scared he's going to make me, you know, disappear in the middle of the night. And blame it on trolls."

"There are no trolls here."

"Metaphor! Literary freaking allusion! God, you're part dragon, and I bet you've never read a fantasy novel in your life." My mind was racing. "Could Davix and Stakrat maybe stay with me tonight? I trust them."

"Neither belongs to Etnep House. They would not be allowed in the living quarters."

"Don't you guys ever have, you know, sleepovers? Dorm parties or whatever?"

"I will watch over you."

I looked up at him, surprised. As usual, his face betrayed no emotion.

"You will?" I asked, incredibly relieved.

"You won't see me, but I will guard you against peril."

"Because I *am* in peril?"

He paused, turning so his face disappeared in shadow. The pause gave me shivers. "I do not know. I have been away from the Realm of Fire for several cycles. Something has changed."

"Like what?"

"I will not speculate. I have said too much already."

"Yeah, if you call almost nothing 'too much.'"

"I must return to the dining room and listen to the discussion. Do not fear. I will keep you safe."

My guest room, at the top of a series of narrow staircases, was a small chamber in a corner tower—just a single bed, a wooden chair, and a small table. On the table stood a pitcher of water, a mug, and a big bowl. It was pretty stuffy, and the bellboy opened the shutters on the window above the bed to let in a cool breeze. When he showed me the chamber pot under the bed, I tried to act cool, despite my sudden and horrified realization there was no en suite bathroom with normal plumbing. I wanted to ask questions, like whether you only pee in the pot or crap, too, and who was responsible for emptying it in the morning, but I chose the coward's strategy of just nodding, like I was a chamber pot pro.

The bellboy left the lantern with me. The glowing rock inside was apparently called a torchstone and never went out. He showed me how to baffle the lantern when I went to sleep. Then, wishing me a peaceful night, he closed the door and went downstairs, his little bells eventually falling out of earshot. There didn't seem to be anyone else in the guest tower, and the silence was eerie. I looked out the window. Could I use it for escape if someone attacked me? Sure. I could leap right out, fall five stories, and crash on the stones below. What kind of lame safety protocols did this world have? I wondered. What if there was a fire?

I kneeled on my bed and checked out the view. Below me, the fog was an unbroken blanket covering the valley. Above, the realm sky was black, criss-crossed by threads, like rivers of blood and gold. There were twinkling stars in it, but also multicoloured tennis balls drifting slowly across the sky. Unlike the view from the roof of the Ambassador, the realms of Air and Water were not visible. *Why not?* I wanted to ask someone. Actually, I would have been happy to ask anyone anything, to talk about our favourite music, or why your own farts smell okay but someone else's are toxic. Anything to break the silence.

It was getting cold, so I closed the window. I examined a set of clothes folded neatly on the chair—pants, a shirt, and what must have been underwear. I unwrapped myself from my fancy-dress duds. It was like undoing a tensor bandage, meters of fabric piling up beside me on the floor as I spun and twisted my way to freedom. I bundled up the material in the corner with my sneakers sitting on top, then climbed back into bed, naked. I didn't want to turn out the light yet, so I just sat with my arms around my knees, the covers pulled up over my shoulders, with no idea of what I was doing there.

Introducing Crispin Haugen, Olympic champion of self-isolation. Due to my stupidity, I had lost Altman, Sylvia, and my whole social circle in about ten minutes. Following that disaster, I could have gone home to the parents who loved me, but I was too chickenshit. So instead I left my goddamned *planet*! And now I was alone, lonely, isolated, cut off, solitary, individual, unique in my patheticness, stuck in a tower like a storybook princess, with nothing to look forward to but an awkward appointment with a chamber pot.

Then I heard a noise. A tap and a hiss of leather on stone. Silence for a breathless five seconds and then again the tap and hiss. Imagining a lone assassin unsheathing his blade, I looked around for a weapon. The glowing torchstone on its brass stand seemed the best bet. Quietly, quietly I reached for it and touched the rim just below the rock, burning my hand.

"Ow, shit!" I shouted, because I have no self-control. *Tiqokh! You better be watching!* But the quadrana was probably still in the dining room. And then maybe he would need to go to the kitchen after and eat his weekly cat or whatever before he went on guard duty. I pulled myself back into the corner of the bed, my back against the cold stone wall, as someone knocked on my door.

"Come in," I said, because I guess even assassins deserve some courtesy. The door swung slowly inward to reveal Davix.

I breathed a sigh of relief. "Oh, it's you," I said, then pulled my sheet higher, blushing and giving him a look of annoyance because I needed to feel I had at least some kind of control.

Davix wasn't exactly a picture of calm himself. Putting a *shh* finger to his lips, he closed the door as gently as possible.

"I thought you're not allowed up here," I whispered. "Aren't you scared they're going to beat you with a stick?"

"It's fine. I got to your room unseen." He moved my fresh clothes onto a corner of the table and sat backward on the chair, crossing his arms on the chair-back and looking at me with those big brown eyes. "Besides, the authorities have not sentenced offenders to the offering the flesh for tens of cycles." He was close enough that I swear I could feel the heat off his body.

"But aren't you violating your precious DragonLaw? And what with you being Grav'nan-dahé's personal assistant or something."

"I actually have two masters: the Prime Magistrate as well as Tix-etnep-thon-dahé, who you met tonight. I fear I will have to disappoint one of them. Maybe both." He suddenly shut down, looking all sad again, and I found the patience to just wait, which is not usual for me. After half a minute, Davix snapped back to life. "Technically," he said, "You aren't part of the DragonLaw, Copper Guest. There are no official rules about you yet."

I tilted my head, either in scepticism or to look at that wonderful nose from a different angle.

"But I'll be part of the revised edition," I said. "Every time I scratched my ass tonight, they wrote it down." That earned me a smile.

"Did you scratch it a lot?" he asked. "Will you be remembered as the Copper Scratcher?"

"Or possibly the Copper Burper."

"Really! I'm sorry I wasn't there to witness it, X'risp'hin."

My eyebrows went right up to my hairline. "What did you call me?"

He looked puzzled. "What you told us to. X'risp'hin."

I collapsed sideways, overcome by laughter that kept growing the more I tried to fight it. *X'risp'hin* meant "adorable little lizard."

"What?" Davix demanded, grinning despite having no clue what I was laughing at.

"Nothing, nothing! It's..." I tried to stop laughing. "It's great. Perfect. Use it."

Davix was laughing, too. "I was surprised by the name, I'll admit, but it kind of suits you."

That made me laugh harder: "Baby iguana, that's me."

Raucous chortles. Guffaw central. We motioned each other to keep quiet but there was no way.

When we finally ran out of laughing gas, we just grinned and looked each other in the eye until suddenly, just like that, my whole body wanted him. There's this thing that happens when someone goes from just handsome, or sometimes not even, to lust object. It's like you just recognized a piece of a puzzle, and you need to fit it in you, *now.* But now wasn't going to happen, obviously. Probably never would. But tell that to my dick, which had become stunningly hard. I bunched up the sheets into a better screen and turned away so he wouldn't see me blush.

"Why are you here, Davix?" I asked the stone wall.

"You had a hard day. And I thought you might be lonely."

I dared a look back at those deep, dreamy browns. "Really?" His caring moved me. It also excited me. "No, I'm fine. I got a nice room and, um, fresh clothes and..." My heart was beating stupidly fast.

"Well, it wasn't an *easy* day, I'll admit it."

"And I made it worse, I'm sorry."

I sat up straight, my blanket slipping down to my stomach. "Huh? No, you didn't. I mean, I was screwing up all over the place, and you were just doing your job."

"We're not used to strangers here. I should have realized how odd this place must be to you. When you went in to dinner, Stakrat said she felt sorry for you, and that surprised me. How could that be? I thought. You're the Copper Guest, flying across the strands from the original realm with a quadrana. I thought you might even look down on us."

"Of course I don't. And I'm not anyone special. I'm just a high school kid with an average GPA and relationship problems. Sometimes they think I'm Chinese or Korean, and I'm supposed to be good at math. Even my teachers are disappointed."

He smiled a little. "I don't know what any of that means," he said, "but Stakrat made me realize that you're just another person, one who left everyone he knew to come here. I don't think I'd last a day without seeing my friends."

"Well, it's not forever. At least I hope not. But once I knew that I had this, uh, copper blood thing, and I could even speak a bit of the language, I guess I had to come and check the place out."

"More than a bit. You even understood the bidahénas."

"Well, yeah. I mean, I understood the words, but they were weird as a third nipple."

Davix reached out with his long, fine fingers and lifted the wolf's head off my chest, examining it carefully. "What is this?"

I was holding my breath and had to remember how to speak. "Uh, it was a gift from my parents. You know, what do you call them? My genetic forbearers. It's a wolf."

"Wolf," he repeated, unsure. "I don't think we have 'wolf' in the Realm of Fire. Unless…yes, it may be one of the accidentals."

"Oh, Korda mentioned those. What's accidental about them?"

"When the great dragons gathered up pieces from the Realm of Earth to build the Livingworld here, some creatures were carried along unintended. They mostly live in the Chend'th'nif Mountains. That is why only the most experienced rangers trek there." He let go of the necklace, and it dropped back to my chest, warmed by his fingers.

"Davix, sorry if this isn't my business, but you guys were talking about someone named Rinny…"

"Rinby. She died. Just fifteen days ago. She was the Lead Apprentice in Atmospherics. She was my friend."

"And that's why you don't want to dance." We were silent, and I wished I'd said I was sorry instead of the thing about the dancing. "Tix-etnep-thon-dahé said you should bring me to the Atmospherics Tower tomorrow."

Davix seemed surprised. "He said that? Why would he…? Okay. I'll meet you outside the front gates of Etnep House at second bell. And now it's late, X'risp'hin, and it's a long walk back to my bed."

He reached out his hand again, and I took it in mine, feeling its strength, glad the blanket hadn't slipped any farther and revealed what was going on down below.

"I'll try to be nicer tomorrow," Davix said, giving my hand a squeeze before letting go.

"Okay. And I'll try not to mess up and get you in trouble."

He smiled at that and got to his feet. With a little formal bow, he touched his head, his heart, and then, after a micro-pause, his stomach. His smile grew mischievous, and I was dying to know exactly what that gesture meant.

"Peaceful dreams, X'risp'hin," he said and slipped out, leaving me amazed and aroused.

I strained to hear the tiny noises of him on the stairs. Then everything was silent but the croaking of frogs in the treetops. I figured I better call it a night; tomorrow was likely to be another big day. I baffled the light, leaving just a faint, comforting glow, lay back, and went to sleep. After taking care of some urgent business.

CHAPTER 13: *The Intruder*

the copperblood is right there, where the light went out. The Intruder lowered himself until he hung just outside the shuttered window. *we do not take orders from the demi-dragons. I will lay the earth boy's bloody body at their feet and remind them who is in charge. no no, quiet, quiet yet. secret.* He sensed a presence above him and froze. Something on the move, an unexpected hunter. The Intruder dropped to a roof below, silent and alert, and disappeared into the shadows. *yet secret, yet secret.*

CHAPTER 14: *Optimal Pairings*

When I awoke early the next morning, bells were ringing across the city, and I felt entirely at peace. The bellboy who knocked on my door informed me that it was first bell. That gave me lots of time for breakfast, a bath, and a tour of Etnep House—Etnep, queen of the Five Dragons, my fiancée according to Tiqokh, but not according to Grav'nan-dahé.

This was the first time in ages I had slept through the night. Most nights, I spent a good hour in panic some time around three in the morning. I'd go over everything I did wrong that day or might do wrong the next, and list all the ways I was useless and generally doomed. You'd think that a trip to another world full of lizard men and scary clothing choices would have caused even worse insomnia than, say, an upcoming trig test. Maybe it was my copper blood. Maybe for the first time, some deep part of me felt like it was home.

By the time second bell rang, I was already at the main gates of Etnep House waiting for Davix. First time in my life I was early for something. Beyond the gates, with their fancy copper mouldings, was a wide platform, almost like a stage, that looked out on a huge, cobblestoned square called the Retreat of Tarn. I scanned the square obsessively, not wanting to miss the moment Davix stepped out between patches of fog, smiling, to beckon me close and take my hand in his.

But it was Stakrat who showed up.

"Peace and balance, X'risp'hin!" she called.

Adorable Little Lizard managed to mask his devastating disappointment behind a happy smile as he climbed down the wide staircase to meet her.

She asked, "You sleep well?"

"Yeah, where's Davix?" I said, oh so casually. "I thought he was meeting me."

"He flew me a message from the Atmospherics Tower. Said he had to get there early, and I should bring you over."

"Don't you have to work? You know, defend the realm and stuff?"

"You're my work. Master Korda assigned me to watch over you today. She liked you, by the way."

"I liked her, too. But I figured all the masters thought I was a moron by the end of dinner."

Stakrat looked around and lowered her voice. "Some of them felt Grav'nan-dahé acted with disrespect. But we shouldn't talk about it too much. At least not in public." She began to walk us quickly across the square.

But as I bounced along beside her, I was full of curiosity. "So, some people don't like the Prime Gravy Boat?"

She bit her lower lip. "Don't misunderstand, Copper Guest. Grav'nan-dahé is a pious man whose strict devotion to the DragonLaw is an example for us all. We in Defence of Realm are duty-bound to enforce the law according to his interpretation." I took the message and shut up. The last thing I wanted was to start stepping on toes before the People had even finished their morning coffee. Actually, the local equivalent was called barnberry, and I'd had a mug with breakfast. It was both earthy and fruity and could have used a lot more sugar.

We exited the Retreat of Tarn and began heading downhill through a neighbourhood of steep, narrow streets. In a lane filled with small craft workshops, a chubby guy wearing a lot of necklaces reached out through an open window and grabbed me by the arm, spinning me around to face him. He was sitting at a messy table making things out of silver—necklaces, rings, tools, statues.

"Copper Guest," he exclaimed, his long eyelashes blinking rapidly. "Please touch my offering!" With his other hand, he shoved a little statue at me with the head of a lizard and the body of a busty, wide-hipped woman. "With your blessing, I hope I will be granted a mate."

I stammered, uncertain what any of that meant, and Stakrat said, "Brother, let go of the Copper Guest. Don't pester him with superstition. Trust the Arbiter of Blood to find you a mate. Trust the DragonLaw."

The man ignored her, gripping me harder and thrusting the statue in my face. "Please, I need this!"

Stakrat moved so quickly, I didn't know what was happening, but a moment later the man wasn't gripping me anymore. His statue had fallen to the street with a clang, and he was rubbing his hand and grimacing in pain.

"Be warned!" she said, and her voice had turned all hard and official. "The Prime Magistrate calls on us again to prosecute those who openly practice the Fire Revealed."

The man was bowing over and over. "Please, I'm sorry," he whimpered.

With my heart still beating hard, I said, "S'okay, Stakrat. I don't mind." I bent down to pick up the statue and handed it back to the man, who took it, tears glistening in his eyes.

Stakrat put a hand on my back and got me moving again. "Sorry about that, X'risp'hin."

"He's looking for a girlfriend? Is that what that was about?"

"He is hoping the Arbiter of Blood pairs him with a woman so he can have offspring."

That sounded the same to me as *looking for a girlfriend*, but I might have been missing something.

"And what's with the statue?"

"He believes you have blessed it. And now he'll go home and put it in his secret shrine and pray to it."

"And that's against the law?"

"It's…not clear. Defence of Realm awaits further direction from Grav'nan-dahé." We had descended into a street so thick with fog that I practically had to glue myself to Stakrat not to lose her.

"Can I ask you a question?" I said.

"Of course."

"It's kind of…delicate…" Embarrassment almost stopped me, but I powered through. "Are there, uh, gay people here?"

We arrived at a fence, and Stakrat unlatched the gate and led us through.

"One moment," she said, and I thought maybe I offended her. But the word "gay" had that funny feeling on my tongue, like it didn't translate. Stakrat picked up a lantern with a large torchstone that was hanging on one of the fence posts. "Be careful, X'risp'hin, this road is shared by riders on horseback. I'll hold the light so they don't run us down in the fog, but you may want to keep an eye on the ground, too." I could already smell what she was talking about.

"Now," she continued. "What are these *ghey* people you mentioned?"

I reminded myself that this shouldn't be so hard to talk about. "You know, people who, uh, do it with someone who has the—the same equipment. Who get it on with the same sex."

"Oh, I see. Yes, of course. We are all *ghey*."

Startled, I almost stepped into a fresh pile of manure and had to do a crazy parkour jump to avoid it. "What?"

"Males and females aren't allowed to breed freely," she said. "One of the bidahénas, called the Arbiter of Blood, determines optimal breeding pairs. The dragons want to improve the People's strength and health, enhance positive characteristics and eliminate weaknesses."

"Oh my God, that's...creepy. Is that why those chaperones follow everyone around?"

"Yes, but they only supervise young people. It is assumed desire speaks too loudly for us to control in the two cycles following Consolidation."

In other words, the adults, as usual, didn't trust teenagers not to fool around given the chance.

"Don't they think you and I need a chaperone? Sorry, I'm not suggesting anything." We could hear hooves approaching, and Stakrat pulled me up against the wall, holding her lantern high as the horse passed.

"Oh, we do have one. I noticed Frelga a few turns back. She's one of the sneaky chaperones who watch in secret, in the hope of catching us slipping up."

Creeped out, I glanced around, trying to play spot-the-perv. "But if no one can have sex without the Arbiter guy's say-so, don't they get...you know...*frustrated?*"

"The great dragons understand the People's need for carnal bonding. Vixtet especially finds our hunger for skin contact and mutual pleasuring fascinating. That's why, other than when we are paired or on temple visits, we all take pleasure with our own sex. We *ghey.* Is that the Earth word?"

"More or less," I said, suddenly distracted. I couldn't help it. I started imagining everyone I'd met so far in the Realm of Fire paired off same-sexually, Kriz'mig with Stakrat, Grentz with the bellboy, Grav'nan-dahé doing some crazy bondage scene with the schoolteacher, and Davix... I cleared my throat, which had suddenly clogged up. "So I guess you and Davix are hoping that the Arbiter of Blood matches you up someday."

"Why? Do you think we're tangled?" She laughed. "No, Davix is my oldest friend. Besides, he is exclusively attracted to males."

"Oh," I said—the nonchalantest, most disinterested "oh" in history—even as my heart started dancing with hope. We stepped abruptly out of a fog bank, and before us was the wide expanse of the valley. The road we were on continued to descend the mountain, but

Stakrat pointed to our right. There, at the end of a winding path, at the top of a long, stone staircase stood a thin tower, alone on the rocky peak.

"The Atmospherics Tower," she told me. The appropriately weatherbeaten stone structure was maybe ten stories high, with only a few windows down at the bottom and up at the top. The roof was crowded with weathervanes, lines of triangular flags, glass cylinders, and other impressive technical doodads. It reminded me of my grandma's pincushion.

"So, Davix is working up there?"

"He is, but wait a moment. I see his master coming."

At the end of a winding path, Tix-etnep-thon-dahé was closing the door of a small hut, built up against the rocky wall of the hill. A solitary tree with a thick, gnarled trunk shaded the building. Beneath it, a chestnut horse and a dark grey mule stood side by side, nibbling at the patchy grass. The old man walked toward us slowly but with great dignity, not always appearing to need the cane he carried.

"Peace and balance, children," he said when he reached us.

Stakrat and I repeated the greeting more or less in unison, and I gave the formal bow, which brought a rueful smile to the master's face. He said, "You are like a medieval courtier, Copper Guest. I am charmed by your manners."

"Could you tell my mom that, please?"

"Young Stakrat, is it?" Tix-etnep-thon-dahé said, turning to her.

"Yes, Master-da."

"I will take the Copper Guest up to the tower. You wait here for his return."

Stakrat clearly didn't like this. "But Master-da, Korda says I'm supposed to stay with the Copper Guest today, to make sure nothing happens to him."

"Nothing will happen to him in the Atmospherics Tower. At least not while I'm around."

"But she said—"

"I heard you the first time. If Koras-inby-kir-dahé asks, you will tell her I make the decisions in my domain. If you like, you may sit at the table in my hut and read my books. You may even have a piece of honeycomb from the larder. But now I am taking the Copper Guest up. Alone."

CHAPTER 15: *The DragonLaw*

Old as he was, Tix-etnep-thon-dahé didn't seem to mind the climb up the long, steep staircase. I supposed he did this every day, probably for decades. I looked back down at Stakrat, who shrugged at me and sat down on a low rock to sharpen her knife.

The Atmospherics Master stopped for a rest at a landing halfway up the hill, and I took a moment to survey our surroundings. We had left Cliffside, apparently. All its buildings were clustered farther up the hill to our right. Or maybe that was considered downtown, and we were in the suburbs. Fog danced along the hill in little clumps, sometimes descending on us, sometimes parting to let the sunshine through.

Tix-etnep-thon-dahé said, "A very unusual season. Nothing is as it should be."

"Isn't the fog supposed to clear when that festival ends? What's it called?"

"*Sarensikar.* The conjunction of the festival and the atmospheric conditions is more coincidental than determined, young man. *Sarensikar* will arrive on schedule, but we've never had such a hard time predicting when the season of fog will actually end. The other disciplines are all waiting for our wise counsel so they can begin their planting, their construction, make cyclical pilgrimages. But now, especially following the death of T'lexdar-inby-thon, we are…in a fog." He smiled darkly at his own joke.

"Why is the fog different this, uh, cycle?"

"Ah! That's the crucial question. All I can say is that we are gathering data—when we're allowed." Before I could ask what he meant, he began climbing again, and I followed, feeling stupid. Tix-etnep-thon-dahé, I noted, was different than he had been at dinner. I'd taken him for some dozy professor who knows pi up to five thousand places but shows up to a lecture still wearing his lobster bib from lunch. Had he been putting on an act? Or was he just sharper on his own turf?

When we reached the door of the tower, a window opened above us and a pair of arms released a kingsolver into the sky. I watched it circle up on a thermal, a scrap of paper tied around its leg. It cawed twice, angled into a dive, and took off across the valley.

A voice came from the window above. "Master, stay there, I'm coming!"

I *thought* I had recognized those arms. It was Davix. I waved, but he had already retreated into the tower. My heart began to pound, and I listened carefully to what it was saying in its particular Morse Code: "Davix is not Stakrat's boyfriend. Davix is only attracted to males. Davix snuck up to see you in the tower last night, despite being a good boy who loves rules more than triple-fudge chocolate ice cream." Also, "Will he notice you didn't brush your teeth this morning?"

Tix-etnep-thon-dahé leaned on his cane, sighing. "I don't need help." He turned to me. "Quite a coincidence, don't you think, that a prophecy should lead you to the Realm of Fire just now when the very weather refuses to behave?"

Before I could say a slack-jawed *I dunno*, Davix burst through the door. "Let me help you, Master-da," he said, offering an arm, and Tix-etnep-thon-dahé, despite his show of independence, seemed grateful for the help. Davix smiled at me over his shoulder. "Welcome, Copper Guest." Our eyes locked just long enough for it to get deliciously embarrassing before he returned to the task of helping his master up the spiralling central staircase to an office on the third floor.

There, Tix-etnep-thon-dahé lowered himself with relief into a large chair behind a huge desk littered with books and charts. Davix put a mug of water in front of him and stuffed a pillow behind his back. I looked around the comfortable old room, with its curved outer wall and high ceiling. Checking out one of the big bookshelves, I saw that not all the books were in the Tongue of Fire. Some were Earth languages, mostly Latin or Italian or something.

I heard a scratching above me and almost jumped out of my skin when I noticed one of the black and red birds sitting on top of the bookshelf.

Tix-etnep-thon-dahé raised a hand in the air. "Flak, to me!" The bird flew across the room and landed on his forearm, then stepped off and began marching around the desk like a little sentry on guard duty. "Flak is my personal kingsolver. Unlike me, he has visited Farad'hil, the dragon abode. In general, though, he is too independent and stubborn to be a reliable courier."

Davix, standing in front of the big desk, cleared his throat, like he had no patience for chit-chat. "Master, I arrived early this morning to review the logs for anomalous incursions. When I compare Rinby's results with—"

"Apprentice, don't leave our visitor standing there."

"Oh, forgive me, Copper Guest." He ran over and pulled a chair from the corner and placed it to one side of the desk. He touched my shoulder with his warm, firm hand as I sat.

"Good," the old man said and gestured at another well-stuffed seat. "And you can sit here to my right." Davix stared as if the chair was full of snakes. Tix-etnep-thon-dahé said, "Come, you used to spend many hours there, reading and pestering me with questions, before you began your studies with the Prime Magistrate."

"But that's Rinby's—"

"Sit."

Davix sat shyly. He was blushing.

"Good, and now you can explain to the Copper Guest what it is you have been investigating."

"You want me to tell him…?"

"As I said."

Davix looked at me, a bit flustered, and leaned forward in his seat. "We—the Atmospherics Discipline, that is—have noticed strange fog patterns this cycle. You know this is the Season of Fog, yes?"

"Hard to miss it," I said, which seemed to amuse the Atmospherics Master, though not Davix.

"Well, we began recording unusual incursions of this sheep fog, as the People sometimes call it, descending every few days from the anti-spinward range of the Chend'th'nif Mountains, and we've been trying to find the cause. Since Rinby died…" He lost his composure for just a second, but then recovered himself. "I've logged sudden heat spikes accompanied by winds from greenward, gusting to five. Within half a day of these events, sheep fog descends into the valley."

Tix-etnep-thon-dahé was staring out the window during this speech, absently scratching the bird's head. He asked, "How many of these events have you noted?"

"Six, Master-da, since I took on these duties."

"All following the same pattern?" Davix nodded. "Yet when you consult the DragonLaw for T'lexdar-inby-thon's observations—"

"Rinby made no mention of the heat spikes or the anomalous winds."

I blurted out, "Even though there were sheep fogs then, too?" Davix nodded again and sat back in his chair.

"Isn't this exciting?" The Atmospherics Master said drily, clapping his hands slowly. Flak jumped and squawked a reprimand at him. The old man took a seed ball from his desk and fed it to the bird. "And what date shall we give pious Grav'nan-dahé for the coming of clear weather, Apprentice?"

"I-I don't know, Master-da."

"Nor I." Tix-etnep-thon-dahé opened up one of those leather books with the jewel in the corner, this one green. He started writing, the jewel blinking as he did. Without looking up, he said, "Leave me, I have work to do. Give the Copper Guest a tour of the tower." We stood, and he added, "And do your work here in my office, Davix. You and I have always studied well together."

Davix was quiet as we left Tix-etnep-thon-dahé's office and began to climb up the circular staircase.

"Everything okay?" I asked as we completed our first circuit. "You going to tell me stuff about this fine, old building?"

"Sorry. I was just…thinking."

"Hey, don't worry, I can do it myself!" I wanted to crack him up, get him back to the mischievous visitor of the night before. I began gesturing with outstretched arms, putting on the most chipper of Tina Tour Guide voices. "On your right, you will find a stone wall. Note the way the stones have been laid really evenly, just like everywhere else in the Realm of Fire. Note how each successive step in this beautiful staircase is just a bit higher than the previous, creating an overall *rising* effect. And here"—I stopped to check out a series of diagonal scratches on the wall—"is where Grav'nan-dahé slipped on a banana peel and—"

I shut up my stupid act because Davix, a few steps ahead of me, had frozen to examine the marks with knitted brow. I had a chilling thought. "Is this where Rinby…?" I couldn't finish.

"Apparently not," he said in a low voice. He reached out his hand and touched the wall, splaying his fingers so that one was on each of the scratches. "Apparently not," he repeated, but now he sounded angry. He continued to climb the steps, and I followed, totally confused, right up to the top of the tower where a door stood open.

"This is the measurements room," he said as we walked in. "Where I used to work." Two younger apprentices looked up and went wide-eyed when they saw me. I felt like a Hollywood celebrity spotted at their local burger joint. I gave them a friendly smile, and they grinned back excitedly until a sharp look from Davix made them drop their heads back to their work.

Davix said, "We record raw weather data here in these notebooks.

Also, we send and receive birds with data from remote weather stations across the Realm."

Near the window stood a series of wicker cages with more kingsolvers in them. Several of the cages were empty, and I remembered how Stakrat had said Davix flew her a message.

On our way out, one of the young apprentices brought Davix a notebook, and Davix passed it to me. Every page was filled with neat tables of characters.

"Thank you, Zent'r," he said to the kid. "This is yesterday's data, Copper Guest," Davix explained, taking back the notebook as we walked down one level. "The charting room," Davix said, holding the door open for me. The room was full of books and maps and elaborately rendered diagrams on sheets of paper, some of which looked a hundred years old. Davix sat down at the desk in the centre of the room, adding the notebook to a pile of them accumulating there.

I said, "This is your office?"

"It is now, yes."

"Now that you're Lead Apprentice."

He knit his eyebrows, face twisting between annoyance and sadness. "I suppose so, yes. I take the raw data and perform calculations on it. Then I bring it to my master, who checks the work and sends it off for inclusion in the DragonLaw. Rinby could do the calculations in her sleep, but it's taking up all my time. I've had to cancel my study sessions with the Prime Magistrate. He isn't happy."

"Is he ever? Those books with the blinking lights, like Tix-etnep-thon-dahé had—that's the DragonLaw?"

"No, that's called a grace book. Everything entered in a grace book goes to the dragon abode of Farad'hil, where the dragon, Renrit, the Great Collator, reviews it and adds it to the sacred DragonLaw."

"And the DragonLaw has everything in it? All the history and laws, plus what I had for dessert last night? Must be a big book."

"See for yourself," he said, pointing to a heavy tome sitting on a stand by the wall.

"That's it? That's a copy of the DragonLaw?" I approached it slowly, like holy flames might leap out and burn me. It was a big book, all right, but not *that* big. Davix came up behind me and put a hand on my lower back, which made my knees go a little weak.

"Don't be afraid, X'risp'hin, open it." I did, at random, impressed by the golden beauty of the vellum pages, elegantly penned in the Tongue of Fire.

"What does it say?"

Davix looked over my shoulder. "*When the polar fires ebb for more than three days, cold will fall on the land, rarely rising above nine bars. The cold-blooded will enter their still-time, the warm, their burrows.* Rinby was training the new apprentices in the basics of Atmospherics. I guess that's why this passage is flowed."

I was trying to follow. "You mean…other times when you open the book, something else is…flowed?"

He reached around me to flip the pages of the book, and I couldn't help leaning back into his chest. On the book's first page was a drawing of a tree, annotated with text I couldn't read.

"That's the table of contents? Hey, can we read what I said last night at the dinner?"

"That won't be entered yet. Would you like to read how the People came to the Realm of Fire?"

"Yeah, okay. I was actually wondering about that."

He touched the tree, close to the bottom of its trunk, running his finger up a low branch. As he did so, I was startled to see the text—which looked like ordinary ink on paper—continually vanishing to be replaced by new text. He stopped his finger on a set of characters that had just appeared, and after a second, they glowed. A line of light ran from the text and down the edge of the book, stopping about a third of the way through.

"This is how you tell the Book what section of the DragonLaw to present."

"Like a big e-reader," I said.

"A what?"

"Never mind."

Davix opened the book to the indicated spot and read, "In a time of calamity, the People were rescued by the beneficent dragons. Hail to the Fire Lords. Great are their Five Names. Their voices shook the ground, and lava touched the skies. Lo! said They to the People. We will build for you a world of peace and balance. Be our servants in this holy enterprise. And the People were raised up along the strands and brought to their new and eternal home."

Davix's face was a bit flushed as he closed the book, like he had just read the most heartbreaking fanfic you could imagine. But I had to spoil the mood, because…*what?*

"So, that's all the detail it gives about how some population on Earth ended up here?"

Davix looked confused. "Well, yes…"

"But who were the People? What part of Earth were you from?"

Davix was knitting those eyebrows again. He was doing so much knitting, I expected Christmas sweaters to start dropping at his feet. "I-I don't know. The DragonLaw doesn't expound on—"

"What kind of calamity was it? Earthquake? War? Did the People have time to grab their vinyl collections before the roofs came down? And did they *want* to come or was it more like, you know, alien abduction?"

"I have read you all that is recorded in the DragonLaw, X'risp'hin. No more is known."

"You mean the dragons haven't told you any more."

"The great dragons tell us all we need to know."

"So, they hide important details about your past, but you can look up every dull detail about last year's wind speeds."

"Wind speeds are not dull," he said. "And we weren't abducted!"

My mouth was just dropping open to argue more when I realized what an idiot I was. Why the hell was I offending Davix with all these questions about his religion? Why wasn't I making amusing small talk and finding a place to drop in lines like, *Just so you know, I'm also exclusively attracted to males.* Davix closed the book and returned to sit behind his desk.

"Don't you believe in anything, X'risp'hin?" he asked after a painfully silent minute.

"You mean, like God or something? I tried once." I sat down on the cool stone floor beside his chair, my arms around my knees. "There was this kid—Timothy—at school when I was thirteen, and I liked him. And I think he liked me, too, but he was one of the Jesus kids."

"Jesus?" Davix asked.

"A god on Earth. One of the popular ones. Anyway, the closer we got, the more Timothy talked about Jesus. One day, I think we were really close to kissing for the first time, but he pulled away and told me, 'If you pray, you won't be confused anymore.'"

Telling the story was kind of shaking me up, making me feel the uncertainty and guilt of that time all over again. I wished I hadn't started. But Davix was looking down at me with those big, warm eyes, so I continued.

"Every night for a week, I kneeled on the floor beside my bed and tried to find Jesus in my heart. That's where Timothy said he hung out. But I never did find him. And when it felt too stupid and my knees started to hurt, I just got up and played video games instead."

"Did you ever kiss Timothy?"

"No. My friends all laughed at the Jesus kids, and the Jesus kids didn't talk to us either, so we drifted apart."

"Sometimes my friends laugh at me for my devotion," Davix said. "I wasn't always so devout. When we chose our disciplines, only the mysteries of Atmospherics interested me. I was determined to grow up into the best forecaster in the Realm. Then, when my friends and I reached our sixth cycle and began preparing for our Consolidation ceremony, the beauty of the DragonLaw opened before me like a flower, full of answers for those who took the time to look." He was smiling now, like he could see the beauty in front of him.

"I understand your friend Timothy, X'risp'hin. I too have no taste for confusion. The balance and certainty of the DragonLaw offers light in the darkness when we feel lost." He straightened the pens on his desk and rotated the ink bottle nervously. "I know you don't feel welcomed by Grav'nan-dahé, but he is a great man, believe me. Pious and dedicated. After my Consolidation ceremony, I decided to model my devotion on his. I pulled back from my studies in Atmospherics, and the Prime Magistrate took me on as his special pupil."

"And that's why Tix-etnep-thon-dahé made Rinby Lead Apprentice instead of you," I said, and his smile went flat. *Way to go, Crispin.*

"We make decisions," he answered. "They have consequences."

I tried to figure out how to climb out of this hole. "So, you're not confused anymore? That's good."

"I wasn't for a long time. Living in the clarity of the DragonLaw gave me peace. But since Rinby died…" He started straightening a pile of already straight notebooks, and I wanted to grab his hands and hold them against me. "For the first time in cycles, X'risp'hin, I am filled with doubts. The bidahénas say her death was an accident, but that doesn't make sense. Grav'nan-dahé has forbidden me to investigate, and I feel so much anger!"

"Trust me, I get it," I said. "Your hero is being a jerk to me, too."

But what I thought was solidarity just made him angrier. "He doesn't want you disturbing the balance of the Realm, like you did when you disrupted the classroom!"

"Look, I didn't ask for this copper blood. They told me I had to come here and be your Dragon Queen's stud horse. And what's my thanks? Some cranky priest makes a laughingstock of me."

"But prophecy is not supported by scripture."

"And I don't care about your stupid scripture," I shot back, exasperated.

Davix's eyes locked onto mine, full of rage, but I also thought he might start to cry, and maybe if we had been seated at the same level, I would have leaned in right then and kissed him. But the idea of hiking myself up awkwardly off the floor to get into position shot me full of hot, red, self-consciousness. I looked away, into the shadows under his desk. And that's when I noticed something weird.

"What's that?" I asked.

"What?" He pushed his chair back and joined me on the floor.

"See? It's a piece of wood under the drawer in your desk. It's probably supposed to be there, right? I'm dumb."

"No, it's not," he said, reaching up to take hold of it. The square of thin wood was cut to the same size as the drawer, but it was a hack job, held in place with a few bent nails. Sliding the wood back, Davix found a small stack of papers.

We stood, and he spread the sheets out on the desk. They looked like the notes in the apprentice's notebook, only messier, hastily scrawled rows and columns without the neat table enclosing them.

"What is this?" I asked. "A rough draft?"

"No, we write directly into the notebooks. This is Rinby's handwriting!" he said, distressed. "I-I don't understand what we're looking at. Why would she have these?"

"And why was she hiding them?"

I'm not sure what he was going to say, but he never had the chance. From eight stories down, we heard Stakrat shouting.

"Davix! Klar's Blood, Davix, come to the window!"

We both ran over and saw her below, at the base of the tower.

"What is it?" he called back.

She was actually jumping up and down in place, her outstretched finger moving as it tracked something crossing the sky. From our vantage point inside the tower, we couldn't see it at first, but then a great creature of green and copper wheeled into view, flying with slow, mighty beats of its wings, a mane of leathery strips trailing back from its head and neck.

It was a dragon.

CHAPTER 16: *The Intruder and the Curator*

The Curator of Sites Historic was in his workshop in the Citadel. It was the quietest place in Cliffside, and he appreciated its peace. But the time he spent cocooned in silence made him acutely aware of changes in the background hum of the city. Sensing a charge, an air of excitement, he left his work to investigate.

He crossed the courtyard and climbed up the steps to the top of the Citadel's walls. The sight of the dragon caught him off guard, and he had to steady himself on one of the flagpoles lest he topple to the rocks below. How magnificent. How unexpected. Why was the dragon here, days before *Sarensikar*? Why this dragon in particular? He knew his services would be required, and he would have to work quickly. Did the dragon require a throne be brought forth? A dining table sufficient to her status laid out in Etnep House? Were the crowns and other emblems of majesty all in good repair?

Focussed as he was on his inventories and task lists, he was unaware of the Intruder's stealthy approach. He tried to grab for the retaining wall as he tumbled forward, but he had been hurled too far into space. The jagged stone below came at him too fast. This was death. How unexpected.

CHAPTER 17: *Sur*

I was excited that a dragon was coming to Cliffside. Who wouldn't be? But I had no idea what kind of freaking insanity I was about to witness. We hurried out into the stairwell. Davix said, "Wait here!" and ran up the stairs. I could hear him shouting to the other apprentices, hear their chairs clattering to the floor as they ran to the window. Then Davix was racing past me, yelling, "Follow!"

We took the spiral stairs so fast, I was dizzy by the time we reached Tix-etnep-thon-dahé's office.

"Master-da!" Davix yelled, but the old man was already at the window with Flak on his shoulder. Both were staring out, both nodding.

"It is Sur," The Atmospherics Master said. "She is here for the Copper Guest. Go! I see the Defence apprentice already has the mare saddled."

Davix hurried me out into the fog-streaked sunshine. I wanted to take a minute and catch my breath, but the chestnut horse appeared out of the fog and almost ran us down.

Stakrat brought it to a halt, shouting, "Climb up, X'risp'hin! I have to get you to Cliffside."

"How exactly do I get up there?" I said, looking for a ladder or a forklift or something. I had zero experience with equestrian shenanigans. Davix squatted and cupped his hands for me to step into, and somehow between him and Stakrat, I climbed into the saddle behind her.

"I'll follow directly," Davix said, running off in the direction of Tix-etnep-thon-dahé's hut.

"Hang on tight," Stakrat called, and we were off. Stakrat reached back and handed me a brass bell on a short stick. "Ring this every few seconds when we're in fog."

And right away we were, so I began ringing loudly and nonstop, terrified of a sudden collision.

"Not that much ringing," she shouted.

We broke through the fog as we rounded a corner, almost immediately catching sight of the dragon flying in circles over the city. As we climbed through the streets, more and more people poured out of every building, blocking our way.

"Stand aside! Let the Copper Guest through," Stakrat yelled in her best soldier voice as the crowd pinned us on all sides. Walking would have been faster, but I didn't want to be down there. Everyone had a kind of desperate longing on their faces, like when middle-school me and a thousand girls lined up for autographs from boy bands. I was impressed with the horse's chill demeanour as we picked slowly through the throng. Stakrat, on the other hand, looked ready to pull out her knife and start hacking us a path. Somewhere in the distance, I heard the sound of hundreds of voices singing.

Suddenly! A deep thumping whoosh, and the sky above us darkened. The dragon, Sur, flew directly overhead, close enough that I could see big, coloured jewels pressed into the scales on her chest. A wave of gasps and shouts washed from street to street as she flew over, and finally a resounding cheer and redoubling of the song. The minute we were free of the narrow street, Stakrat urged the horse into a gallop. I rang the bell to get people out of the way, almost falling off as we took a tight corner. And there we were, back at the Retreat of Tarn.

"Holy crap," was my summation of what lay ahead of me. Stakrat and I climbed off the horse onto the raised base of a statue where we could watch the action. Every one of Cliffside's residents was either present or just arriving, filling the Retreat of Tarn all the way to the stage in front of the gates of Etnep House. As one, they sang their rousing hymn:

You, the Five, who saved us from calamity
You who built this haven for the People
You the dragons whom we love
Accept this song as our token

Sur, sitting serenely on the stage, was huge, at least six metres from head to tail. The long leathery strips on the back of her neck were swept elegantly to one side, like a shawl, and the sun glittered off the jewels on her chest. From her broad shoulders to her heavy tail, she radiated power. Yet she was also graceful as she surveyed the crowd with her hooded, red eyes. People were coming forward to lay down presents on the steps. Even the fog seemed to be showing its respect, hanging above the square without touching down.

"Isn't she wonderful, X'risp'hin?" asked a voice behind me. I turned and found that Grentz had joined us on the statue base, tears spilling from his eyes.

"She really is, yeah," I said, moved by his big, wet display of emotion.

"My full name is Agren-sur-dez. You understand?"

"You mean you're part of Sur House? She's your dragon?"

Nodding like a bobble-toy, he said, "This is a day without parallel!" and pulled me into a smothery hug.

Extricating myself from him as politely as I could, I asked Stakrat, "I know they do flyovers, but when was the last time a dragon actually landed in town?"

She grinned at me, so wide-eyed, she looked stoned. "Not for generations, X'risp'hin. The last one was Queen Etnep herself, receiving blessings from the People before she retreated to the Matrimonial Tunnels. That was when she laid Sur's egg. And Sur is now one hundred and eighty cycles old!" Even though she was shouting in my ear, the rising crowd noise almost drowned her out.

Up on the stage, an official-looking group emerged through the gates of Etnep House, walking with measured steps in precise formation. Grav'nan-dahé and some other humans were in the lead, all dressed in fancy-ass robes with glittery bits. They were followed by a bunch of mixed beings including the bidahénas Kror and Throd I'd met the night before. Bringing up the rear was the little interpreter in orange. He squeezed his way to the front, standing close, but not too close, to Sur. The songs continued, and the gifts piled up on the steps. For next few minutes, the group of officials did elaborate bows and prayers, until Sur raised a hand, silencing them. The crowd shut up, too, the cacophony dropping to a low, excited hum.

Sur began scanning the crowd, her search coming to an abrupt halt when she turned my way. Coincidence, I hoped. But then she spoke, and the others on the stage followed her gaze. The interpreter walked to the front of the stage. He was shouting something into the crowd, and everyone in the crowd turned my way, picking up the call.

"Copper Guest! Copper Guest!"

"What am I supposed to do?" I said, leaning close to Stakrat.

"You have to get up there."

"Shit," I murmured, feeling sick.

"Copper Guest!" called a man in front of me. "Let us lift you over the square." He raised his hands toward me.

"Uh, that's, um, nice of you…no, I-I can walk…"

But then everyone around him was raising their hands, and I realized I was supposed to crowd surf.

"Do it, X'risp'hin," Stakrat said. "They won't drop you."

"No, no way, forget this," I said, trying to climb higher on the statue, but time had smoothed the stone until there was no foothold, and right away I slipped.

Screaming, I fell into a sea of hands, soft but firm, that lifted me into the hazy sunshine and carried me over the square. At first, I was terrified, passed hand to hand, face turned up to the foggy sky, moving inexorably to my rendezvous with the giant lizard. The voices from below were ecstatic, calling up, "Bless our realm, Dragon Groom," and "You are the peace, you are the balance," so I tried to let go of my fear and get into it. I was the mighty Copper Guest and this was a big day. But then the whole religious experience tilted into the creepy. The crowd, growing more feverish as I got closer to the stage, began to snatch souvenirs off me. I felt the belt being pulled loose from my pants, then felt a tugging and tearing at the decorative hem of my shirt. A few hands took liberties they should not have on my bum and environs.

"Stop that!" I shouted, as the gentle sea of hands grew turbulent. They yanked my hair and pinched my flesh. One of my shoes began to come loose in someone's hand, and I kicked until the sneak thief yelped in pain. I felt like I was fighting for my life. But suddenly, all the grabby hands were wrenched loose and replaced by a single pair. Before I knew it, I was being flipped upright to sit on Tiqokh's knobby shoulders.

He pushed through the crowd like his arms were scythes and he was cutting a path through a cornfield.

"Wow, am I glad to see you!" I said, balancing myself with a hand on his scaly head.

He answered in his cool, thoughtful way. "The psychodynamics of human crowds is an area not well enough understood here in the Realm of Fire, but I recognize it from Earth."

"Yeah, this is a total hockey crowd." I ran a hand through my messed-up hair and refastened the buttons on my tunic. One button had been torn right off. We were approaching the stage; everyone was looking my way. Including the dragon.

"Hey, Tiqokh," I said quietly into his ear. "I don't suppose we could go anywhere other than up there, could we?"

"There is no point, Crispin, in delaying what must be."

"I know, I know. Once you break Mom's favourite porcelain, it's only a matter of time before she notices it's missing."

Tiqokh lifted me off his shoulders and deposited me on the steps among the flowers and statues and cakes wrapped in coloured paper, like I was one of the presents. I had an epic wedgie, and the only non-gross way to fix it was to jump up and down until my underwear settled, holding up the beltless pants so they wouldn't fall down in front of everyone. My jumping seemed to excite the crowd, who roared in approval.

And then Sur spoke.

"*DRAGON GROOM,*" she said. The voice wasn't just deep. It was like the world had built me a private earthquake with its epicentre in my bowels. And there was more to it—something not vocal or vibrational at all, but like the message had been beamed right up my nose and into my brain.

"*THE CRACKED FRACTALS OF DESTINY/THE THREADS OF HISTORY, SPUN AND SPINNING/TANGLED IN YOU, YOU IN US, WE IN ALL/BRING YOU HERE.*"

I recognized her speech as ancient dragon, but it also sounded like poetry—the modern kind without the rhymes. I dared a look at Sur, who was examining me with her head tilted to one side. I could feel the hot breath she exhaled from her nose and hear the EDM bass thud of her enormous heart. When her tail swished to the side, the hiss across the marble was like the world's biggest librarian shushing the reading room.

"Join us," said a bidahéna, clicking its long claws at me in a way that didn't exactly put a spring in my step.

"Tiqokh…?" I muttered, turning and finding him gone.

Then I felt a hand on my shoulder and heard murmurs in my ear. "Climb the steps. Bow with each step. Repeat after me." It was Grav'nan-dahé. And it's funny how even your worst enemy can be an ally when the situation is this weird. "Oh, Great Sur…"

"Oh, Great Sur," I repeated, full-voiced as Gravy-man fed me the lines in a whisper. "Far have I travelled and grateful am I…" My toe hit a gift—a little metal statue of five dragon heads in a circle, and it toppled over and clanged all too audibly down the steps.

"Sorry," I said to whomever.

"Grateful am I to see your shining countenance," the Prime Prompter hissed into my ear with bonus saliva. And soon I was standing beside the bidahénas, Sur's shadow falling across me. With three thousand people watching, I awaited my next order ("Dance the merengue covered in peanut butter!"), but then five people in some kind of ceremonial robes climbed up the steps and kneeled in unison.

The guy in the front of the group held up an amazing, translucent yellow rock the size of an ostrich egg. His hands were shaking as he said, "The people of Sur House dedicate this stone to our patron, to commemorate this wonderful day. Please take it as a token of our love and devotion."

One of the bidahénas took the stone from the man in its clawed hands. Sur raised her chest like she was about to receive a medal, and that was more or less what happened. The bidahéna placed the stone in a blank spot on her chest, amid the red, blue, and green stones that seemed to be embedded in her scaly skin. The stone began to glow as soon as it touched her, and smoke rose from the scales around it. The bidahéna let go of the stone, and it sank slowly until it was half-buried in Sur's chest. The dragon's eyes were closed, and she seemed to be humming in her bones-deep voice as the smoke cleared.

Sur said, *"THE BOND IS TRUE / THE HOUSE ENDURES."*

The Interpreter translated for the delegation from Sur House, most of them weeping freely. "Sur proclaims that your offering strengthens her bond with you, and that she will forever protect your house."

The bidahéna dismissed the delegation, and they moved down to the bottom of the steps.

"AND NOW THE UNBRACEABLE SHALL BE BOUND / SUR IS NOT DOMESTIC / YET SHE WILL BEAR / BRING FORTH THE RIDER'S SEAT."

The bidahénas looked at each other, and then turned as one toward Grav'nan-dahé. He made a sour face and said to the Interpreter, "The meaning?"

The little guy was so nervous, he was tapping the ground with his foot like a rabbit in heat. Maybe this was his first time translating for an actual dragon. "Well, the—the subtleties are numerous. There are the multiple meanings of 'bound,' as in 'bound for a destination' or 'fated.' So, I suppose—I mean, I believe—Sur tells us that though she must leave, she will not forget—"

"Sorry," I said, loud enough to catch the attention of everyone on the stage. "Uh, I'm not an expert or anything, but is she asking you to put a…a saddle on her?"

All the mixed beings stared at me, then closed themselves into a group and began arguing. The head of the Sur House delegation climbed back up to the stage, bowing low with every step.

"Honourable beings, great masters," he said. "The Copper Guest reminds us that there is, indeed, such a holy apparatus in Etnep House."

Grav'nan-dahé straightened and called out, "Where is the Curator of Sites Historic? He must bring forth the relic!" This led to another minute of confusion, and from what I could figure out, it was really surprising and really bad the Curator guy was missing this whole party.

Grav'nan-dahé said to the man from Sur House, "Inquire of the Etnep House Porter. She will have the keys to the reliquary." While the delegation ran past us and through the gates, someone with a beautiful tenor voice started singing another hymn, and the crowd picked it up. Sur seemed to be infinitely patient through all this.

In the meantime, I was busy scanning the crowd for a particular set of eyes, a certain distinctive nose, a smile that was hard to coax, but worth the effort. Where was Davix? Despite being in the centre of a revival meeting for dragon fanatics, a large part of my brain was worried about how I had talked to him up in the Atmospherics Tower. I had questioned his religion, told him the DragonLaw wasn't so impressive—he probably hated me. The thought burned like acid.

The gates banged open again, and the delegation from Sur House emerged, carrying a complicated contraption of leather and wood with ornate copper fittings.

With a hot blast of breath and a gut-churning "*HURUMPHHH*," Sur fell forward to crouch on all fours. Her folded wings separated, and she tilted to one side. Have you ever watched a family on a camping trip trying to set up their tent as the last bit of sunlight is leaving the sky and the kids are already screaming for supper? That's sort of what the delegates and the mixed beings looked like putting the saddle on Sur. I stood well back.

But let me ask you, how dumb am I? Why hadn't I guessed who was going to be sitting in that saddle, which was probably seeing the light of day for the first time in centuries? Why was I surprised when Sur said, "*DRAGON GROOM/THE FIVE PREPARE A WELCOME/COLLATION, CREATION, POETRY, BALANCE, AND TRANSFORMATION*"?

"Um, oh yeah?" I said, feeling light-headed. I must have looked at everyone onstage, begging for a way out, but only Grav'nan-dahé responded, gesturing me toward the dragon with foul impatience plastered across his face.

I moved slowly forward, like my pants were full of crap, and Sur called, "*THE SKIES ARE LONELY/THEY WRITE YOUR NAME IN FOG/YOU WILL RIDE ME, RIDE ME/THOUGH NOT AS LAVA-BLOODED GROOM.*"

I stopped. "Wait, did you just make a sex joke?" Someone placed a big cape on my shoulders, and someone else handed me a cloth sack, pointing out the provisions inside, the food and drink I would need during the journey. And then, still holding my beltless pants up with one hand, I was helped up into the saddle, which was more like one of those riding baskets they put on elephants in India.

The helpers scrambled back down Sur's flanks, retreating to a safe distance like you do before a helicopter takes off, and I think I called out, "Hey, wait... " But destiny doesn't wait, at least not for someone as insignificant as Crispin Haugen. Sur's wings snapped open, and their wind made my hair rise and fall. We lurched backward, my feet rising in the air, and then forward. I grabbed the edge of the basket, just saving me from slamming my face into its ornate woodwork. And we were airborne.

Sur made a sharp turn above the square at a terrifying angle, and below me, every face was turned upward in awe. The wind in my ears was loud, the ground retreating, but I leaned over the side of the basket and saw Davix at the back of the square, sitting on Tix-etnep-thon-dahé's grey mule. He was waving at me, the smile on his face visible even from that distance. Daring to let go one of my clutching hands, I waved back. And there was a connection between us, as real as the strands that linked the Realm of Fire to the Earth. Sur gained altitude, and we disappeared into the ceiling of fog. I prayed wherever I was being taken, the thread tying me to that peculiar, beautiful boy would stay strong.

PART III

HIGH IN THE MOUNTAINS, DEEP IN THE FOG

CHAPTER 18: *Farad'hil*

Sometimes I have this image of myself as a wimp who's afraid of everything. But I'm not afraid of heights. In fact, the ride on Sur's back was totally kick-ass.

We began by flying low over the fields outside Cliffside, the landscape of the Realm of Fire playing hide-and-seek beneath us under the shifting layer of fog. Farmers, hammering at fence posts, pulling weeds, and otherwise getting ready for planting season, dropped their tools and gaped as Sur passed overhead. With two days of nonstop amazement behind me, it was hard to remember that seeing a dragon was a rare, red-letter day for the People. Beyond the farmlands, we passed over hilly meadows dotted with wildflowers and small gatherings of trees. Fog patches drifted by, revealing deer munching on the daisies. A fox chased a rabbit through the low bushes, and I cheered when the little bunny got away.

Abruptly, the greenbelt ended, and we were flying over bare rock, grey and pitted. This terrain was empty and lifeless as the moon. Dry heat rose around us, and Sur caught the thermals like a hawk and circled higher into the sky.

"That's a depressing view," I muttered to myself, and what with being up on her back with the wind howling by us, I didn't think she would hear me. I was wrong.

"WE PLANT OUR LITTLE GARDEN, DRAGON GROOM/ CHERISH ALL FROM WHEAT STALK TO KINGSOLVER/ONE DAY, THE LIVING WORLD WILL BE COMPLETE."

I felt a hot flush of embarrassment. "Sorry, didn't mean to disrespect the, uh, realm. Can I ask you a question, ma'am…I mean Dragon-dahé…"

"WHY USE ANY NAME BUT 'SUR'/WHEN 'SUR' ENCOMPASSES/ALL MY GREATNESS?"

"Okay, Sur, awesome. And you can skip the whole Dragon Groom thing and call me Crispin."

"KHARIS'PAR'IH'IN," she repeated, which meant something like, "That itch on your back you can't quite reach."

"Um, close enough," I said, giving up on anyone in the realm getting my name right. "Where are we going exactly?"

"FARAD'HIL CALLS TO US/AND TO ITS HALLS WE FLY."

"How far is that?"

"NO MATTER HOW FAR/FARAD'HIL IS AS CLOSE AS/THE BEAT OF YOUR PULSE."

"Like, should I ration my food or can I eat my sandwich?" I asked with a hopeful lilt. Sur didn't answer, so I pulled the food from the cloth sack. I held off on drinking, because I wasn't sure how I'd ask the dragon to pull into a rest stop if I had to pee. We were way up high now, flying parallel to a distant range of jagged mountains covered in thick forest, the tallest of them with bare snowy peaks.

"What're those?" I asked her.

"THE CHEND'TH'NIF MOUNTAINS/THE SPINE OF THE REALM/A GREEN WALL BETWEEN US AND THE BADLANDS."

"Badlands?"

"A DESPERATE INFERNO WHERE NO CREATURE WALKS/ BUT THEY WISH THEIR HOURS SHORTER./THE TRAVELLER'S SKIN ERUPTS LIKE THE GROUND/THEIR TEARS DRY IN BLISTERED SOCKETS."

"Yeah, let's give the Badlands a miss, then."

I didn't realize I had fallen asleep until I found myself tumbling sideways. I peeked over the edge of the basket. Sur was banking sharply into the Chend'th'nif Mountains. Snowy peaks rose high over our heads, and forested valleys slid by beneath our feet. Up ahead, something glittered in the sunlight, dazzling my eyes. It was a huge dome made up of triangular glass panes, the only thing in the mountains that wasn't, you know, nature. I didn't have much time to wonder about it before Sur went into a sudden dive, and I had to grab the basket rim for support. We plunged into a long canyon, narrow as a bowling alley, zooming straight at a sheer rock face. Before I had time to scream, Sur made a last-minute upward climb, spread her wings wide, and landed with a stomach-lurching deceleration.

We were on a wide ledge of rock, like a balcony halfway up the mountainside. In the big stone wall of the mountain stood a massive and intimidating gate made of criss-crossing beams of copper and steel. Sur sat placidly as seven mixed beings ran out through a small door in the gate. Three octonas began undoing the saddle, while a quadrana lifted me out of the basket like I was a Pomeranian. Unlike Tiqokh, this quadrana had an impressive set of leathery wings. Still dizzy from the ride, I was happy to just sit on the ground, taking in the scene.

One of the freaky bidahénas was up front, wiping Sur's head and shoulders with a large damp cloth, while a second quadrana ran his clawed hand through the leathery cords of her mane. This busy crew reminded me of hair and makeup, touching up the movie star between shots. Everyone was wearing shimmery tunics, like the costume designer had been given the direction "glamalicious Bible epic."

"Welcome, Dragon Groom," said an octona in a long green robe with a matching big-shoulder jacket. "I am X'raftik, the Chief Valet of Farad'hil." She reached out a hand and pulled me to my feet like I weighed nothing. Immediately, my beltless pants fell to my ankles. Never say I don't know how to make an entrance.

"Do not be distressed," X'raftik said as I pulled up my pants, blushing. "We have new vestments for you, more appropriate to the dragons' domain." She clapped her hands twice, and two of the octonas came forward, carrying a folded set of the shimmery clothing—imperial purple, shot through with threads of silver and copper. The pair were young, maybe college age, and I realized all the mixed beings I'd seen so far were adults. Was Farad'hil where the mixed beings grew up?

"Please change into these garments, Dragon Groom," said one.

"Change? Out here?" I watched a hawk sweep through canyon, eyeing our party suspiciously.

The other young octona said, "You may not pass through the gate dressed as you are. Do not worry. We will take care of your clothing during your stay."

So I stripped down to my dragon boxers right there under the foggy sky. I guess I was starting to get over my body shyness. But as I stood in my skivvies with the chill wind whipping around my skinny legs, I made an awful discovery.

"My necklace. It's gone!" It had to have been one of those grabby souvenir hounds when I was crowd surfing. They probably had the little wolf's head hanging from their showerhead by now, praying to it so they could get some mating action.

X'raftik made a tutting sound. "I'm sure all will be restored when we return you to Cliffside. But now, let us not keep Great Sur waiting." She shoved one of the young octonas forward with my new clothes.

The outfit felt all kinds of rich and yummy, and I hoped there would be a full-length mirror in my near future. I did a fashion model spin and came back around to find Sur looking me up and down through her big slitted eyes. She nodded solemnly.

"YOU SHINE LIKE THE GREAT ABODE ITSELF/ KHARIS'PAR'IH'IN/NOW ENTER FARAD'HIL/AND BE AMAZED!" The ground shook as the big gate began to open up, the horizontal and vertical elements pulling apart, like a shredded wheat unweaving.

Okay, I'll admit it. Despite having dragon blood myself, I was still making assumptions about my scaly cousins. I expected Farad'hil to be stony and primitive—dank, dark caves, maybe stinking of dragon guano. Stereotypes, I know! I'm a dragophobe. In point of fact, the place was better than a Vegas hotel. The walls of the curving entrance tunnel started as rough rock but soon gave way to a smooth pattern of long waves that sparkled in a dozen shades of fuchsia. The waves led us around the corner to a wider hall with crystal statues three times my height. There were realistic subjects like birds and flowers, but also wild abstracts. Moving lights glinted through the crystal so they seemed to be dancing.

The corridor took a last turn, and we arrived at the enormous central cavern. I looked up and down at what seemed to be a city in an open-pit mine. A wide and winding road hugged the walls of the cavern, spiralling round from top to bottom. The cavern was narrow at the bottom and widened as it ascended, like the inside of a big ice cream cone. And up at the top was the glass dome I'd seen from the air, the mid-afternoon light pouring through, lighting up the whole of Farad'hil.

The design theme was natural versus artificial. Stands of trees planted along sections of the road were interspersed with pillars of polished stone. Shiny metal sculptures of birds hung from the high ceiling, and flying among them were live storks who landed in perfect pools set in outcroppings on the terraced wall. A narrow waterfall across from us fell with a bright splash from the top of Farad'hil to a small lake at the bottom.

Despite the size of the place, it didn't appear to have much of a population. I saw maybe a dozen mixed beings moving around. Some were pulling small wagons or carrying bundles of lumber and cloth. Others wrote in grace books as they walked the roadway. A pair of winged quadranas flew up from the depths, circling once when they saw Sur and calling out, "The city throbs with pleasure as you enter, great Sur." I won't comment.

I felt hot breath on the back of my neck, and Sur said, *"OH,*

FARAD'HIL / YOUR GOLDEN HALLS GIVE BIRTH TO DREAMS/ YOUR LIGHT ILLUMINATES THE REALM."

"And I haven't even seen the food court," I murmured, unnerved by her looming presence behind me. Maybe the joy of coming home was making her playful, because she suddenly ducked her head and hooked me on one of her rounded horns, lifting me off the ground and flipping me onto her wide back.

Before I had time to lodge a protest, she said, *"TAKE HOLD OF MY MANE / OR PLUMMET TO ECSTATIC DEATH / IN THE ABODE OF DREAMS."*

She leaped from the roadway into space, and I chose the holding-on option, doing a roller-coaster scream to show I was a good sport. Or maybe I was just petrified. She circled the great cavern, swooping low over the lake and then climbing again. Sur landed on the spiral roadway not too far from the cavern floor, in front of a high triangular cave mouth cut in the wall of the chamber.

"HERE THE DRAGONLAW COMES HOME / ASHES AND SMOKE RUNNING BACK IN TIME TO MAKE AGAIN THE TREE."

I slid off Sur's back and approached the opening curiously. The dragon followed me inside. The rocky chamber was dim, with a ceiling high enough that dragons wouldn't have to worry about bumping their heads. What lights there were came from a series of…I guess they were workstations, maybe twenty-five of them packed tightly like a call centre. Each desk was occupied by an octona, flipping the pages of grace books, making notations in green ink. Small torchstones cast just enough light to illuminate the open books.

I was looking over one of their shoulders when he suddenly called out, "Proofed entries from Textiles on the rise."

He swept his hand across the page from the bottom to top, and the text vanished. The blue light in the corner of the grace book flashed. It might have been my imagination, but I thought I saw the letters swirling into the air, like a swarm of translucent bees, rising through a big hole in the ceiling that led to an upper level.

From that second level, a deep, flat voice responded. "Entries from Textiles received." I followed Sur up a wide ramp to this second level, keeping far enough behind so I didn't get flattened by her swinging tail. Upstairs, there were only three desks, but much bigger than the ones below. At every desk, a quadrana sat, poring over texts in the four or five grace books arranged in front of them. Eyes inches from the page, they ran clawed fingers across each line, calling out requests for reference books. Octonas scrambled up ladders to fetch the dusty old volumes from the floor-to-ceiling bookshelves that lined the walls. There was a chilly draft running through the room, and I looked up into a huge airshaft over our heads, so high and dim, I couldn't see where it ended.

"Likh'tik!" called a quadrana to his colleague. "Can we refer to a second mate-match as that human's 'inevitable'?"

"Was the first pairing without issue? If so, then yes. Otherwise, use the phrase 'consolation spouse.'"

Sur spoke up, her rich voice filling the chamber. "*CONSOLATIONS OF RIVER AND TREE/THE BIRD THAT RETURNS/THE FERTILE DECAY.*"

Everyone in the room had paused to listen to her poem. After a momentary silence, they all gave a short round of applause before returning to their work. I don't think anyone wrote down these words of wisdom.

I said, "So this is where all those entries for the DragonLaw go?"

It wasn't Sur who answered, but one of the octonas. "Here we collate and cross-check, Dragon Groom. And when our work is done, the work goes up...up to Renrit, the Great Collator." He gestured at the airshaft.

A quadrana to my left called out in a nail-scratch monotone, "Results and interpretations from Atmospherics on the rise." He swept his clawed hand across a page of the grace book in front of him, and this time, I could clearly see the swarm of letters fly from the page, glowing as they spiralled into the darkness above.

Atmospherics? I wondered if I was watching Davix's words in the air. I almost waved at them.

"*CLIMB ON, DRAGON GROOM!*" Sur cried, and I had barely scrambled onto her back before she lifted into the air. Taking off in such a cramped space was obviously a bad idea, but all the octonas and quadranas in the room seemed to be used to it. They grabbed books and cups of water off their desks and ducked. Of course, as Sur climbed up into the narrow airshaft, the problem was no longer theirs but mine. I hung on tight to the ribbons of leather on her neck and pressed myself close to her back as we sped upward with just a snot trail of space between my head and the jagged lava rock walls.

The stomach-turning journey lasted maybe thirty seconds before we burst into another dark chamber. Sur righted herself and came in for a landing so abrupt, I rolled off her back and landed face down on the floor. Luckily, it was carpeted, or maybe it was some kind of thick moss. It did taste vaguely organic.

A voice shook the air and the floor beneath me. *"REFRAIN FROM BREAKING THE DRAGON GROOM, YOUNG SUR <ref. inertia; ref. human anatomy & trauma; cross-catalogue: 1. history of dragon grooms (5). list of humans who have visited Farad'hil (9)>"*

"Renrit?" I ventured, sitting up. The only light in the room was a single torchstone in a standing lamp, but I got a good view of the dragon. He was huge, twice Sur's size, both taller and considerably heavier in the bum. In fact, he looked so heavy I wondered if he ever left his chamber. His wings, puny in comparison, didn't look like they could keep him airborne. Not only was he, um, generously proportioned, his skin was covered from basement to attic in coloured jewels like the ones Sur wore, only she had the good taste to know more is less.

"<article. History of Dragon Names>INDEED, I AM RENRIT! <cit. 3rd oldest Dragon of the realm; mother: Sekhnet; sibling: Queen Etnep; trivia bred racing llamas for 271 cycles> WELCOME TO THE EDITORIUM."

Renrit sat behind a desk the size of a pool table with an enormous book open in front of him, its pages blank. The ghost letters I had seen rising from below were circling above his head. Sur was tracking their progress with glinting eyes, like a cat eyeing birds on a fence. Renrit gestured at one of the circling word swarms, and it dived at his open book, laying itself out into neat lines of text.

"Wow. And now it's in the DragonLaw?" I asked Sur in a whisper, but she was still watching airborne words as they sailed past her nose. It was Renrit who answered.

"FIRST I WILL PERFORM THE FINAL BLESSING OF THE PASSAGE. <ref. style book; ref. omega reader>"

He ran a finger swiftly across the lines of text, stopping once or twice to change or rearrange a character. He then gave a deep, satisfied *harumph* and looked up from the page, fixing me with a cold, penetrating stare.

I cracked a nervous smile, "All good?"

"I SHALL RECITE: 'Though I alone of the twenty who carry the blood was selected to travel the strands, the gracious hospitality of the Realm humbles me. My role, like any of yours, is service. I must be your apprentice, and you my masters, instructing me how I may better serve the will of the mighty dragons—gracious is the world they have built.' <Book of Visitation, 4th epoch, Ch.XLVII, Incident XXXII>"

I nodded vacantly. "Um, nice. Very…exciting." A lead pipe of comprehension banged me upside the head. "Wait! Was that me? My speech after dinner last night?"

Before Renrit could answer, Sur flung herself across the room, pinning one of the swirling word clouds beneath a clawed hand.

Renrit raised himself up in protest, his jewelled chest flashing. "*SUR! UNHAND THE HOLY TEXT <ref. Genizah of lost and damaged words; cit. the 100-cycle debate of 'excoriation' vs 'excess oration.' body count: 56.*"

But Sur ignored him, busily picking through the little glowing wad of words, which squirmed like baby mice under her claws.

"*POSSIBILITIES, RENRIT,*" she said. "*SO MANY PRETTY PHRASES/BETTER USES THAN IN YOUR PAGES.*"

Renrit, apparently at the end of his patience, growled. The growl shook me right up to the eyeballs, and my vision vibrated. Sur stared back at him and hissed. But she relented, releasing the letters, which arced through the air, landing in the open book at a gesture from Renrit.

"What are those?" I asked.

Renrit smoothed his palm over the text, like he was comforting it after its ordeal. "*SEED TALLIES FOR THE PLANTING. SARENSIKAR IS ALMOST UPON US. <comment: net yield of +15–25% expected>*"

Sur tossed her mane like a diva. "*A THIN AND TASTELESS HARVEST/COMPARED TO ANY I MIGHT HAVE REAPED/WITH THE PRETTY WORDS.*" Without warning, she lifted me onto her back, my hands windmilling as I found my balance. She said, "*WE MUST EAT AND REST/COPPER GUEST./LET OUR MINDS PAUSE AND WANDER/BEFORE THE NEXT TEST.*"

"I could eat," I agreed, straightening my clothes and grabbing her mane.

Sur pulled aside a curtain that stretched across the whole wall, revealing a huge window with a view of the central core of Farad'hil. Light streamed into the Editorium, causing Renrit to howl in indignation. With the room lit up, I saw his big, unmade bed in the corner, surrounded by half-eaten plates of food and bottles of drink. I was right; Renrit was a shut-in, a total *otaku* nerd.

Sur unfastened a latch and gave the window a push. It swung outward on its enormous hinges, and she called, "*HOLD FAST, KHARIS'PAR'IH'IN!*"

As we swept out into the cavern, I could hear Renrit bellowing behind us, "*CLOSE THE WINDOW! BANISH THE LIGHT!*"

The noise Sur made beneath me might have been chuckling.

CHAPTER 19: *Safe Space*

Davix started awake in the armchair by the fire in Tix-etnep-thon-dahé's study. A workbook was open in his lap, and piles of weather data surrounded him, stacked up on the floor. Embarrassed, he looked at his master, who was poring over Rinby's secret data, cross-checking it column by column with the DragonLaw, open on its stand beside him. Master and apprentice had worked late into the night. Then, after too few hours of sleep in the cottage, Davix had been back here, striving not to fall behind with the new weather data, which never stopped coming in. He knew he needed to stay sharp, but Tix-etnep-thon-dahé's study was too familiar. It was too easy to feel safe and drowsy in its warm confines.

He had practically grown up in this room. The other apprentices were content to learn their discipline by day and play by night. Stakrat and Grentz, even studious Rinby, loved to joke and wrestle and race each other up the cliffs. But Davix wanted nothing more than to spend his hours reading silently, hungrily beside an old man, surrounded by dusty bookshelves and ancient maps. What a strange child.

It wasn't that he didn't want friends, or that he was not as consumed with the growing needs of his body. His desire to touch another boy's flesh was, in fact, so intense that sometimes he would jump from his chair as if on fire and race out of the tower. And if he had no fleshmate at the time, he would just run...run down into the valley and back up again until he was exhausted. But always he was driven to dig deeper into the mysteries of the world. Always he would return to this room.

Now he was back, drawn by mystery and *ekdahi*. And this time, the balance of the whole realm might be at stake.

"Hmm," Tix-etnep-thon-dahé breathed. Davix knew well the meaning of the old man's every sound.

"What have you found, Master-da?" He hurried over to stand in front the desk.

The Atmospherics Master was holding one of secret pages close to his face. "Rinby's figures are, needless to say, far different from what she submitted to the DragonLaw. Unfortunately, these secret data are more consistent with the unusual weather patterns we have witnessed this season."

"Unfortunately…?"

"Such a conclusion is heresy, Davix." Tix-etnep-thon-dahé watched him register the shocking words before continuing. "They are at odds with the data that appears in the DragonLaw…"

"And the DragonLaw is the true and eternal word of our Dragon Lords."

His master nodded. "Only not in this case. Here is an entry, for instance, from a quarter cycle back. Rinby notes a massive heat spike, coordinates high in the spinward Chend'th'nif."

Davix felt a knot tighten in his chest. The theological problem should have been his main concern, for as Grav'nan-dahé had taught him, *All houses are built on the foundation of the DragonLaw.* But he couldn't stop his atmospherics mind from engaging.

"A volcanic breach perhaps?" he asked. "The molten substrate of the Realm could have broken through a crack."

"It was definitely not a spontaneous geological breach. We would have noted a change in air composition. Krar's Claws!" the old man said. "Everyone in Cliffside would smell the sulphur from an eruption that size."

Davix dropped into the low chair beside the desk in frustration. "Why would Rinby have hidden such important data? Why didn't she tell you? How could she keep it from its rightful place in the DragonLaw?"

Tix-etnep-thon-dahé pushed the pile of scrawled notes to the side. He reached for the heavy earthenware teapot and refilled his small cup. He poured another cup of the strong brew for his apprentice, but Davix raised his hand in refusal.

"Drink," he ordered, so Davix did. The rich, bitter tea warmed his throat and then his stomach, strengthening him. "You are right, apprentice, Rinby would never have done such a thing on her own. No, she must have been following orders."

Davix couldn't believe his ears. "Yours?"

"Of course not. Someone who spoke for the dragons. Or so she believed."

"One of the bidahénas?" The idea was preposterous.

"I have a different thought. You will not like it, D'gada-vixtet-thon."

"Master...?"

Tix-etnep-thon-dahé's ancient fingers were pressed against his cup, the story of a long life of learning told in their tracery of wrinkles.

"There is someone in Cliffside who seeks to disrupt the balance of our realm, who would risk everything for his misguided beliefs."

Quiet, Davix wanted to say. *Stop talking, please.*

The old man's voice dropped to an urgent whisper. "Many, many cycles ago, when he was still seeking his spiritual path, Grav'nan-dahé—"

"Master, no!" Davix called out, like a dam was about to burst and only by squeezing himself into the widening crack could the world be saved. He would not hear words spoken against the Prime Magistrate. He lowered his head and closed his eyes tight.

Tix-etnep-thon-dahé continued without mercy. "Grav'nan-renrit-dez, as he was then known, was an apprentice in Stonework, my friend and sometime fleshmate. Browsing in the old libraries one day, he found an ancient book by the heretical scribe Brontlo. This book predated the DragonLaw by a hundred cycles. Not surprisingly, it was not included when the Law was collated."

Despite himself, Davix was listening intently.

"Brontlo's short book was written in a time of famine and imbalance, when the People's very survival was in doubt. Brontlo blamed the dragons, claiming their narcissism and decadence had brought these calamities upon the Realm. He dared suggest a purge. All but the Queen should be killed and a new Five raised who would fulfill the promises made to the People when they were brought from the Realm of Earth. Grav'nan was an angry boy, Davix, idealistic and given to extremes. For a time, far from any ears but mine, he would wonder if such action as Brontlo suggested might someday be called for again."

Davix was shaking. "He would never...Grav'nan-dahé loves the great dragons!"

Tix-etnep-thon-dahé flipped quickly through the pages of notes, pulling one out and laying it before Davix.

"In addition to her alternate data, Rinby provided a one-page summary of her theories. It was written, I believe, on the day she died. In it, she suggests some deliberate earth work was happening in the Chend'th'nif, likely near the Red Hammer, though she didn't have the background to guess what it might be."

"But you have a guess," Davix said. It sounded like an accusation. Tix-etnep-thon-dahé sounded weary. "Brontlo's book included a proposal for a dragon trap." He let these unthinkable words hang foully in the air before continuing. "It would require the release of tremendous energy, but in a controlled manner. A hidden pool of destructive power."

"Would such a structure be enough to account for the heat spikes and the sheep fog?"

"Perhaps. Yes, if it were large enough. Davix, believe me, I do not wish to trouble your heart like this. But remember, Grav'nan-dahé was the one who ordered you to stop asking questions about Rinby's death."

"No, you're wrong! Kror and Throd investigated and—"

"Or so claims the Prime Magistrate. He also told me the bidahénas had rejected my request for a routine data-gathering expedition into the Chend'th'nif. I believe now Grav'nan-dahé did not want us to find his dragon trap."

Davix had no idea what to do. He could run to Grav'nan-dahé and report Tix-etnep-thon-dahé's heresy; the Atmospherics Master must have realized that. Or he could accept this new version of reality and harden his heart against the Prime Magistrate, the man who had filled that same heart with light in its darkest hour. He could even choose to ally himself with Grav'nan-dahé and join him in toppling the dragons. What did he love more: the man or the principles he had learned from him?

The fog had grown thick in the late afternoon sky, and the room was full of shadow. Davix rose and walked to the window. He scanned the redward sky in hopeless hope. He wanted to see the magnificent form of Sur breaking through the fog, and riding on her back, the boy from the Realm of Earth. Impetuous, fearless, with his roving eyes and expressive hands that were always in motion, his body lithe as a fox. X'risp'hin had only been gone two days, but already Davix ached for his presence.

"If that's what you believe, then report it to the bidahénas. Or directly to Great Renrit."

"That course carries perils of its own."

"What? Are you afraid?" He couldn't hide his contempt.

"Yes, and so should you be. If treason is afoot, the treacherous will defend themselves."

That gave Davix pause. He had no experience facing such momentous decisions. "What if I don't want to believe you?"

"I can tell you many things, Davix," the old man said. "But I can't tell you what to believe."

The cozy, familiar room suddenly felt like a prison to Davix. "I have to leave." Then pausing at the door, he asked, "What will you do, Master?"

"I will watch and listen. I will take this gift Rinby has handed us from beyond the grave, and I will honour her sacrifice. And you, D'gada-vixtet-thon, what will you do?"

"I-I will prepare for *Sarensikar*, the time of renewal. I will join my friends and all the People in welcoming the season of sunshine. And we will await the coming of the gracious Dragon Lords."

"And gracious is the world they have built for us," the old man replied. Davix hurried from the room, leaving all his workbooks and maps behind.

CHAPTER 20: *The Poet's Garret, the Biologist's Workshop*

On my third day in Farad'hil, I woke up in my luxurious corner of Sur's rooms, or the Abode of Great Sur, as it was known locally, feeling rested but restless. Day one had been amazing with meeting Renrit and hearing my own words recited from the DragonLaw. So naturally, I had expected more and better on day two. But when I'd woken up, I was told Sur had left Farad'hil early that morning.

"Where did she go?" I asked X'raftik, the Chief Valet.

"No one knows. Of late, she often makes solitary excursions. Usually she returns within a day."

Usually. "Great. What am I supposed to do?" The best she'd been able to come up with was a tour of the vegetable gardens and the kitchens. If it had been a school field trip, it would have been fine, but I had come to expect a lot more of the Realm of Fire. And because they didn't want me wandering Farad'hil alone, I was shut back up in Sur's quarters for the rest of the day, without even internet access.

"Why did Sur bring me to Farad'hil in the first place?" I'd asked X'raftik as a fox walked up to me with a ball in his mouth, hoping for some fetch.

"It is not my place to speak for the great Dragon Lords and their motives."

Now it was morning again, and I was bracing myself for another day of twiddling my thumbs and other bits of anatomy. The light from the stained glass window above the bed bathed me in rainbows. I pushed several foxes aside so I could get up, and they barked sleepily in protest.

Oh, I should say something about the foxes. Sur liked them a lot. A pampered pack, maybe nine in total, had free run of her quarters and their own dedicated octona to groom them, prepare special food, and pick up their poop. You couldn't sit still for a minute without two or three of the demanding little brats cuddling close and whimpering for head scratches. But they were crazy cute, and I didn't even need blankets during the night, as I had my own squadron of warm critters packed in tight around me.

Octonas came and went, bringing me warm stew for breakfast and laying out a fresh set of funky dragon duds. Today's outfit was all about forest colours and featured shoulder pads which made me think of Consul Krasik-dahé back on Earth. As I climbed into the big, sunken bathtub, I realized I didn't know anything about her. How old was she, for instance? She obviously came from the Realm of Fire, but how long since she'd been back for a visit? Why was she the only "dahé" among the mixed beings? Maybe when I got home, my parents could invite her for dinner, and I would tell them all I'd seen on my adventures. I liked the idea of bringing Krasik-dahé news from home.

X'raftik entered with a head and heart bow, just in time to help me with the buttons on the back of my tunic.

"Thanks, X'raftik," I said. "How are you doing?"

"If the Dragon Groom is content, then I am, too." My mom would have called that unhealthy codependence.

"Is Sur back?"

"Great Sur is sequestered in her Sanctum. She may not be disturbed."

I gritted my teeth in exasperation. "Why did they even bring me to Farad'hil if I can't—"

Sur's voice filled the chamber. "*THE DRAGON GROOM IS TO ASCEND AND JOIN ME.*"

It was like she was standing beside us even though she was clearly not in the room. X'raftik, unsurprisingly unsurprised, led me to another big corner of Sur's abode where there was a large hole in the high ceiling, obviously for Sur to fly up to this sanctum.

"Um, how do I…?" I said, and the octona pulled aside a glittery blue curtain to reveal a ladder bolted to the wall.

I climbed up and looked around curiously. Every bit of Sur's Sanctum was teeming with words in the dragon tongue script. Some of them were on scraps of paper pinned to canvas bulletin boards and some were graffiti scrawled on the copper-plated walls. But in addition to these reassuringly stationary texts, thousands of words were in flight, like the ones that had been circling in Renrit's Editorium. But these loose words weren't polished prose waiting for their place in the DragonLaw. They were loners. Some shot around the chamber as if desperate to escape, and others were so much dandelion fluff, floating lazily through the air before coming to rest on a random surface, like they'd lost the will to describe.

There was a pervasive background hum of the words whispering and muttering to themselves. Closing my eyes and concentrating, I could just make out: "corroborate," "incredulous," "stem and bowl." One of the loudest was a "the" that just kept saying its name over and over like an annoying three-year-old.

Sur sat on the floor in the middle of this chaos, grabbing at phrases, licking their backs, and slamming them down on a huge sheet of paper. When nothing useful was at hand, she would beat her heavy wings and fly into the air to nab a juicy adjective circling a torchstone fixture. I kept out of the way, sitting in the corner and occasionally swatting at a stray word that flitted around my eyebrows.

Spotting me, Sur rose up on her hind legs, holding the big sheet of stiff paper to the light.

"DRAGON GROOM! I WILL READ YOU MY NEW POEM." She took a deep breath. *"IN NIGHT'S OBSCURE PASSAGES / YOU BEAT AGAINST THE CREEPING SPECTRE / PROPHECIES LIKE THORNS IN FLESH / FESTERING WHERE YOU CANNOT REACH."*

After a long pause, I realized she was waiting for me to say something. "That's great. Uh, five stars."

"ONE FOR EACH DRAGON," she said, pleased, I hoped.

I'd never had much luck with poetry—you remember what happened with my last attempt—so I decided to change the subject. "Hey, what are we doing today?"

"FOLLOW," Sur told me, spreading her wings and flying down through the hole in the floor. I scrambled down the ladder, but by the time I reached the floor, she was nowhere to be seen. While searching for Sur, I stumbled across a huge horse who seemed just as unnerved to see me. It reared up on its hind legs, spread a huge pair of dragony leather wings, and emitted a very unhorse-like roar.

Back away slowly, I thought, backing away fast.

I finally found Sur. She was staring out a huge picture window that looked out onto the central cavern of Farad'hil, petting the fattest fox I'd ever seen. Two octonas were hard at work, tying jewelled balls to the leathery strips of her mane. I came to stand beside her head.

Sur spoke without looking my way: *"TODAY, WE VISIT THE DOMAIN OF INBY AND VIXTET / WHERE WONDERS ARE BORN."*

"Awesome," I said. "Listen, can I ask you something? About your poem?" She didn't answer, so I blundered on, hoping I wasn't being inappropriate. "You mentioned the, um prophecy. Flesh tearing and stuff. Do you mean the prophecy about a dragon dying? That's why I'm here in the Realm of Fire, right?"

"*WE ARE MARKED BY FATE/A RED JEWEL IN OUR BREAST/PAIN/THE FALL OF A MIGHTY TREE.*"

"Grav'nan-dahé doesn't believe in the prophecy. He says if it isn't in the DragonLaw, then it's bullsh...Uh, nonsense."

"*LITTLE GRAV'NAN LOVES US SO/HE WANTS US IMMOR-TAL/LIKE THE ROCK BENEATH HIS FEET.*"

The octonas, finished with their hairdressing duties, bowed to us and left.

"But you're not immortal, right? Do you think the prophecy is true?" I suddenly felt sad for her. "Are you scared it's you?"

"*I ONLY FEAR THAT I WILL NOT FINISH/A POEM I LA-BOURED UPON WITH LOVE./I DO NOT WANT TO DIE/BEFORE I FIND A RHYME FOR 'K'RIZAT-ZHIS'.*"

"Yeah, that would suck," I said. "Wait. How about *'D'zastat Zhis'*?"

"*AN IDENTITY IS NOT A PROPER RHYME, DRAGON GROOM.*"

It turned out the flying horse was meant for me, but I declined the offer as politely as I could. No way was I getting up on that thing. I climbed onto Sur's back, which at least I was used to. We flew past Renrit's Editorium on our way to our destination, and I asked Sur, "You guys fly over Cliffside during *Sarensikar*, right?"

"*WE ARE THE PEOPLE'S BLESSING AND INSPIRATION.*"

"So, Renrit...He's kind of on the big side...and he wears all those heavy jewels. Can he even get airborne?"

"*WE THROW HIM FROM HIS WINDOW/AND HOPE THAT HE'LL FIND LIFT/BEFORE THE GROUND COMES UP TO MEET HIM/THERE'S A PRICE TO EVERY GIFT.*"

I wished I could read her inflections better, because that sounded like straight-up shade. She beat her wings heavily, and we climbed to the highest part of the central cavern. Sur came in for a landing on a wide ledge in front of a huge oval mirror. I slid off her back and approached my reflection. Something was different, and it wasn't just that I was decked out in Farad'hil's fall line. I looked good. I mean, I wasn't *hot* or anything, but...Here's the thing, usually I avoid mirrors—

one quick look on my way out the door. And even if I'm dressed right and it's a good hair day, some little voice in my head always tells me, "You're an ugly loser."

Was it possible the voice hadn't made it across the strands?

Sur reached over my shoulder with one big clawed fingertip and touched the middle of the mirror. The whole surface swirled like a cappuccino in progress, and then the glass was gone. Just gone.

"FOLLOW ME/TO WHERE THE MIXED ARE MADE MANIFEST."

Beyond this doorway was shiny darkness. Everything was metallic black, dimensions barely discernible by complex patterns of light in the walls that winked on and off in inscrutable sequence. It could have been a machine display or it could have been art. In either case, there was a sense of power, like mighty forces were at work behind the walls.

As we walked, the space opened up into a chamber several stories high. Spotlights illuminated work areas on different levels accessed by wide, curving ramps. In the dimness, mixed beings stood before panels of black glass, and as they passed their hands across them, the lights jumped and danced in response. Up to this point, I had seen nothing in the Realm of Fire that looked so sci-fi, and I felt an odd annoyance, like the world couldn't decide on its genre.

I followed Sur up a ramp to a balcony that overlooked an even larger cavern, its far end invisible in the black distance. A sci-fi console to my left lit up, and I was shocked to find another dragon had been standing beside me in the shadows. It was as long and tall as Sur but probably only weighed a third of what she did. This skinny dragon was all lanky limbs, sliding against each other with a sound like sandpaper on glass. The bones of its torso opened and closed like umbrella ribs as it breathed, and its skinny hands, though still five times as big as mine, worked the controls of the console with delicate precision. It reminded me more of a stick insect than a dragon.

Sur didn't seem like she was about to introduce us, so I said, "Hi, I'm the Dragon Groom. What's your name, Dragon Sir? Ma'am?"

The dragon turned a pair of eyes on me that shone with so much intelligence, I felt smarter just looking at them.

"¿¿DO YOU KNOW WHY WE KEEP THE BLOOD OF THE GROOM ON THE REALM OF EARTH??"

"Uh, no."

"¿¿WHAT WOULD HAVE HAPPENED DURING THE GREAT REALM WARS HAD ALL OUR GENETIC MATERIAL BEEN HERE??"

It was like being called on in class on the exact day when you forgot to read the homework. "Uh, nothing good, I guess? I guess invading dragons from some other realm might have wiped you all out." The skinny dragon blinked for the first time, and I hoped that meant I was right.

"So, which dragon are you?" I repeated. "I mean, you're probably not Queen Etnep. So..." I counted dragon names off on my fingers, like Snow White's dwarfs. "You're either Vixtet or Inby, right?"

"*¿¿IF I TOLD YOU THAT VIXTET MANAGES THE BALANCE OF THE LIVINGWORLD, AND INBY OVERSEES THE BLOOD- LINES, WHICH DRAGON WOULD YOU INFER I WAS, EARTH BOY??*"

"Well, since this place seems more Frankenstein lab than test garden, I'm going to guess you're Inby. Sir." Eye blink.

Inby dropped a claw on the console, and the cavern in front of us lit up. The wavering green light came up through the waters of a narrow stream that cut through the featureless black floor. The stream snaked toward us in a gentle zigzag from the dim distance, reminding me of the lazy river ride at the water park. I half expected to see little dragons floating our way in big inner tubes. In fact, this guess wasn't completely wrong.

"Why do those look like bodies?" I whispered, and the answer was because they were. Three figures, floating on their backs, were coming our way down the stream, feet first, single file. They were naked. No inner tubes. Unmoving as they were, somehow I knew they weren't dead. They were bursting with life like ripe fruit, ready to jump up and break into a dance routine.

"What's going on?" I asked, astonished.

"*¿¿IF INBY DESIGNS THE MIXED BEINGS AND FORMS THEM FROM THE MATERIALS OF THE REALM, ARE THEY TRULY ALIVE??*"

"You mean, you make the mixed beings?" I asked, a bit slow on the uptake.

"*¿¿HOW DID YOU THINK THEY CAME INTO BEING, EARTH BOY??*"

I was too amazed to answer. The river was a literal birth canal, and I was watching mixed beings being born. Having never seen a naked mixed being, I had to check out their junk. It was kind of half-formed down there, even the mostly human-looking octonas.

A creepy question occurred to me. "Inby, could you grow humans that way, too, if you wanted?"

"¿¿OF COURSE, BUT HOW WOULD THE LIVINGWORLD EVOLVE IF THERE WAS NO UNPREDICTABLE ELEMENT??"

Sur, who had been silently watching the parade of newbies rising from the birth canal, said, *"THE MIXED BEINGS ARE BORN TO LOVE THE DRAGONS, KHARIS'PAR'IH'IN/DEVOTION AND LOYALTY WOVEN INTO THEIR VERY FLESH."*

I was working hard to keep up. "But humans need to learn to love you?"

"WE CHERISH THE IMPULSE OF THE PEOPLE/THE BEAUTIFUL ILLOGIC/THE LEAP OF FAITH/A SUBLIME CRY OF WONDER/THE NIPPLE HARDENS."

I couldn't decide which was more irritating, Inby's question-answers or Sur's poetry-answers. There was a narrow spiral staircase leading down to the dock, and I went down it without asking permission.

The air smelled of lavender. Or was it the newborns that smelled that way? The older mixed beings were helping them from the water, and I got splashed in the face by some of the warm liquid, which I decided *not* to think of as amniotic. There were two new octonas and one quadrana, and they were already teenagers at birth. That saved time, I guess, but they had no parents, no childhood with teddy bears and tantrums, no secrets shared with best friends. I felt kind of bad for them.

The adults dressed the newborns in pale silver robes and fed them their first meal, a thick green soup in an earthenware bowl which they slurped up hungrily. They didn't look confused or dazed like you might imagine. They weren't drooling, wide-eyed infants, pointing and going "Wazzat?" No, they looked happy and ready to play their part.

The quadrana in charge told them, "You are in Farad'hil, home of the great dragons."

The newborns beamed. "Oh! I *love* the great dragons!" one said.

The quadrana looked at me and then said to the newborn, "What would you do if I told you to harm this human?"

"Hey!" I shouted, stepping back and almost falling into the water.

But the newborn looked more horrified than me. "I could never do that!"

"That is correct," the quadrana answered. "Boy from Earth, the mixed beings will never let the humans come to harm. Remind them in Cliffside."

I nodded, but I couldn't take my eyes off this fresh-from-the-farm creature, born loyal, loving, and ready to serve. I didn't like it at all.

❖

Just before Sur and me exited through the mirror gate, I noticed another corridor leading back into the mountain, pulsing orange lights glowing from deep within.

"Hey, Sur, what's there?"

"*THE DOMAIN OF VIXTET/WHO KEEPS THE BALANCE/ WHO MOVES THE PIECES ON THE BOARD/SO THE LIVING-WORLD MIGHT THRIVE.*"

"When are we going there? Maybe after lunch?" I realized I was hungry again. Were there any good restaurants in Farad'hil? If I was designing this place, I would have built one behind the waterfall. I'd call it "Sprinkles." Or "Make a Splash!"

But Sur's answer caught me by surprise. "*GREAT VIXTET IS ILL/SHE BATTLES INFECTION/FIGHTS FOR THE INTEGRITY OF HER BEING/FIGHTS TO KEEP THE DRAGONS FIVE IN NUMBER.*"

"She'll be okay, though? The prophecy isn't about her, right?" I thought about Davix. He was a member of Vixtet House. Did he know his dragon was sick?

"*SHE WILL LIVE OR SHE WILL DIE/THIS TOO IS BALANCE/ ALL ELSE IS A LIE.*"

"Sur, Inby didn't ever call me Dragon Groom. Doesn't he believe in the prophecy?"

"*SUR ALONE CONSULTS THE SEERS/SUR ALONE HAS BORNE THE FEARS/WHO BELIEVES? IS THERE ANOTHER?/ ONLY SUR AND HER GLORIOUS MOTHER.*"

So even the dragons didn't all believe in the prophecy. That sounded good to me. Maybe I'd get to go home without doing the deed, like when Dad was dismissed from jury duty. For once, I wanted that jerk Grav'nan-dahé to be right. But as I climbed onto Sur's back, I swear I could feel her tension. Sur believed. And so did Queen Etnep.

CHAPTER 21: *Two Days before* Sarensikar

After leaving Tix-etnep-thon-dahé's office, Davix had climbed the path back to Cliffside and wandered its streets alone. When people came his way, he hurried around corners or ducked into dark alcoves. He was sure they would see in his face all his renegade thoughts, his impurity, his impiety. He spent the night in a quiet room of the Comfort House, turning away young men who wanted to bond with him, sometimes with a gentle demur, sometimes with unearned harshness.

He did not return to his duties in the Atmospherics Tower the next morning. He was so inexperienced with defiance that he couldn't gauge the seriousness of his absence. He just knew he couldn't be in the tower with Tix-etnep-thon-dahé. Nor could he be with Grav'nan-dahé, who was undoubtedly blessing sites and preparing rites for *Sarensikar.* Davix walked down to the anti-spinward gates of the city and sat with the guard there, watching the dance of fog on the unplanted fields. The guard shared a rumour about the Curator of Sites Historic and his disappearance, a possible unsanctioned love mating, the couple escaping in the night. But none knew of a missing woman to complete the tale.

When the guard changed, Davix rose and walked the city perimeter until solitude finally broke his spirit, and he went in search of friends. He thought he knew where he'd find Grentz and perhaps Grentz's closest ally, the mischievous Ragnor, apprentice in Health and Healing. As expected, they were high up in the city, sitting on the ground in what had once been a tool hut, a narrow, stone room whose roof was half gone. This space, forgotten by everyone, was a perfect clubhouse for their little gang, providing it wasn't raining.

When he entered, the boys whooped in surprise. Their surprise was matched by Davix's own. He had expected Grentz and Ragnor, but he was shocked to see Stakrat, sitting peacefully beside the boys on the old straw mattress, and Kriz'mig, painting a mural of the four realms on the wall.

"You are unchaperoned!" he stammered.

They all laughed, and Stakrat said, "Davix, you're so stiff-backed, I'm scared you'll snap in two. Sit down and have a drink." Stakrat looked utterly relaxed. Her feet, almost always clad in soldier's boots, were bare. She reached a flask up to him, and he drank a long swallow of the musty water, warily lowering himself to sit against a wall.

"*Sarensikar* approaches, Davix!" Grentz said. "The rules bend, the watchers' eyes grow cloudy." As if demonstrating, Grentz turned his own eyes to the sky and became silent, drifting into a reverie, as if his friends weren't there.

Stakrat put an arm around Davix. "Stop looking over your shoulder. Kriz'mig and I are theoretically still on work rotations. Everyone's running around so much, no one noticed we slipped away." She smiled and stretched her legs out, wiggling her bare toes.

Kriz'mig's voice was even dreamier than usual as she dabbed at her mural with a brush of bone and fur. "See? The three wandering realms await their glorious homecoming." Davix handed her the flask, and she drank deeply, smiling up at him. "I'm so glad you're here. I thought we wouldn't get you out of the Atmospherics Tower until the fog lifted."

Davix pushed past his guilt and answered her with a proverb. "*Sarensikar* knocks on the door. The People answer with garlands and sweets." It sounded like he was imitating a Temple elder, and they all laughed except Grentz, who was still staring at the sky. Davix felt like he had passed a test.

The truth was, he was tired of feeling guilty. The last days had proved years of devotion and obedience did not protect you from grief. In fact, they set you up for it. So, why shouldn't he have a life, the same as his friends?

A sudden flashing light startled him, and he threw a hand out, as if to ward off a blow. Looking up, he saw little falling stars of blue and gold. The sound of the sky was a low chuckle. Or was that his friends laughing still?

"What…? What is this drink?"

Grentz, snapping out of his distracted state, grabbed Davix and pulled him to the ground in an affectionate wrestle. "Hast'nan mushrooms," he said.

Davix licked his lips and found they were growing numb. "You… you stole the sacred mushroom from the Temple?"

Stakrat snorted. "Stole! From the Temple! You're so, so terribly, terribly serious, D'gada-vixtet-thon. Ragnor was on cleaning rotation there last week, sweeping up the crumbs. He suspended them in water, and now we share the revelation!"

Ragnor's mushroom smile was wide and easy. "To waste such a gift would dishonour the dragons."

Davix felt a familiar voice of reproach somewhere in his breast. *Disobedience. Impiety.* But the voice came at him from an unaccustomed distance and was drowned out by his own ecstatic laughter. He rolled out of Grentz's arms and lay on the stone floor, holding his friend's hand, staring up at the sky.

"*S'zista farad dr'kaden,*" he said in a dreamy voice, watching the shapes of giant frogs dance in the sheep fog overhead. "You honour the way of our beneficent lords." He laughed again, his spirit free in the cool, moist air. Free like Stakrat's toes.

Then the sky started wailing, a heartbreaking, insistent lament, a cry that rose and fell and rose again. Davix raised his hands in the air, expecting tears to fall as rain. Stakrat was on her feet in a moment, and her quick movements left trails in his vision. He had to concentrate to take in her words.

"Alarm! Urgent call!" She was pulling on her boots, her leather harness, and knife belt.

"Where?" Grentz asked, letting go of Davix's hand as he stood, too. The sudden withdrawal of its warmth felt like a rebuke.

Stakrat was at the door. "Renrit House."

"There's movement on the Citadel walls," Ragnor said, pointing up. They were gone before Davix could even sit up. It had not been the sky lamenting. It was the horn of alarm, blown rarely and never to be ignored. Kriz'mig squatted before him, glowing in her dress of orange and green, her smile gentle and sympathetic.

"Come, Davix, your head will clear as we run."

Despite the others' head start, he and Kriz'mig had no trouble finding them. A crowd had already gathered, held back from the scene by officers of Defence of Realm. Davix saw Stakrat beside Korda, who was shouting orders, coordinating the traffic of physicians and investigators. They were at the back of Renrit House, at the base of the Citadel's wall. Only the legs of the body were visible from where he stood, but by their unnatural tangle and utter stillness, Davix knew they belonged to a dead man. People were pointing upward, speculating on the trajectory of his fall.

Davix was still unsteady on his feet. Light played tricks with his eyes, and time moved in sickening jerks. Convenor Zishun stood by Korda over the body, his sibilant voice clearly audible above the murmur of the crowd.

"I fear I must assume some responsibility. Quadranas such as I do not fully understand the hearts of humans. When the Curator of Sites Historic told me of his sadness, of how he sometimes could not rise from bed in the morning, I was not wise enough to send for a physician. I did not realize he would take such desperate measures. Poor man."

They all shook their heads slowly—in unison it seemed to Davix's altered senses. He almost laughed. But the sky had ceased its wailing, so Davix cried in its place.

CHAPTER 22: *Train Entering a Tunnel*

There was no restaurant behind the falls, not even a snack bar. Sur was away again, but this time she must have left instructions, because a quadrana named Bars'torm had been recruited to hang out with me. First stop, a bench behind the falls, where the light was blue and peaceful and the crash of water irritating. The quadrana wasn't a lot of fun, but he was good for answering questions.

"Why do only some of the quadranas have wings?" I asked, shouting above the noise. Bars'torm didn't have wings, by the way.

"It is an adaptation expressed in only a few. It is not planned but revealed."

"And you were born there in Inby's lab? Already mostly grown up?"

"There is no need for a human developmental period when the parameters of our lives are predetermined."

"I guess, yeah. And you love the dragons, right? Like, automatically."

"I want nothing more than for the dragons to rule our realm effectively."

I was about to say *Doesn't that make you mind controlled slaves?* but that would have been pretty presumptuous, even for me. And also, Tiqokh and Krasik-dahé seemed to have minds of their own.

I'd had enough of shouting. "Can we get out of here?" We began walking down the road, and I said, "I know Vixtet is too sick for visitors, but maybe I could meet Queen Etnep. What do you think?" Sur had already said no to this request, but it never hurt to ask, right? For the first time, the quadrana didn't answer, so I dropped the subject.

Over the next few hours, I saw a garden of flowers that could sing harmony and a training academy for racing birds. Our lunch was mushrooms and mosses, picked straight off a rock face. Weird but tasty. We left the spiral roadway and walked down a long set of steps hacked out of the stone wall, until we came to a sculpture garden. Bars'torm left me to wander around and check out the art. One sculpture in particular stopped me in my tracks.

It was like a stop sign, except there was a huge, writhing wad of raw meat on top instead of a red hexagon. I couldn't figure out if it was really alive or if it was just a lubed-up, glistening machine. As I watched, a slit appeared in the surface and opened like a mouth, smiling red, then gaping, then peeling back until the opening vanished behind the wad to reveal a new, unmarked surface. After a short pause, the new surface opened, and the whole process began again. The sight was revolting, but it was also hypnotizing.

The sculpture, as my art teacher would have said, affected me at a visceral level. Translation: It scared the shit out of me. It made me wonder things I didn't want to wonder. Like, what if life has no set form? What if every version is temporary, a lie you're telling to hide the truth underneath? But then that truth turns out to be another lie.

They tell you that graduating from high school with a good GPA is all you need to focus on, but as soon as you graduate, you find out that your future is anything but secure. They tell you love is all you need, but maybe love is just a pretty skin on horniness. The more I thought about it, the farther back the process began. You play husband and wife in kindergarten with Amy Dorkman, and everyone calls you the handsome little husband. They hand you a baby doll, and you set up house. But you don't care about Amy Dorkman. You really want to lie beside Eric Petrovic at nap time. Jump forward six years, and Jesus-loving Timothy makes your heart bleed. A year later, Dražen rips the Band-Aid off with his kiss. Then everyone knows. It's awful, but it's over. Only, it isn't. They don't know about Altman. Then they do. But your parents don't know...*but then they do!* You come out and come out and come out, and it's never done.

I was pretty exhausted by the time we reached the bottom of the central core. On the shores of the lake, Bars'torm showed me a memorial garden for long-dead dragons. They weren't really graves, he said. Dragons kind of disintegrated when they died—auto-cremation. But some of their ashes and various mementos were buried there. Altogether, there were maybe twenty-five markers, representing around a thousand years. I did the math and understood the significance. Dragons didn't die that often, and it was a big deal when one did.

I asked Bars'torm, "Do you believe in the prophecy?"

His answer was enigmatic, like a dragon's. "Eras come to an end. Death burns down life, and new possibilities grow in the ashes."

I was about to press him for a bit more detail when I heard something. At first it sounded like my mom calling me for dinner, but just at the edge of hearing. I turned and walked back through the gardens that circled the memorials. I heard the sound again, but this time I could have sworn it was Altman, shouting to one of his wingmen as they surged down the ice, or maybe calling out in orgasm. A great redwood stood in front of me, and in the deep shadow of its boughs, I felt a chill. The path curved around its girth, and on the far side, I found the entrance to another cave. It was narrow, jagged as a lightning bolt, and the voice was coming from inside.

It called my name—all my names: Crispin, Puppy, Cris, Crisper, Dork, Goober, X'risp'hin, Kharis'par'ih'in, Copper Guest...*DRAGON GROOM*. I twisted my body, shaping it into the key that fit the lock, and entered the cave mouth. Another voice was calling, a voice deep inside me. It was the copper blood, and this time it wasn't calming me down. This time I was scared. But I couldn't stop. I was called, I was compelled.

Dark, cold. I lurched across an anteroom and through another singing mouth, holding myself to stop my shivering. But no matter how hard I held, precious pieces of me flew away, lost forever. And even as I fell apart, other pieces rose from some secret source deep inside to take their place. A mouth that opened and opened endlessly, telling truths within truths: one of twenty, the one chosen. Changing, growing, growing hunger, growing unbearable. And still the voice called, so loud you could call it a scream.

"WHY ARE YOU HERE?"

Eyes! Yellow eyes in the dark, far down the corridor in the dark. Etnep, Queen of the dragons. Etnep, my mate. And I couldn't help it. I wanted to be there in the dark with her, even though it could mean my death.

Sur, Tiqokh, Davix, Altman, Mom, *help me...*

CHAPTER 23: *The Darkest Night*

The dancing lights in his vision and the feeling of buoyant peace were all but gone. The holy effect of the mushrooms was leaving his body, and Davix felt only great heaviness. It was the middle of the night by then. He could have lain down in the grass, on the rocks, or in a cold corridor and been asleep in moments. But something had driven him to the Atmospherics Tower. Back in Cliffside, seventh bell rang and all was silence in its wake. Davix pushed open the tower's heavy door and entered.

Climbing the steps to Tix-etnep-thon-dahé's study, Davix opened the door with greatest delicacy in case his master was still inside, working through the night. But the study, this home from which he had exiled himself three days earlier, was empty. His heart pounded. If he was going to do this, he had to be quick. Above all, he had to silence his doubts and be true to the instinct that drove him to this blasphemous act.

In the lowest desk drawer, Davix found Rinby's notes and Tix-etnep-thon-dahé's elegant summary of their findings. Then he opened the grace book. The green jewel in the corner flashed, as if the book was waking up, surprised to be called upon so late. Davix had watched his master make hundreds of entries, but he had never done so himself. He was but a youth and an apprentice, and this act of holy transmission was far above his station.

Not that it was difficult. It merely required a firm hand and clear resolve. Copying carefully from the notes, he watched the light blink as the words of his hand travelled across the realm to the holy mountain, faster than any kingsolver could have carried them. By this act, he connected himself to a power so pure, he feared it would set his heart on fire. His master would find him here in the morning, a black husk.

But there was no fire. There was just the scratch of the pen, the blink of the light, and Rinby's words set free to do what they would.

CHAPTER 24: *Homemade Biscuits of the Seers*

I was awakened by an annoyed fox nipping sharply at my fingertip. I swatted at it, and the beast ran off with an indignant swish of its tail, a streak of orange-red in the morning light. I realized I had been hugging it for dear life in my troubled sleep.

Sur's voice rang in my ear. *"LIKE LIFE ITSELF/THE FOXES LOVE TO BE LOVED/UNTIL THEY DON'T/AND YOU TUMBLE INTO THE BLACK EMBRACE/OF INCONSOLABLE ETERNITY."*

Through a half-cracked eyelid, I saw the dragon looming above me. Either her poetry was hurting my head or my head was doing it all by itself. I tried to sit up, but the room spun, and I let myself collapse back on the pillows. Immediately, an octona rushed forward with a mug of water and helped me drink. Her dark hair was cut in a cute bob, and her eyes were kind.

"What happened to me?" I asked, and it sounded suspiciously like crying.

X'raftik answered, somewhere to my left. "Against explicit orders, Bars'torm took you to the lowest levels of Farad'hil, where you penetrated the abode of Queen Etnep."

"And how'd I get back here?"

"Great Sur entered the Matrimonial Tunnels and rescued you in time."

My vision was clearing, and I saw at least fifteen mixed beings around my bed, with Sur towering above the group like a kindergarten teacher in a class photo. I pulled the covers up around me.

"The Matrimonial...the Queen? But what did I...why was everything...?"

I turned away and caught sight of myself in a mirror. It looked like I had gotten drunk-tattooed. An image in black blood covered most of my face, an evil butterfly, or one of those Rorschach blots psychiatrists use to figure out if you're a psychopath. I tried to speak, but I doubled over in agony, like someone had stabbed me in the solar plexus. I rolled into a ball, gasping as my body supplied some terrible remembrance of change, my limbs stretched beyond their limits, skin cracking, movement in my guts like a huge worm forcing its way to the surface. I screamed, and the room retreated into darkness.

I think only a minute passed, but I had definitely been right out. I was drenched in sweat, and the same octona who gave me the water was holding me and putting a cool, damp cloth on my hot forehead.

Sur leaned down, assessing me with her cold, clear eyes.

"TO CHANGE BEFORE THE TIME IS RIGHT/COULD CRACK YOUR FRAGILE MINDBODY/A WASTE OF POTENTIAL/A TRAGEDY FOR QUEEN AND REALM."

"So why did Bars'torm take me there if it was so dangerous?"

X'raftik shrugged, a more human gesture than I had been expecting. "An error was made."

"An error? I almost died!" I was, admittedly, going for melodrama, but no one jumped in to deny it. A chill passed through me. "Where is Bars'torm?" I asked.

"Great Sur has punished him."

The dragon was picking at her teeth with one long claw, and I hoped she wasn't dislodging bits of Bars'torm from her incisors.

"Sur, why did you even bring me to Farad'hil?" I was shaky and scared, my voice a weak croak.

"YOU NEED TO UNDERSTAND/ALL THAT MIGHT BE LOST."

A fresh wave of fatigue hit me, and I muttered, "Want to sleep…"

"LET HIM SLEEP AWAY TRAVAIL/THEN PREPARE HIM FOR TRAVEL."

"Yes, Great Sur," X'raftik replied, and that was the last thing I heard.

When I woke up again, the sun was coming through the window from a different angle. Hours had passed. I rolled over and looked at my face in the mirror. The devil butterfly was mostly faded. Now it looked like I had been shovelling dirt and just needed to wash my face. I sat up and saw my clothes from Cliffside were laid out on a side table. The octona with the bob cut was sitting in a chair beside me.

"Your garments have been washed and mended, Dragon Groom," she said. "I have prepared a meal that will help you regain your strength. Then we must hurry back to the gates of Farad'hil, where you will fly again with Great Sur."

"Can't we go tomorrow?" I asked, my voice cracking a bit with fatigue. "I just want to sleep some more." My limbs were achy, like I'd run a marathon, and my back and shoulders itched. I ran my hand down my side and felt something, like a bit of extra bone on my lowest rib. I tried to calm myself. Maybe it had always been there, but I didn't think so.

"Great Inby has ordered your leave-taking. He fears you will not recover if you stay in Farad'hil." The octona placed a tray of food in front of me. It was just bland soup and dark bread, but I felt stronger after I'd eaten it. A horse and cart were waiting outside Sur's abode. The octona put a long, hooded cloak over my shoulders as I climbed aboard.

"What's your name?" I asked her.

She hesitated and looked away. "Soon it won't matter." I was groggy, or else her answer would have struck me as strange.

Sur was waiting outside the gates of Farad'hil with the basket-saddle on her back. Cold winds blew down the cliff face, and I snuggled down under a heavy blanket inside my little nest. Sur's takeoff was turbulent in the whirling gusts, and I hung on as best I could, fighting back nausea.

The winds grew calmer as we climbed high above the mountains. I sat up and watched the scenery for a while before I got up the nerve to ask Sur the question weighing on my mind.

"So, how am I supposed to, you know, fulfill my Dragon Groom responsibilities if being near the Queen is going to kill me?"

"THE DEATH OF A DRAGON/WILL REALIGN THE REALM/ YOUR BODY WILL RESPOND/WITH INEVITABILITY/WITH GLADNESS."

"Gladness, right…" What about this whole process could any sane person think of as glad? And *realign*? Realignment did not sound like a safe process. What was it I'd been turning into in the Matrimonial Tunnels? Something capable of being baby daddy to the Queen of Dragons, obviously. But what was that form? Winged? Scaly? Heterosexual? I pulled the curtains over the ugly pictures in my brain and swore not to think about it until I was myself again, whatever that meant.

"Are we going back to Cliffside now?" I asked, thinking, *because there's this boy I really need to kiss.*

"FIRST WE VISIT THOSE APART/ALONE BUT FOR EACH OTHER/AND THE VISIONS THEY SHARE."

"A party. Great. I hope I wasn't supposed to bring the chips."

The cold was starting to get to me, so I curled up at the bottom of the basket wrapped in the blanket, with the hood of my cloak pulled low. I could feel a comforting heat rise up from Sur's back and I wondered if there really were fires down in her belly she could breathe out if she felt threatened. Or if someone didn't like her poetry.

I fell asleep like that, dreaming Davix and I were in Farad'hil together. I was super excited to flip the script and be his tour guide for once. But when we visited the different dragons' abodes, the rooms were abandoned, bare to their cold stone walls. In Renrit's Editorium, there were no desks, no books or flying words; there was no glowing machinery in Inby's science caves; Sur's poetry loft was still as a tomb.

I started awake and sat up to see where we were. Sur's wings were extended straight to the side, and she was gliding into a snowy valley, somewhere farther along the Chend'th'nif range. Ahead, a tall cloud of steam and gas rose into the air, climbing high above the treetops before it broke up in the breeze. Sur circled the towering white pillar once and then flew on, bringing us in for a landing in a clearing beside a small wooden cottage. It was straight out of a Christmas card—neatly built of rough logs, with smoke rising from the chimney. I could see the big pillar of steam climbing into the sky over the tops of the trees to our right.

The door of the cottage opened, and a woman with a large basket made of woven branches stepped out into the snow. She was dressed in bulky furs, and her long grey hair stuck out from under a fur hat. She crossed through the deep snow to a neat woodpile and began filling her basket. Old as she was, she looked strong and healthy. Only when she started walking back to the door did she see the dragon in front of her house. I expected her to scream or drop to her knees and start praying.

Instead she wrinkled her nose and turned back to the house. "Arjee! Sur's here."

The door opened again, and an old, bald man with a messy salt-and-pepper beard poked his head out.

"Does she want a biscuit?" He turned to Sur. "Do you want a biscuit? They're fresh."

"*THE DRAGON GROOM IS HERE/TESTED BEYOND WHAT HE DESERVES/BRING HIM FRESH PASTRY/AND YOUR BERRY PRESERVES.*"

The woman put down her basket and crossed to us. "So, Dragon Groom, you've come to the Realm of Fire. I'm Glei'hak. My husband,

Arjee, will bring you a biscuit. He just made them." She squinted her eyes, appraising me. "He looks ill, Sur. We better bring him inside and bundle him up in bed."

"THE TIME IS SHORT/WE COME FOR ILLUMINATION/ THEN WE FLY."

"I'm okay," I assured her. I climbed awkwardly from the basket and slid down Sur's back, making a clumsy landing in the thick snow. I still had my hood up and the blanket wrapped around my shoulders, but when the snow snuck into the back of my shoes, I gasped at the cold. Glei'hak took my face in her furry mitten.

"So young," she sighed. "Humans shouldn't visit Farad'hil, not that anyone's asking my opinion." Sur ignored her and started marching toward the tree line in the direction of the pillar of the steam.

"Oh, llama dung," cursed the old woman. "Arjee! Her Highness needs a prophecy. Get out here!" Sass turned up to ten! Clearly, these folks didn't think they had to treat the dragons as A-list celebrities, much less gods.

The old man hurried out of the cottage, stomping his feet into his boots and pulling a fur coat over the baggy grey onesie he was wearing.

He said, "Sur, we gave you everything the emanations showed us. There won't be any more yet." But the dragon didn't turn or slow her pace. I figured I wasn't going to get my biscuits any time soon.

The three of us hurried after Sur into the woods, though we stayed far enough back that the big branches she was bending out of her way didn't knock us over like bowling pins when they snapped back. We came out of the woods in front of the pillar of steam. It was rising from a pool maybe four metres in diameter, in the middle of another, smaller clearing. Its steaming surface bubbled, giving off a strong smell of sulphur that stung my nostrils and made my eyes water. The snow at the edge of the pool was melted, revealing wet, black earth.

Sur started waving her head back and forth, her chin high, like she was getting off on the fumes. When she lowered her head toward the old couple, her eyes had turned a dark red, flecked with spots of gold.

"ASK, ASK THE EMANATIONS/STUDY THEIR VIBRATIONS/IS A DRAGON STILL DOOMED?/WHICH OF THE FIVE?/DOES IT HAPPEN ALL TOO SOON?/WHAT ROBS THEM OF THEIR LIFE?"

"You know it doesn't work that way, Sur," Glei'hak grumbled.

Husband and wife both closed their eyes and started preparing for whatever it was they were about to do. Glei'hak rocked back and forth from toe to heel, arms wrapped around herself, slapping her shoulders from time to time. Arjee, meanwhile, was lowering and raising his arms and mumbling little mantras as he hopped from foot to foot like a sparring boxer.

He said, "This may be pointless, Sur. I hate to disappoint—"

"*SPEAK TO THE LAVA./THE ROCK OF THE REALM KNOWS THE STORY/FROM THE DAY OF SEPARATION/TO GLORIOUS REUNION.*"

"Yes, we know," said Glei'hak, taking her husband's mittened hand and walking toward the stinking, steaming pool. They stood on the muddy black earth, right at the pool's edge, breathing in the vapour. I wasn't surprised when they started coughing and retching. But they didn't give up. They spread their legs wide, raised their arms, and tipped their heads back in unison. They were breathing deeply now, chests rising and falling, and the steam that poured from their mouths joined the towering column over their heads. Someone on Earth could market the whole ritual as a trendy wellness thing, but tranquility wasn't on offer here; whatever was happening, it clearly hurt.

Glei'hak began to cringe as if someone was flicking hot embers on her face. Arjee swayed unsteadily, moaning.

Suddenly, he cried out, "The hot flow, the red river…"

She answered, "History will not be told. History will tell us."

"The history of a dragon…the course stopped, the flow cooled, hard and unforgiving."

"From five to four, the realm staggers."

Almost in unison, they dropped to their knees. Their eyes were open now, and holy shit, they were white and blank. Not surprisingly, they seemed to be blind now, and the man reached for his wife, pawing the air until he found her hand. They leaned on each other for support, tears flowing from their blank eyes.

"Death crosses, hides in the fog, springs with claw and tooth upon the unwary."

"From the sky, in fury and vengeance, a dragon drops."

"Falls, falls…"

"Betrayal of the beloved, the heart cries in shock."

"Betrayal…Darkness…Farad'hil grows quiet."

The woman fell forward, catching herself before she face-planted into the mud.

"Enough, enough," she called. "Help us!" She reached a hand out to anyone. I looked at Sur, but she seemed busy, puzzling over all the mumbo jumbo she had just heard. So I hurried over to the old couple, holding my breath and squinting against the acrid fumes as I took Glei'hak's hand. She was still holding Arjee's hand, and I led them back to the relative freshness of a nearby snow bank, where they sat heavily. Arjee dropped his head into his wife's lap.

All the normal parts had returned to her eyes, though they were red, streaming with tears. She turned and snarled at the dragon. "I hope that was worth your time, Sur. Because I'm not letting him do that again anytime soon."

"*WORDS, WORDS TO CONTEMPLATE./MEANINGS NESTED, EMERGING/DANCING TOGETHER IN THE SEARCH FOR TRUTH.*"

"Dancing," she scoffed. "You should dance this poor boy back to Cliffside. He's pale as a night frog and shivering. That's no way to treat the Dragon Groom."

I was going to say I was fine, but the truth was, I was completely drained. I wanted to sleep again, and I wanted to get far away from the craziness of dragons. After everything I had seen in the last three days, getting back to Cliffside felt like going home.

Arjee coughed and sat up. "Did we give her what she needed?"

"You did fine, husband." Glei'hak heaved herself to her feet and brushed the snow off her butt. "Come, let's get the boy up on Sur's back. I'll be glad to see them gone."

Her words kind of stung. It hadn't been my idea to make them do their prophecy thing. But I also understood what it was like to have your life hijacked at the whim of a bunch of dragons.

"Wait, love," Arjee said, coughing again. "The body. Sur should take it back."

"Do what you like!" the woman snapped at him. "I'm done here." With that, she turned her back on us and trudged into the woods.

"What body?" I asked, helping him to his feet, though I almost fell over myself in the process.

"Sur!" he called. "There's a body. Human. Down at the base of the cliff. Must be a ranger had an accident. Stumbled to his death in the fog, I figure. Or maybe in that storm t'other day."

"*I WILL INVESTIGATE,*" she said, for once without a word of poetry, and took off over the trees.

As the sound of her wings vanished in the wind, Arjee opened his eyes wide.

"I forgot!" he exclaimed and reached into his coat pocket, bringing out a fat biscuit, a little squashed on one side, but still warm. He handed it to me. "Grow strong, lad. The rock of the Realm is saying that troubled times are coming."

The only problem with the biscuit was that there was only one of them. If I ever wrote a travel blog on the Realm of Fire, I'd definitely give the food four stars.

"You will return to Cliffside?" Arjee asked.

"Yeah, have you been there?"

He surprised me by laughing. "Oh, not for dozens of cycles. Do send our warmest regards to Grav'nan-dahé." He laughed again, though it was a bitter kind of laugh. I half remembered something. Arjee and Glei'hak—their names had come up during the fight between Tiqokh and the Prime Magistrate on my first night. Yes. The couple had been banished for prophecy by Grav'nan-dahé himself.

We waited in silence for Sur's return. I finished up the last buttery morsel of biscuit and then searched my blanket for crumbs, like some crazed drug addict. But when Sur reappeared in the sky, carrying a corpse in her talons like she was an oversized hawk with a squirrel, I almost threw up all the goldeny goodness.

Sur laid the body out in the snow and lowered her head to investigate. The old man walked over to join her, but I stayed where I was. I had never seen a dead body before, and I was kind of curious, but even from a distance, I could see the bloody wounds across the neck and face, the furs torn aside to reveal more torn flesh and gore. Not this time, I decided.

"Could be the cougars," Arjee said, fingering the corpse carefully. "Or else a bear."

"*THE ACCIDENTALS ROAM THE LAND/BEYOND KNOWL-EDGE/OUTSIDE THE PLAN.*"

"Mmm. Whatever beast, it was more angry than hungry. All his parts are here. Or maybe he beat it off, then bled to death overnight. Tragedy however it happened. I met him a few times. His familiar name was Twis'wit, but I wish I had his proper name to say now. Send him off right."

He strapped the body to Sur's flank with ropes and belts tucked into a compartment of the saddle basket. I tried to help, but I got light-headed and had to sit down before I fainted. That was pretty embarrassing, since fifteen minutes earlier Arjee had been fainting, too. Now he was apparently fully recovered, and clearly fitter than this sixteen-year-old suburban rat. I climbed into the basket from the opposite side, but my stomach still heaved when I caught a glimpse of Twis'wit's frozen, staring eyes.

I turned to Arjee. "I'll make sure they take good care of him back in Cliffside."

"Thank you." He wrinkled his brow. "Twis'wit was stationed up by the Red Hammer, higher up the range and some days' march to spinward. It's strange he should have been down this way so early in the season. Almost like he was heading back to Cliffside already. Why would he be doing that?"

Obviously I had no answer to this, so I just said, "Thanks for the biscuit," and held his gaze, hoping he got that I was saying more: *Thanks for being kind* and *Sorry Sur made you do all that.* And then the world reeled as the dragon flapped her powerful wings and launched us into the air. She never even said thank you.

CHAPTER 25: *One Day before* Sarensikar

Davix sat cross-legged atop the heavy wall surrounding the Citadel, watching the sky go through its changes. The thick fog glowed orange and red as the sun began its final descent. Soon another wasted day would be over, another day with his own heart as clouded as the realm. Out of habit, he estimated the speed and direction of the wind from the fog's rolling dance. Out of habit, he muttered the sunset prayer.

Below him was the place where the Curator of Sites Historic had met his death, body smashed on hard stone. He hadn't planned on coming to the very spot where the man must have jumped, but it hadn't exactly been an accident either. Instead of looking down, he stared out at his world. If the weather had been clear, he'd have been able to see as far as the greenward edge of the Chend'th'nif Mountains. But while the fog remained—whether by chance or conspiracy—his world was smaller than that. He could glimpse all five of the city's houses; the Retreat of Tarn was already decorated for *Sarensikar*, and looking right, Davix could see the Atmospherics Tower. Tall and shadowed, its unwavering rectitude rebuked him:

I have stood here, loyal and unflinching, through hundreds of cycles. Wind and war have battered me, yet I stand. While you, boy, cannot take the smallest blow to your ego before you run off.

He squeezed his eyes shut against the tears forming there, and another voice spoke in his head: "When your soul is burdened, D'gada-vixtet-thon, recite the Litany of the Generations."

Davix, barely out of childhood, had been crying alone in an empty classroom when he'd first heard those words. He couldn't even recall now why he'd been crying. The man had entered quietly, sitting in a nearby chair to offer the solace of ritual. It was Grav'nan-dahé, a person so exalted, Davix almost regarded him as a myth.

The man said to the weeping boy, "There is great comfort in acknowledging the pious ones who came before us, building the citadel of the law brick by brick. Come, I will say it with you: *Griit, Gram'jn, Novh'it'dafan, Stemmik, Disnof, Tren'fas-xak-dahé…"*

It had been the start of a new path to peace. The Prime Magistrate's piety had been lodestone to his lost soul. But no more.

"Traitor," Davix accused that inner voice. "You betray the trust of the People. You betray the Dragon Lords. You betray me."

If it was true, that is. If Tix-etnep-thon-dahé's wild theory was not just an artifact of some ancient jealousy. The ache in Davix's chest was unbearable. His stinging eyes snapped open and he found himself at the edge of the wall, staring into the fatal drop. How could someone seek such an end? What kind of despair would have to shroud your heart to make you take that final step? To jump. To fall. To let fate have its way.

"Do not be reckless, D'gada-vixtet-thon," Grav'nan-dahé's voice said. "Youth seldom comprehends how slim is the line between life and death." But the voice was not in his head.

Davix spun around and looked down into the courtyard where the Prime Magistrate stood, peering up at him with those hawk-sharp eyes. At a loss for words, Davix simply stared at him. What he had once found noble in the solemn line of posture and dress now seemed sinister.

"Teacher…" he finally managed, his voice tight with discomfort. He stood and walked along the wall until he came to a narrow staircase. Descending, he found Grav'nan-dahé speaking to Convenor Zishun, gesturing out into the courtyard where a half dozen mixed beings were placing barricades around the entrances to the Citadel's underground bunker.

When Zishun went to join the others, Davix approached Grav'nan-dahé and asked, "What are the mixed beings doing?"

"Some repairs to the support structure, apparently." Grav'nan-dahé turned to Davix. "But you and I must speak of serious matters. This is the third day you have absented yourself from your duties in the Atmospherics Tower."

Davix gave an involuntary gasp. Somehow, having run away from his life, he believed the world had forgotten about him, too.

"Who told you of my absences?"

"It is my business to know what goes on in Cliffside. Especially the actions of those I have come to depend on."

Davix straightened from his embarrassed slouch. To stand tall before the Prime Magistrate, accepting the rebuke, was a gesture of obedience. Yet rising to his full height also changed his perspective. For the first time he saw Grav'nan-dahé not as mentor, not as avatar of the living DragonLaw, but as a man. Davix noted with surprise that he had grown taller than his teacher.

The older man was watching him carefully. "You quit your studies with me in order to aid the Atmospherics Master, but now you shirk those duties as well. You wander lost, D'gada-vixtet-thon, and grow unproductive. I know the anticipation of *Sarensikar* can distract a young heart, but I thought you were stronger. Perhaps a cycle of work on the silence farms would serve to focus your soul."

Davix was shaken by the threat, and it was hard to keep his voice steady. "Are you banishing me, Prime Magistrate?"

"I am saying you are drifting like fog and are perhaps in need of some solid ground beneath your feet."

"I wouldn't be the first you banished," he shot back, surprised by the anger rising in him.

Grav'nan-dahé stepped back in surprised. "Acolyte! Do I even know you? Where once stood a pious lad, now a rude brute faces me, eyes clouded by pride. This may be the way you speak with Tix-etnep-thon-dahé, but it is not how you will speak to me."

Davix felt a power and autonomy he had never known. "My Master of Atmospherics tells me you were great friends, many cycles past." He was toying with the Prime Magistrate, like a sly kingsolver buffeting a frog he would eventually kill. He could hardly breathe.

"And I hope we remain friends. Is there something you wish to ask me, Apprentice?"

Davix almost said it: *Are you plotting to kill the holy Dragon Lords?* But how could he? Right here in the courtyard of the Citadel, hours before the holy rites of *Sarensikar* were set to begin?

Instead, he said, "Teacher, I am worried about the Dragon Groom. I hope he is safe."

"He is not to be called by that name. Do not become caught up in the fog of superstition that chokes the city. He is the Copper Guest, and soon he will leave for the Realm of Earth. He never should have come here."

"But he is not just the Copper Guest. Great Sur herself called him Dragon Groom. Do you not dishonour the wisdom of the Dragon Lords by refusing this name?"

Davix had never contradicted Grav'nan-dahé so brazenly, and he watched with equal parts terror and wonder as outrage flashed in the man's eyes.

"Child!" the Prime Magistrate barked, the echo of the word

slapping back a moment later from the far wall of the courtyard. "When you have lived more than a dozen cycles, then you may begin to question me. Question instead the dangerous influences that have played on your mind. This boy from the Realm of Earth—you should avoid his company and the gaudy reverence that follows in his wake. You are too impressionable, D'gada-vixtet-thon, and the paradoxes of faith require, above all, moral strength."

Davix's jaw tightened. "Are you saying I am weak, Prime Magistrate?"

"I am saying I am your elder, and you must trust I will guide you on the path of righteousness."

"I am not a child, Prime Magistrate."

"Are you not? I know you visited the Copper Guest on his first night in the realm, knowingly trespassing in a house not your own."

Davix, caught off guard, felt a flash of fear. This wasn't a game. He was suddenly conscious of the forces he opposed and all he might lose.

"The voice of the flesh is strong," Grav'nan-dahé said. "But it must not be allowed to cloud your judgement. The boy from Earth is a threat to your clarity." He almost sounded sympathetic.

"Teacher…" Davix began. He wanted, *needed* to explain the feelings growing in him for X'risp'hin, how his thoughts these past days had been full of the Earth boy's voice, his smile, the way his skin of pale gold shone in the moonlight. But his voice was choked by tears, and he could not speak.

"From this moment forward," the Prime Magistrate commanded, "I'm afraid I must forbid you his company."

Grav'nan-dahé's words went through him like a knife. Could Davix doubt anyone who would say such a thing might also plan to murder a dragon? He started to shake.

"Davix, my boy, let us not succumb to anger." He put a hand on Davix's neck and drew their foreheads close. The intimacy of the gesture confused Davix, made the tears fall. The old man's voice was quiet and sure. "Come, recite with me the Litany of Generations. It will unburden your soul."

Davix almost laughed. This uncanny echo of inner and outer voices was more than he could take. He pulled himself from the embrace.

"Keep your tired litanies and your pious corpses, old man. I believe in the Dragon Groom, and I will be with him."

Grav'nan-dahé reared back and swung his hand wide, slapping Davix hard on the face. Davix staggered in shock. The sound of the blow echoed through the courtyard before he even registered the sting. He brought a hand to his cheek. The mixed beings had stopped their work to watch. He breathed hard, his face now full of fire. There were so many words he wanted to say—words of apology, words of defiance, of blasphemy—that they tangled on his tongue and left him mute.

So without a word, Davix turned and walked to the citadel wall where he stared through a narrow window. Archers had once stood in this spot, drawing back their mighty bows to repel attacks from the Realms of Air and Water. And through this window he saw, silhouetted against the clouds in the last of the day's light, the great dragon, Sur. Her mighty wings cut through the air, pushing her toward Cliffside. On her back was the saddle, and in it, he knew, was X'risp'hin.

Davix did not even look back at Grav'nan-dahé. He ran. He ran as though fuelled by the Realm's mighty fires, ran down flights of steps and through winding streets, pushing past surprised citizens, determined to be there when the dragon landed.

Chapter 26: *Slow Motion Interrupted*

The lights were coming on in Cliffside as we flew in across the foggy fields. Sur's spiral path ended with a bumpy landing in a dark corner of the Retreat of Tarn. "You're not going up on the stage this time?" I asked, and her only response was a low growl. She'd hardly said a word since retrieving Twis'wit's body. I wondered if she was depressed or angry or some other flavour of emotion particular to dragons. Still growling, Sur walked us into a shadowed alcove between buildings.

I didn't understand why she was hiding, and I didn't feel like asking. All I wanted was to get back to my room and collapse for a week or three. I figured if I made my presence known, someone would come and escort me, but I didn't want to wait. I hoisted myself out the basket and climbed down the dragon's haunches. As soon as my feet hit the cobblestones, I got dizzy. Nonetheless, I was determined to find my own way.

"Hey, Sur," I called over my shoulder as I began my journey, my vision already growing cloudy at the edges. "Thanks for the lift. I don't mean to be rude, but I've got to get some sleep."

I stumbled out of the alcove and made it maybe ten more steps before my legs just gave out, and I found myself sitting on the cold stones. My body's inability to follow simple orders was annoying, like I was walking a labradoodle that refused to heel.

From the shadows of the alcove, Sur broke her silence. *"DO NOT HURRY, DRAGON GROOM / YOUR BODY REALIGNS / LISTEN TO ITS SIGNS / CARE AND COMFORT WILL BE HERE SOON."*

Now, I doubt she meant her words to cue the action so exactly, but at that very moment, I turned and saw Davix running across the square toward me in the last scraps of daylight. Not jogging, mind you, not a careless lazy lope. No, he wanted to get to me as fast as humanly possible. My heart swelled like one of those compressed sponge dinosaurs when you drop them in water. I'll tell you a secret…I might have had a little crush on him.

Okay, shut up.

I suddenly understood that cliché slow-motion reunion run, where the guy and the girl—it's always a guy and girl, right?—race toward each other, taking five minutes of screen time to cross the train platform. It was the kind of bullshit that made me laugh when I watched old movies with Mom, but that was because I didn't understand back then. Now I got it. Everything was slow because I had so much going on in my brain.

In that scant ten seconds, I had time to watch his legs pumping, his cloud of hair rising and falling with his stride, covering and then revealing his big brown eyes, his big brown nose, and those amazing lips. I marvelled that I was the goal of all his passionate action, that he demonstrably wanted me. Sure, an ugly voice in my head was saying things like, *He's going to run right past you and into a porta-potty.* That voice, thankfully, was drowned out by the rising surge of my body, which was being flooded with hormones and emotional lubricants, making me feel beautiful and worthy.

The movie moment was, of course, spoiled by the fact that I wasn't running to him in return. And as much as I would have loved to shoot up like a rocket into his arms, I didn't have the energy. Instead, Davix dropped down into a squat in front of me and, momentum lost, we both got shy.

He was panting, hugging his knees and staring anxiously into my face. "You're back!"

I gave a tired laugh. "I know. I missed you." Ack! Why had I started with that? But maybe truth was the right way to play this unfamiliar game.

"X'risp'hin, you're shivering!"

"Yeah, I've been sort of sick. Dragon Groom troubles." A thick blanket of fog was starting to flow into the square, which made me shiver even more.

"I must get you to Physician-da Raglar." His forehead was wrinkled up in worry. It was pretty cute.

"How about just taking me back to my room?" I said and blushed. Was there anything I could say that didn't drip with sticky innuendo? "I mean, I just need some sleep."

He pulled me to my feet. When I was standing, our hands stayed clasped, and the closing of that particular circuit lit up every string of Christmas lights in my body.

Sur took that moment to lumber out of the shadows with an oversized, bone-rumbling sigh. Davix, who hadn't realized she was even there, dropped instantly to his knees and bowed until his head was on the stones.

"O, Mighty Sur," he moaned. "I didn't realize you were there. Forgive me."

Sur ignored him. She looked twitchy and agitated, and raised her snout in the air, sniffing loudly.

"Is everything okay?" I asked her.

"*THE BALANCE TEETERS/THE REALM GROANS AND CRACKS!*" She rocked from foot to foot.

Davix raised his head cautiously. "Is the great Dragon Lord angry?" he whispered, as if it was his fault.

"She's definitely in a mood." He got up and put his arm around me protectively.

People were now running into the square from every direction. Sur might have flown into Cliffside without any warning, but all it took was a couple of sightings for word to spread like lice in a daycare.

"Great Sur!" called one approaching person.

"We are your humble servants!" said another.

"Mighty Sur brings us blessings at *Sarensikar!*" shouted a third.

And inevitably I was roped into the proceedings. "Dragon Groom, bless my consummation," which was just…*ick.*

"Let's get out of here," I begged Davix. "Before another mob tears my clothes off."

Already dozens of people had arrived, but the gathering horde left a wide, cautious circle around the dragon, and we were safe inside the circle. Well, safe other than the fact that Sur was definitely not her usual chill self. Even I was nervous to be within smiting distance. Abruptly she rose up and, with a sulphurous snort, turned in a half-circle, revealing the corpse tied to her other flank. The smiles, woo-hoos, and hosannas turned to gasps and groans.

I felt Davix's body stiffen. "Another death…"

"Another?"

"While you were gone…The Curator of Sites Historic. Please tell me what happened."

"We were up in the mountains, visiting some friends of Sur's." I didn't have the energy to start explaining about the prophecy. "They let us know about the dead guy—Twis'wit. Do you know him?"

"Not well. He brought some weather instruments up to the mountains for us. Sometimes we sent birds to each other." He did a head and heart bow and said, "Twis'wit—Tarsen-renrit-kee—may your spirit know peace."

Stakrat and another officer from Defence of Realm pushed through the silent crowd and entered our VIP circle. Davix went to greet them at the same time as my legs gave out again, and I sank back down. I could hear Davix repeating my story, gesturing in my direction. I gave Stakrat a little wave, and she nodded back with a serious police face.

The older officer approached Sur, looking like he might mess his drawers. "Great Dragon Lord, what can you tell me about the deceased? Where was he found and what were the circumstances?"

I didn't need my dragon blood to read Sur's contempt. *"HE DARES TO TREAT ME LIKE AN EQUAL / TO A BIDAHÉNA ALONE I SPEAK WILL."* The man threw himself into a super bow, face down on the cobblestones.

"My most abject apologies, Great Sur!" He craned his neck around and shouted to Stakrat. "Get Korda and ask her to call one of the bidahénas and the Interpreter. I'll secure the scene." She ran off, and he got cautiously to his feet. "May I…if Your Eminence allows… untie the body?"

She glared at him, her eyes a hot volcanic red. *"YOU MAY DO YOUR DUTY / NO MORE CAN ANY OF US DO / SUCH ARE THE LIMITS OF FATE / OF DESTINY."*

He looked confused, and I called out, "That means yes."

"Thank you, Copper Guest," he answered, bowing low to me, which was, frankly, just embarrassing.

The officer and Davix freed the corpse, constantly bowing and apologizing to Sur. She wasn't even paying attention. The only help I could offer was asking Sur to stand up so they could get the leather strap out from under her belly.

The square was now packed with spectators, and enough were carrying torchstones that the whole scene was lit in a warm, fog-diffused glow. Compared to the last time they had gathered to greet the dragon, they were unnaturally quiet. The officer and Davix were just laying the corpse gently on the steps of the nearest building when I heard a commanding voice call out.

"Let me pass!"

The crowd parted to allow Korda through on her horse, the Interpreter seated behind her. A moment later a bidahéna flew in. Kror, Throd? I had trouble telling bidahénas apart. Korda was already getting her debrief from the officer as she dismounted. The Interpreter clambered off the horse more awkwardly, buttoning up his official orange jammies as he hit the ground. His hair was a mess, and he had smears on his face from whatever he'd been eating when the call came. Soon, the bidahéna was speaking to Sur, and the Interpreter was relaying the information to Korda. Meanwhile, Korda's deputy was bent over the corpse, doing his CSI thing.

"Multiple deep lacerations," he called out to Davix, who had been pressed into service to take notes. "As from a clawed animal. More likely feline than ursine."

"Like Rinby," he said, his face grim enough to make a team mascot weep.

A growing hum of agitation rose from the crowd. Still dizzy, I got to my feet and lurched to the edge of the circle. I'm not sure what I was intending to say, but I figured the least I could do was offer some words of comfort.

"Dragon Groom! We welcome your return!" said a woman in the front row, and everyone around her agreed loudly. She hadn't called me Copper Guest, I noticed.

Someone else asked, "Has a dark demon thrown the realm out of balance?"

The first woman was horrified by this suggestion. "Is that why the fog remains, Dragon Groom? Are we being punished for our sins?"

I tried to reassure them. "No, it was just some animal up in the mountains. It's dangerous there." But then I thought of the prophecy of the old mountain couple. Something about death in the fog, attacking with tooth and claw. *Betrayal of the beloved.* No wonder Sur was upset. Everything started spinning around me, and I stumbled closer to the crowd and their wide, frightened eyes. Hands reached for me, and I thought maybe I'd just let go and fall into their octopus embrace. I was grabbed firmly from behind and turned around.

"Don't go that way, X'risp'hin," Davix said, walking me back toward the dubious protection of Sur's presence. "Tarn's blood, you're white as a sheet. Is there anything I can do to help?"

With my teeth chattering, I told him, "Th-there's a blanket in the basket."

When I saw him bowing deeply to Sur, I realized I had basically asked him to climb up on God's back. But he did it for me, hero that he was, scrambling up her leg and into the basket. Sur turned her head to watch him suspiciously, and I felt like asking her, "What do you think? Isn't he cute?"

Davix was out of the basket holding the blanket, balancing on her back, looking right up at Sur's glowing eyes when his face twisted up.

"What's wrong with X'risp'hin?" my foolish hero shouted in the great dragon's face. "You were supposed to take care of him. He's important!"

I heard Korda gasp. Everyone stopped what they were doing to watch the scene play out. Sur pulled her head back for a better look at him, her eyes tinged flame red.

"*CAUTION YOUR TONGUE/FRAGILE AND YOUNG...*"

"Davix, it's okay," I said, but I couldn't make my voice loud enough.

"The Dragons are supposed to take care of us," he continued, his voice full of anger and tears. "But we endure death after death. Everything in the Realm is out of balance."

Even though she'd basically said the same thing five minutes earlier, Sur clearly did not like to be talked to that way.

"*WHO IS IT THAT SPEAKS/THAT SQUEAKS THUS?/WHO INVITES A ROASTING/FOR HIS MINDLESS BOASTING?*" She was rhyming in more modern dragon tongue so he could understand his imminent peril.

Clouds of steam, rich with sulphur stink, poured from her mouth and nostrils as she talked, and Davix, who must have been waking up to what he'd just done, started coughing. The dragon straightened her front legs, and he tipped off her back and slid inelegantly down her sleek side, landing heavily on the cobblestones.

I crawled to him and wrapped my arms protectively around his chest.

"Why did you talk to her like that?" I whispered anxiously in his ear. He was shaking. Impressively, he had managed to hold on to the blanket.

"I didn't mean to. The words just came out."

Sur reared up to tower over us. "*STAND ASIDE, DRAGON SIRE/VENGEANCE COMES WITH DRAGON FIRE!*"

I grabbed Davix tighter. "Come on, Sur, don't make a big deal out of this!"

And that's when Tiqokh appeared out of nowhere and stepped between us and the dragon as we huddled together on the ground like rats.

"Great Sur, please forgive the boy. He is concerned for the safety of the Dragon Groom, whose future could be the future of us all."

His voice was calm and clear, and his words hung in the air with their own humid weight. She nudged Tiqokh to the side with her snout, and bent to take a long sniff of Davix.

"*THEN I LEAVE THE FATE OF KHARIS'PAR'IH'IN IN YOUR TINY HANDS/SHOULD HARM COME HIS WAY, WE'LL KNOW WHERE THE CONSEQUENCE LANDS.*"

Davix stood slowly and bowed. "I will not fail, Great Sur. Does he need any special care?" How he'd pulled this confident voice out, I have no idea, but he was shaking as hard as I was.

"*A NIGHT OF PEACE AND WARMING FIRES/IS ALL HIS WOUNDED FLESH REQUIRES.*"

She stood on all fours and shook herself like a wet dog. The antique basket her followers had guarded for a century or more flew through the air, splintering into kindling as it hit a nearby wall.

Sur had, apparently, had enough of humans for the day. With a mighty flap of her wings, she took to the air, flying low over the cowering crowd, and disappeared into the fog and darkness.

"Sorry," I said as I got to my feet, "I don't know why she's acting so…so…" And with that, the world faded, or I faded. There was fading.

I woke up, wrapped in the blanket, being carried through the square in Tiqokh's arms, out of reach of the crowd.

Tiqokh asked Davix, who was walking just behind, "Do I take him to his room?"

"No, we'll go to the Comfort House."

"The Comfort House," I mumbled, smiling in my delirium. "That sounds comfortable…" and faded out again.

CHAPTER 27: *The Absence of Euphemisms*

When I woke, it was just Davix and me in a warm, cozy room. Tapestries covered the walls, lit by the gentle glow of torchstone lamps with orange shades. Most of the floor was a big mattress, and I was propped up like a prince on a pile of pillows, covered by a silky, fringed blanket. Across the room, Davix crouched in front of a burning hearth, stirring a pot that hung over glowing coals at the edge of the fire. The smell of whatever he was cooking made my mouth water.

"Hi," I said, and he looked up and smiled. His eyes reflected the twinkling light of one of the lamps, and the fire made a halo behind his thick hair. "Was I sleeping long?"

"Since sixth bell. Physician-da Raglar just left. I thought he would mix you some medicine, but he said if Sur thinks rest is all you need—"

"And food. Definitely food."

Davix tipped the contents of his cooking pot into a bowl and brought it to me. I drank it down without a spoon, sticking my face right into the smoky, earthy aroma.

"It's good. Is this the Comfort House?"

"Yes."

Through the walls, I heard a long, moaning sound. "What is it? A hospital? It doesn't look like a hospital."

He laughed. "That wasn't a sound of pain, X'risp'hin. Never mind; finish your soup."

"No, tell me!"

"The Comfort House is a place not under the auspices of any of the houses. Here the People can come together to enjoy the pleasures of the flesh."

On cue, the guy in the next room moaned again, the moan immediately joined by a groan, mixing together into a porny little radio play. Davix reached out a hand and straightened my soup bowl, which I was on the verge of spilling down my front.

"And it's all guys with guys?"

"On this side. The women's rooms are in the building's other wing."

I did a full-body blush. "And you brought me here to—"

"Oh! No, no. Sur tasked me with your care, but I'm not allowed in your quarters in Etnep House, remember? It's warm here, and I can cook for you."

He said all this in one fast exclamation, and I realized I'd embarrassed him, which sort of pleased me. I wasn't the only doofus in over his head.

"Right, right, I get it."

"You're still weak. And I didn't mean to presume that you would want to…mingle with me…"

"No, right. I mean…not tonight, but…"

We both paused to breathe, looking into opposite corners of the room. I felt his eyes drifting back to my face, and I dared a peek in return.

"Not tonight? You mean, you would be interested in exploring the pleasures of our bodies another time?"

They did not go in for euphemisms in the Realm of Fire. "Uh, yeah. I mean, I would like that…if you would." The heat of the room and the soup were making my eyes grow heavy again. It was a very strange feeling to be both horny and sleepy. "Are you staying here tonight?"

"I will watch over you, yes." Tiqokh had said something similar on my first night in the Realm, but this was definitely more romantic. In fact, it was the most romantic thing anyone had ever said to me.

"We could, uh, cuddle a bit if you like," I ventured.

"I would like that very much, X'risp'hin. But I will not move to stimulate you sexually until you are stronger."

I cringed.

"Did I say something wrong? How would you express it in the Realm of Earth?"

"I don't know. Something like, 'I promise to be a gentleman.'" The whole conversation qualified as the worst discussion ever about the best idea ever.

He put my soup bowl away and added more wood to the fire. Then he climbed in under the blanket and made me the little spoon. I'm not poet enough to explain how good it felt to have those long arms wrapped around me.

"I promise to be a gentle man," he said, his voice both intimate and confident. Then he kissed the back of my neck with lips as soft as a summer smile. I thought, no way am I falling asleep and missing a minute of this, but the delicious warmth and the feeling of complete safety conspired within the minute to send me off into blissful, dreamless slumber.

CHAPTER 28: *The Intruder, Eighth Bell*

The city was gaudily draped. *"toys for children,"* the Intruder whispered to the last of the night, *"so so."* In his own land, such display would be an embarrassment. Festivals were meant for victory in battle, no decoration necessary but the corpses of the vanquished.

It was laughably easy to slip unnoticed by the few people awake at this hour. Even the so-called Defenders of Realm were oblivious. He could slice off one of their ears and be gone before the sting registered in their slow wits.

The Intruder knew he should temper his arrogance. The plan was not unfolding with precision. Their accomplices were too cautious. But if he and his troop had to compensate for this caution with greater violence, so much the better, so much sweeter the festival of victory to come. *soon soon.*

PART IV

SARENSIKAR

CHAPTER 29: *The Day of Devotion*

I woke slowly, curled like a cat under the blanket. The fire was embers and the torchstones shuttered, casting the windowless room in the palest of glows. I was alone. The ache in my limbs was gone, and my mind was sharp and clear. Sur was right. I just needed a good night's sleep to feel like myself again. After the incident in the Matrimonial Tunnels, it was like all my parts had been put back together by a drunken mechanic. If something didn't fit, he just whacked it in place with a hammer. But through the miracle of sleep, and quite probably my hours spent pressed up against that delicious boy, my whole system seemed to be restored to factory settings.

But where had Davix gone? Maybe he was getting me breakfast? *Croissant and three eggs with strong cheese, please. Orange juice and chocolate milk to follow.* The door opened, and I felt my smile tug up hydraulically. But it was Grentz. Sorry, I didn't mean that to sound like Grentz was anything less than "Yay!" but you know what I mean. Grentz crossed the room and unshuttered the lights.

"X'risp'hin, you're awake. That's great. Get dressed. It's *Sarensikar*, and everything's already starting." He was excited, hopping up and down and humming what was probably some holiday tune. *Rudolph the Bat-Winged Bidahéna.*

"Where's Davix?" I asked, my voice betraying my disappointment.

"He asked me to take you around today. He's busy."

I climbed out of bed, hunched over as I shyly pulled on my clothes, aware that Grentz was watching me unapologetically. As I pulled on my shirt, my hand brushed the extra bony bit on my rib and my enthusiasm dimmed. I wasn't totally back to normal.

"Busy with what?"

"I don't know. Maybe he finally went back to the Atmospherics Tower." I wanted to ask more, but Grentz was tapping an anxious staccato with his foot. "You need a bath or anything?" he asked. That actually sounded good, but I could tell he wanted me to say no, so I did. There was a mirror on the wall, and I checked my face. The last of the discolouration was gone, which was enough of a relief I didn't even care about the new zit on my cheek. I felt a pang about leaving the cozy room. It was, after all, the first place I'd ever cuddled overnight with a guy. There ought to be a plaque or something. And just then, I saw a big, purple flower sitting on the cool hearth. It had maybe a hundred petals, all curled around to form a ball, open just enough to reveal the copper stamens inside.

"What's that?" I asked Grentz.

"Oh, nice. Davix left you a Divinity. It's something friends give each other at *Sarensikar*, to wish them well in the coming season. Friends and the looped."

"Looped?"

"He sure is!" He laughed at his own joke, but didn't explain it.

Grentz helped me pin the Divinity flower to my shirt. I felt like a prom queen with her corsage. For his part, Grentz was wearing the long, orange scarf he'd picked up in the Textiles workshop, and we both looked sharp and ready to party.

The Comfort House was quiet as we exited, although I thought I could still hear low moans coming from behind some of the closed doors. We crossed the building's foyer, with its mosaic floor whose pattern seemed to be copulating doves, and opened the front door.

"Wow," I gasped as we walked out into the street. Because it wasn't there. Nothing was but thick, white fog, so dense I couldn't see the buildings on the other side of the narrow street.

"Impressive, right?" Grentz said. "Haven't seen sheep fog this thick in five cycles. Don't worry. Nothing's going to stop our fun today. Besides, think how dramatic it's going to be in three days when *Sarensikar* ends and the fog blows away."

I thought about what I'd heard in Tix-etnep-thon-dahé's office. There was no way of knowing when the fog would lift. Judging by Grentz's unshakeable conviction, there would be a lot of disappointed people in three days.

But for now, everyone was in a holiday mood, and if there were a few minor collisions as people stepped out of the fog, they laughed them off and called a festive greeting. "May your heart be light!" or

"Here comes the sun!" and other phrases that got Earth songs stuck in my head.

Every time the fog parted, I saw more holiday decorations—twists of coloured cloth hanging between buildings, garlands of flowers pinned to doors, and dramatic hanging banners with messages in Tongue of Fire I couldn't read. Little groups were singing two- and three-part harmony on every corner, accompanied by drums and bells.

Grentz dropped a friendly arm over my shoulders and steered me toward a long line of people that snaked through a square into a street beyond. And that's where we found Kriz'mig, holding a place for us.

Grentz sighed with relief. "I was scared we wouldn't make it in time."

"Blessings of *Sarensikar* on you, X'risp'hin," she said, and then to Grentz, "Are you joking? We'll be standing here until second bell."

"But it's worth it, X'risp'hin," he told me, licking his lips. "They only cook up one batch of *skrin'drin* a cycle, and then we have to spend every hour in between dreaming of it."

Kriz'mig ran a finger gently over the petals of my purple flower. "That's a lovely Divinity. Who gave it to you?"

"Davix," I said, beaming like an idiot. "Do you know where he is? I-I want to say thank you."

Grentz laughed and punched my arm. "For last night? You never forget your first time at the Comfort House."

My face burned. "No! We didn't…It wasn't like that." But he and Kriz'mig clucked like amused chickens, and I knew my denials were falling on deaf ears. Embarrassed by my blushing, I looked away and saw everyone nearby in line was staring at me, openly or shyly.

"May *Sarensikar* make your heart light, Copper Guest," a nearby woman said. She was with a little boy of maybe four, and when I smiled at him, he buried his face in the woman's skirts.

"Thanks." Immediately, a dozen more people got up the nerve to greet me.

One guy said, "How blessed you are to have visited the Dragon abode."

"Yeah, totally. *Farad'hil* is amazing!" I think I tried to say something like "It's the bomb," but my mouth couldn't find an equivalent in dragon tongue.

"Tell us what wonders you witnessed," he asked. And so, as the line snaked slowly along toward to the *skrin'drin* vat, a select group got to hear my travel blog about their holiest of sites, a place none of them would ever visit. Years later, I got to see some of my story, twisted by imperfect memories and thousands of retellings, in the DragonLaw. But at the time, I had no understanding how much each of my words weighed.

Skrin'drin was completely worth lining up for. It was a sweet and tangy pudding, with dried fruits in it that exploded with flavour in your mouth. We tried to make our portions last, but it wasn't humanly possible. By the time we reached the first of the "offering sites," we had licked our bowls clean.

There were something like ten offering sites in different parks and public squares, and the three of us, along with everybody and their uncle, wandered from one to next, in no particular order. At each, people threw flower petals and dried nuts into the flames for good luck. After the fifth site, I could sing along with the offering theme song:

> *Mounting fire, take this gift*
> *Lift it on the air*
> *Carry it to Farad'hil*
> *Fill dragon hearts with bounty*

At one stop, I started beatboxing over it. The worshippers seemed to appreciate my efforts, but maybe it was just because I was the Dragon Groom. Everything I did was by definition holy and next-level cool. For instance, when we came across some merchants selling religious trinkets, I blessed a few of them and the merchants almost started crying. I could see how easy it would be to get high on your own celebrity.

The fog grew thinner as the day grew warm, and the three of us stopped to check out singing groups, acrobats, and puppet shows. And it would have been a day of perfect happiness, except that I kept overhearing hushed conversations about Twis'wit and Rinby and the Curator guy who killed himself.

"Ill luck," someone said.

"No, it is demons. The thickening fog is proof."

"Punishment for heresy."

"Disrespect for the Fire Revealed!"

"Shh!"

If I leaned in to listen, they shut up, like what they were saying was illegal. Wasn't that what Stakrat had said? Grav'nan-dahé was cracking down on "superstition."

I was also less than perfectly happy because I couldn't find Davix.

Lunchtime came and went, but we were too full of *skrin'drin* and other festival snacks to bother with a sit-down meal. Then Grentz announced he had to go.

"I have my bonding time with one of the sacred priestesses," he said, and his eyes were practically bugging out with excitement.

"That sounds...fun?" I said. "Is it far?"

"The Greenward Temple is just outside the city gates. It's been a quarter cycle since my last bonding."

"Then go," Kriz'mig said, giving him a push.

Grentz was practically skipping with excitement, calling, "Blessings of *Sarensikar!*" as he disappeared into the fog.

When he was gone, I asked Kriz'mig, "What happens at the temple?"

"He will receive instruction in heterosexual congress from a priestess."

"Okay..." I said, stunned again by how casually they talked about sex on this world.

"Most of us enjoy same-sex pleasure, but for those who are partly or mostly attracted to the opposite sex, it is considered both physiologically and emotionally necessary to experience that domain of physical pleasure."

"Isn't a temple a weird place to do it?" I was imagining the big Catholic church where my grandma prayed.

"Why? All human pleasure is sacred and beloved of our Dragon Lords."

Do they get off on watching us? I wanted to ask. Then it occurred to me that in this world, gay people had an advantage. We could do it whenever we wanted as long as we had a fleshmate to hook up with. The unpaired heteros only got to four times a year.

Kriz'mig said, "And now I have to go, too. I'm sorry. My Master, Lok'lok-sur-nep-dahé, needs my help to decorate the stage for the Prime Magistrate's sermon. All the People will attend, and it has to be perfect." She looked around. "Will you be all right on your own? Do you know where you are?"

I did a 360 and realized I had no idea. But not wanting to hold her up, I pretended I was totally oriented. She gave me a big, unchaperoned hug, and then I was alone.

I chose a direction at random and started walking, figuring I'd hit a square pretty soon. But my brave marching soon faltered. Every turn just seemed to take me into more and more remote alleyways. Was I getting paranoid, or were eyes watching me from upper windows?

And if they were, why wasn't anyone calling out "Merry Sarensimas!" or anything? I heard a scraping sound, like someone was dragging a fork along the bricks. Something leaped across the gap between roofs, casting a faint shadow across my path. I walked faster. I wanted to run, but that would make me look like I was scared. *To who?* I asked myself. *Shut up*, I answered.

I came to an intersection and gave in to a desire to find a hiding place. To my right were four steps leading down to a door, but it was protected by a heavy cage and a large brass lock. To my left, a narrow passage led up toward the light. I took three or four deep breaths and began to climb the steps as swiftly and bravely as I could. A huge silhouetted figure stepped into my path, raising its clawed hands in the air. Was this Grav'nan-dahé's assassin, come to finish me off?

"Let me pass," I shouted, hysteria evident. "I am the Dragon Groom." Or was that the worst thing I could have said? Had I made myself more of a target? I should have yelled, "I'm Latrine Cleaner #8. No point killing me!"

But the figure replied, "Yes, I am aware of your identity, Crispin." Tiqokh stepped out of the fog and shadow. "You appear to be lost."

CHAPTER 30: *Heavy Thoughts in Thick Fog*

Tiqokh guided me out of the back alleys to the main streets.

"Where's everyone going?" I asked him, because the streets were full of people all heading in the same direction.

"It is time for the First Day Blessings. All of Cliffside gathers in the Retreat of Tarn where Grav'nan-dahé will speak his sermon and then offer the traditional prayers."

"Um, okay, how about we skip that?" We had been noticed by then, and people were waving to me, heading over for blessings.

Tiqokh sniffed the air. Maybe he smelled my lack of enthusiasm, because he said, "Come," and led me quickly down another laneway. We climbed a ladder on the side of a building and stepped onto a meandering path of wooden slats, narrow bridges, and short staircases that crossed from roof to roof through the city.

"Where are we going?"

"To attend the blessings. I know a shortcut."

"But…"

"Your absence would be noticed."

"So? I don't really care what Gravy Boat thinks of me."

"No, Crispin, I meant noticed by the People. They have already come to depend on you as a stabilizing influence."

"But I'm just a tourist." I stepped off the path and sat at the edge of the building we were crossing. "Sorry, Tiqokh, they'll just have to do without me."

I'd gone on strike like this a couple of years back during an argument with Mom at the mall, planting my butt on a bench and passive-aggressively texting friends. She called my bluff and left me there, threatening to rent out my room if I didn't find my own way home by sunset.

Tiqokh, in contrast, was a picture of patience. "Consider, Crispin, what your presence in the Realm of Fire means," he said. "Remember the prophecy. The Dragon Groom has ascended from the Realm of Earth because a dragon may die. Such a calamity would shake the People's world."

"Then they should hate me. I'm, like, this harbinger of doom."

"True, you are the harbinger, but also the way back to balance. Without you, there is no new dragon."

"But only if the prophecy is real," I said, louder than I meant to. Swinging my feet over the edge of the roof like a toddler, I watched the crowd streaming by in the street below. I had come to this world to get away from my own problems. What responsibility did I really have to these strangers?

"A lot of people are freaking out, like the realm is in trouble. They're whispering about balance and demons and the fog. It's just more superstition, right?"

The quadrana was silent for a moment. "Perhaps not," he said. "I have been investigating clues disparate and disconcerting. But if there is a conspiracy, the conspirators are guarding their secrets well. I have a question for you, Crispin. When you were in Farad'hil, and Bars'torm brought you close to Etnep's lair, what did he say to you?"

"I don't really remember. Something about ashes, I think?"

"Shh," Tiqokh hissed, not that I was talking loud or anything. He placed two fingers on my cheek and tapped lightly on my temple with his long nails. "Remember the warmth of the great mountain. Remember the song of the stone, for Farad'hil is always singing. Remember Bars'torm's scent as he stands behind you."

The rooftop seemed to pull away, like a tide going out, and suddenly I was in Farad'hil, in the memorial garden with that other quadrana, who, I now remembered, smelled like roasted almonds. He was speaking, and I repeated his words to Tiqokh.

"Eras come to an end. Death burns down life, and new possibilities grow in the ashes."

The world of Cliffside returned, like an elastic snapping your finger when you undo a bunch of asparagus. I looked up at Tiqokh, who was mouthing my words silently.

"New possibilities," he said. "Good. Thank you, Dragon Groom." He began walking the path again, and I hurried to catch up. I guess my strike was over.

"Davix gave me this flower," I said, pointing at the purple ball, which had started to wilt.

"Yes, I saw your Divinity."

"It's a sign between friends or, you know, fleshmates." It sounded dirtier when I said it. "Can I ask you something else?" I said as we crossed a rickety rope bridge single file.

"You may."

"Do they have, like, condoms in the Realm of Fire?"

"What, Crispin, is the purpose of the prophylactic protection? You do not intend to copulate with a female of the People, do you?"

"What? No!" I sputtered as we stepped onto the next roof.

The quadrana turned and sniffed me. "Ahh. You have lain with the Atmospherics apprentice."

I pulled away. "God! Can't a boy have a few secrets? Well, yeah, but 'lain' is all we did. I think maybe we're going to do more. So…"

"I understand what you are asking. You do not need barriers from disease here in the Realm of Fire. The properties of the air and water act as a defence against both viral and bacterial maladies. There are few illnesses that afflict the People. Hurry, or we will be late."

So, I didn't need protection. Good. Now I just had to figure out everything else. Until I asked about condoms, the detailed mechanics of what me and Davix might do hadn't really crossed my mind. I was going to be an awkward nerd our first time, that much was guaranteed, but maybe not a total failure. I could kiss okay, and I knew how to give a blowjob. But I didn't know how to, like, be *romantic.* I didn't know how to take someone's clothes off them in the sexy way you see in movies. I didn't know when it was my turn do something to them, or when I was supposed to lie back, swooning. And would I look like a fool swooning? What if I swooned and he laughed? Then there was the whole question of butt sex. Would Davix expect it? And which way? I mean, I understood it in theory, but I was missing some basic, practical info.

We crossed a bridge over a main road, and I knew we were near the Retreat of Tarn, because I could already hear the rumble of the crowd gathering. Tiqokh stepped off the path and opened a small wooden door in a wall beside us, bending low to enter.

On the other side was a dark and dusty room full of furniture covered in drop cloths. "Where are we?"

"Etnep House. Come." Tiqokh led me through a crazy labyrinth of rooms and hallways in the castle until we emerged on a little covered porch that overlooked the Retreat of Tarn and the big stage in front of the gates of Etnep House. It reminded me of a box seat in an old theatre. Hidden behind a pair of translucent curtains, we sat down on two chairs. I peeked through the gap between curtains.

The big cobblestone square was as packed as the day Sur had

flown in to take me to Farad'hil. But instead of the football-hooligan mood of that day, today's crowd was quiet and respectful. Every person was holding a long, upright reed in their clasped hands, so the whole square looked like a marsh. In fact, I heard some frogs croaking, but that was probably a coincidence. Kriz'mig and her guild had hung colourful tapestries over the stage, and I hoped that Grav'nan-dahé would have something equally cheery to say. The fog was proving to be a problem, and muscular guys with big fans were waving it away from the stage whenever it got thick enough to block the show.

The opening act was onstage at that point—three priest types wearing crazy big hats that looked like stilt houses. When they raised their hands, the crowd hummed louder. When they lowered them, everyone grew obediently quiet. It reminded me of a kindergarten game.

When it was over, Tiqokh abruptly stood me up and pulled our curtains open. The hum of the crowd grew into a little cheer as they all turned my way, shaking their reeds in the air. A few people started singing, and the sound spread out like a wave, until everyone had joined in.

"The song of the Five," Tiqokh said. "It is meant to convey the gratitude we feel to be living in the Realm of Fire, part of the great plan of the dragons. They sing in your honour."

I'd made some great playlists in my time, but this had to be one of the most beautiful songs I ever heard. So I stood there, letting the People bask in my counterfeit glory, because Tiqokh said it was important to them. I looked all around for Davix, but I couldn't see him. The crowd's attention turned to the front again as Grav'nan-dahé stepped through the gates of Etnep House and crossed to the podium in the middle of the stage.

There were no microphones, obviously, but the acoustics were pretty impressive because I could hear everything he said. His sermon wasn't the happy pep talk I'd been hoping for. After some lines about the planting season and the return of the sun, he started giving everyone shit.

"Fog has been with us for too long," the Prime Magistrate said, lifting his arms in the air so his long, loose sleeves slipped down and revealed his bony arms. "It has blinded our path and dulled our senses. We have come to rely not on faith and truth, but on rumour and superstition. But know this, People of the Realm of Fire. The absence of light cannot be mitigated by stories of light. The hands of the shadow puppeteer make demon shapes, but these are not proof of actual demons. Nothing can replace the wisdom of the Dragon Lords and their holy DragonLaw."

I whispered to Tiqokh, "He's saying the same thing again, right? Don't believe in the prophecies, don't believe rumours about Rinby. Or Twis'wit."

"Precisely, Crispin."

I wanted to scream in frustration. "But the People are scared. He can't just say, 'Stop being scared because the DragonLaw says so.' That's not what they need to hear."

After the sermon, Gravy Man and the priest guys recited some prayers and played a round of pass-the-ritual-object. My mind had wandered by then, as it does in church situations. Then the crowd was on the move, beating a hasty retreat for whatever was next on the *Sarensikar* agenda.

Tiqokh led me down the stairs of Etnep House. I was anxious to get out and find my friends and especially Davix. If he still wasn't around, I was going to march right over to the Atmospherics Tower and grab him. As we crossed the foyer, Tiqokh was called over by a group of mixed beings. He left me leaning against a pillar, wishing I had my phone to kill the time. After a couple of minutes, who should enter the foyer, surrounded by his priests and various assistants, but the Prime Douchebag himself. I stepped away from the pillar to catch Tiqokh's attention. If I had to talk to Grav'nan-dahé, I didn't want to do it alone. But Tiqokh and the mixed beings were gone, like they'd never been there in the first place.

CHAPTER 31: *The Choreography of Faith and Desire*

Grav'nan-dahé stepped toward me, leaving his priests to wait for him. "Copper Guest, I am pleased you attended the blessings. I hope you are quite recovered from your ordeal at Farad'hil."

"Yes, sir," I replied, working hard at politeness in the hope of ending the conversation faster.

"Let that unfortunate incident be a reminder that you do not belong here. Peace and balance endures in the Realm of Fire, and your presence just confuses the People."

I took a deep breath and then said in one fast exhale, "Listen, Your Prime Magistrateness, I don't want to keep contradicting you, but I was up on the mountain. I saw the prophecy happening."

He shot me a stern X-ray of a look. "You witnessed the ritual of the heretics?"

"Yeah, me and Sur did."

My news might have rattled him for a second, but his arrogance was quickly back in full swing. "And you think that after four days in our realm, you are experienced enough to interpret the words of that mad, old couple? I knew them in their youth. Even then, they revelled in their heresies. That is why I had to banish them. They were infecting too many of the uneducated with their ideas. Now they live out their days clinging to the side of a mountain, imagining all manner of nonsense."

"Sur finds them pretty interesting," I said, my voice edging into anger.

His voice grew quiet and hard. "Copper blood or no, Earth boy, do not pretend you have the smallest idea what goes on in the mighty heart of a dragon."

But then out of nowhere, Ol' Gravy Train produced a warm smile, like we were buddies just doing some trash talk. "Copper Guest, you are troubling your soul over worries that are not yours. I absolve you of this responsibility." He waved a hand over me. "I will talk to the bidahénas, and they will order Tiqokh to return you to your world as soon as *Sarensikar* is over. Someday, if tragic circumstance does take one of the Five, perhaps we will meet again. Or another of the blood will be chosen. In any event, you have our gratitude."

He didn't wait for my response. He just gave a fast head and heart bow and turned on his heel with a swish of his swishy gown, tap-tapping away across the marble floor.

"Grav'nan-dahé!" I called after him. He stopped. "Have you seen Davix? He...he's been kind to me. I don't want to leave without saying goodbye."

He turned, and his eyes were shining like he had already won. "The young apprentice has not been seen today. Perhaps he is making amends in a solitary retreat in the foothills."

Amends for what? "Okay, how can I find him, then? You have a map or something?"

"Copper Guest, I have instructed D'gada-vixtet-thon to abjure your company." My breath caught in my throat, and Grav'nan-dahé smiled—a smile as cold as the snow on the Chend'th'nif. "The apprentice was grateful for my advice and understood its wisdom. Davix is a young man whose feelings burn more brightly than his wisdom, and he knows this. I see he gave you that Divinity. One of its meanings is 'Farewell. We part with no ill feelings.' You would be showing him the greatest respect by honouring his decision."

Having sunk these poisoned spikes into my heart, the old bastard turned again and marched off down a dark corridor followed by his entourage. I couldn't breathe. As much as I wanted to believe everything Grav'nan-dahé said was dragon dung, maybe he was right this time. After all, where was Davix? I knew he liked me all right, but what if I was an obstacle in his religious path? Just a terrible temptation messing up his career?

Or maybe Davix didn't like me the way I liked him. He had done his holy duty and cared for the Dragon Groom in his time of need, but now that I was healthy again, he took the advice of his magic father figure and made himself scarce. Grav'nan-dahé was right. I would be doing Davix and everyone a favour by flying right the hell out of here. Who did I think I was anyway? Some saviour of the Realm? I was no one but the pathetic fag clown of my high school. I didn't even deserve a friend, much less an honoured place in some ancient pantheon.

Tears rolling down my face, I walked out of Etnep House onto the stage. The last of the crowd was leaving the Retreat of Tarn, and I was happy to be alone. *Happy.* Wrong word.

A voice below me said, "Dragon Groom?"

I looked down and saw two kids at the foot of the stage, different in age, but so alike they must have been brother and sister. Both had long, straight hair that hung halfway down their backs, and they were wearing two or three garlands of fresh cut flowers each. In Earth years, the girl looked around twelve, just starting to get some curves and that challenging stare girls suddenly find at that age. The boy was more like nine, all sweet enthusiasm.

"Blessings of *Sarensikar*," I said without much feeling, wiping the tears from my eyes.

"Holy One, we would be honoured to lead you to the dance," the girl said, offering me her hand.

"Thanks, but I just want to go back to my room. I don't know how to dance anyway."

The boy cracked up, like I had said the funniest thing in history.

"No, Dragon Groom, *you* don't dance. You watch the dancers and cheer for the one you think should win."

"Be polite, you little wheat weevil. This is the Dragon Groom, not one of your smelly slashball teammates."

"The Dragon Groom knows I was joking. He's not brainless like you."

"Hey, hey!" I interrupted. "Don't fight, I'll go to the dance." It wasn't like I had anywhere else I needed to be. I climbed off the stage to stand between them, and their animosity immediately turned to excitement. The boy reached out a hand and I took it, offering my other hand to the girl.

The time of my return home was coming, and I was already disconnecting from the Realm. I no longer felt like I had any place here. But when I tried to imagine myself back on Earth, I couldn't make that picture come into focus either. Had I made a horrible mistake coming to this world? Maybe my copper blood, once ignited, would refuse to cool down again. Maybe I would never again be Crispin of the Realm of Earth. But if I didn't belong here or there, what the hell was I?

My escorts were very serious about their duties, so I didn't feel bad about not making conversation as we walked. Still, every now and then, one or the other would sneak a glance at me. After a few times, I timed it so I was making a face when they looked. This quickly turned into a game, and I shook off my gloom before too long and let silliness take over. The road grew steeper, and we broke into a laughing run, speeding perilously down the winding streets until we caught up with the tail end of the crowd, still on the move from sermon to dance. Together with most of the population of Cliffside, we exited through the city gates and emerged onto a flat field.

In the centre of the field, a circle was marked off with stones. Some of the crowd was staking out places around the circle, while the rest were sitting up on the adjacent hill, like it was the bleachers in a ball park. Musicians—drummers, string players, flute players—were laying down a chill groove.

The vibe in general was pretty chill. Instead of going ape when they saw me, everyone was just smiling and saying hi. Kid after kid let their curiosity overcome their fear, and soon I had a junior army around me. Meanwhile, every adult in the crowd wanted me to sample some specialty they pulled from their picnic baskets, and soon I was blissfully stuffed.

The sun was setting behind the Citadel, way up at the top of Cliffside, and it got dark fast. The musicians kicked it up a notch, the beat insistent and funky. Torchstone lanterns were brought out, and a crew in red uniforms fired up a big bonfire in the centre of the circle. The crowd's excitement grew, more and more of them stamping their feet to the beat and whistling in anticipation.

Suddenly, a quadrana strutted to the front, raising his hands to quiet the crowd. He wasn't like any mixed being I'd seen. Tiqokh and the other quadranas dressed simply and moved kind of gracelessly. This guy, on the other hand, wore a long green cloak covered with jewels, almost the same colour as his green skin, and on his head was a crazy tall, feathered hat. His movements were all high fashion catwalk, and after every turn or sweep of his hand, he paused for a second, like he was posing for the cameras. Impressive dragon drag.

The brother and sister were standing beside me, and they stared in delight.

"Who is that?" I asked.

"That's Farkol," said the girl. "He's the organizer of the annual dance."

Her brother added, "He used to live on the Realm of Earth, Copper Guest. Didn't you ever meet him?"

"Uh, no. Did he always dress like that?"

"Only after his time on Earth," the girl said. "I heard he got in trouble with the bidahénas last year because he told everyone to call him dahé. Only the Dragon Lords can bestow that honour."

Farkol-*not*-dahé swung his arms to the side and shouted, "Let the first competition begin!"

A line of ten women were climbing up the road from farther down the hill, and the crowd opened a path for them to reach the circle. They hopped over the stones and formed their own circle, dancing to the rising beat around the bonfire, facing outward, arms linked.

"What are those costumes?" I asked the brother and sister. The dancers were dressed in light, short dresses, but over these they had strips of fur, elaborate headdresses, and face paint.

"They're dressed as animals. See? She's a bear, and she's a deer."

The crowd began singing along with the musicians, a wilder and sexier tune than any of the prayer songs I'd heard all day. The dancers stepped forward two at a time, busting out whatever special choreography they'd invented to annihilate the competition. The crowd cheered or booed, and one out of every pair was eliminated. The vanquished animal would then leave the circle in humiliation, fake tail between her legs. With each elimination round, the beat got faster, the dances more athletic, and the crowd went crazier.

I got right into it, the way you do with a reality TV contest, screaming or booing. My favourite dancer, a sinuous and strong mountain lion, made it to the final four, but the spotted rabbit who could practically kick herself in the nose proved unstoppable. The music ended, and sweating and panting, the girl was crowned with a ring of purple Divinity flowers, her brown bunny ears poking out through the middle of the crown.

It was fully dark now, and Farkol the fashion forward quadrana had changed into a purple outfit covered in little glittering stones that caught the light of the bonfire.

He sashayed to the centre of the circle and called out, "Let the second competition commence!" The musicians dropped the beat again, and the male dancers appeared, snaking their way toward us. As they got closer, I could see that they were dressed pretty skimpily under their costume pieces. I was, suffice it to say, even more ready to cheer for this group.

The line of dancers was coming right toward me, revealed one at a time as they jumped into the ring. Decked out in feathered headdresses, I realized they weren't animals of the ground, they were birds. They had pieces of wings hanging off their backs and fastened to their wrists. When they spread their arms, the wings opened to reveal amazing shapes and patterns woven in the feathers. I got to appreciate each one in turn, older and younger, skinny or muscular. The seventh one in line was Davix.

I screamed.

He was clearly a kingsolver, with the familiar black and grey wings and a red headdress. A brief skirt of matching red leather strips hung from a belt at his waist and flew up into the air to reveal his loincloth whenever he turned or jumped. He wasn't wearing anything else. As he passed me, our eyes met, and he grinned like this was my surprise birthday party and he'd been planning it for a month. The smile was lava that flowed through me, melting my sadness and my doubt.

The kid brother tugged at my shirt to get my attention. "Davix told us to bring you here."

And his sister added, "He said to tell you he is dancing for you."

I have never cheered so hard at any competition in my life.

Davix wasn't really a dancer, okay? I mean, the guy was basically a scholar and a science nerd, but he could jump higher than anyone, and keep on jumping. He held nothing back. And he was the most beautiful, his long limbs glinting gold and red from the bonfire's flames, his mouth gaping open, his hair shaking loose from his topknot in a black waterfall, his dark nipples rising and falling with his breath. I was mesmerized and turned on.

The crowd was pretty amused at the way I screamed myself hoarse and jumped up and down as if I was in the competition myself. It didn't even matter when Davix came in second, beaten by a guy who danced with the true grace of a bird in flight. In fact, I felt bad for the winner because, when Davix left the circle and came forward to give me a sweaty hug, no one was paying attention to anything else.

"Come with me," Davix whispered in my ear. He walked us out of the crowd, moving faster and faster until we were running back through the gates of the city and up its steeply climbing streets.

Here are things I knew: Davix wasn't following Grav'nan-dahé's orders. He wasn't off on a monk's retreat to avoid me. Davix hadn't just taken care of me last night out of religious obligation. Davix wanted me. *Me.* Crispin Haugen. X'risp'hin. Kharis'par'ih'in, the Dragon Groom. And he wanted all of me. Through our sweaty, intertwined hands, I could feel our bodies calling to each other. This primal conversation had started the night before, maybe earlier. And even if I knew dragon tongue better than this new language of the flesh, I still understood. I won't lie to you. I was scared. But I was buoyant. And ready.

CHAPTER 32: *Take My Hand and Touch You*

Seeing as Davix and I had left the dance ahead of everyone, I wasn't surprised Cliffside was deserted. Most of the torchstones were still baffled, and I had to trust my guide to lead me through the dark. Trusting him felt daring and sexy. In the middle of the dark city, the Comfort House was the only building all lit up, and that's where we were heading.

Men were on their way in and out of the big doors, and a line of women were going around the corner to their wing. In the lobby, guys of all ages sat on the couches, talking, eating, and laughing. They sprawled across each other in a way that would have been too intimate for just buddies back on Earth.

"I thought everyone was still at the dance," I said.

"The Comfort House is so popular during *Sarensikar*, people skip ceremonies to get a room. And you have to reserve your place a quarter cycle in advance."

"Oh yeah? Then how did you know you were going to need a room?" I eyed Davix with a little pang of jealousy. Who was the guy I was replacing?

He looked abashed. "I, uh, arranged it earlier today. I said the Dragon Groom needed a room. Several people offered me their reservations right away. I think you'll like the one I accepted." The celebrity thing did have its advantages. Also, this meant he had been counting on us needing a room, a fact I found both thrilling and terrifying.

"Blessings of *Sarensikar* on you, Dragon Groom," called a guy seated on cushions in the corner. He was young enough to still be pretty hot, but old enough to be going grey. Another dude had a hand in the guy's tunic, casually stroking his chest hair, and a third was climbing onto the cushions to join them. I blushed.

"Uh, yeah, blessings."

We passed many doors, with stuff happening behind every one. I should also say that even though all the rooms were in use, not all the doors were closed. I admit letting my eyes stray a little.

Still, I was feeling pretty overwhelmed. "Can we be somewhere alone? Just us?"

He stopped and ran a hand down my cheek. "Of course. That's what I've arranged." *Do that again*, I wanted to say, but I was suddenly so shy I almost called the whole thing off. Almost.

We were in front of a set of double doors inlaid with red tiles in a spiral pattern. Davix pushed the doors open, and I looked into a tiny paradise. He laughed again when he heard me catch my breath. Woven runners in red and gold criss-crossed the tile floor. Curved beams of cedar wood arced overhead like they were the ribs and we were in the breast of the beast. Steps led down into a wide round tub whose water was steaming in the torchstone light. Beyond the tub stood a huge bed, covered in fabrics and pillows. The heart of the beast, you might say.

"Oh my God, what is this? The Harlequin Suite?"

"*Khar'le'gin?*" Davix said, perplexed, and no wonder, since *khar'le'gin* means "meat beginning to spoil."

"Gross. No. Never mind. I love it." We entered our little paradise. "I'm kind of nervous. I'll probably say a lot of dumb things like that." He put a hand on my shoulder, one finger straying to slide across my neck. I got goosebumps.

"X'risp'hin, I'm nervous, too. But listen, you don't have to do anything—*anything*—you don't want. You could even tell me you'd rather just go for a walk through the city and talk about our lives. That would be fine."

"But…but you want stuff to happen. Here, I mean, with me. Right?"

"Very much. Yes."

"Me too." I had never spoken words like this out loud in my life. It felt like I was breaking the laws of the universe.

"I would like to take a bath. Will you join me?"

My voice got all chokey. "Yeah…"

I watched him walk across to a bench beside the tub. He sat and unlaced his dancing shoes with their red leather tassels. He wiggled his toes on the cool tile while he undid the vest with its beautiful, feathered wings and untied them from his wrists. The hair under his arms was damp with sweat, shiny black against his brown skin. Removing the wings, he looked like an angel transforming into a man. Then he untied the loincloth with no sign of self-consciousness and let it drop to the floor.

Tonight, I was meeting a new Davix. As he danced, as he got naked, he seemed twice as alive. The daily Davix machine that measured itself off by hard rules of the DragonLaw, by the strict tables of weather figures, had become a flowing dance of muscle and flesh. He looked like freedom. Watching him, I could barely breathe.

He saw me staring as he stepped down into the water, and there was clear evidence he liked me watching. He lowered himself until he was sitting on the floor of the tub, the surface of the water cutting those beautiful nipples in half. Seriously, I had never realized a guy's nipples could occupy so much of my focus. He sighed, and a smile of pure pleasure lit up his face. He looked at me, waiting patiently. So I undressed, not nearly as gracefully or unself-consciously, but with my own arousal metre displaying a similar reading.

I sat on the opposite side of the circular pool, and when I stretched out my legs, our toes touched. I reflexively pulled them back, but then I remembered I wasn't bumping feet with stern, old Auntie Carmen under the dining room table. I let my toes slide back over his, and we toe wrestled for a few seconds. More smiles. Dumb boy smiles this time that felt a lot safer. I let out a breath. I was doing fine. Then Davix slid around to sit beside me, and my heart started pounding.

He picked up a soft cloth from the edge of the tub, wet it, and handed it to me.

"Would you wash my back, X'risp'hin?" He turned away, pulling his long hair off his neck. I washed his back in slow circles, marvelling at the play of muscle under the smooth skin, and he hummed with pleasure.

"I haven't danced that hard in half a cycle. I'll be sore tomorrow."

"Uh-huh," I said, my cloth circling lower, breaking the surface of the water. Through the ripples, I could see the top of his ass crack, but I didn't let my circles go that low. My face was close to his skin, and I smelled it, like I was a dragon who could figure out hidden secrets that way.

He turned my way and took the cloth. We stared into each other's eyes until I got shy and lowered my head. Through the distorting lens of water, I could see we were, um, pointing at each other. He began washing the side of my neck, my chest, my stomach, and it was so good for a minute, and then it was too much. I pulled away.

"Sorry, seriously, sorry." A deep shame ran through me. But when I looked back at Davix, he was calm and smiling.

"There's nothing to be sorry about," he said. "Your body said you needed some space, and you listened. The body is wise. Keep listening to it."

I felt like crying for just a second, but I took a deep breath, and the feeling went away. "Thanks."

"Have you never mingled with anyone, X'risp'hin?"

"No, I totally have. Of course."

He looked skeptical. "It's no shame if you haven't. There are a few people our age who still don't feel ready."

"No, yeah, totally ready. And experienced, yeah. There's this guy, and since, like, September we've been really, you know…going at it."

Shut up. He doesn't need to know about Altman. He doesn't even know what a September is!

"That's good. Do you bring each other a lot of pleasure?"

"Well, he didn't have any complaints," I said with a weird sitcom leer that made me want to rip my own face off. "Sorry. I mean, he basically liked it when I gave him a…" And I got hung up on the word. It was one of those times I forgot I wasn't speaking English, and "blowjob" didn't produce the usual auto-translation into dragon tongue. Maybe dragons didn't do oral sex.

"Yes?" Davix asked, raising his eyebrows.

"You know, with my mouth. On his…" Ahhh! Frustration. *Dick, cock,* and *junk* produced no effect, so I had to go clinical and think "penis" before I could produce any translation. Why does that word always seem dirtier than any of the alternatives?

"Oh, that's good," Davix said, which sounded absurd. "And what did you ask him to do for you?"

"Um, yeah, well we didn't really get that far. I mean, I'm not complaining…"

Davix knitted his brow. "Wasn't there anything you *wanted* him to do? Were you content with being the one to provide—"

"Oh, I wanted stuff. Even just, you know, kissing. I love kissing. There was this other boy, Dražen, and him and me kissed a lot." Something knotted up in my chest. I felt all the humiliation of both relationships—two boys so wrapped up in themselves, they barely realized I was also a real person. Still, I felt the need to defend Altman. "It's not his fault. He doesn't like guys, at least that's what he says. So, it kind of didn't come up."

"But we always owe each other pleasure when we mingle. There is a proverb, 'You find your own smile in the mirror of your partner's regard.' X'risp'hin, you have to feel free to express your own desires. Your needs."

I sank lower in the water, until it covered my chin. He was waiting for me to say something. Otherwise, I would have sunk until the water closed over my head and I drowned.

"I kept hoping, right? I thought if I gave him enough time, maybe he'd want to do more. If I loved him enough..." I didn't mean to choke up, but I did.

Davix stood, water dripping off him. He climbed from the tub, and I thought for an awful second he was done with me. He dried himself with a big red towel and then picked up a big blue one and held it open for me.

"Come," he said, the most caressing of commands. So I got up, still hard despite the sadness. He was, too. I stepped onto the tiles and turned backward into the towel. He closed it over me like I was the knight and he was the squire setting my cloak in place. With his arms around me from behind, drying me with the towel, he kissed my neck like he had the night before in bed. My breathing got faster.

Davix led me to the bed, and we sat on its edge, our towels falling off our shoulders. I couldn't look right at him. It was too bright, like looking at sun. I was in danger of screwing up the whole event, and I would hate myself forever if that happened. Action was required, and I knew what to do. I put a hand on his hip and started to lower my face to his excitement. But Davix stopped me, and I sat up, surprised.

"There's time for that later. Take my hand," he said, "and touch me with it."

I was confused, but I did what he said, holding him by the wrist, placing his hand on his chest, like he was a Southern belle going, "Oh my!"

"Where?" I asked.

"Wherever you like."

So, I became the puppeteer and he was my puppet, clumsily pleasuring himself. At first it was totally absurd, but then I really got into it, caressing his face with his hand, his neck, his chest, the inside of his thighs. He was watching me, his mouth hanging open, making little noises when I hit a good spot. I put his hand on his hard-on for a second and then took it away, in case that was going too far. I laid his hand on his thigh, giving it a little pat before withdrawing my own hand.

"Who taught you that?"

"A temple priestess. I was as nervous as you my first time."

"Did it feel good? What I did?"

"Yes," he said, with no embarrassment, with nothing but simple honesty. "It felt beautiful. Like it was me and not me. Now, X'risp'hin, take my hand and touch you."

I looked down at the hand. I picked it up as before, just holding it in front of me, not moving. I was afraid but I couldn't exactly say why.

"Where do I touch myself?" I asked.

"Wherever feels good."

I started on my chest and my stomach. Then I slid his beautiful, long hands across my shoulder, up the side of my neck and onto my cheek. I turned my nose right into it, smelling his warm palm, letting the heat transfer into my skin. I got bolder as my excitement grew. It felt like I was climbing the ladder on the biggest slide in the water park.

Davix said, "It's good. You're beautiful. Keep going." And I did, and I made a noise which should have embarrassed me but didn't.

And then his arm was too short to reach farther, and we froze for a second, staring into each other's eyes. I let myself fall back on the bed, opening my arms to him, and all his patient reserve vanished. He climbed right over me, our bodies shouting with the hungry joy of touch, our lips coming together.

It wasn't rocket science. I told him I liked kissing, and now he was kissing me. What would I ask for next?

CHAPTER 33: *The Day of Jubilation*

This time, Davix wasn't gone in the morning.

Sex aside, do you know what's amazing? Waking up with your body all rested and glowing, and looking across the disaster of sheets and blankets to see his beautiful face there. And how awesome was it to roll back into his arms and say, "Don't tell me if my breath smells bad, okay?" And if you don't know yet, don't worry, you will. And you're going to love it.

I guess I had the idea from movies that it's always awkward the morning after sex. Well, not for Crispin and Davix. We were gorgeous and goofy and grinning into each other's bleary faces. And kissing and getting turned on and doing it again.

Okay, wait a sec. Time out.

I don't want to hold back and hide behind empty phrases like "doing it." On the one hand, it's not really your business, but on the other, maybe it's important. What would it mean if I told you, in all my usual excruciating detail, about sheep fog and the architecture of Cliffside and how the DragonLaw works, but I made the sex all winking and metaphorical? I think it would mean I'm a hypocrite. So, I'll tell you some real stuff. Even the clumsy parts, like where I accidentally bashed Davix in the balls with my elbow.

We kissed a lot, of course. And our tongues left the safe territory of our mouth and lips and went on epic journeys around jawlines, behind ears, down necks, and across nipples. At first, my mind wanted me to be grossed out by all the saliva and sweat and tastes, but my body assured me it was all amazing. We were literally hungry for each other. What then? I did get to show off the specialty I perfected on Altman, and if I do say so, I was inspired. His hands were in my hair, clenching and releasing as he made these awesome noises. Oh! And you know what's insane fun? Just lining up your junk and grinding. There's a word for it, but I can't remember it in English or dragon tongue.

So, there, you satisfied? No metaphors, just bodily fluids. Look, Mom, I'm a pornographer. But I better stop now before we get too distracted.

No, wait, there's one more thing. At one point, my panic started rising, and I stopped everything to say, "Look, Davix, I don't want to do anal sex. Not now."

Of course, I didn't have to worry. "I don't usually like to enter the nethers the first time with someone, anyway."

"Nethers? Oh, you mean…got it." I blushed and cracked up.

And that was it. My panic vanished, and we got back to business.

When we were done and done again, I picked up an imaginary bedside telephone and said, "Hello, room service? Eggs Benedict and champagne, please."

"I only understood 'eggs,'" Davix said with a dopey smile, disentangling himself from my arms and dabbing at us with a dry corner of the sheet. "Are you hungry?"

"Dying."

"We'll get some food soon. But first, let's bathe again. And then we must clean the room."

"The hell? What kind of resort is this? My review just dropped a star."

So, in case you think being Dragon Groom is all glamour, you should know the job doesn't exempt you from draining the tub, scrubbing it with sandy powder stuff, stripping the bed, remaking it with fresh linens, and taking the ones you stained to the laundry room.

As we headed back down the hall, we heard bangs and crashes from a nearby room. The door burst open, and out tumbled Grentz and another guy, rolling across the floor as they wrestled in nothing but their underwear.

"Relent!" Grentz shouted.

"Never!" the other guy called back.

"Come on, admit you've lost," Grentz said, twisting the guy into a pretzel and climbing on top of him.

"I relent!" the guy finally shouted, his voice muffled by Grentz's thigh.

They stood and did a friendly forearm shake. Grentz noticed us.

"Davix! X'risp'hin! You guys going to get breakfast? Give me a rabbit dash, and I'll go with you."

"A rabbit dash?" I asked Davix as Grentz and his friend headed back into the room, where I noticed a third guy still asleep on the bed.

"A very short interval of time."

Grentz emerged almost immediately, wrinkled and mussed but ready to roll, wrapping his orange scarf around his thick neck as he closed the door behind him.

"Let's go," he said.

"You don't have to clean the room?" I asked.

"Nope, I won the wrestling match."

Soon, we were sitting on a bench, people-watching while we ate spicy eggs on a fresh bun.

"Can I ask you something, Grentz?" I said. "Something personal."

He looked wary. "Maybe. About what?"

"Sex."

His face lit up in a broad, dopey grin. "Oh, sure. I thought you meant, like, whether I pray in Open Heart style or Dawn Revelation style. That's kind of private."

"Yeah, no, I don't even know what that…Never mind. See, I just don't get how you can have sex with guys if you're really into women."

He looked confused. "Well, few people are totally exclusive. And even then, you can still give and take pleasure. I mean, that's easy. That's what friends do."

"But it's not the same feeling as when you, uh, visited the temple yesterday?"

"Oh, no, of course not. Being with a woman lights up all the fires in my body and soul. I'm so looped, I can barely speak. You know, like Davix is when he looks at you."

I turned to grin at Davix and saw him blush for the first time. That was so cute, I had to lean in and kiss a drop of hot sauce off his upper lip.

"What's 'looped'?"

Grentz pulled off his scarf and lassoed me with it. "Like this. But with feelings instead. And frankly, I think Davix isn't just looped with you. He's tangled."

"Practice some silence, fool," Davix said, growing even redder. "We should get going. There is a prayer meeting after second bell. I think we'll avoid the crowds in the Retreat of Tarn and attend a smaller service in the Park of the Five."

"Smaller sounds good," I said as we set off. "I hope you can find your way. The fog is worse than yesterday. It's not going to lift, is it?"

Grentz said, "Of course it will. At the end of *Sarensikar.* Didn't your time in Farad'hil deepen your faith?"

I tried to catch Davix's eye, but he obviously didn't want to get involved. We hadn't talked about the weather or about his master,

Tix-etnep-thon-dahé, or Atmospherics at all since I came back to town. But ever since we left the Comfort House, I had noticed him doing little weather testing things like licking a finger and raising it to feel the wind.

Everyone we passed seemed to be in a good mood. How many of them had had their own special nights with friends after the dance? We came across Stakrat and Kriz'mig buying jars of preserved fruit from a vendor. I wondered if they were also fleshmates. Stakrat was in her usual practical clothes with the Defence of Realm sash across her chest, but Kriz'mig had made an effort. She wore layers of silky material in green and yellow, a bunch of jangly bracelets, and a kind of turban on her head.

"X'risp'hin!' she cried, jingling over to hug me. "Are you ready for the second day of *Sarensikar*? We call it the Day of Jubilation!"

"I was just noticing that people look jolly."

Over Kriz'mig's shoulder, I saw Stakrat giving me the once-over, her head tilted to the side.

She said, "I know why the Copper Guest and D'gada-vixtet-thon are jubilant."

Grentz punched her on the shoulder. "Shh, you'll make Davix blush again. He was red as lava spew before."

Davix, annoyed, walked past them, calling over his shoulder, "We're late. Follow, you juveniles."

The four of us stumbled after him like a gang of puppies, deliberately bumping into each other, feeding each other spoonfuls of the preserved fruit. A chaperone fell into place behind us, but I ignored him just like the others always did.

Soon, we came to the Park of the Five, a square I hadn't seen before. Wait, is it still called a square if it's round? You could call it a round, I guess, but that's a kind of song. Or a cracker. Anyway, the floor of the circle was light-coloured stones, with darker stones laid into them, forming a five-pointed star. At each star point was a huge fir tree, and on each thick trunk hung a big rectangular panel with a painting of a dragon. I recognized Sur, Renrit, and Inby. Renrit, I should point out, looked a lot slimmer in the painting than in real life. Was the artist trying to be flattering, or had the editor of the DragonLaw gained all that weight since the painting was done?

"Oh, wow," I said. "Is tonight when they do their flyover?"

"Yep!" Grentz shouted, jumping up to try and touch the bottom edge of one of the paintings. "It's the culmination of the second day of *Sarensikar*."

The park was filling up now. I gave Sur's painting a little wave and then moved on to the biggest painting of all, lavishly decorated with gold and jewels. The dragon in it had twice as many fringes as Sur, all tied with golden bangles. It had to be Etnep, the Queen, my mate. I wondered what I would feel when she flew over that evening. Would my copper blood respond? Would she "light up all the fires in my body and soul," like the priestesses did for Grentz?

I did a test: I looked at Davix, who was standing across the park. My gaze wandered over his legs and butt, his narrow hips, his wide shoulders, the hair falling across them. Maybe he felt me looking, because he turned and pierced me with those dark eyes. Oh, yes, fires lit up. All of the fires. If any dragon could make me feel that, I'd be more surprised than if I found Tiqokh doing an open mic night at a comedy club.

I walked over to Davix and put my arm around his waist. Together, we looked up at the dragon in the last painting. She was a deep green, like a mysterious forest. Her long tail curled in an S-shape, and her face was serene.

"I love this image of Vixtet, X'risp'hin. She looks so wise and powerful. It is so propitious that my first union with you should be on the same day I see her again."

"So, that's Vixtet. She's…"

And that's when I remembered Vixtet was sick. Maybe dying. I couldn't believe I'd forgotten, and forgotten to tell Davix the news about his house's official dragon. If I told him now, he'd think I was a totally self-centred asshole. But if the dragons flew over, and she wasn't there, what was I going to say?

"She's what?"

"Beautiful." I turned away. "It will be great to see her again. Them. All of them. Hey, look, there's Tix-etnep-thon-dahé."

The old man sat on a low tree stump in the middle of the park, wrapped in a fringed, blue shawl, smiling up at the painting of Etnep. The kingsolver Flak was on his shoulder, tugging at the old man's earring with his beak.

Davix ran over, kneeling on one knee in front of him.

"Master-da! How did you get here? I would have fetched you if I knew you wanted to attend the morning prayers."

"I am happy to see you, D'gada-vixtet-thon." The old man put a hand on Davix's shoulder. "Do not worry yourself. I awoke very early, and the mule and I had a slow and pleasant journey. That's twice I've come to Cliffside in eight days. I will lose my hard-won reputation as a misanthrope. You look well, Dragon Groom. Flak tells me you had adventures and trials in Holy Farad'hil."

I doubted the bird was really his news source, though he did look pretty sharp for a bird.

"Yes, sir. I feel much better."

"No doubt my wayward lead apprentice has aught to do with your recovery. But I think you would do well to avoid the Prime Magistrate today." He reached up a bony old hand to feed his bird a piece of fruit.

"That's why we came to the Park of the Five for our prayers, Master-da."

Surprised, I asked Davix, "Wait, did something happen with you and Grav'nan-dahé? Are we avoiding him?"

The kingsolver opened its wings and cawed loudly. Tix-etnep-thon-dahé squinted into the distance and sighed.

"I fear your stratagem was in vain, Apprentice."

Grav'nan-dahé was striding into the circle now, followed by a couple of his stilt-hat priests. They all carried fancy leather volumes.

"Tarn's blood," Davix muttered. He looked around nervously. "Come on, X'risp'hin, let's go to the back of the crowd."

"We could just leave."

"No, I don't want to miss the prayers."

Why? I wasn't raised with any religion, and it was hard to imagine risking trouble just to say nice things to the dragons. Did they even know or care? Maybe they had some kind of baby monitor to listen in on the service. Grav'nan-dahé and his buddies were standing on a flat rock under the painting of Etnep, and we were positioned behind two tall people at the other end of the circle.

The service wasn't much fun—not even any good tunes—and my mind wandered to the previous night. I think I was trying to count from memory how many freckles Davix had on his lower back when I heard the Prime Mugwump's voice rise from its monotone.

"D'gada-vixet-thon, remain where you are." I snapped out of fantasyland fast. The service was over, and people were busy blessing each other.

"He saw us." I gasped.

Davix didn't answer. His face turned into an unreadable mask.

Approaching us, Grav'nan-dahé said, "It is less than two days since you and I last met, D'gada-vixet-thon. At the time, I was shocked by the change in your ways. I hoped my intervention might make you reflect on your behaviour. I am sad to see it has not. You are in danger of throwing away all you have worked for."

His beautiful, warm eyes grown cold and hard, Davix loudly answered, "I throw away nothing, Prime Magistrate. I am using all I have learned from my elders and making decisions for myself."

"Silence! You will speak if and only if I ask you a question."

I said, "Hey, easy. He didn't do anything wrong."

As I had learned the day before, Grav'nan-dahé no longer felt he owed me any special politeness. "Copper Guest, you will cease to involve yourself in matters you know nothing about."

I wanted to tell Grav'nan-dahé to fuck himself. But he was one of those people who just make your tongue tie itself in knots. Basically, I was a chickenshit and backed away, joining Kriz'mig, Grentz, and Stakrat in the crowd of onlookers. They didn't look any braver than me.

Grav'nan-dahé turned his spotlight-of-nasty back on Davix. "Counting your misdeeds would take me all day. But I will remark on one. The young men and women who dance in the competition do so for the glory of the great dragons. To dance, as you did, in a state of spiritual imbalance is to mock the gifts of our holy lords. You danced purely for your own glory. Were they not fair and equitable, the dragons would punish the People for your blasphemy."

Davix just stood there like a waxwork and took it. I wanted to throw my arms around him and tell him he was the best boy in the world.

Finally, Tix-etnep-thon-dahé stepped forward to speak. He seemed older and more feeble than ever.

"Prime Magistrate, this has been a trying time for my apprentice. He has known loss and confusion. Show him some patience." The kingsolver on his shoulder was glaring at Grav'nan-dahé like he wanted to fly over and peck out an eye.

"Atmospherics Master, your apprentice has not been at his post for many days. He has abandoned you, but your compassion blinds you to this insult. I will deal with the situation." He took a step closer to Davix. "D'gada-vixtet-thon. You will, without comment, turn and leave this place. You will return to your quarters to retrieve minimal supplies and leave Cliffside. You will undertake a forty-day retreat and daylight fast. You will reflect on your actions and change the course of your life. This is the last chance you have to make amends. Do you understand?"

Davix was still as a statue. The deadness of his eyes scared me. After a short pause, he gave a shaky nod and turned. He didn't look at me. He just walked away, pushing past people who were staring in shock at the scene. Then he was gone.

I stared up with hate at the Prime Magistrate, and still I didn't speak. He threw me a contemptuous look, like I was a mouse, or a single piece of mouse poop, and then turned oh so casually to talk to others in the crowd who were waiting for a chance to fawn over him up close and personal.

Stakrat put an arm around me, and I almost started crying.

"Just before Sur brought you back, Grav'nan-dahé and Davix had a confrontation."

"What kind of confrontation?"

"I heard Grav'nan-dahé slapped him. In public."

"I want to kill him," I hissed. "How does he get away with acting like that?"

My anger clearly upset Grentz. He said, "He's the Prime Magistrate. He wants what's best for the People. I love Davix, but he has to follow the law, the same as us."

I shot him eye daggers, and Kriz'mig got between us, as if I might start a fight.

"It's because Grav'nan-dahé also loves Davix," she said. "And feels betrayed by him."

"That's what he calls love?"

I dropped to the ground with my back against Sur's tree, wishing she was there to recite an inscrutable poem. My misery felt like tar in my stomach. Then someone tapped me on the shoulder. I was about to bark, "Leave me alone," when I looked up into a pair of twinkling, mischievous eyes, the eyes of the best, cutest guy in the realm, peeking around from behind the tree. He was smiling like the cat who ate the prize parakeet.

"Don't look so troubled, Dragon Groom," Davix said. "It's the Day of Jubilation!"

He pulled me to my feet, and I looked around to see if Grav'nan-dahé had heard. Of course he had.

"D'gada-vixtet-thon!" he screamed, his face red. Holding hands, we ran from the park, laughing, free, and perfect. Totally tangled.

Soon we were high up in the city in this tiny, broken old building with most of its roof missing. We were sitting on a straw mattress, our backs against the stone wall. My head rested on his shoulder, and his arm was around me. He had just told me a story that made everything worse.

"Do you think it's true?" I asked. "Grav'nan-dahé built a trap to kill the dragons?"

"I don't know. I don't even think Tix-etnep-thon-dahé is sure. I keep going over and over it in my head. On one level it makes sense. It would explain why sheep fog is still flowing from the Chend'th'nif. If Grav'nan-dahé believes Dragons are violating the spirit of the Law… The implications, X'risp'hin! For one thing, it would mean the Prime Magistrate is responsible for Rinby's death." I felt him shudder.

"Yeah, I hear you." I looked up at a mural Davix told me Kriz'mig was painting. The picture represented the four realms. Earth was the big mama in the middle, surrounded by her three kids: fire, water, and air. I looked at the Earth and thought about all the places I would like to show Davix, everything from a movie theatre to the shore of the Atlantic Ocean.

I kissed his cheek. "I'm sorry you have to go through this. What will Grav'nan-dahé do to you?"

"I don't know. My lapses are minor. Truly. Tix-etnep-thon-dahé will talk to him, calm him down. They're old, old friends."

He kissed my forehead. "I'm just glad I'm here with you now."

"Me too."

We lay down on the mattress, and things got serious fast. When we were done, I tucked myself back under his arm.

"D'gada-vixtet-thon," I said.

"Yes?"

"Just saying it. I never called you by your whole name before. 'Thon' is the old word for 'storm.' That stands for Atmospherics, right?"

"Correct."

"And Vixtet is your Dragon Lord. Lady."

He laughed. "Patron of my house, yes."

"So that leaves D'gada. Your name." I felt him tense up a bit. "Can I just call you that? D'gada?"

"No," he said, like he was kind of pissed off.

"What? Why not? It's a cool name: 'Hey, D'gada!'"

He pulled away. "Don't, it's embarrassing. It's too personal, like you're seeing me without my skin."

I sat up and looked at him. "I don't get it."

"Then I can't explain. It's our way in the Realm of Fire. Just… please."

"Okay, sorry," I whispered, kissing him softly on the mouth. "You sure no one knows about this place? We're safe from Grumpy-dahé?"

"Some of the apprentices come here, that's it." Bells rang out all over the city, and Davix's face lit up with excitement. "The dragons arrive!" He went to sit in the doorway, scanning the sky. "We'll be able to see from here, but no one will see us."

I didn't say anything. I had been working hard not to think about Vixtet and what I would say if she wasn't there. She wasn't going to be there, I knew it. She was probably already dead, and it felt like it was somehow my fault.

"Come here, quickly," he said. "The first moment they appear is the best."

I joined him reluctantly, sitting in front while he wrapped his arms and legs around me. The fog had, thankfully, thinned, leaving just a misty, cloud-filled sky. The moment seemed to stretch on and on. The whole of Cliffside was silent, like it was holding its breath. And then I saw Sur. She was high overhead, but clearly visible. Behind her was skinny Inby, flying an S-shaped course. Renrit was next, lumbering along with fast strokes of his wings. I wished I had been there to see them toss him from his window.

I recognized the next dragon by her picture, and relief washed through me. Vixtet, flying strong and steady. Cheers were rising from the city like when the home team scores. Davix was squeezing me so hard, I thought I'd squirt out of his arms like a watermelon seed.

After a gap in the formation, Queen Etnep came into view. She was the largest and most majestic of the dragons, and I gasped when I saw her. A noise was growing in my head. Gradually, it became words, poetry, incantation, in a form of dragon tongue so old, I only got the rough gist:

Sk'l'akh't attakla Khev'nin Dwark'a Kiir.—The ache of separation, the longing for union.

"Etnep…" I breathed, light-headed, like I was untethered from the earth, floating away. But Davix held me tight, and I came back to myself. "She's beautiful," I said, and I was shocked to feel a tear running down my face.

The dragons didn't stay long. They circled the city, and we lost sight of them for a bit. Then they were back, flying home to Farad'hil the way they had come. Night, descending swiftly, swallowed them whole. Davix and I stayed there in the doorway, not speaking. Lights winked on in the city, and still we didn't move.

Then there was a noise. Davix scrambled to his feet and peeked around the doorframe. He signalled me to be quiet. We slipped into the darkest corner of our little house and stayed absolutely still as the sound of footsteps approached.

It'll be okay, I told myself. *Davix has it under control.* But I was so wrong. Three figures were in the doorway, then in the room, carrying torchstone lanterns, lighting us up like mice on the kitchen counter.

They wore sashes and knife belts. Defence of Realm. One of them was Stakrat. She wouldn't meet our eyes.

I jumped forward, putting myself between them and Davix. "But his lapses! They're totally minor!" I shouted. They ignored me.

The lead man, a severe-looking guy with short hair and a scar under his eye, said, "D'gada-vixtet-thon, you are under arrest for insults against the DragonLaw. You will come with us. Any resistance will be answered with force."

CHAPTER 34: *The Day of Reckoning*

Night was falling like an axe. I followed behind the Defence of Realm officers who were walking on either side of Davix, marching him off to dragon jail. Stakrat was one of them, and I couldn't help totally hating her.

A third officer shadowed me, saying, "I have orders to escort you back to your quarters, Copper Guest." I ignored him and kept walking. My face was a stiff, angry mask, and after a while, started to actually hurt. I was afraid I'd start crying if I let up on the fury for even a second.

Word of the arrest had spread ahead of us, and by the time we reached the next square, a big group of hushed people were staring. That's where Kriz'mig ran up to me.

"X'risp'hin, don't worry," she said. "Tix-etnep-thon-dahé knows. He'll talk to Grav'nan-dahé and get Davix released."

"This afternoon in the park, *Grav'nan* wasn't too interested in what the old man had to say." I had deliberately left off the "dahé." My open disrespect shocked Kriz'mig. Good.

Davix and his two officers had pulled ahead during this conversation, and I was losing track of them in the crowd. I was about to run and catch up when I suddenly lost my will. What could I do on my own? Stick out my tongue at them? Write dirty graffiti on the prison building? I had to rely on the people who cared about Davix.

"Fine," I said to my escort. "Take me to my room." I turned back to Kriz'mig. "Sorry if I was a jerk. You'll send me a message if you find out anything, right?" She nodded solemnly and gave me a hug.

When we reached my room at the top of Etnep House, I was surprised to see another guard already standing on duty outside, a young woman with close-cropped hair and thick eyebrows. My officer gave her a head and heart gesture and left.

"Copper Guest," said the new guard. "The Prime Magistrate has requested you stay here until the end of *Sarensikar*, at which point, you will be escorted back to the Realm of Earth." She held the door to my room open.

"I'm a prisoner?"

"Please don't think of it that way, Copper Guest. The People love you and are grateful for your visit."

I'm the Dragon Groom, I wanted to shout. *Not the Copper Guest!* The Primate Maggot was getting his way right down the line. I glared at the guard with a stare as cold as a blue and white Popsicle, then went inside, slamming the door behind me. I heard a click. *Great. Locked in.*

The room felt smaller and more suffocating than ever, not a romantic fairy tale tower but a jail cell. It reminded me of when my family went to England and saw the Tower of London. I knew it had been a prison for rich traitors, and I was disappointed by what a low and ordinary building it was. I had been expecting a real tower—shiny black stone, fifty stories high, blocking out the sun. There should have been spiked gates and a moat. It should have been guarded by...well, dragons.

I sat on the bed and sulked until they brought me some dinner, the lock clicking again on their way out. I would have left the food untouched as a sign of protest, but I reminded myself I'd need my strength to save Davix. And it smelled really good. After dinner, I sulked until bedtime. As I fell asleep under the open window, I heard a sweet, high voice singing an unaccompanied lament:

As Tarn lay dying
Spear in her side,
The people crying,
Her arms opened wide

"Weep not, my children,
I have saved the realm
From Air and Water
In their armour and helm

"As I leave you, my People
Do not dwell on your pain.
Realms torn asunder
Will be made one again."

"Hey, shut it!" I yelled out the open window. "People are trying to sleep here!"

In the morning, they brought me breakfast and exchanged my chamber pot for a fresh one. Silently, I dedicated the departing excrement to Grav'nan. The door closed and clicked. I looked out the window, but my view was useless: rooftops in the foreground, and beyond it, the fog-shrouded valley. They would keep me here all day while Davix was…who knows what? Locked in a dungeon? Sent to the mines? Then Tiqokh would carry me home on the strands, and I'd never see him again, never feel his skin against mine. It was like I'd held the ultimate treasure in my hand, only to find out it wasn't mine at all—just pay-per-view.

"Tiqokh," I whispered. "Are you watching?" Of course not. Not when I *really* needed him. "Tiqokh!" I repeated, shouting this time, my outrage catching fire. I paced five fast circuits around the room and then pounded on the wooden door. "Let me out of here! You have no right to lock me in!" I leaned on the door and rattled the door handle, which, much to my shock, depressed easily. The door swung out into the hall, and I crashed forward on my hands and knees.

The guard outside immediately jumped to his feet. It was a different guard now, an older guy with uneven teeth.

"Do you need something, Copper Guest?"

Still angry, but also feeling stupid, I glared at him as I climbed to my feet. I stepped back inside the room and closed the door again, listening to the mysterious click. I pulled the door open again. "Wasn't this locked?"

"No, Copper Guest."

I glared more, blushing at the same time. "If I leave, will you try and stop me?"

"No, Copper Guest, I wouldn't presume…I wouldn't dare…"

"Right. So. Um, I'm leaving. And you can't stop me." I closed the door behind me and saw a little table next to the door wobble on its uneven legs, the short leg tapping the floor. *Click.*

I ran down and down the stairs and out of the castle, into the final day of *Sarensikar*. I didn't know where to go, so I just started wandering out of the Retreat of Tarn and through the streets. Day Three's holy feature were these flowers that looked like dandelions in their white and fluffy stage, except they were bigger and had blue stems. Everyone was saying prayers over the flowers and then blowing the tufted heads to send the seeds flying.

I stopped to watch, but everyone acted nervous around me. No one greeted or asked for blessings or anything. They clearly knew about Davix's arrest, and the whole realm probably knew Davix and me were doing it. I had become tainted by the whole messy affair, and it felt disturbingly like when Sylvia told the school about me. But this time I didn't care. This wasn't about me. I had to save Davix.

I didn't know who to ask for help until, finally, this man and woman approached. They were holding hands, leaning into each other. In love. I had only spent a few days in this land where male/female pairs are rarely seen, and already this couple's boring, old heterosexual affection looked bizarre.

"Dragon Groom?" the man said, and I felt grateful to be called that, like it was my real name. "We wanted to bring you our greetings and blessings."

In her free hand, the woman carried a bunch of the special dandelions. She said, "We are so sorry for the troubles you and D'gada-vixtet-thon are experiencing. We saw you leaving the dance together, and your affection reminded us of our own when we were young."

"Thanks," I mumbled. And even though their sweetness was welcome, seeing all that happiness while Davix and I were about to be ripped apart made me want to scream. "So, how come you guys are allowed to be all touchy-feely?"

The man beamed a satisfied smile at the woman. "We are truly blessed by the Dragon Lords. From early in our youth, we were desperately tangled for each other. When the Arbiter of Blood declared us compatible, it was almost a miracle."

"We are one of only three opposite-sex couples who live together as spouses," said the woman. "We have already produced two fine children for the glory of the dragons."

On Earth, I would have guessed them to be in their early thirties. The guy was kind of a DILF, with his muscular arms and dusting of grey hair at his temple. I looked at them again and saw how *right* they seemed together. I imagined myself at their age and imagined it was Davix standing with me arm in arm. Maybe we'd have a few kids, too, or maybe not. But I definitely wanted to be part of a couple. With Davix. I felt my eyes tearing up.

"Please," I asked. "Can you tell me where they took him? I have to try and fix this."

The woman put a hand on my arm, and it reminded me of the way my mom would touch me when I was upset, just a small contact to let me know I wasn't alone.

"I believe you will find him at the Citadel," she said, drawing me out to the middle of the street where we could see over the surrounding buildings. She pointed to the highest part of the city, higher even than

Etnep House. "Grav'nan-dahé will be pronouncing sentence in the afternoon, and the Citadel is the most consequential place he could choose."

I took a deep breath to calm myself. "But Davix is already there?"

"Probably," the man said. "There are holding cells in the Citadel for those who break the law."

"I better run, then. Thanks for helping me."

The woman took my arm again. "Dragon Groom, wait. Join us in the blessing for the third day of *Sarensikar*, the Day of Reckoning. It will bring us all good luck." She handed me a flower, gave one to her husband, and kept the third for herself.

I held it up in front of my face. "Do I blow on it?"

The man said, "Wait until I've said the blessing. Oh, Mighty Dragons, as these petals fly far and wide, so may you lift the fog from before our eyes and reveal the perfect balance of your world."

"May it be so," said his wife, and the three of us blew.

I watched the little parachutes floating away. "You really think the fog will lift tonight?" They nodded, their faces solemn and filled with hope. Wouldn't it be great if they were right?

CHAPTER 35: *Blood in the Citadel*

Whatever it was planning to do later, the fog was still dense around me as I hiked up to the Citadel. When it parted momentarily, I caught glimpses of heavy rectangular walls that looked like they really meant business. The huge gates of wood and iron stood open, and just inside them I met Grentz.

"X'risp'hin!" he called. "I was hoping you'd find your way."

Clammy with sweat from my climb, I steadied myself with a hand on his muscled shoulder and caught my breath. "Is Davix here?"

"Yeah, follow me."

Inside the gate, the street continued rising steeply, but now it was banked by those steep stone walls. The road ended in a wide courtyard with a square tower in each corner. Walkways criss-crossed the inner surface of the walls with slit windows at eye level. For archers, I knew, like in that medieval first-person shooter game I used to play.

"What's the story of this place, Grentz?"

"Back in the days when the strands were strong, the Realm of Fire was often attacked by the other realms. All the People gathered in the Citadel to fend off the foe."

I looked up at the open sky. "But dragons fly. How do the walls help?"

"Most of the time, the wars were fought with ground troops. But if an attack came from above, the People went down those stairs to the bunker." He pointed to a half dozen stairwells scattered across the courtyard, the steps vanishing into the darkness below. The entrances were all blocked off by wooden barricades, like there was construction happening. Grentz pointed to the far corner of the Citadel. "Come on, Davix is being held in that tower."

We found Kriz'mig there, dressed less flouncy today, in a kind of green silk pyjamas. She was talking with Stakrat, who stood one step above her in the narrow doorway of the tower, wearing her knife and uniform sash. When Stakrat saw me, she blushed.

"Copper Guest…" she began.

I hated her calling me that. It was Grav'nan's name for me, and it told me which side she was on. "I want to talk to Davix, Stakrat."

"Not possible, I'm sorry. I really am. You'll see D'gada-vixtetthon when he's brought out for his sentencing."

Kriz'mig touched my arm. "They won't let anyone see him. I've been trying to get in since first bell. It's crazy. All he did was miss a few days of work!"

I took a step back and looked up at the tower. A small crowd was watching us now. I didn't care. In fact, I was glad.

"Is Korda up there?" I asked.

Stakrat looked startled by my question. "Well, yes, but…"

"Call her. Tell her the Dragon Groom is here."

Stakrat lowered her voice. "X'risp'hin, there's nothing she can do. Nothing anyone can. If the Prime Magistrate says—"

I did a slow circle, taking in the crowd, calling out in the most arrogant voice I could manage, "Tell Korda the Dragon Groom demands an audience!" I realized by using that name I was openly declaring my opposition to Grav'nan. The thought made me afraid, but I tried to keep the fear from showing.

Stakrat looked at the growing crowd watching intently. She was gripping and releasing the handle of her knife while she made up her mind. "All right. Just…just wait a minute." She went inside, closing the heavy door behind her with a low thud. The *clunk* that followed? That's what a *real* lock sounded like.

I turned to Kriz'mig and Grentz, expecting some kind of high fives for my little victory, but Grentz was looking at the ground, and Kriz'mig's mouth was compressed into a distressed prune. Soon, the door unlocked and flew open. Korda, standing on the step, stared down at me with a look of irritation I'd seen from authority figures all too often in my short life.

"There's something you wish to say to me, Copper Guest?"

"Yes! Why is Davix under arrest? He didn't do anything wrong."

"He is guilty of many serious breaches of the DragonLaw. The least of these is disobeying a direct order from the Prime Magistrate to cease contact with you and to leave the city."

"But those orders weren't even about Davix. Grav'nan is just taking it out on him because he doesn't like me." Leaving off his

"-dahé" definitely had a reaction. Everyone's eyes widened except Korda's, who closed hers and sighed.

"Copper Guest…" she began, a note of sympathy in her voice.

"Come on, you know it's true! Just let Davix go." It felt like negotiating with my parents. *You know, if I had the more expensive laptop, I could also learn game development.*

Korda stood up tall, looking past me at the gathering crowd. "You don't have all the facts, Copper Guest. I suggest you return to your room."

I also turned to our audience. "So Grav'nan can whisk me out of here tomorrow without ever seeing Davix again? Not going to happen."

"It is not our place to question the wisdom of the Prime Magistrate."

"Why don't you try thinking for yourself for a change?"

"I am a soldier! *Ekdahi* demands I obey my superiors and defend the DragonLaw."

"Even if the DragonLaw is wrong? Or in this case, Grav'nan is wrong?"

Korda abruptly stepped down from the step and threw an arm around me, leading me away from the tower to a nearby bench.

"On the Realm of Earth," she said, "There must be laws you are compelled to obey."

I looked back toward the tower door, like this might be a trick to get me out of the way. But Korda was a straight shooter, so I decided to trust her. "Well, yeah. You can't just go around stealing, or…or peeing in swimming pools."

"And there are those who enforce these laws, mete out the punishments for inappropriate urination?"

"But," I said, "now you're talking about bad guys, criminals. Not kids like me and Davix."

"So, in your life, you answer to no one?"

"Well, yeah, my parents—um, genetic forbearers—I guess. The school principal."

"So, if you were urinate in this public pool, there would be consequences."

"I guess I might get suspended from school. Or grounded or something."

"Correct, because how would society function if everyone made water wherever they pleased? The smell alone would be distracting and dispiriting."

"Can we change examples, please?"

"The point is, we must bow to some authority if the world is to have order. The DragonLaw is true, and Grav'nan-dahé its arbiter." I was filled with that kind of mad frustration where you can't find the words, can't even squeeze your thoughts through all the dried toothpaste at the top of your mind.

"But what if the authority can't be trusted?" I sputtered. "What if Grav'nan's the criminal?"

Her eyebrows came together. "What are you saying, Copper Guest?"

I couldn't tell if she was angry or alarmed, but then Grentz yelled, "X'risp'hin!" and I swung around to see a line of people emerge from the tower door. Between two pair of guards, one in front and one behind, stood a barefoot Davix, his hands bound together in front of him with thick rope.

"Davix!" I shouted, running to him. The four guards turned their spears sideways in a slick, coordinated move, forming a wall around their prisoner.

"X'risp'hin," he said, and his voice sounded rough, like he'd been crying, like he hadn't slept since his arrest. "Go away. I don't want you to see me like this."

"Don't be an idiot," I told him, reaching out a hand, but the guards blocked it with their spear handles. "I'm with you. If they throw you in jail, I'm coming, too!"

Davix actually smiled, but then his eyes filled with tears and he looked away.

"Move on," he told the guards. The group got back in formation and walked across the courtyard, the crowd parting as they advanced.

"Davix!" I shouted again, but Korda had her hand on my shoulder. I snapped at her, "Isn't this kind of over the top? He's not a murderer. He's just a kid who skipped study hall."

"Copper Guest, I'll leave the choice up to you. Do as D'gada-vixtet-thon asks and return to your quarters, or—"

"I'm staying," I said with a good dose of F-you in the intonation.

At one end of the courtyard was a wooden stage with a small dais in front, like where a preacher would make a sermon, and beside the stage, a wooden pole was sunk into the paving stones. Davix was marched up the eight steps to stand at the centre of the stage, while the guards took places at the four corners. The crowd had grown, maybe to a couple hundred people. Some of them were dressed formally, like they had an official role, but most were just ordinary folks. They looked grim. I doubted *Sarensikar* usually ended like this.

Growing murmurs announced Grav'nan's arrival. He was marching briskly across the courtyard from the same tower where Davix had been held. The Prime Asshole stepped up onto the dais with his back to Davix. He was frowning into a grace book, opening and closing it and turning it over.

"Someone take this," he said. "It's not working."

Behind me, Korda murmured, "That's odd…"

Some little minion took the busted book, and Grav'nan smoothed out his black silk robe, like there was going to be a photo shoot. Was he enjoying this? My anger was as black as his robes.

Grav'nan's voice carried, cold and crisp, across the courtyard. "We gather here in the name of the DragonLaw, in the sight of the Holy Five who watch us ever and guard our lives. Today, we address blasphemies against the DragonLaw committed by one of the People."

I recognized other apprentices from Atmospherics in the crowd, the kids who worked on the top floor of the tower. And off to the side was their master, Tix-etnep-thon-dahé. He leaned heavily on his stick, looking extra old and broken, squinting and blinking as if he couldn't quite bring the scene into focus. On his shoulder, Flak took it all in with cold spite.

"The prisoner has been found guilty of seven separate counts of wilful transgression against the DragonLaw," droned Grav'nan, who never seemed to get sick of his own voice. "He entered areas of Etnep House forbidden to him to meet with the Copper Guest. He neglected his duties to his discipline, showing disrespect to his master and to the holy balance of the realm. He disobeyed orders to undertake a pilgrimage of self-reflection. He disobeyed orders to abjure the company of the Copper Guest."

Grav'nan said all this like they were major crimes, but they were bullshit. Just the kind of stuff any kid does during a bad week. I was furious, but also, I felt kind of guilty. Davix was mostly in trouble for doing stuff with me.

The Prime Hoo-ha paused dramatically, and then shocked everyone including me, saying, "But these actions, while demanding punishment, pale in comparison to the final crimes. D'gada-vixtet-thon is guilty of speaking in support of the heretical belief in prophecy."

The crowd starting whispering to each other, and I felt myself growing cold.

"And most serious of all, D'gada-vixtet-thon did deliberately seek to taint the purity of the DragonLaw by accessing his master's grace book and transmitting false information directly to the great dragons."

This made people gasp, and even I got confused. What the hell had Davix done? I tried to catch his eye, but his head was hanging on his chest, his hair covering his face.

Tix-etnep-thon-dahé stepped forward. "Prime Magistrate! The fault is mine. I exposed the youth to my own wild theorizing and inadvertently drove him to rash action!"

Grav'nan looked utterly satisfied. "Silence, honoured master. The Apprentice's actions were his and his alone. Perhaps you must answer for your actions within your own soul, but he must answer to the law." Grav'nan raised a hand in the air, and the crowd shut right up. "The prisoner's crimes are even now being transcribed in the great DragonLaw as a lesson for future generations. That leaves only the sentence. D'gada-vixtet-thon!"

Davix raised his head, and I don't think I'd ever seen anyone braver. He held Grav'nan's gaze without faltering as the old crow cawed in triumph.

"You are hereby stripped of your recent rank as Lead Apprentice of Atmospherics. You will leave this guild permanently. Your future and diminished role will be determined on your return from exile."

I saw someone else crossing from the tower, but I ignored him. Korda's hand tightened on my shoulder, like she was restraining me.

"With but the most humble possessions, you will leave Cliffside today to embark on a solitary pilgrimage to the most distant of the Silence Farms, at the anti-spinward extreme of Chend'th'nif. There, you will spend three full cycles in solitary prayer and contemplation. It is hoped this time of reflection will cleanse your spirit of the rebellion that makes our holy Dragon Lords weep."

Davix finally broke eye contact, turning to look at me. And I don't know if it was really some psychic thing or just my dumb, romantic imagination, but I swear we could each other's hearts talking: *I will not forget you. Your voice, your laughter, your kisses, your touch, the oh-my-god orgasms. The way we fought and the way we made up—if this is the last time we see each other, still, we will always be together. Tangled.*

But Grav'nan wasn't finished. Grav'nan was never finished. "D'gada-vixtet, whose name will not be spoken during the entirety of his exile, must also be made an example today." Something in Grav'nan's voice, a kind of shaking excitement.

I was suddenly aware of the guy I had spotted before, crossing from the tower. He was dressed in a long purple robe so dark it was almost black. On his head was a tall, flat-topped hat, and a veil covered most of his face. He was carrying some kind of high, narrow container with a couple of sticks poking out the top. When he came to a halt beside the stage, water slopped out the top of the container, splashing on the cobblestones.

"The seriousness of the prisoner's crimes must be answered publicly," Grav'nan said.

What the hell does that mean? I wondered with mounting fear.

"The prisoner will undergo the offering of the flesh. Ten strokes." The crowd gasped, and I remembered Davix telling me about the bad old days when they used to beat people in the public square.

"What?" I said out loud, but my voice was lost in the rolling sea of chatter. "*What?*" I said louder, as the guards in red took rough hold of Davix and hustled him off the stage toward the pole that stood beside it.

He was staggering as if his legs couldn't support him, and before they turned him around to face the pole, I caught one glimpse of his frantic, terrified eyes. They stripped his shirt off, raised his tied wrists, and hung him on a hook high up the pole, leaving him straining for balance on his tiptoes.

When the veiled guy lifted one of the dripping sticks from the container and shook the water from it with a sickening *whish, whish*, I truly freaked out.

"What the fuck? You can't do that!"

Some people in the crowd turned and hurried out of the square, but most of them were glued in place, shock or disgust or fascination on their faces.

"Hey! What's wrong with you people? You can't let this happen." No one would look me in the eye. "Korda! Master Tix, help!"

"There is nothing anyone can do," Korda said in a tight voice as the guy in purple approached Davix "That is the sentence of the Prime Magistrate."

I screamed a lot of things—a bunch of swearing, and then Davix, his face against the wood, shouted, "X'risp'hin, leave. Go! I don't want you to see this." And his voice was scary, hoarse, in a place beyond anger or regret—heartbroken, allbroken.

And that's when Grav'nan spoke directly to me in a voice cold with triumph. "You heard his words, Copper Guest. The last strand tying you to this world is broken. The Transgressor himself has no use for you." To the guy in purple, he shouted, "Carry out the sentence!"

"Stop," said my voice. "Stop! The Dragon Groom *commands* you."

And it worked. The guy with the stick actually turned and looked at me. But now that I had everyone's attention, I had to do something. I shrugged off Korda's hand and walked across the cobblestones until I was standing in front of the dais. I turned my back to Grav'nan and spoke to the crowd.

"So, I've got stuff to say," I began, my heart pounding. "You all know there's been a prophecy. I was brought from the Realm of Earth because of it, and it's really terrible, since a dragon is supposed to die. Grav'nan says there's no prophecy, but I was in the mountains with the old prophet couple. I was there with Sur!" Mentioning Sur was a good move. No cred like dragon cred.

"Grav'nan wants to send me back to Earth. But how can he take that chance? If a dragon dies, I have to be here to mate with Queen Etnep or the Five will be, you know, four." I looked around the square, trying in vain to spot Tiqokh. Things usually went better when he was around. In fact, there were no mixed beings to be seen. Weird. I jumped when Grav'nan spoke behind me in a low, seething voice.

"Leave this place, blasphemer," he said. "Koras-inby-kir-dahé, remove him."

More of Korda's guards had come to stand beside her, and I glared back at them all, my heart beating hard. "Don't touch me. I am the Holy Dragon Groom!" The guards looked to her for guidance, but she just stood there with her hand on her knife. And that's when I turned and pointed at Grav'nan, my enemy and the enemy of love. "Why do you think *he* denies the prophecy? Why do you think *he* refuses to call me by my proper title? Maybe Davix isn't the bad guy here. Maybe there's someone who is actually planning to *kill* dragons…the Prime Magistrate!"

The crowd's reaction to my accusation even impressed me. Wails, not only of anger and indignation, but of pain, like someone watching their dog get nailed by a car in the supermarket parking lot. Some people even fell to their knees. Maybe I'd gone too far, but now it couldn't be unsaid. I was desperately trying to remember the details Davix had told me up in the little clubhouse before he was arrested. It was pretty fuzzy in my head, since I'd mostly been focussed on holding his hand and thinking how he looked cute as a puppy when he was sad.

I pushed on. "Back when Grav'nan was young—yeah, I can hardly imagine it either—he found a book by a guy who wanted to kill dragons. A guy named…" Brain freeze. Improv. "Toe-Bro."

"What?" Grav'nan said.

"Bro-lo!"

"Are you referring to the heretic, Brontlo?" His voice was coldly amused, which didn't bode well.

"Right, yeah, Brontlo. You done interrupting?" I turned my back on him again, like I was actually confident. "Brontlo wanted to kill the dragons and so does Grav'nan."

A man in the crowd called out in rage. "Our Prime Magistrate teaches us only love for the great dragons and their holy law. He would never do anything to harm them."

"Yeah, but Brontlo loved the DragonLaw, too. He thought the Dragons in his time were corrupting it. Maybe that's what the Prime Magistrate thinks."

Grav'nan's voice was low and hard and seemed to be made of contempt. "You are a fool, Earth boy. The great DragonLaw had yet to be written in the days of Brontlo. Carry out the sentence."

Shit. I spun around to see purple man approaching Davix, his whip stick raised. My chances were drying up. I had to hurry.

"Up in the Chend'th'nif there's a dragon trap like the one Brontlo planned. That's why we have all this sheep fog. It's the last day of *Sarensikar* and it's supposed to disappear at sunset, but you wait and see. It won't, because of Grav'nan and his trap."

Another audible gasp and moan rose from the crowd, and that was it for Grav'nan's cool. He jumped off his dais and grabbed me where my bicep would be if I had one. The man was like a hundred and sixty years old, but he dragged me squirming back to where Korda and the guards stood. He was screaming, red in the face.

"Get this miserable creature out of my sight lest I do something to offend the Dragon Lords!"

He threw me to the ground at their feet, and my knees hit hard. I cried out in pain and looked up at Korda. Her face was all kinds of confused.

"Rinby knew!" I shouted. "She had secret data about the dragon trap. Now she's dead, and Grav'nan stopped the investigation!" But who was listening anymore? I had fucked up my chance, and now Davix would pay the price.

The Prime Magistrate screamed down at me. "You are the poison that has infected our land! And worse, you have infected a youth of great promise. D'gada-vixtet's life is ruined thanks to you."

I tried to catch a glimpse of Davix through my tear-filled eyes, but surrounded by a forest of legs and robes, I couldn't see anything. I felt like I was alone at the bottom of a well, looking up at all these faces, and no one was going to throw me a rope before I drowned. Below us in the city, bells started ringing.

Grav'nan spun around to face the crowd, his robe slapping me in the face like this was a bad comedy.

"We have lost our way!" he called to his People. "This miserable creature is right. *Sarensikar* will close, but until this poison is expelled from our realm, the fog will not lift. We will be a People without peace and balance, lost in the obfuscating mist."

I craned my neck around him to see how the crowd was taking all this, and what I saw was a couple hundred people gone silent in shock, all looking our way. But they were looking past us. Something was very wrong. I got to my feet, and me, Grav'nan, Korda, and the guards turned in unison and watched as a man lurched into the courtyard from the direction of the gate.

He was still on his feet, but barely. The skin of his chest and arm was shredded and bloody, his shirt in tatters. He stopped moving and fell to his knees. Korda pulled out her knife and stepped into a wide-legged stance, eyes scanning the square.

"We are attacked," the wounded man said, his gasping voice piercing the silence. "Air!"

And that's when the thing literally dropped into our lives. And it was all kinds of WTF, like the wrongpunch line got attached to a joke. It jumped from the wall of the Citadel, landing gracefully on the stone courtyard. What was it? It was shaped like a human and dressed like one, in red and black leather. But its face wasn't human. It was a cat's face—and not a sweet, meme cat. No, it was scarred, one ear half chewed off, patches of brindle fur missing. And the sight of those pissed-off, alley cat eyes sitting on top of a human-shaped body was so intensely wrong, I wanted to throw up.

The cat stared at us all, pinning us in place like we were hypnotized, and spoke in a voice that was never built for the beauty of the Tongue of Fire.

"*so so. too late for humans, too late for dragons. the time of triumph and blood is now NOW.*" And then in one quick motion, it lifted the wounded man up by his hair and slashed open his throat with its claws. A geyser of blood hit the stones with a wet slap.

CHAPTER 36: *We Are All Lost in the Fog*

As the dead man crashed face first into his own spilled blood, I could hardly pick out my own scream from the general wail of terror. In fact, everything that happened in the next few minutes was the action of a crowd reacting as one big, frightened animal. No actual thinking seemed possible in that fog of shock. I only knew I had to get somewhere safe. I scrambled over unnamed obstacles, not stopping to wonder if some of them were people.

The world of order had collapsed into incoherent flashes of horror: running feet, straining hands, wild eyes, and cat soldiers. More and more of them dropping from the walls. How many were there? Three? Eight? Twenty? They were vicious and efficient, and almost defied gravity as they leaped and slashed, corralling us toward the middle of the courtyard.

Air! the dead man had said. This was an attack from the Realm of Air! Was this Grav'nan's doing? Did he bring these monsters here?

And then I heard Grav'nan's voice, shrieking above the chaos. "Leave this realm, beasts of heresy! There is no place for you in the DragonLaw!" Defence of Realm guards were pulling him to the ground, protecting him with their bodies. But if these cats were part of his plan, why did he seem so shocked?

"Form a line! Attack stance," Korda called. "Weapons ready, await my command!"

Yes! Defence of Realm was going to save us! Two guards attacked a cat soldier, stabbing at it with spear and knife. But the unarmed cat tossed one aside like she was a toddler and leaped at the other, tearing his throat out with its teeth.

Then my name being called.

By Davix.

In all that spinning mayhem, he was still hung by his hands, face against the pole. Before I could think better of the plan, I was racing to him, shouting his name, Grentz suddenly running beside me.

"Get him down. I'll defend you both," Grentz shouted, pulling off his scarf and loading a stone into it to make an improvised weapon.

"Help me!" Davix screamed, twisting his neck sideways to find me. I wrapped my arms around him from behind. The sweat of his bare back soaked my face as I heaved him upward so he could free his hands. We strained and squirmed, and I wished I'd taken Altman's advice and worked out sometimes, but then suddenly Davix was free, tumbling to the ground on top of me.

"Are you okay? Are you okay?" I shouted, as he climbed off me, as if any of this could be okay.

"Grentz, don't!" Davix screamed. Grentz was swinging at a cat soldier with his useless weapon. It was the first cat, the nasty brindle that had started this chaos. The cat-man dodged each swipe of the scarf weapon without apparent effort, toying with Grentz, taunting him.

"*weak and slow is the realm of fire,*" it hissed. "*living for luxury instead of war.*"

And then with a lazy, savage blow, it toppled the sweet, strong boy. Time slowed to a crawl as an arc of blood rose high in the air, shining in a sliver of light that had pierced the fog like a slice of hope, even as Grentz's body fell backward and hit the ground with an ugly thud. The cat licked its bloody hand with a mottled pink tongue. Davix and I huddled on the ground and held each other, our breath a single pumping bellows.

"Don't move, don't move," Davix whispered. I could feel him shaking. Or was it me?

Screams and the clang of metal. The smell of iron hanging on the air like a bloody nose. To our left, I saw that three guards had killed a cat, and for the first time in my life, I felt the satisfaction of violence.

"Kill them! Kill them all!" I screamed.

A sickening change in air pressure made my ears pop and my stomach flip. The fog-shrouded sky, already blood-red with sunset, suddenly got darker. Every human and beast in the courtyard of the citadel went silent as a dragon appeared over the high stone walls, roaring like a volcano.

It was nothing like the dragons of Farad'hil. It dwarfed any of them in size and sickness. Its legs were long like a horse's. But there were too many. I counted four legs on one side and three on the other, legs that ended not in hooves, but in talons like a raptor. The dragon's body and wings were more bone than flesh, shining bone over which rippled a flowing skin made of wind and smoke. The dragon was a storm front of screaming tornados, and we were the trailer park going down in its path.

Then it saw me.

"*IT IS AS RRRRHAARSS THE GROOOOM OF FIRE SHUUUUHARRRRR THE BLOODBONE KESSSSSSSRSSSSS.*"

The dragon's voice was part of the wind that surrounded it, a modulated shriek inside a deafening howl. The language it spoke was some ugly cousin of the Tongue of Fire, but even if I didn't understand every word, I knew the dragon was talking to me as it moved my way.

"Help us!" Davix called, and Korda and three guards broke off from the battle to run our way. Cat soldiers leaped between us and our rescuers, holding them off.

"Begone, creatures of Air!" Korda screamed at them. "This land belongs to the dragons of Farad'hil!" And while I really applauded the sentiment, our rescuers couldn't get past the cats. The wind grew louder and a shadow gathered above us as the dragon of Air drifted closer.

Korda and her guards could barely stand in the rising wind, much less fight. Above the howl, I heard her yell, "Retreat!" and she and her guards did.

"No!" Davix cried. "Come back!"

Hunching low against the wind, the claws of their feet gripping the paving stones, the cats too backed away as the dragon floated over us on its portable tornados, one mighty talon opening. I could have yelled like Davix was yelling, but something was already happening inside me. I was abandoning myself to my fate. Abandoning myself as I had when I agreed to this whole trip to the Realm of Fire to be the Dragon Groom, as I had when I'd opened myself up to love with Dražen and Altman, and finally with Davix. No regrets about that last one.

As the dragon descended, I let go of Davix's hand and roughly shoved him aside. I crawled up the steps of the stage and struggled to my feet, arms wide, confronting my fate alone. It was me the dragon wanted. It would just kill Davix.

The claws circled around me and squeezed, the sharp edges cutting into my flesh, the pressure forcing the breath from my lungs. Everything was wind, blinding me, howling like a hundred mocking voices. Helpless mouse that I was, the dragon of Air carried me off into the sky.

PART V

WAR

CHAPTER 37: *The Net Closes*

"X'risp'hin!"

The dragon of Air was clearing the walls of the Citadel and already vanishing into the fog, the Dragon Groom in its talons. Yet Davix raced up the steps, as if he could still pull his fleshmate free from the grip of fate. He tripped on the last step and crashed to the floor of the stage, trying to cushion his fall with his hands still tied together.

Turning on his back, straining to see in the dimming twilight, Davix again cried, "X'risp'hin!" Nothing made sense. He was back on the stage where he had only minutes earlier been a prisoner, his life shattered, like a clay pot dropped in a moment of clumsy inattention. That story already felt like a piece of another lifetime.

"X'risp'hin!" he called a third time, rising to his knees and reaching his bound hands into the gloom. A pair of strong arms circled him and dragged him down the steps, into the shadows against the stage wall.

"Stay down, you fool!" Stakrat hissed in his ear. "The cats attack out of nowhere, at any time." Davix snapped out of his delirium, waking into a nightmare of terrified screams and running feet.

"We have to save X'risp'hin," he moaned, struggling to get free of her.

"We have to not die first, okay? Now hold still." Stakrat unsheathed her knife and sawed through the rope that bound his hands. "Remain here and let Defence of Realm handle this."

She left him clinging to the shadows, shaking, trying to stay as small as he could. But after a minute, during which every cry from the People made his heart jump, he knew he couldn't just hide. He peeked around the corner of the stage and saw Grentz lying out in the open, vulnerable to attack. Davix knew if he stopped to consider his actions, he would lose his nerve, so he scrambled from his hiding place on hands and feet until he was crouched beside his friend.

"Grentz! It's okay, I'm here." Grentz lay crumpled, one arm twisted under him, the other flung across his face. Davix turned him over, and the words of comfort died on his lips. Grentz's eyes were open, unfocussed, his face white but for the sticky clot of dark blood at his temple.

A passage from the DragonLaw flashed through Davix's mind. "When the spirit leaves the body to journey beyond the realms, all that remains is the lonely flesh, an empty gesture, tribute and reminder." He had to clamp both hands over his mouth to keep from screaming. It was too much to bear. He wanted to curl up and let the sobs and tremors wrack his body, but he dragged Grentz's body, panting and cursing, until they were back in the shadows by the stage.

Again, he lost track of time. When he returned to himself, the Citadel had gone quiet. Only low whispers and moans drifted across the air. In the glow of torches, he saw guards armed with knives, spears, and bows, standing in a rough circle to protect the stunned People who were huddled together in the centre of the courtyard.

Davix rose from his hiding place and caught Kriz'mig's eye. Hunched like she was hurrying through a hailstorm, she ran to him. Her hair had come loose from its clips and fallen into her smudged face. The silk of her clothing was torn at the elbows and knees.

She saw Grentz's corpse and burst into tears. Davix held her, asking, "Are those cats gone?"

"No. They're up on the walls, pacing back and forth, watching us." He looked up and caught glimpses of glowing, yellow eyes. A shiver passed through him. Kriz'mig led him away from Grentz's body, and they joined the People, a few hundred sitting stony-faced or crying, hugging their friends or their own drawn-up knees. Some nodded to Davix, but some just stared into the distance with empty eyes.

"What's happening down in the city?" he asked, and a woman named Dral'gofrin answered. She had taught him how to tie knots as a child.

"We heard screams. There might be fighting. But the mixed beings are down there. I'm sure they will defeat the invaders."

"Unless the cats have killed them," a man said. He was holding a blood-soaked rag to his arm.

Davix shook his head. "That's impossible. Even five of those horrors couldn't defeat a bidahéna. Has anyone sent word to Farad'hil?"

The man said, "The grace books have gone dark. And if any

kingsolvers were dispatched, we haven't seen them." Davix realized this man was the guard who had been tasked with beating him. The man's ceremonial hat and veil were now discarded, and he looked ridiculous in his shiny copper gown, like a child playacting.

A cry rose from the crowd as a cat leaped from the wall. The guards all whirled and raised their knives.

"Wait!" Korda yelled. "Do not strike without my orders."

The cat didn't even acknowledge her or her guards. It paraded itself in front of the frightened people, waving a clawed paw and hissing.

"now now the humans know their flesh is soft, their dragons too weak to protect them." It was the cat that had appeared first and started all this terror. Davix recognized the voice, though he had been tied to the pole with his back to the action. It lunged at a woman holding her infant, and she screamed. The cat hissed in contempt and pulled back without striking, strutting in front of the cowering humans.

From the centre of the group, Grav'nan-dahé leaped to his feet.

"Creature of Air! Beast who knows not the meaning of balance! Return to your realm before you are destroyed. You are nothing beside the beauty and majesty of our sacred DragonLaw and the Dragon Lords who love us." The cat stared his way and hissed a warning, but Grav'nan-dahé continued. "Does it pain you and your grotesque dragons to see the beauty of our realm? Do you envy the contentment of our lives?"

Davix watched with fascination. If the cat killed the Prime Magistrate, would he mourn, after all that had happened? What duty did he still owe to the teacher who had banished him?

Korda hurried to Grav'nan-dahé. "Prime Magistrate. I must ask you sit down. Do not provoke the enemy."

"I will stand," he shouted back. "I am the living representative of the law, and I will not be silenced by twisted blasphemies from across the strands!" At first he had seemed calm, but now Davix heard the hysterical quaver in his voice.

Up on the walls, the cats were still squatting, as if ready to pounce. Davix stood quickly and walked a crooked path through the frightened People until he stood beside Grav'nan-dahé.

He grabbed his arm. "Old man, do as Korda says." The Prime Magistrate turned to him with an indignant frown, but when he saw it was Davix, his face twisted in confusion, and he did indeed look old and weak.

"Personally," Davix whispered into his ear, "I don't care what happens to you, but the People need your leadership. Besides, the grace books are dead. Your final speech won't even end up in the DragonLaw."

Teacher and acolyte stared into each other's faces like they were grappling, seeing who would surrender first. After a long moment, Grav'nan-dahé allowed himself to be helped back down to the paving stones.

The cat slapped his paws on his leather vest. *"smart smart is the old man, no longer holy, his claws torn out. all humans will be silent and await their orders. new destiny, new lords, yes yes."*

When the beast left, Davix toured the miserable crowd. Someone gave him a handful of dried fruit, and he ate gratefully. Back near the greenward wall, a makeshift hospital was being set up to treat those wounded in the attack. There he found two of the younger apprentices from Atmospherics sitting with an injured friend.

"Davix," said one, jumping to his feet. "Are you all right?"

"None of us are all right, Zent'r. But I'm as well as can be expected."

The other apprentice said, "We're sorry for what happened to you. Before, I mean. With Grav'nan-dahé. That wasn't just. That wasn't balance."

Davix was amazed how young they looked. He was only two cycles older, but he could barely remember what it felt like to be that age.

He put an arm around the boy's thin shoulders. "Who is to say, at a time like this, what justice looks like?"

A woman from Health and Healing, her clothes bloody and her eyes red, asked Davix and the boys to help carry the seven people who had died in the attack to a makeshift morgue in a corner of the courtyard. The long silence that accompanied this grim parade was suddenly broken by the sound of a large crowd approaching from below. Within seconds, everyone was on their feet, straining to see what was happening.

Thousands of the People began streaming into the courtyard from the city below like driven cattle. Davix saw with surprise that the herders were the mixed beings. There were maybe fifty mixed beings in Cliffside, and it seemed like most were here, along with the rest of the city's human population. The young were helping the old to keep up, as octonas walked on either side of them, holding torches and banging slowly on hand drums usually only heard at harvest festivals. The drums beat in a perfect, inhuman unison.

"Keep together," said the quadrana leading this migration. Though it was dark, Davix recognized the sibilant voice of Convenor Zishun, ringing out with calm authority. "It is important we all reach the safety of the Citadel."

The two hundred or so already in the courtyard ran to greet them, momentary relief winning over fear as friends and fleshmates were reunited.

"What happened down in the city?" Davix asked them, and their stories tumbled out. The cats had attacked there, too. Panic and rumours of slaughter had spread like fire through the final hours of *Sarensikar*, before the mixed beings began issuing orders. *Gather in the nearest square. Bring no belongings. All will be provided. Your safety depends on your cooperation.*

Once everyone was inside, the gates to the Citadel closed with a low, ominous creak and a soul-chilling boom. The tightly packed crowd now stretched from the spinward wall halfway across the courtyard. The mixed beings assembled in three neat rows, facing them, a no-man's-land of some ten strides between the two groups. In the centre of the first row stood the quadrana Zishun. The brindle cat, Grentz's killer, the only one Davix had heard speak in the Tongue of Fire, prowled around behind the mixed beings, licking its paw to casually clean the blood from its face.

At the front of the human ranks, the guards from Defence of Realm were gathered around Korda, exhausted and dishevelled, some of them injured from the fight with the cats. They looked as confused as everyone else.

Grav'nan-dahé broke from the crowd and marched right across no-man's-land to stand before Convenor Zishun.

"Explain what is happening," he demanded.

"Prime Magistrate," Zishun said, "remain with the People and await further instruction."

Grav'nan-dahé was so startled by this command, he staggered back a step. "Convenor, do not forget that you speak to the holy representative of the Dragon Lords."

"This realm," Zishun said with a calm that belied the explosive force of his words, "is no longer under the rule of the dragons of Farad'hil. Our allegiance—and yours—is to the dragons of Air."

Davix's breath caught in his throat.

Grav'nan-dahé's eyes went wide, and he leaned closer, staring up into the face of the Convenor. His voice shook with anger. "Listen carefully, blasphemer, as I speak the words of the DragonLaw—"

The quadrana raised his hand, as if to forestall a misunderstanding. "Do not waste your energy, Grav'nan-dahé. The DragonLaw is dead." And he turned his back on him.

CHAPTER 38: *Prisoners in the Citadel*

The People were prisoners. Zishun sent mixed beings to guard the gate of the Citadel and others to guard the steps that led down to the bunkers. The brindle cat, the commander of the cat soldiers, conferred with Zishun in the Tongue of Fire and then called out in Air's language of hisses and moans. The cat soldiers climbed down the walls and began circulating among the crowd, snarling and shoving, making feints with unsheathed claws and once or twice delivering stunning blows to those who did not get out of the way fast enough.

Careful to avoid the prowling cats, Davix made his way through the crowd and stood behind Grav'nan-dahé, in conference with Korda and the other masters on the human side of the square.

Lok'lok-sur-nep-dahé was fingering the blue beads strung on his beard. "This is impossible. The mixed beings would never...could never—"

Korda cut him off. "But that's how it is, Lokré."

The Prime Magistrate said in a low voice, "Do you have a plan to defeat them?"

"Look at the numbers!" she said. "It took three of my men to bring down one cat, and they were lucky. And now the mixed beings? Would you want to tangle with a quadrana? I have no suggestion for now but cooperation."

Grav'nan-dahé nodded. Given the circumstances, Davix was impressed how quickly the man had regained his composure. "But you *are* keeping your eyes open for possibilities?" he asked.

"Every single second."

Davix pushed closer. "Has anyone seen Tix-etnep-thon-dahé? I'm worried about him." The masters looked at each other and shook their heads.

"I haven't," Korda said, surveying the crowd. "Not since your sentencing. Say nothing about it to anyone else for now. My guards will make a search." Davix grew even more worried. He wanted to ask what they were going to do about X'risp'hin, but he knew the Dragon Groom was beyond their reach for now.

An octona Davix recognized as Librarian of Etnep House approached them.

"Masters of Cliffside," he said. "I have come to inform you that you may no longer meet together. Korda, Convenor Zishun orders you come stand with the mixed beings."

Davix caught Korda's eye, hoping to see an angry glint of rebellion there, but she just followed the octona.

"And what are we to do?" Grav'nan-dahé called after him. Davix could hear the rage lurking beneath the surface. The octona didn't answer.

As Korda took her place by the mixed beings, a piercing cry shattered the air above them. Davix's heart raced, and his legs urged him to run for cover. Was it the Air dragon returning? No, it was the bidahéna Throd flying in over the walls and spiralling down to the stage. Zishun and the cat commander climbed the steps to join the bidahéna onstage.

"It is time for Throd's proclamation," Zishun called, in a voice that filled the Citadel. The bidahéna moved to the front of the stage with his odd, clicking gait and spread his wings wide. Zishun said, "The Interpreter will come forward."

Davix wasn't surprised to see the little man in his best ceremonial gown. If the realm had not been turned on its head, the Interpreter would now be translating as the bidahénas chanted the banishment of the fog, the final ritual of *Sarensikar*.

Speaking in the ancient tongue, Throd's voice was like the screams of forest beasts running from a fire. The Interpreter's mouth fell open in horror at what he heard. Throd closed his wings as the Interpreter stepped forward.

"L-long ago, the one world split asunder, um, birthing the realms in elemental fury. That fury must rage and rage until many is un-, uh, is dis—" The Interpreter had never seemed so intimidated before, even when interpreting for Sur. "Until again comes unity, yes. Fire will rage with the fuel of Air. Long live our new lords, the-the dragons of Air!" Zishun nodded at the frightened man, and he all but ran from the stage.

"People of Cliffside," Zishun said to the crowd, "Cherished human inhabitants of the Realm of Fire. We understand your surprise at the events that have transpired since fifth bell. Fear not. We have no wish to see any of you come to harm." He raised his arms in the air in victorious salute, but his voice retained its even tone. "Rejoice, the time of your deliverance is at hand. No more will we serve the pampered dilettantes of Farad'hil, who have forgotten what it means to be dragons. From this day forward, we are the servants of the twenty-two dragons of the Realm of Air!"

The crowd erupted in a roar, the most prominent sound, a loud "No!"

A woman called out, "We love the Five. We can love no others."

The brindle cat hissed at her. *"silence, meat! or your flesh will feed my cat soldiers!"*

Zishun, in contrast, looked down at her with understanding. "Patience, sister. You will come to see, as we have, that the dragons of Air are the rulers you need and deserve."

But the woman was growing angry. "Never! The Five will fight this invasion, and we will be their soldiers." Voices in the crowd shouted agreement.

The cats were still sliding through the crowd. At a signal from their commander, one abruptly changed course and clubbed the woman in the back of the head with an outstretched paw. The woman howled and collapsed to the cobblestones. The people nearest the violence screamed and pulled away.

As if the display of force had never happened, Zishun continued in patient tones. "We ask only that you trust us. All will be provided. The cooks will now follow the octona guides—guides, please raise your hands."

One of the old cooks, a grim and grizzled man named Xelm, shouted, "Where are we supposed to do this cooking if we can't leave the Citadel?"

"Down in the bunker. Old facilities that have not been used in a hundred cycles have been restored by the mixed beings to working condition."

That meant the mixed beings had been preparing this invasion right under the noses of the People. Davix felt the betrayal like a blow to the chest.

Xelm called out again. "And what is it we're cooking?"

"Behold," the Convenor answered and gestured toward the Citadel's entrance. Four quadranas entered the square carrying enormous canvas sacks and dropped them in front of the stage. From one sack, a quadrana pulled a dead kingsolver. The crowd gasped. The other bags were opened, revealing hundreds more—undoubtedly the city's entire population of messenger birds.

Young Zent'r, who cared for the kingsolvers in the Atmospherics Tower, gave a choked cry. Davix hugged him close for a minute. "Be strong," he whispered. "Later there will be time for tears." He watched Grav'nan-dahé march across the no-man's-land to stand with Korda at the bottom of the steps. Curiosity was stronger than fear. Davix released the boy and hurried to follow.

Zishun descended from the stage and sat on the lower steps in front of them, his attitude relaxed.

The Prime Magistrate said, "The mixed beings are grown by Great Inby to love and obey the Dragons of Farad'hil. Explain how it is possible that your allegiance has changed." Davix felt an unexpected relief to have him there, confident and unafraid.

Cars'tat, the octona porter of Vixtet House, approached "You no longer give orders here, Grav'nan-dahé. Return to your side of the square."

"No, Cars'tat," Zishun said. "It would serve us all if this honourable man understood how these changes came to be. As you know, Grav'nan-dahé, in the days following the harvest, the mixed beings retreated to the Valley of R'atur for our twice-cyclic colloquy. In an open forum, attended by all, the octona Fralox asked a simple question. 'How do our Dragon Lords serve the greater arc of history? In the past, the realms fought for supremacy, each trying to conquer the others, with the ultimate goal the capture of the Realm of Earth.'

"All of the mixed beings realized that this was true. Our Dragon Lords in the Realm of Fire did not strive thus for greatness. Fralox continued. 'We were born to serve the great dragon masters. Would it not make sense for us to align ourselves with the fiercest and strongest of those dragons? The ones most fit to rule?'"

"How was Fralox even allowed to speak those words of blasphemy?" Grav'nan-dahé said, his voice low and angry.

"It is each mixed being's duty to speak his thoughts freely at the colloquy," the Convenor replied. "That is how new ideas are generated. However, a strange thing happened. As I stated, we were each and every one of us in attendance at the session, and from octona to quadrana to bidahéna, every one saw the wisdom of Fralox's words. And because we all had this revelation simultaneously, *we were changed*, down to the very code that shapes our cells. It is true, we are born with unquestioning loyalty to the Dragon Lords, but in an instant, we realized the dragons of Farad'hil were no longer the dragons that deserved this loyalty."

Davix was leaning forward, listening like this was a heroic tale told around a bonfire, and he had to remind himself that the situation was deadly serious.

Zishun continued. "But if the Fire dragons were no longer deserving of our allegiance, who was? The dragons of Earth have not been heard from since the Great Division; they may well be dead. Then there was Water. But the strands between the Realms of Fire and Water were completely destroyed in the last war. That left the dragons of Air, historically the most ambitious and merciless of the dragons."

Korda said, "But the strands between Fire and Air were also damaged."

"Damaged, not destroyed," Zishun said. "Perhaps another can help me tell this story. Bring out the prisoner."

A figure was led up from the underground bunker, head shrouded in a black hood. For a moment, Davix thought it was Tix-etnep-thon-dahé, but it was a tall quadrana, naked, thick ropes wound around his torso, pinning his arms to his side. Two octonas positioned themselves around the quadrana and prodded him with their spears, forcing him to kneel on the hard stones.

Zishun approached the prisoner and pulled off the hood.

"Greetings, Tiqokh. I hope you are well and have been provided with all you need."

Tiqokh's pupils shone blackly from his time in the dark. Now the vertical slits of his eyes closed again, like the pages of a book, to restore his calm, green gaze.

"Yes, other than my freedom, my physical needs have been provided for, though I will need to eat in a day or two."

"It is my hope that by then your coding will have aligned with ours. Do you yet share our zeal to follow the dragons of Air?"

"No, I remain loyal to the lords of Farad'hil," Tiqokh said. He turned slowly, making eye contact in turn with Grav'nan-dahé, Korda, and with Davix. "I am sorry," he told them, "that I failed to uncover the plans of the conspirators in time."

"I have explained to the humans that we have made alliance across the strands with the Realm of Air. Korda asks how this was possible given the degraded state of the strands. Can you provide an answer?"

"I believe so," Tiqokh said. "It is not impossible to restore the strands, Korda. The traitors would have required a source of elemental power both readily accessible and hidden from discovery. For instance, a fissure in the skin of our realm, far away in the Chend'th'nif." He turned to Zishun. "I am correct thus far?"

"Very good. It is unfortunate that our efforts were discovered."

"Yes, Ranger Twis'wit must have found your base of operations. But while his discovery was mere coincidence, you underestimated the intelligence and tenacity of the Atmospherics discipline. Rinby intuited the existence of your power source from its effect on the fog patterns."

Rage flared in Davix. "And so you killed her? You are monsters!"

Tiqokh said, "No, Davix. The mixed beings are unable to harm a human. At first, the bidahénas merely ordered her to remain silent. I assume, Zishun, you were there when Throd or Kror met with the girl, to translate from the ancient tongue."

Davix was overwhelmed, confused. "But who killed her?"

Tiqokh tilted his head, cracking the stiff muscles in his neck. "Shortly thereafter, the first of the cat soldiers—the commander here, I would guess—arrived across the revitalized strands." Tiqokh looked up at Zishun. "Did you have Rinby killed when you discovered her secret notes? No, you never did find them, did you? You would have destroyed them. But you didn't trust her intimidated silence. You dispatched the cat to slaughter the girl in the Atmospherics Tower."

In his mind, Davix saw the flash of cat claws—not a death blow, but enough to unbalance Rinby and send her careening down the steps, screaming in the stone silence of the night. If only he had come to her earlier, convinced her they should call it a night and return to Cliffside.

Tiqokh looked up at Zishun. "More cat soldiers must have crossed over as the strands strengthened. With their involvement, murder was now possible. Twis'wit was killed and left in the woods, as if slain by an accidental. The next victim was the Curator of Sites Historic. With him around the Citadel, the bunker below us could never have been restored."

Zishun said, "Believe me, Tiqokh, we took no pleasure in the deaths of the humans."

"Nor did their deaths upset you much."

The extent of the deception, the murders, all happening right in front of them, staggered Davix. He was barely aware he was speaking out loud. "The open fissure is why the sheep fog descended, and why it persists." He looked at Grav'nan-dahé. "It wasn't a dragon trap." Davix himself had never made the accusation, even though he'd believed it. He almost apologized.

"Do you know, D'gada-vixtet-thon," Zishun said, "your transmission of Rinby's data made us attack Cliffside ahead of schedule?"

"No!" Davix cried. Was he responsible for all the bloodshed they were living through? For Grentz's death and X'risp'hin's abduction?

Misery drove him to the ground, where he sat with his head hanging low.

"Indeed. We had planned to attack only when more Air dragons crossed the strands. But once you sent the data, we knew we could not hide it from Renrit for very long. We had to take the city ahead of schedule. It doesn't matter. The grace books are dark and the kingsolvers dead. Farad'hil is cut off from the rest of the realm, and soon our new lords will descend the strands in numbers sufficient to mount an attack on the holy abode."

Tiqokh's voice rang out, this time with force. "D'gada-vixtet-thon! This is not your fault. Because they have had to accelerate their plans, the traitors have made themselves vulnerable. There is time to for us to act and save the Five!"

"Silence him!" Zishun called. The octonas shoved a gag in Tiqokh's mouth and pulled the hood over his head before dragging him back underground.

Zishun put a hand on Grav'nan-dahé's shoulder. "Do not fear. The People will always be of great importance. We will implement a new breeding program to enhance your numbers."

Korda said, "Our lords keep our numbers in perfect balance with what the Realm can provide."

"Your *former* lords. I advise you not to make that mistake again. The People will be raised into a mighty army. Some will stay here, and some will travel to the Realm of Air, where they will be turned into a matchless fighting force. Together with the cat warriors, you will help the Twenty-Two conquer all of Realm Space."

Davix noticed Zent'r waving at him, a look of desperation in his eyes.

"What is it?" he asked when he reached the young apprentice.

The boy drew close, discreetly pointing up at one of the corner towers. "There! In the window."

Davix glanced up and saw a blue shawl hanging half out of the window, shifting in the evening breeze. He recognized it immediately as Tix-etnep-thon-dahé's.

"Quickly," he said to the boy. They moved as fast as they could without drawing attention to themselves, pausing at the edge of the People's assigned area. To reach the tower, they would have to cross an open space, under the watchful eye of many mixed beings.

Davix had a cold premonition of tragedy. "Zent'r, I need you to go find someone from Health and Healing—Krenlin-etnep-bor-dahé if he's available—and bring him to the tower." The boy slipped away through the crowd. Davix tried to get his nerve up to run, but fear held him like the teeth of a bear. He had been through too much already. All he wanted was to lie down and mourn. But he was certain his master needed him, so he ran.

He reached the tower door and, finding it unlocked, raced up the stairs, even as a voice behind him called, "Stop!"

Tix-etnep-thon-dahé was lying on the cold stones of a dusty storeroom at the top of the tower. Above him was the window where his shawl had caught on a hook. His cane lay halfway across the floor, where it must have rolled when he fell. Davix cried out, thinking he was dead, but then the cloudy eyes opened—one more than the other—and the old man reached out a faltering hand in Davix's direction.

"Master, thank the Dragon Lords you are all right."

But he wasn't. His eyes roamed wildly, and his speech was a garble of incoherent vowels. Mixed beings arrived at the window and door, surveying the scene with cool curiosity. Davix stood between them and Tix-etnep-thon-dahé. He would defend his master to the death if necessary. But a minute later, the Master of Health and Healing arrived with another physician. He pushed brusquely past the mixed beings in the door.

"He has had a stroke," Krenlin-etnep-bor-dahé said after a cursory examination. And then to his colleague, "If you have redstones in your kit, bind two at his left temple."

Davix had no more shock or tears left. Only anger kept him moving. He kneeled again by his master. Tix-etnep-thon-dahé lifted his left hand, the fingers splayed, and waved it up and down, as if he was greeting an old friend seen at a distance.

"Master, rest now, please."

But the hand kept waving, the old man moaning, "Ahh, ahhh."

CHAPTER 39: *Translator*

I have no clever jokes or quips to make about those hours in the talons of the Air dragon. They were too awful and terrifying and their memory will forever haunt me. So, all right? No smart-ass Crispin lines.

Okay, if you insist.

I would say that having flown first class from the Chend'th'nif to Cliffside on Sur Airlines, I was returning like a stowaway squeezed into a golf bag, freezing and faint in the hold of the plane.

I was numb with shock and cold during most of the flight, but woke out of my stupor to scream as we descended like a meteor, my ears and stomach squeezed in misery. The dragon released me without warning, and I rolled across the hard ground, scratched and bruised by the rocks under me. The howling wind that accompanied the creature suddenly quieted, and I turned over to see it flying off again. Good fucking riddance.

I sat up fast, taking in the scene around me. A camp had been set up on a rocky plateau at the base of a mountain with tents and lean-tos, a cooking area, and racks of tools and weapons. I saw half a dozen octonas and quadranas, and a few of those nasty cat soldiers. I was the only human. But the most prominent feature of this one-star holiday camp was the fire pit at the far end of the compound—a volcanic trench which roared like a jet engine and spewed smoke and fire.

As cold as it had been in the air, I was quickly baking in the dry heat. The glow from the pit was intense enough to obscure the stars above, and I had to remind myself it was still the middle of the night. Above us, I could see the strands. I'm usually slow on the uptake, but I quickly realized these were not the strands back to Earth. These strands connected the Realm of Fire with the Realm of Air.

In all the noise and confusion, I didn't notice the calico cat soldier until it was looming over me, sniffing at my scent, raising a big clawed paw. All the carnage I'd just seen at Cliffside replayed in my mind. I shrieked and wrapped my hands over my head, but the cat only snarled and gave me a kick in the ribs. I think it was making sure I knew my place in the social order.

My shriek must have attracted more attention. Two octonas walked my way.

"Look, the mighty Dragon Lord has brought us the Dragon Groom," said one.

"An important prize indeed."

They were looking at me like I was a slice of beef on the butcher's counter.

"Help," I said, "cats from the Realm of Air attacked Cliffside. An Air dragon carried me here!" But nothing made sense. They saw the cats, so they had to have seen the dragon. One of them turned toward a big tent, decorated with purple banners and gold tinsel, the only thing in the whole camp that could be described as pretty.

"Farkol-dahé!" the octona called, and out of the tent stepped the fashion forward quadrana I'd last seen running the *Sarensikar* dance contest. He wore long yellow robes and an ornate war helmet with three big feathers sticking up from it.

"Why do you disturb my wise deliberations?" he asked.

"We have an important prisoner, honoured one. The Dragon Groom."

Farkol clapped his hands together like a thrilled toddler. "Excellent. Put him in the cage, and we will decide how he may be of use."

Panic seized me by the throat. "What? You're supposed to be our friends. What about—"

The octonas didn't wait for me to finish. They each grabbed one of my arms, dragged me across the compound, and tossed me into a cage.

"Hey," I shouted, trying to hide my terror. "Let me go! I'm friends with Great Sur!" But clearly, they didn't give a frog's ass.

Did I call my room in Etnep House a cage? Is that the word I used? I'm not sure, but if I did, I was begging karma for a kick in the pants, because this was the real deal. It was made of discarded bits of rough lumber and twisted lengths of rusted wire. One crumbling brick wall was a leftover from some previous building. Some of the bars were actual bones, long bones like from the thighs of a cow, white except for blackened bits of gristle at the joints. And as the octonas closed the big, ugly metal lock and walked away, I shook the bars and screamed at them, but I could hardly hear myself over the noise of the fire pit. Sweat dripped down my forehead and stung my eyes, and when I wiped them with my sleeve, I saw a face glaring at me from the shadows to the side of the cage. It was a tortoiseshell cat, a savage scar running from below one eye and across its cheek.

The cat reached into the cage and grabbed my arm. His mouth stank of foul meat, and I could feel the tips of his claws pierce my skin.

"Human of copper blood," it hissed. "Stop your useless howling."

I screamed some more and broke loose from its grip, falling down and curling into a ball. Maybe I scared the cat away, because it didn't speak again. I cowered on the ground, drenched in sweat from the heat of the pit which roared and roared until I wanted to stuff my ears full of stones. After moaning in a delirium for God knows how long, I begged the universe to let me escape into sleep. I imagined Davix curled up next to me, stroking my hair and telling me we would be together again, and eventually I passed out. But when I woke up crying later in the night, I thought about my mom, not Davix. Maybe my sweaty, fractured sleep reminded me of when I was a little kid, sick with a fever. She would sit at the edge of my bed, laying cool cloths on my head and singing softly. It was the only time I ever remember her singing.

I slept again, not waking until the sun was up, though it was hard to tell. Thick fog mixed with black smoke from the fire pit darkened the sky. The glowing pit was the major source of light. One small mercy was the pit was not as loud this morning. I watched the camp waking up. An octona was doling out food from a big pot to the mixed beings and the cats. Eating would have been terrific, but what I desperately needed was a drink. Dehydration was giving me a headache.

"Good morning, Copper Blood," said a voice above me. I looked up and saw the tortoiseshell cat sitting on top of my cage. "I am Translator. We talked when you arrived last night."

My heart started pounding, but I was damned if I was going to cower again. "You better let me go. I'm an important person, and they're going to come and rescue me. Defence of Realm. Or the mixed beings. Or Sur."

The cat jumped to the ground, landing almost silently. He was dressed in brown leather, his feet were bare, and he wore a cloth backpack. The tortoiseshell fur made his face into a chaotic map with no place to put your focus other than the red-rimmed eyes or the shining fangs that showed when he spoke.

"You are stupid, human. Your mixed beings have aligned with conquerors from the Realm of Air. The dragons of Fire sit in ignorance in their mountain, placidly awaiting their deaths." I was stunned into silence. The cat reached toward me with a bulging waterskin. "Drink?"

Much as I hated to cooperate in any way, I grabbed the waterskin and practically drained it in one swallow. Handing it back, I couldn't help saying, "Thanks, Translator."

"You are welcome. Would you like to eat, too?" He uncovered a dish, and the smell of stew hit my nostrils, making my stomach sing a little ballad.

"Yeah, for sure."

"Well, then, you have to help me." Translator pulled a fat, leather-bound book from his backpack. "This is a dictionary I have compiled myself. Tongue of Air to Tongue of Fire." He stroked the cover tenderly with the pads of his hand. "I have little opportunity to speak to anyone in the Tongue of Fire. You could help me confirm some pronunciations."

"And if I do, you'll give me the food?" He pushed the bowl through the bars, and I grabbed it, scooping up chunks of meat with my fingers before bringing the bowl to my lips to lap up the greasy broth. Under other circumstances, I don't think I could have choked this mess down, but beggars can't be restaurant critics. "Uh, did they give you any bread with the soup?"

He handed me the end of a dark loaf from a side pocket of his backpack, and I wiped the bowl with it. The world, while still bleak, didn't seem quite as hopeless.

"Finished?" the cat asked, turning his dictionary so I could see it. It was open to a page with three columns of neatly penned words. "Now, Copper Blood, say each word slowly and clearly for me, so I may verify my pronunciation. And don't touch the pages with your filthy fingers."

Before I could say anything, another cat soldier passed by with dramatic black-and-white fur and a crest on its head, like a mohawk. It hissed something at Translator and pushed him up against the bars of the cage. Translator hissed back, but I had the impression he was scared. When the black-and-white raised its claws like it was going to give him a smack, Translator mewed and raised his arms to protect his scarred face. The black-and-white swaggered away, making little grunts of satisfaction.

Not that Translator was my friend or anything, but I knew bullying when I saw it.

"You okay?" I asked him.

He hissed at me, his pink tongue lolling like Japanese tentacle porn. "I don't need human sympathy. I am a cat warrior of Air."

"Whatever," I muttered. "Look, I can't help with your dictionary. I only speak Tongue of Fire. I can't read it."

He shot me a fierce, carnivorous glare. "Then what use are you?"

"It's not my fault! Why don't we just talk? You probably don't get much chance, right?"

He growled low. "Agreed."

"Wait, what about that other cat at Cliffside? The brindle one? He speaks Tongue of Fire. Well, sort of."

"Exactly. He has no grasp of the idiomatic language. He speaks word-for-word translation, and with only the most rudimentary vocabulary. I should have been sent to the city in his place." Apparently, I had uncovered a sore spot.

"So, why weren't you?"

"They think because I am a scholar, I am no warrior. But I am a cat soldier of Air, same as he!" Translator puffed out his chest and roared in my face.

"Hey, you have me convinced," I assured him, my heart racing. "How many cats came over the Strands?"

"Twenty-nine. Though there are only four at this camp." He glanced around, his bravado suddenly not so brave. "But I should not tell you strategic information."

He handed me back the waterskin, and I drank the last of it.

"Then let's just talk everyday stuff," I said. "What's your real name?"

"Only my family calls me by my given name. You will call me Translator."

"Oh, okay. I'm Crispin, not that anyone on this world ever gets it right."

"Kras-pa-han," the cat said with a nod like he had nailed it. I sighed.

"So, you're from the Realm of Air. Nice place?"

He looked up into the sky, like he could see his world floating there. Now it was his turn to sigh. "Air is a world of impressions. We move through the coloured mist, finding our way by scent and feel. The wind makes the mist dance, and in those cyclonic movements, tales are told." The cat clearly had the soul of a poet under his motley hair and scars.

"Are there trees?" I asked. With all the violence and fear I'd been living through, making small talk was a relief.

"Yes. Majestic evergreens, whose tops pierce the mist and bring us news of the sky."

"I love forests. It sounds like a beautiful place."

"Indeed. But how much more beautiful it would be were we allowed to sleep every night in our lairs with our spouses and our kits.

By hand have I written a modest but wide-ranging library, and as each of my children grows to cognizance, I read with them the histories and the fancies. But not every kit has received my tutelage. All too often, I am called away from home to translate, sometimes for more than a cycle." He brought his face closer to the bars and whispered, "Kras-pahan, you do not know. Air is a land without mercy. Our only value is how we may serve the twenty-two dragons and their obsessive quest to rule all of Realm Space. If they intend to bring you there…"

This awful possibility hadn't occurred to me. "Let's talk about something else," I said quickly. "Do you sing songs in the Realm of Air?"

"Oh yes, songs martial or songs romantic. Farces and roundelay japes. Perhaps that is what keeps us from going mad. Here, I shall sing you a song about an aerialist named Aaaf-thal-asoff Softhal-mas."

The song, which he sang in a surprisingly sweet voice, got faster and faster as it went. I think it was basically a joke song, made up of crazy tongue twisters. At one point, it got so fast and complex, my eyes widened. Translator finally messed up and started laughing. The difference in his personality now that he was talking about things that mattered to him was a shock. I realized how lonely he must be.

A quadrana showed up out of nowhere and prodded Translator with his spear handle. "At attention. Farkol-dahé comes, requiring your services."

As we awaited the boss's arrival, our good mood grew dark again. "Translator?" I asked.

"What is it, human?"

"I was wondering, am I the first prisoner you've had in this cage?"

"No, there was another. A ranger named Twis'wit."

Great. I knew how his story had ended.

The big, glam quadrana emerged from his tent and crossed the compound to us, surrounded by a retinue of mixed beings. Today's outfit featured lots of mauve, and he was leading a pet deer on a silver leash.

"You are well, Dragon Groom?" Farkol asked. Every other quadrana I'd met spoke in a flat voice, just this side of bored, but Farkol's ranged up and down like he was performing Shakespeare. "I trust the accommodations, though simple, suffice." He gestured at the cage like he was a spokesmodel showing off a designer kitchen.

"Sure. It's a terrific holiday resort you have here. I'd love a bubble tea, if the kitchen's still open." I realized I was angrier now than scared.

"Oh, and congrats on the 'dahé.' I thought only dragons could give you that."

He let out a high, fake laugh and explained to his retinue, "The humour of the Realm of Earth is most subtle and particular." He laughed again, like a barking Chihuahua. His pet deer, I noticed, kept big, wary eyes on Translator. The cats must have been drooling over this tasty meal.

"Seriously, Farkol-dahé," I said, giving him his title as well as a head and heart bow. "Why don't you let me out of the cage?"

"The cage is for your protection, Dragon Groom," he answered in his sing-song voice. "If you were to escape, you could only die trying to scale the cliffs into the Chend'th'nif or by running into the Badlands, where the arid heat and burning ground would kill you before the sun had set. Your safety is important to us."

"Oh, gee, thanks a lot then," I muttered. Still, it was good to hear I was being kept alive, which was more than Twis'wit got. Why bother kidnapping me if they were just going to kill me, right? Maybe I was going to be ransomed. What would the dragons of Farad'hil pay to keep my copper blood safe?

The air was torn by a long, grinding screech louder than the sound of the fire pit, and the dragon of Air came in for a landing on a rocky ledge above us. Its swirling skin of tornados thinned to a writhing mist and what was left over looked bony and disgusting. The deer tried to bolt, but Farkol held the leash tight.

"Well, Translator?" the quadrana said, and I realized the dragon's screech had actually been, you know, words.

"Yes, Farkol-dahé," Translator responded, his voice clear and loud. "The mighty dragon of Air, destined to rule the Realms forever asks, 'Why should we bring this flap of wriggling flesh back to our magnificent land?'"

Yeah? I thought. *Well, you look like a broken umbrella in a dust storm.* But then I thought about more than the insult. Was Translator right? Were they planning to take me across the strands to the Realm of Air? I desperately wanted that not to happen.

Farkol addressed the dragon. "Eminence, as I explained before, the copper blood is powerful in this one. Introducing his bloodline into that of the Twenty-Two could only strengthen you." My tortoiseshell friend relayed his words to the dragon, his rolling cat tones making the language almost attractive.

Another gut-shaking, smoky exclamation from above, which the cat translated. "So slaughter him now, and I will drink his precious blood. My soldiers are in need of fresh meat." Translator gave me a quick look and whispered, "The dragon's words, Kras-pa-han, not mine." That was sweet, but cold terror had come over me so fast, I could barely nod in reply.

"Yes, Eminence," Farkol explained carefully, "I see your point. But first of all, I'm not sure you could absorb the benefit of the blood that way, though of course you are free to try."

Not helping!

"But might I also point out he could be a valuable hostage in the event this conflict becomes prolonged."

The tornados began forming around the dragon, and his smoky wings filled and lifted. Within seconds, the whole camp was swirling with dust and volcanic gas. Everything from racks of weapons to shelves of cooking utensils tumbled over in the wind.

"*LLL-AAAAA-SSFFFAAARA-KHALLLOOOO-SOOOAHHH!*" screamed the dragon as it lifted into the air.

Over the noise, Translator shouted the translation to Farkol, who was holding his plumed helmet in place with one hand. "Within days, my siblings will arrive. We will slaughter the dragons of Farad'hil, and the wind will sing our victory." The dragon was still screaming as it flew away, and the tortoiseshell cat cupped his ear to make out the words through the rumble. "And I don't care about the human. Make him your pet, eat him, copulate with him, he is beneath my notice."

I had already dropped to the ground, bent forward till I was kissing my kneecaps, both hands covering my head. I was protecting myself from the blowing dust, but I was also a five-year-old, chanting to himself, "I'm not here! You can't see me! I'm not here."

CHAPTER 40: *The Five Day War*

Day 1

When the Bear Star rose in the redward sky, the apprentices were still awake. The entire human population of Cliffside lay around them in the Citadel's courtyard, shifting and moaning in uneasy sleep, exposed to the damp night. There weren't enough of the musty blankets to go around, so the apprentices were huddling together for warmth, whispering stories about Grentz. When a mixed being or a cat soldier approached, someone would chirp like a night frog in warning, and they would fall silent until the danger passed.

"So what did Grentz do with the stolen spice-cakes?" Zent'r asked.

Kriz'mig said, "The answer is obvious, bean sprout." The boy, clearly baby-looping on her, giggled at the insult. "He ate all twelve of them, one after the other, in the time it took the teacher to walk to the library and back."

Zent'r had to put both hands over his mouth and bury his face in the blanket so as not to give them away with his snorting laugh. What a gift it was, Davix thought, that the boy could still laugh at this terrible time.

"I remember it well," Davix said. "His flatulence the rest of the day is the stuff of legend."

Stakrat stepped out of the dark and joined them, tucking herself against Kriz'mig under her blanket. Davix had been watching her and the other guards closely. He'd observed them meeting stealthily in twos and threes, passing intelligence through the ranks about the cats and the mixed beings. With Stakrat's arrival, the talk turned from tales of their dead friend to rumours of the war.

"How many cat soldiers are there?" Ragnor asked.

Stakrat looked around again, making sure they were unheard.

"Somewhere between twenty and forty. Davix, I've been told to ask you what the DragonLaw says about previous attacks from the Realm of Air."

She didn't look him in the eye, nor did he seek out hers. Even with all that had happened, her involvement in his arrest was still a wall between them. Would they have the chance to heal this rift before the war destroyed one or both of them?

He cleared his throat. "In the Book of Recitations, there are accounts of a siege which lasted half a cycle, with almost six hundred of the People dying. There is also a much-disputed passage in the Canticle of Infamy about ritual sacrifices which became popular for a time. Some say this section of the DragonLaw is evidence that Air ruled our realm in the time of the spectral dragon, Frazz'laf."

They finally closed their eyes around seventh bell—the automated bells down in the city were still doing their job, as if nothing had changed. Davix didn't think he'd get any sleep, but suddenly it was morning, and he was being awakened from thick slumber by the banging of hand drums. In the cold damp of the foggy dawn, the whole human population of Cliffside was prodded into long straight lines for a count. They were allowed to descend into the bunkers in groups of ten to use the lavatories, while the cooks and those seconded to help them served up breakfast.

The mixed beings, under the leadership of Convenor Zishun, divided the humans into work groups. Some were tasked with setting up a proper camp in the Citadel, and some with meals and cleaning. Octonas and quadranas supervised, while the hissing cat soldiers intimidated the humans into obedience. A small group was allowed down into the city to feed the animals in their barns. They were even more heavily guarded.

Grav'nan-dahé and the masters of all the disciplines—with the exception of Tix-etnep-thon-dahé, who was in the healing tent—were ordered to join Zishun across the no-man's-land. Grav'nan-dahé was assigned a desk just to the left of Zishun's, while the others were clustered together farther away. The group was guarded by two octonas, while an extra octona with a spear guarded Korda specifically. Soon, all the masters were filling blank notebooks with text, like they were sitting for a commencement exam. Davix, busy with a building crew, was burning with curiosity to know what they were up to.

❖

Day 2

Right after breakfast on the second day, Davix was told to leave his work unit and join Grav'nan-dahé at his desk by the stage. He almost objected. How could he assist the man who had been on the verge of destroying his life? But they were all lackeys to the traitorous mixed beings, so what choice did he have?

Grav'nan-dahé was reading through a delicate book with a cracked leather binding, and greeted Davix with the faintest of nods as the apprentice sat down across from him. The desk was covered in more dusty old books, stacks of paper, ink bottles, and pens.

"Welcome, young apprentice," Zishun said. "We are glad of your aid. The former masters of Cliffside are compiling documents for the great dragons of Air so they may decide how best to use the resources of the realm when they arrive." Behind Zishun, Tiqokh kneeled, still as a statue, his head in the shroud, his arms still bound to his side.

Zishun continued. "D'gada-vixtet-thon, your task is to compile a list of prayers and rituals—daily and cyclical—that the People perform. Rather than banning these rituals, we plan to adapt them to suit the worship of our new lords. We hope this will make the transition less traumatic for the People."

Davix didn't dare show his contempt to Zishun, but when the quadrana left, he let his frustration out in unaccustomed insolence to his former teacher.

"Prime Magistrate," he asked with a curl in his voice that already made Grav'nan-dahé's shoulders stiffen in anticipation. "Should I include the domestic rituals of Fire Revealed? After all, these are part of the daily devotions of much of our population."

"D'gada-vixtet-thon, while your levity might make our situation seem more bearable, you and I must be exemplars to the People. Act with some dignity."

Davix wanted to throw his pen at him. "Why are we cooperating with these traitors?"

"We have little choice," Grav'nan-dahé answered without looking up from his work. But then he lowered his head and whispered all but inaudibly, "And Korda told us to…for now."

Davix fought the urge to spin around in excitement and look at the Defence Master. But as the morning went on, he watched guards coming to speak to her and caught her covertly passing them notes. The sudden surge of hope made it hard to sit still.

After lunch, as the day grew hot and muggy, members of the People began to break down. One by one, people would come to a halt in the middle of their work and sink to the ground, weeping uncontrollably, or just stare into space and pick at their clothing. Krenlin-etnep-bor-dahé, Master of Health and Healing, walked them back to their sleeping area, talking softly to them while his assistants ran for hot, sweet tea.

"What ails these people?" Zishun asked Grav'nan-dahé with curious surprise.

"Humans come into this world like seeds sown on the wind," Grav'nan-dahé responded. "Their potential is only realized when they find good soil. The DragonLaw is that soil, and in its nurturing embrace, a human grows productive."

Zishun said, "Book of Comforts, 13th Lesson. What is the point of your quotation, Grav'nan?"

"You have torn the People loose from the soil of the law. Rootless, they wither, starting with the most delicate."

Zishun grew still as a statue, as quadranas did when thinking through a problem. "Then you must find words to comfort them. We cannot afford any diminution of our workforce."

Grav'nan-dahé examined his fingernails. "And what words shall I use, when you have banned the DragonLaw?"

Zishun shifted one of the piles of paper on his desk and found a thin notebook with a red leather cover. "Here. These are collected thoughts of Kaaarhh-als-sssssiiii, the greatest philosopher dragon of Air. We have been translating the book for the last quarter cycle. I'm sure you will find something suitable in its pages." He handed the book to Grav'nan-dahé, who took it distastefully between two fingers, like it was a squirming insect, and passed it to Davix.

"D'gada-vixtet-thon," he said, "Read through this…*mighty* tome and find words of comfort for the People."

Davix suppressed a smile at the Prime Magistrate's theatrical gesture and opened the book at random. "Blood! Blood and entrails to anoint the general. What satisfaction it is to wash your feet in the gore of the vanquished." He and Grav'nan-dahé locked eyes and almost laughed. "I will try and find something more appropriate."

Despite the tension between them, Davix had to admit that amid all the blood and chaos, there was comfort in being again at the old man's side.

As he thumbed through this book, whose philosophy of conquest was so foreign to him, Davix looked up repeatedly to observe the People. While some were felled by the stress of the attack, others were fuelled, their faces full of anger and resolve, awaiting a moment when they might act. And, too, he saw Korda and Defence of Realm passing whispers and notes, nodding to each other across the courtyard. A growing readiness hung in the air.

Day 3

Something was about to happen. Davix could almost taste it on his tongue as he sat down to begin another day of work on behalf of the dragons of Air. He looked around, but everything seemed calm. Then he caught a little thread of electricity passing through the courtyard in a series of glances from guard to guard, each discreetly putting a hand to their chest before passing on the signal to the next person in the chain. The chain ended with Korda, whose hand strayed longer over her leather breastplate and then closed into a fist.

"Good morning, Tiqokh," Zishun said just behind him, and Davix turned to watch the octona guards bringing the bound quadrana up from the bunker. At a gesture from the Convenor, the shroud was removed from his head.

Tiqokh squinted at the sky and around the courtyard before turning his attention to Zishun.

The Convenor asked, "Has your time here with your kind brought you around to our way of thinking? We are eager to add your skills to ours for the glory of our new lords."

"Fortunately, I find myself unchanged."

Zishun shook his head. "Your time may be running short, my comrade."

"I cannot be other than what I am." Hearing this, Davix felt a stab of guilt. Tiqokh was loyal and true, while he and the rest of the People were doing whatever they were told in aid of the Realm of the Air. But something, he reminded himself, was about to happen.

"Convenor!" shouted an octona, arriving in haste. He sounded as distressed as an octona could. "We have completed count, and six humans are missing."

Davix's heart began to beat faster. His senses were sharp and alert. Grav'nan-dahé arrived at that moment from his morning trip to the bunker, a dollop of shaving foam behind his left ear.

"Six of the People are missing," Davix told him, trying hard to keep his voice neutral.

Zishun said, "It is nothing. Resume your work." Davix lowered his head to his pages, but kept peeking discreetly.

Three of the humans were soon found in bed, apparent victims of the spreading melancholia. Two more were discovered to have taken lavatory breaks without permission. A final one returned to her work crew having wandered, by her own account, in search of a hammer. But these minor mysteries were distractions.

Korda's insurrection began mere minutes later, as second bell sounded.

The goal was twofold: first, to capture or kill as many cats as possible; second, to take Convenor Zishun prisoner. Korda reasoned that without Zishun, the mixed beings' rebellion would be thrown into chaos.

The attack's first wave targeted the mixed beings near the stage. A group of guards and others deputized into service ran at them, shouting and wielding improvised swords and spears. As cats from all across the Citadel surged forward to repel the attack, Korda tipped over the tables where the masters were working and pulled them into this improvised fort for cover. Davix followed suit, knocking over his desk and dragging Grav'nan-dahé down behind it. The last thing Davix saw before they curled themselves into hiding was Korda racing across the courtyard toward one of the corner towers.

The brutal battle of claw and cudgel filled the air with screams and flying blood. The odds of success for the first wave soldiers were practically nil, but their attack was just a feint. Within minutes, the soldiers of the second wave struck. They had used the distraction of the missing people to get into position up on the walls, in two of the corner towers, and behind a stone storehouse near one of the bunker entrances. From these positions, they prepared to fire a coordinated volley of arrows down on the cats clustered together in front of the stage.

From the high window of the redward tower, Korda shouted, "For the dragons of Fire!"

Arrows were striking Davix's tipped desk with ringing thuds. Even so, he peeked around to watch the battle when he dared. He wished he could join in, but he was a scholar, not a warrior. He had no training and no weapon at his disposal other than a large book of ancient furniture design. Still, he was prepared to hit any cat or mixed being with it should they invade the shelter and threaten him or the Prime Magistrate.

Davix spotted Tiqokh in the middle of the melee, clambering awkwardly to his feet, his arms still bound to his side. Run, Davix thought, but he stood his ground, bending forward, face twisted and straining, as cats and humans fought around him. Suddenly, with a cry louder than the sounds of battle, Tiqokh raised himself up. The ropes holding him snapped, torn apart by the new wings bursting from his back. With a shower of gore, the wet wings spread wide, glistening. Tiqokh grabbed a spear from a fallen human and began battling three cats, killing one with his first strike.

Hope soared in Davix. He began to believe the tide would shift and the People would win the day. But it wasn't meant to be. An octona of Etnep House, a most bookish of mixed beings, climbed onstage. Standing behind a bidahéna who protected him with an enormous shield, the octona pointed out every secret hiding place of the second wave guards. Cats immediately bounded across the courtyard and attacked these positions.

Davix peered over the edge of his shelter and caught Tiqokh's eyes.

"I am yet too weak, Davix," he called. "I'm sorry. Don't give up." He delivered one final blow to the last cat fighting him and leaped into the air, his new wings carrying him shakily over the walls of the Citadel.

With the second wave soldiers under siege, Korda's plan collapsed, and the battle was over in minutes. Three members of Defence of Realm were dead, as were four of the deputized volunteers. And then the final humiliation—Korda captured in her command tower by the bidahéna Kror. The great winged creature disappeared inside through an upper window and emerged moments later holding the Defence Master immobile in his mighty arms as he flew to the stage. Zishun, not appearing to be overly distressed by the whole incident, climbed the steps to join Kror.

A wave of nausea washed through Davix as Korda was shackled in irons. Cats in front of the stage hissed and clawed the air in her direction. She ignored them, her face revealing no emotion, but Davix hoped she was furious inside, swearing revenge against the traitorous mixed beings.

Zishun put a hand on Korda's chin and gazed into her controlled face.

"You probably think I am upset by your revolt, Koras-inby-kir. On the contrary, I believe it proves your bravery and spirit. You, of course, miscalculated. Your battle strategies could easily be predicted by those mixed beings who are familiar with the history of Defence of Realm as recorded in the DragonLaw. In fact, we were expecting this attack as early as yesterday."

Davix wished she would spit in his face.

"But, Koras-inby-kir," the Convenor continued, "a glorious destiny awaits you—leading your troops on behalf of the twenty-two dragons of Air. I will give you two days to decide. Either swear allegiance or be the first of the holy sacrifices. Do you have any questions?"

Korda spoke at last. "Yes. How many cat soldiers are here in the Realm of Fire? Was the Air dragon we saw the only one that's crossed the strands so far? Where is your base in Chend'th'nif? When and how do you plan to attack Farad'hil?"

Zishun's eyes sparkled. "Yes, much bravery. Much spirit. Take her away."

Day 4

Korda was being held in the same tower where Davix had been imprisoned. There had been no sign of her since her capture the previous day, and the mixed beings would reveal nothing of her fate.

After lunch, Davix was given permission to visit Tix-etnep-thon-dahé in the healing tent. On his way there, he passed Lok'lok-sur-nep-dahé. The Textiles Master was sewing some kind of ceremonial garment, decorated with bear's teeth and bones. The garment was being recreated from a drawing in a coarsely bound book annotated in strange script. Davix looked over his shoulder and marvelled at the unknown language.

"Is that the Tongue of Air?" Davix asked the master who, lost as he was in concentration, yelped in surprise. "I'm sorry," Davix said. "I didn't mean to scare you."

"Indeed, my nerves are fragile, D'gada-vixtet-thon." He ran his fingers along the line of teeth, which rattled softly. "It is a terrible garment, though a beautiful one. I wish I knew what it was for. Or perhaps I don't wish to know."

It was cool in the healing tent. The Master of Atmospherics lay on a low cot with a blanket pulled up to his chest. His left hand was raised in the air, waving weakly as it had when Davix discovered him in the tower. The fingers danced like stiff grass in the wind, and the old man watched their dance in the way of an infant who doesn't realize the limb is his own.

Davix took the dancing hand in both of his, as much to make contact as to stop this meaningless, heartbreaking motion.

"Master-da, how are you feeling today?" Tix-etnep-thon-dahé smiled with half his face, and Davix was not sure the old man recognized him. "You were right, Master. There is a rift in the Chend'th'nif. That is why the fog remains." Tix-etnep-thon-dahé gave a high wheezy sigh which Davix could not interpret. "But Grav'nan-dahé was not responsible. We were wrong to blame him." *You were wrong*, he wanted to say, aware of his anger. Davix was sickened by the way the two old men had spent the last quarter cycle standing over him, two puppeteers fighting for control of the strings. He let go of the old man's hand, and it fell to the bedding, like a frog shot from the sky.

"Oh, Master-da," Davix said. "What will happen now? Korda's revolt failed. The balance is shattered, the future unknown."

Tix-etnep-thon-dahé gave a mischievous half-smile. He raised his hand again, extending and relaxing the fingers as the hand climbed higher, like a wave on a lake. Like a wing.

"F-flaak…" he murmured through lips only half awake. "F-fly, Flak…" His left eye was clear and bright, turned skyward, though there was only the roof of the tent above. Davix, too, looked upward for a sign of hope.

When Davix returned to his desk, he saw that Lok'lok-sur-nep-dahé had finished the ritual cloak. It was displayed on the stage, hung on a T-shaped post. The cloak filled and billowed in the rising wind, as if animated by a malicious spirit. The white bones and gleaming, fearsome teeth that decorated the garment clattered in the breeze. Davix felt a sinister chill pass through him.

Day 5

It astonished Davix how quickly even the most terrible circumstances could settle into routine. The People ate their meals, slept, and prepared for the coming of their new lords. Was it really only five days since the cats attacked and the mixed beings betrayed them? It felt like a lifetime.

"Davix," the former Prime Magistrate said as they finished their lunch. "Go bang the drum to commence the afternoon work shift."

"No," Zishun replied, standing. "We have holy business to conduct first." Davix and Grav'nan-dahé exchanged worried glances as the quadrana located a small sheath of papers on his desk and reached into a drawer for a stone knife with a dark metal handle. He stepped forward, and his voice boomed across the courtyard.

"People of Cliffside, put down your bowls and stand, facing this way. Bring forth she whose glory awaits!"

From the door of the nearest tower, two tall octonas and the brindle commander cat emerged with Korda, her hands shackled. She was dressed in a long gown of coarse grey cloth. Her hair was loose and had fallen to her shoulders. Davix had never before seen her without it tied tight on the top of her head. Korda was marched before them and up on the stage, where Zishun joined her along with two octonas and three cats.

Korda stood with a soldier's bearing, staring forward, showing no fear. Zishun ordered her shackles removed and took the ceremonial cloak from its post.

"Spread wide your arms, Koras-inby-kir." She hesitated a moment, then did as she was told. Zishun placed the cloak over Korda's shoulders so that it hung down on all sides, cold and regal. The gruesome decorations glittered in stray flashes of sunshine that pierced the fog. Standing to one side of the stage, the cat commander licked his paw and began to clean himself.

"Hold her," Zishun said, and the octonas each grabbed one of her wrists to keep her arms extended. Zishun pulled a sheaf of papers from his pocket.

"Forgive my unfamiliarity with the ceremony, Koras-inby-kir. We all have much to learn about the customs of our new lords."

Davix's heart pounded. Despite his best efforts to marshal his emotions, he was pulled back to the hour, not six days past, when he had been the prisoner with bound hands. The memory made him nauseous and sweaty. But Korda did not flinch, even when Zishun lifted the stone knife and touched it to her forehead.

"Koras-inby-kir, you led an aborted rebellion against the twenty-two dragons who rule this realm. You are now offered two sacred paths to glory. You may publicly denounce your allegiance to the decadent dragons of Farad'hil and swear to bring your brilliance and ferocity to the service of the Twenty-Two…"

He brought the knife point down so it lay upon her breast. Davix reminded himself no mixed being could harm a human. Still, his breath caught in his throat.

"Or you may consecrate this stage with your blood, making of it a sacred altar for the worship of the Twenty-Two. This is an equally holy path, though I hope you choose the former. Great triumph awaits us if only we accept our new destinies."

Had she already been told of this choice, Davix wondered, or guessed it? Because she didn't seem surprised. Still, she must have been scared, for her face was ashen, and her voice betrayed the slightest tremor as she replied.

"My blood flows for clever Inby. It flows for wise Vixtet. My heart beats for Sur and for Renrit. My life is Queen Etnep's life."

Somewhere in the crowd, someone said, "Gracious is the world they built us."

Only then did Korda raise her voice to the crowd, her cold soldier's gaze turning hot. "And when my blood of Fire falls on your stinking altar, I hope it burns to the ground and takes you with it!" She spat at the feet of the Convenor. The cat soldiers snarled and took a step closer, but Zishun waved them back to their places.

He gave the smallest of nods to the octonas, who tightened their grip on Korda's wrists and drew her arms to full extension. Zishun handed the knife to the cat commander, who let out a low, guttural laugh and brought the point back to Korda's breast, this time pushing slowly through the material. She winced, and a small stain of red marked the spot.

"*weaknessss,*" the cat hissed.

Restless anger swirled through the crowd like cream in hot chicory as Zishun read from his paper, hissing words in the Tongue of Air, pausing occasionally to correct his pronunciation. Cat soldiers menaced the crowd with claw and spear, warning them to stay where they were.

"Do something," Davix hissed into Grav'nan-dahé's ear.

"What would you have me do?"

"Say something!"

"And precipitate a slaughter? We must cooperate. For now."

Davix's voice notched a little louder. "Yes, you're content to watch, aren't you? Just like you were content to sacrifice me."

Grav'nan-dahé's voice also rose, from whisper to growl. "How can you compare the situations?"

"Can't I? You claim to care about the People, but first you abuse your authority and now you abandon it." Davix was aware they were drawing attention. He didn't care. "You're the one with all the words. Speak!"

At some point during this exchange, Zishun had switched to Tongue of Fire. "The Realms were born in blood, torn loose from Mother Earth and expelled into the harshness of the Realm of Sky. Since then, blood has been our lot—the blood of battle, the blood of sacrifice. O Twenty-Two! O Dragon Lords of Air! Take the blood of this warrior woman and let it feed your hunger for conquest and domination!"

He nodded at the cat commander, who raised the knife high, ready to plunge it into Korda's heart, and that's when Grav'nan-dahé stepped forward.

"Stop! You creatures of chaos, you living violations! You will *not* kill this woman." Davix, despite having encouraged this intervention, was suddenly terrified for the old man, who continued in a high, tight voice. "You will not sully the realm of the Five with your unbalanced devotions." He turned to the People and raised his arms high. "Hear me, beloved children of Etnep! Do not submit! If they kill Korda, if they kill me, do not submit!"

The cats were headed his way, and Davix felt ice flow through him. Grav'nan-dahé was about to die, and it was his fault for goading him. And why? Because Davix wanted revenge on him? He couldn't stand by and watch. He lurched forward and raised his own arm, intertwining their fingers.

"Step back, Davix!" Grav'nan-dahé told him, almost pleading. But Davix stood his ground.

Zishun spoke behind them, his voice calm and clear. "Grav'nan-dahé, D'gada-vixtet-thon, the ceremony cannot be interrupted. Return to your place, or I will not restrain the cat soldiers."

Everything slowed. It seemed to Davix he had ample time to consider his life. With startling clarity, he looked back at all the turning points that had led to this moment—sending Rinby's data to Farad'hil, defying Grav'nan-dahé to be with X'risp'hin, daring to open his heart to love—and in no case could see how he might have acted differently. Were these truly decisions, or had he acted the way he, Davix, must act? Maybe he had stumbled on the meaning of destiny: to truly know yourself and then be true to that knowledge in your actions. Davix was not the person who could let Grav'nan-dahé die alone, so he stood with him. And if this was to be the end of his life, then it was the only way events could unfold.

Davix gripped Grav'nan-dahé's hand. His teacher was no longer a semi-god to him, but an ordinary, flawed human. He looked at the People, and they returned his look, anger or sympathy in their eyes. Standing among them, as they had always stood, were the mixed beings, creatures of honour and power whose lives had always represented the balance and harmony of the Realm of Fire. Their betrayal was unbearable.

"Do not throw away your lives for nothing," Zishun said to their backs. "Surely you must see…"

The voice stopped abruptly. Had the Convenor run out of lines to read? In his peripheral vision, Davix saw a strange movement. He turned to watch an octona tip sideways and fall to the ground. Then, in the middle of the crowd, a quadrana crumpled and vanished among the People. Then another. Like a rain that starts with scattered, single drops and then cascades into a downpour, the mixed beings began to collapse. Their eyes rolled back in their heads, their knees buckled, and they all fell dead.

Davix spun around to face the stage. The octonas holding Korda had released her, one dead at her feet, the other on its hands and knees, gasping for breath. Korda threw off the cloak and moved to the front of the stage, staring out into the courtyard in surprise.

And in that moment, Zishun, the last mixed being standing, grabbed the knife from the confused brindle cat. He shouted, "My life for Air!" and staggered toward Korda, bringing down the knife. But Zishun couldn't overcome the discipline of his blood. At the last second, he turned the blade, and it plunged into Korda's shoulder instead of her heart, as he fell dead on the stage.

Chapter 41: *A Game of Cat and Mouse*

Farkol-dahé was pacing back and forth in front of the dead deer, waving his hands around like he was conducting the Realm of Fire All-Star Band. "You have no right! This creature was *mine*! I am your superior!" "Honourable one," a worried octona murmured. "Be careful of the hem of your gown."

I almost laughed as Farkol hopped backward, only just avoiding dragging his fancy outfit through the puddle of blood. Yes, I know it wasn't funny, but life-and-death tension does weird things to me, okay? All the cats other than Translator had chased the poor deer around and around the compound before the calico cat finally jumped on it and tore out its throat. The killer cat was all pumped up after that, carrying the little drooping body around over his head to show off to the other three soldiers, licking at the blood that dripped down his arms. When Farkol and the mixed beings arrived and starting yelling, the calico dropped its kill and marched off in a huff.

Translator was hanging out in front of my cage, which was where he'd spent most of his off-duty time since I'd arrived. I wouldn't call it friendship, but we were the two nerds no one talked to, so we needed each other. It was hard to get him to open up about his life, although he did like to brag about his kids. When it came to his wife, he was more guarded. He called her a loyal and fierce mother, but he never said he loved her or missed her. I think he did, but those were the kinds of airy words that could get you beaten up by the other cats.

He appreciated it when I said she sounded brave.

"But what are you guys, anyway?" I had asked one long afternoon, after he got bored listening to me recount boy band relationship rumours. "Why are there big, talking, two-legged cats in your realm?"

"As the dragons of Fire needed the mixed beings, so our dragons needed their own army. Cats from the Realm of Earth were augmented, shaped slowly and in great agony until the design was complete. The feline martyrs are much revered."

Every story from Air included pain and glory.

I lost track of the days, but it felt like a week had gone by in that cage. Mostly I was ignored, which was fine by me. Even before the killing of the deer, the atmosphere had been growing tense. The Air dragon had not been seen in days. Farkol-dahé had no idea what was going on in Cliffside or Farad'hil, and his pep talks to the troops were less and less convincing. Maybe it was this lack of leadership that made the cats grow so bold and rebellious. That and a shortage of fresh meat.

Farkol screamed at the cats. "You are savage and undisciplined!" Their reply was a chorus of threatening growls.

The black-and-white cat finally got sick of Farkol's rant and bounded up to him, claws raised, hissing and spitting in the tongue of Air. Farkol's eyes went wide, and he and his underlings took a nervous step backward.

"Translator!" Farkol called in panic as the cat continued its pissed-off, spit-hiss symphony.

Translator was no fool. He didn't want to get in the middle, so he shouted his translations without leaving his place by my cage.

"The black-and-white says, 'We do not follow orders of fruit-eating philosophers.'"

Farkol actually stamped his foot. "Tell this cat he should run a comb through his greasy hair!"

I could already see the situation was going to devolve quicker than a YouTube comments thread. Translator repeated this reply in the sibilant, snarly Tongue of Air. Judging by the cat's furious reaction, he should have softened his words a bit.

"You will all be meat beneath our claws," came the translation of the furious black-and-white. "We will slash your soft bellies like we did your deer."

But fierce as the cats were, the mixed beings were not to be messed with. All over the compound, octonas and quadranas drew weapons except Farkol, who stepped behind one of the burlier quadranas. Up on the cliff face to my left, the one and only bidahéna at the camp gave a frightening call, which translated to: "Prepare to fall, low creature!" The bidahéna spread her wings and pulled back the string of a huge silver bow, ready to let her silver arrow fly.

I felt sick. I could practically see the big "Collateral Damage" sign hanging over me and Translator.

The black-and-white cat hissed an answer. "No, Fire-fool. It is *you* who will fall."

And you know what? The cat was right. As if the power had been cut in the wacky animatronic Hall of Dragons, every mixed being collapsed to the ground, dead. The cats stood frozen for a minute before they dared approach the bodies, kicking them, at first experimentally and then with gusto.

I was in shock. What could have killed all the mixed beings? Was this slaughter happening everywhere in the Realm? What about Tiqokh? But I didn't have time to think about it, because suddenly we were in the middle of a full-on cat victory party, and that's one party I'd advise you to skip. With a sickening crack and splat, the black-and-white cat cut off Farkol's head with the quadrana's own sword, and before you knew it, it was being tossed around like a gory basketball. They all looked sickeningly happy for a while, but then a fight broke out between the calico and the black-and-white, complete with that kind of angry mewing cats do before they pounce on each other.

"What's happening?" I asked Translator, the hairs on my arm standing up.

"A struggle for power, Kras-pa-han. We are in great danger. Wait here."

He ran off, leaving me defenceless. I crouched in the darkest corner of my cage, which wasn't all that dark. Several cats gave me the once-over as they ran by, and I swear they were sizing me up for a stew.

Translator was back, a fat iron key in his paw. "Hurry, hurry," he said as he unlocked the cage and swung the door wide.

The fur was literally flying in the middle of the compound as the two cats fought for leadership, but it was clear that whoever won, I was just going to end up so many steaks in the fridge. I ran after Translator to a little cave in the base of the cliff.

"What's in there?" I asked him, panting.

"My study."

I had to duck to get inside. The low-ceilinged space was even smaller than my cage, with grass mats on the floor and a one-row bookshelf with four more of Translator's handmade books.

"I will stand guard," Translator told me, seating himself in the cave's entrance. We were safe, at least for the time being. Safe, but trapped.

CHAPTER 42: *Reclaiming the Realm*

Davix, stunned into immobility, stared all around at the corpses of the mixed beings, many of whom he'd known his whole life. Up on the stage, Korda dropped to her knees, the knife deep in her shoulder, a growing bloodstain colouring the ceremonial robe. With sweat pouring from her brow, she crawled to the front of the stage and half rose, pushing the hair from her eyes.

"Defence of Realm, arm yourselves!" she shouted hoarsely. "Deputies, gather your squadrons and chase these stinking cats from the Citadel!" The brindle cat looked around, weighing the sudden shift in power, and called out orders in the Tongue of Air. Every cat in the courtyard followed him up and over the walls.

Grav'nan-dahé ran up the steps, followed by a physician who hurried to aid Korda. The Prime Magistrate shouted into the courtyard in his preacher's voice.

"People of the Realm, seek shelter in the bunkers! Protect the children and the elderly!" He looked down at Davix. "Go, help move your master and the other patients in the healing tent." Davix hurried to obey.

The People were frightened as they scurried into the barracks, but Davix knew he wasn't alone in feeling real hope for the first time in days. Still, the mixed beings dead? Another realm attacking for the first time in hundreds of cycles? It was hard to believe anything could ever return to normal.

The cats regrouped to attack at nightfall. But Defence of Realm was ready for them. They successfully repelled the attackers, killing two.

At dawn, Davix followed Grav'nan-dahé up into the foggy daylight where they found Korda, her shoulder bandaged and her arm in a sling, in weary conference with her deputies, including Stakrat.

"I doubt we'll hear from those animals while the sun is up," she told them. "Even so, I want the People to stay underground today."

"Agreed," said Grav'nan-dahé. "But we are not safe as long as a dragon of Air remains in the Realm."

"It's worse than that," Korda said. "If Zishun could be believed, the strands to the Realm of Air are fully restored. If we can't shut them down, more cats and probably more dragons will come."

The Prime Magistrate asked, "How can we break the strands?"

"I don't know. Without access to the DragonLaw, we can't read any relevant history. Someone among the People will probably have an idea." She looked up at the sky, shining weakly through the fog. "I must eat. Stakrat, I want you to rest until third bell."

Stakrat stood taller. "I'm fine, Korda. You're the one who was injured. I'll stay with you."

"That's an order. You're useless to me if you're exhausted. Davix, find a quiet cot where your friend can sleep."

The two apprentices walked together in silence, until Stakrat finally said, "Are we still friends?"

"I don't know," Davix conceded. "My thoughts of you weren't kind when I was a prisoner in the tower."

"You know I had no choice. I'm a soldier."

"You don't need to remind me."

"Please, Davix," she said, her voice growing throaty. "With all we've lost, I couldn't bear losing you, too." Her words made his heart ache. "It wasn't me who told the guard where they could find you. It was Grentz." Davix winced. "He thought he was doing the right thing."

Davix stopped walking and closed his eyes. He had never known this feeling before—sorrow and anger and desolation, swirling together in a gale so strong, it threatened to knock him to the ground. It finally passed, leaving only fatigue. He turned to Stakrat.

"I don't care what Grentz did. Or what you did," he said. "Everything in my life was already upside down, even before my arrest and this awful war. I've changed, Stakrat."

"Changed how?"

He sighed. "I thought I understood the world and my place in it. Atmospherics made me useful. The DragonLaw gave me purpose. I was so sure before."

"Before?"

"Before Rinby died...and before the Dragon Groom came to our realm. He smashed my certainty. He broke the shell I had built around myself, and everything spilled out in chaos. At first, it only felt like a terrible loss. But then I realized, with the shell broken, the light could finally come in."

"So, isn't that good?"

"Good? I'm undone, Stakrat! What does this new life mean if X'risp'hin is gone?" Davix felt himself dissolve, the tears bursting from him with a harsh, guttural bark of pain. Stakrat held him until he calmed down. Through his exhaustion, he remembered his task. Davix took her hand and led her to the nearest bunker entrance.

Before they could descend, the alarm horn sounded.

"From the anti-spinward sky!" a guard on the walls cried. Stakrat jumped in front of Davix, knife drawn, eyes tracking upward. Davix expected the return of the terrible Air dragon, or maybe all twenty-two come to destroy them in a final assault. But that's not what flew up over the walls of the Citadel. Appearing like a dream, beautiful and strange, were seven winged horses. They broke formation as they descended, landing in a clatter of hooves, breathing hard, damp with sweat and dew. Brown, black, piebald, white—each was uniquely lovely, in equal parts muscular and graceful. With brays and whinnies, they pawed the ground, shaking out their magnificent, leathery wings and then folding them on their backs.

The people had heard of the sky steeds of Farad'hil, but none had ever seen one. But as marvellous as the beasts were, they were still horses, and the stablekeepers knew to wipe them down, to feed and water them. In a pouch hanging from the lead steed's saddle, one of the grooms found the special grace book.

Grav'nan-dahé had taken over Zishun's desk, and there he opened the book. Davix and the assembled masters arrayed themselves around him and leaned in closer. On the first page, in calligraphy almost too elegant to read, were the words *GREETINGS FROM FARAD'HIL. THE KINGSOLVER REACHED US. DESCRIBE THE SITUATION IN CLIFFSIDE. <instruction: turn to the first blank page and write.>*

Grav'nan-dahé did as instructed. *The People are again in control of the city. Do I have the honour of addressing Great Renrit?*

As he wrote, the jewel on the cover winked on and off until Grav'nan-dahé's message faded into the paper to be replaced by more of the beautiful text.

INDEED, THAT HONOUR IS YOURS. THE OTHER DRAGONS WILL JOIN ME SHORTLY.<alert: all dragons, immediate attendance in Renrit's Editorium, RSVP regrets only>

What happened to the mixed beings? Grav'nan-dahé wrote on the next blank page.

THEY WERE TERMINATED BY INBY WHEN THEIR DEFECTS BECAME KNOWN TO US.<compare: elimination of hopping snakes, cycle 27, adjunct inquiry: mass production of antivenoms>
The masters and Davix straightened in shock as the meaning of the words sank in. The Dragon Lords had killed all the mixed beings. With the blink of a crystal in one of Lord Inby's mighty machines, the individuals they had always known and counted on, the nearest most ever came to standing before a dragon, were all dead. For the first time in his life, Davix felt doubt in the beneficence of the Dragon Lords. They were the saviours of the People and maintained the balance and beauty of the realm, but theirs was the power of life and death, a power they could wield with frightening nonchalance.

Grav'nan-dahé alone remained focussed on the grace book. He turned to a blank page, but before he could write any question, Renrit's next message appeared:

YOU MUST FLY SOME OF THE PEOPLE TO FARAD'HIL IMMEDIATELY. WE FIND IT DIFFICULT TO PERFORM OUR HOLY DUTIES WITHOUT SUPPORT. WE ARE ESPECIALLY IN NEED OF COOKS AND CLEANERS. <ref. Delicacies of the Dragon Palate, by Khel'hoon-satrap-dahé>

"No," Korda said. "We must find the stronghold of Air in the Chend'th'nif. We don't have time to fly to Farad'hil first." Davix wanted to cheer. Flying off to challenge the Air dragon also meant flying to X'risp'hin's rescue.

The Prime Magistrate was less impressed. "I am sure the Great Ones have taken these concerns into consideration."

"No offence, Grav'nan-dahé, but the dragons are locked away in their mountain, with the grace books dark. They have been blind to the outside world. Does Great Renrit even know where we may find the breach that powers the strands?"

Davix blurted out, "Wait, yes, he does know." He hadn't asked permission to speak, and the Prime Magistrate was clearly irritated, but Davix had caught the spirit of Korda's directness. "Rinby made rough calculations of the coordinates in the margins of her secret data. I copied them into the grace book."

Renrit confirmed this. In fact, they had replicated Rinby's work and produced a more precise calculation.

THE RIFT WILL BE LOCATED AT THE BASE OF THE MOUNTAIN KNOWN AS THE "RED HAMMER," DIRECTLY ADJACENT TO THE BADLANDS. <ref. Courting sites of dragons in the Decorous Era.>

Korda placed her hands on the table and leaned closer to the Prime Magistrate. "Grav'nan-dahé, please apologize to the Five, but we must use their sky steeds to mount an attack on the stronghold of Air."

Lok'lok-sur-nep-dahé, his voice full of agitation, said, "But we have been ordered to serve our lords! They are hungry!"

Grav'nan-dahé banged a fist on the desk. "Silence. I have made my decision. Four of the horses will fly to Farad'hil, three to the Chend'th'nif." Davix alone might have realized how much it cost Grav'nan-dahé to deviate at all from the Dragons' command.

With some kind of nascent plans in place, excitement spread through the group. Grav'nan-dahé wrote their decision in the grace book, and amazingly, Renrit and whatever dragons were with him agreed.

THOUGH WE DO NOT JOIN YOU IN BATTLE, KNOW THAT OUR PRIDE IN YOU IS WITHOUT COMPARE. BELOW, FIND THE EXACT COORDINATES OF THE RIFT AND AN OPTIMAL FLIGHT PATH. YOU WILL FLY TODAY, LED BY THE QUADRANA TIQOKH.
<compare: the Siege of Flar'far, Cycle 432.>

"But," stammered Krenlin-etnep-bor-dahé, "all the mixed beings are dead."

"Not I," Tiqokh replied, and they all turned to see him land gracefully on the stones of the square, folding his new wings on his back. "I remain. And I remain loyal."

CHAPTER 43: *Siege*

I awoke on the second morning in the cave with my stomach rumbling, sore and cold from sleeping on the damp ground. I wished I could sleep some more and not have to face the misery of our situation. A single torchstone lit our refuge. I already knew every bump and crack in the rock that surrounded us, and I had a complete mental inventory of every object in the cave: Translator's four bound volumes, his notebook, pen, bottle of ink, the cage's iron key, the almost empty sack of mystery-meat jerky, and the equally diminished barrel of rusty water.

Translator was awake, sitting in the front entrance of the cave, sharpening his improvised spear. He spent all his time near that entrance, slept there—probably badly—alert for attacks by his nasty comrades.

The other three cats had spent the first hours after we ran under-ground trying to convince him to come out and give me up. Sometimes they promised to just keep holding me hostage, and sometimes they tempted Translator with an invigorating human hunt followed by yummy barbecue. I have no idea how tempted he was, but he kept refusing even when their cajoling tones turned hostile. I know all this because he translated a lot of it for me. Maybe that's the main reason I believed he was on my side.

They tried attacking a couple of times, but they couldn't get past Translator's spear in the narrow entrance. Just to clarify, I was pressed up against the back wall during these attacks, whimpering and struggling not to piss myself as claws and fur and bone-chilling snarls filled the air. But my tortoiseshell cellmate could keep us safe as long as he stayed alert.

In between cat attacks, we spent a lot of the time discussing the Tongue of Fire. We were both of us student and teacher, him giving me insights into the history and grammar of the language, me supplying him a lot of new words he dutifully copied into his notebook. He had a theory that the tongues of the various realms had a common lineage, from the time before the realms separated from Earth. As school went, it was more interesting than usual, but I preferred talking to him about our lives, our families.

"Kras-pa-han, our situation is dire. I may never see my wife and kits again. Thinking of them fills me with despair and weakens my resolve."

"You don't know. We could still get out of this." I wasn't sure if I was saying that for his sake or mine. This was the third day of the siege, and I could feel hopelessness setting in.

"You should eat the last piece of jerky," I told him, a level of self-sacrifice I didn't know I had in me. "You're the one protecting us."

I handed him the dry, brown hunk which, under normal circumstances would have been highly unappealing. He tore off two-thirds for himself, and I gratefully ate the rest.

"I'm more worried about our water," he said, betraying no emotion. "What do we do when it runs out?"

He changed the subject, and I didn't object. "We have not talked about the Tongue of Earth. Is it difficult to pronounce?"

"It's not so simple," I said. "There's something like six thousand languages in the world. And sometimes there's more than one way of speaking the same language. Like, I speak North American English, not British English."

He considered this. "In the Realm of Air, we have but one goal: that our Dragon Lords conquer all of creation. For that, we need a common tongue. In a world of six thousand languages, are there an equal number of competing goals? Your world must be constantly at war with itself."

It was hard to argue with the insight.

Translator gave me an easier question to answer. "Is *inglish* the only Earth language you speak?"

"Pretty much."

"What words would you use to describe me in *inglish*?"

I grinned. "Oh, definitely *bad-ass*. And *moody*."

"I am a *bad-ass moody*," he ventured.

"Other way around, but for sure."

We got quiet again, each of us lost in his own thoughts. Cats came to the door sometimes, but Translator had stopped talking to them. He wouldn't answer me either the next time I tried to start up a conversation. He had gone inside himself, and it frightened me.

After what seemed like hours, he announced, "I will attack." He said it without any excitement, like calling in a pizza order.

I sat up abruptly. "What do you mean? You can't fight all three of them. We'll both be killed!"

"Our situation will not improve. Either I will be caught unawares in an attack as I grow weaker, or we will die for lack of water. I must take my chances in battle."

I wanted to tell him he wasn't a fighter, but I knew that would be an insult. I tried to prepare myself. We were probably about to die, but at least something was finally going to happen. Translator started flexing his muscles, cracking his neck, and checking the point of his spear. He was very methodical.

"Hand me the second volume on the bookshelf," he said, and I wondered how this played into his strategy. "This book is a treatise on the use of infixes in the Tongue of Fire. Of all my writing, I'm most proud of this. I hope it lives on even if I do not."

He put down the book and coiled himself at the entrance of the tunnel, ready to pounce. *You didn't say goodbye to me*, I thought. Translator sprang from the cave.

Immediately I heard howls of feline outrage, the sound of a high cry, and something toppling over with a bang. My heart was pounding, and I couldn't sit still. I grabbed the empty water container—a lidless cube of clay—and lifted it over my head, ready to brain any cat that entered. It wasn't long before the black-and-white pushed his head and shoulders through the door, his mohawk springing up to brush the ceiling.

"*Khssssssss-ffaaaff,*" he told me with a sick, toothy grin.

"Your mama plays with balls of yarn, asshole!" I screamed back, swinging the water container. He dodged it effortlessly and climbed farther in.

Another scream outside. More shouts and commotion than three squabbling felines could possibly make. Black-and-white must have agreed with this assessment because he paused, ears twitching, and started pulling himself backward from the cave. But just before his grotesque fright mask of a face disappeared, the eyes went wide. His paws flexed wide and he coughed a spitball of blood into my face before collapsing dead.

"Dragon Groom!" came a cry from outside. Someone was pulling the dead cat out of the entrance of the cave, and a moment later, the mask of horror was replaced by Stakrat's sweet and sweaty face.

I crawled out into the fresh air, standing for the first time in days, and surveyed the scene. The black-and-white cat lay at my feet, three arrows in its back. The calico cat lay on a pile of broken rocks, its neck clearly broken. Above it, on the ledge overlooking the camp, was Tiqokh…and he had frickin' *wings*! And in the middle of the compound stood Translator, his spear piercing the throat of the striped tabby, whose blood stained the stony ground.

Two guards from Defence of Realm had arrows notched in their bows, pointed at Translator.

"You will lower your spear and drop to your knees," shouted Korda, standing behind them, one arm in a sling. Translator didn't answer. He stood, panting heavily, looking down at the cat he'd killed. Korda shook her head. "He doesn't understand. Archers, prepare to fire."

I ran forward, screaming, "No! Don't kill him, Korda, he saved my life. Translator, do what they say!"

He dropped the spear and looked at me. "Kras-pa-han. I am most tired."

If Korda was surprised to hear how well he spoke, she didn't show it. "On your knees, cat, or we will kill you."

"Please, Translator."

He put his paws on his head and slowly sank to his knees in the blood of his fellow soldier of Air. The guards ran forward and bound his arms and legs. He didn't struggle.

"Korda," came a familiar voice. "Please, can I come down there now?" My heart, which had been heavy as lead, floated up like a silver balloon in the shape of a unicorn. It was Davix, standing above us on a ridge, half hidden in puffy white sheep fog, surrounded by three sky steeds, their muscular wings spread wide. It was like those pictures of heaven they used to paint, and Davix was my angel on high.

CHAPTER 44: *The Tables Turn and Turn*

The sun was already setting, and we lit a fire and cooked up a stew out of salted meat and root veggies the good folks from Cliffside had brought along. I don't know if I can begin to describe the relief of having been rescued, not to mention having a hot meal in my belly. While four guards watched the perimeter for any stray cats or the return of the Air dragon, I told Davix, Stakrat, Korda, and Tiqokh everything I knew, including the fact that the dragon had not been seen for seven or eight days. Davix sat behind me with his arms wrapped around my chest. There was nothing you could have said, including "Hey, doughnuts!" that would have made me move. Above us, the strands to the Realm of Air were brighter than I'd ever seen them. I could just make out the sphere of the cloudy world hanging distant in the realm sky.

"What's the plan?" I asked. "Are the dragons coming from Farad'hil to kick the invaders' asses?"

Korda shook her head. "No, they trust us with this fight."

"But there's a war on," I said, surprise turning to outrage. "And they're just sitting safe and sound in their mountain? They *trust you* to fight for them?"

Tiqokh cut me off. "And we are honoured by their trust. Do not fear, Crispin, we have a plan." Tiqokh led us back to where the sky steeds were tethered. From a big leather bag, he removed two coiled metal tubes. When he untied the cord wrapped around one, the coil sprang out open to form a broken circle. At one end was a shiny metal clasp with a red jewel in it, and when he closed the circle to create an outsized hula hoop, the jewel started glowing.

Tiqokh said, "This is an explosive device. It will be detonated in the realm fissure." We all looked over at the big, glowing firepit, which chose that moment to sneeze out a lava booger. "The explosion should seal off the energy stabilizing the strands to Air. We must stop more dragons from arriving in our realm."

"Will that kill any dragons already on their way over?" I asked.

"Oh, no, X'risp'hin," Davix said. "Don't worry. If they are already crossing, they will fall unharmed back to the Realm of Air."

He gave me a reassuring squeeze, and I made a fake sigh of relief. Actually, I had been hoping the answer was yes.

"Why do you have two of the, uh, explosion hoops?"

Tiqokh said, "The other is backup, but I do not think we'll need it." He took two translucent stones, about the size of chicken eggs, from separate pockets in the leather bag and handed them to me. One was a beautiful twilight blue, the other a vivid crimson.

"Crispin, I will give you a role to play. Please tap the trigger stones together so we can test the connection." I took them and was about to bang them together when the quadrana touched my arm. "Very gently. Or else the detonation will occur now and kill us all."

"Uh…right. Okay." Holding the rocks at arm's length and cringing, I gave them the tiniest of taps. The assembled ring glowed for a second. After remembering to breathe again, I tried to hand the stones back to Tiqokh. He ignored me—deliberately, I thought. My "role" wasn't over yet. I put one stone in each of my front pants pockets so they wouldn't accidentally hit each other.

Tiqokh said, "There is no time to waste. I will enter the fissure and decide on the placement of the explosive. If we shut down the strands tonight, we can fly to Cliffside at dawn."

"Do you need help?" Stakrat asked him.

"The heat inside the fissure is too intense for a human body. I must work alone."

He took the assembled hula hoop and crossed the compound until he was standing above the pit, his face lit red by the fires below. Spreading his wings wide, he flew down out of sight.

Davix and I didn't have anything to do, so we took one of the bedrolls and lay down. Despite the heat of the night, I burrowed deep into his arms. Now that I'd been rescued, all the fear I had been pushing down in the last days was rising to the surface. I kept bursting into tears, and Davix would stroke my hair and my chest, kiss my neck, and whisper, "You're safe. I'm with you." I was embarrassed by my out-of-control emotions, but he didn't make me feel ashamed. "You were so brave to be here on your own, X'risp'hin," he said.

But I hadn't been alone. I looked over at Translator, squatting forlornly in the same cage where I'd been held, and knew I had to do something. We found Korda at a desk in what had been Farkol-dahé's tent, reading through his notes by torchstone. Half of the tent was given over to Farkol's outfits. It was like being backstage at a Vegas show.

"Can me and Davix bring Translator some food?" I asked.

"Yes, but you may not unlock the cage."

"Thank you, Kras-pa-han," Translator said as he ate. "Please tell your commander I will do whatever is asked of me."

"I will, I promise," I told him. "Hey, this is Davix. He's my boyfriend." My heart had started pounding before I said this, because it was supposed to be a big announcement—said as much for Davix's sake as the cat's—but the word had no *oomph* in the Tongue of Fire. It just meant he was my friend and he was a boy. I concentrated on saying the word in English, "*Boyfriend...*" but, of course, this meant even less to him. It even felt weird to me, like English had become some foreign language I was studying for extra credit. For the first time, I wondered how different things would be when I got back Earth. Now that my copper blood was used to life in the Realm of Fire, would it make me feel like a stranger in my own home?

Davix surprised me by bowing to Translator. "X'risp'hin told me you saved his life. I am grateful to you."

"You may not believe this, human of Fire, but there is honour in our world." He looked up at the strands and at his realm, which lay beyond them, out of sight. Suddenly, the hair on his neck and back rose, and he exhaled a long hiss.

"What is it?" I asked, alarmed.

"Kras-pa-han, go to the tool chest. In the top drawer on the left side, you will find a far-glass."

"What's a far-glass?"

Davix said, "It's a metal tube with glass lenses so you can see at a distance."

"Oh, a *telescope*. Is something wrong?"

Translator's voice was tight. "Hurry, human. And tell your commander to join us."

After finding the far-glass, I spotted Stakrat counting arrows and asked her to bring Korda to the cage.

"We are all very busy, X'risp'hin," she said. "What is it?"

"I don't know yet. Just...come." She followed me back to the cage, and I handed Translator the far-glass. He focussed on the strands and began mewing low, ominous tones.

"What do you see?" I asked, looking up into the sky, dread creeping into my chest.

Translator put his paws around me from inside the cage and pushed the far-glass in front of my face. The light through the eyepiece was bright enough to blind me for a few seconds, but then, just above the strands, I thought I saw something. I twisted the interlocking tubes, and the image came into focus. I swore in English. Four more Air dragons were flying our way on smoky wings. And floating around them, like nasty little attending angels, was another bunch of cat soldiers.

"Oh shit, look, look!" I handed Stakrat the telescope, and she gasped at the coming horror. Calling to Korda, she ran into the night.

"Let me out!" Translator said. "The penalty for capture is death!" But I didn't have the key, much less the authority.

Korda was out of her tent, scrambling up on a rock in the middle of the compound.

"Tiqokh!" she screamed, and despite the loud roar of the pit, he must have heard, because he flew up into the air and landed a little ways off. His skin was so hot from being down near the lava, steam was rising off him.

Korda pointed to the strands. "Four Dragons are on their way, and another ten cats. Are you almost ready with the explosive?"

The quadrana looked up, apparently able to see the coming creatures without the far-glass. "Not yet. I must be sure I've set the device correctly. We no longer have time to set the second explosive if the first fails."

Stakrat said, "How long until they get here?"

"Less than an hour, I believe. Dimensional parallax does not allow for a more precise estimate. Crispin, when next I emerge from the fissure, you must immediately bring the trigger stones together with force. That will set off the explosion."

Before I could object, Tiqokh flew into the air and back down into the fissure.

"I have to go check in with the guards on the perimeter," Korda said. "Dragon Groom and Davix, I want you back up on the ridge. Stakrat, you're guarding them. Signal if you see the Air dragon or another cat. Go!"

We climbed up a winding path to the ridge and crouched behind some rocks, watching the fissure. I held a trigger stone in each fist, fussing with them nervously. "Tiqokh should have given these to someone experienced. What if I accidentally hit the stones together and blow him up, and then everyone dies because of me?"

"Don't be foolish," Davix said, reaching over to stroke my head, but I pulled away. It bugged me how he underestimated my talent for fucking up.

But Stakrat understood. "You won't, X'risp'hin," she said. "Many times in these past days, Korda has given me duties I worried were too much, given my own lack of experience. But war is new to all of us, and no one is truly prepared. Korda believes in me, so I have no choice but to believe in myself. Perhaps that is the lesson Tiqokh wishes to teach you."

"Okay," I said. "I'll try." A small pebble hit my head. Streams of falling dust began falling from above, making us cough. "What's going on?" I said and looked upwards.

Something was happening to the cliff face. It seemed to be shaking, as though an earthquake was passing through. But the ground under our butts wasn't shaking, so it wasn't an earthquake. The shaking turned to writhing, like squirming snakes embedded in the rock were waking up. Wind rose around us, whirling into shrill dust devils that grew into twisting, grey columns as they scooped up the earth. We stared, stunned, as the twisters merged with the form detaching itself from the cliff face. The muscle and dust resolved into a familiar shape, camouflaged in plain sight for more than a week. It was the dragon of Air.

CHAPTER 45: *Beasts of Heaven When They Fall*

The dragon spread its massive wings, jumping down on the ridge, almost crushing us under its talons.

"*FFFFFFFFSSSAAAAAAAHHHAAA-KLOOOOHHHHMMMM-AAAAAHHHHHHFF-FAAASSSSSAF!*" it shrieked, staring up at the strands, and maybe Translator was right about the common mother tongue of the realms, because I thought I could almost understand. I think it was saying, "My family comes!"

"This way!" Stakrat screamed over the whine of the wind. The earth shook beneath us every time the dragon moved. We followed her across the ridge, which narrowed and narrowed until we had to cross in single file, our backs against the cliff face, a steep hill at our feet. We were finally putting some distance between us and the Air dragon when the ledge crumbled away under my feet, and down I went.

I heard Davix screaming my name as I tried to control my descent down the almost vertical hill. Blinded and choked by dust, I fell faster and faster, finally snagging my foot on a root and tumbling head over heels into the main area of the camp. My left arm hit the ground first, and the rest of my body came down on top of it. A spectacular light show of pain shot through all my senses.

"Kras-pa-han! Are you hurt?" shouted Translator from the cage, just off to my left.

But before I could say anything about my busted arm and the blood pouring from my nose, the dragon of Air leaped down from the ridge like it was no more than a step-stool. The repulsive leviathan danced around my head, although I don't think it even knew I was there, and began to spit single syllables in the Tongue of Air:

"*KHAFF! SKEH! ARRSSFFF!*" And again, buried in these sounds were words I could just understand through my pain. "*Unity! Blood! Conquest!*"

The collision happened so close to me, I felt the *WHOOM* of displaced air deep in my guts. I pushed myself into the ground as a mass of flesh and scales, steam and dust rolled past, surging across the compound, crashing into another of the enclosing cliffs. Only then, as they got back up on their giant feet, did I see who the headliners were in this Wrestling Extravaganza of the Realms. In this corner, the butt-ugly, nameless dragon of Air! And in the far corner, for the first time in this tournament, that lizard living large, that pyrotechnic poet, Sur of Farad'hil!

"THE SKY SPLITS/INFECTION ENTERS THROUGH THE WOUND/BARBAROUS STENCH OF BATTLE/THE PRIMITIVE PAST UNAPPEASED!"

Sur's juicy poetry shook the rocks. But any hope this would just be a rap battle was quickly dispelled. The dragon of Air leaped up from where it had fallen and crashed back into Sur, knocking her on her back. Despite having paid plenty for ringside seats, I decided it might be wise to get the hell out of there. I tried to push myself up, but I had forgotten about my arm. My scream mixed with the roar of the dragons and the howl of the fissure as my vision went black and starry for a few seconds. I got to my feet more carefully and limped over to the cage. Translator was pressed up against the bars to watch the fight.

"K'FFFSSSSAAAAAA-RAHHHHHASSSSAAL!" the Air dragon spat back at Sur, poised above her with its wings raised. Long, curved spikes emerged from the tip of each wing.

"Weak child with no sense of history," Translator interpreted in the cage behind me, screaming against the whine of the wind.

"FRR'AHHHHHATLA-KHOOOOOLII-KRAI!"

"It is war alone that writes the truth, writes it in blood."

Sur's tail snapped out like a snake and grabbed the Air dragon by one of its five ankles, pulling it off balance so it crashed on the rocks with an ear-splitting wail. That's when I realized I was in a Japanese *kaiju* movie, but without the buttery comfort of popcorn.

Sur jumped to her feet. *"A WAR FOR PEACE?/CHAOS IN THE NAME OF BALANCE?/NO CONTRADICTION LEADS TO DICTUM/NOR ERUPTION TO REASON!"*

The Air dragon growled long and low, birthing multiple mini-cyclones all around the compound. I tried to game out the odds on the fight. Both were physically strong, although the Air dragon was bigger and had those spikes on its wings. Plus that whole crazy wind power. Sur, on the other hand, had muscle and…rhymes? Yeah, I didn't like the odds. I squinted through the growing dust haze toward the fissure.

Was Tiqokh almost ready? I briefly panicked I'd maybe lost the trigger rocks when I fell, but they were still in my pockets.

The dragons circled each other, the earth trembling with each step. Arrows rained down from the ridge, fired by Stakrat and the other guards, but they passed through the Air dragon's skin of wind, bouncing off its bones or flying straight through the gaps.

Translator and I clung fearfully to the bars of the cage in the growing hurricane. One guard had climbed down from the ridge, spear poised, trying to find a meaningful place on the Air dragon to aim for. With a shout I could see but not hear, he hurled the spear at the Air dragon's head. But before it reached its destination, a gust of wind slapped it aside. The dragon screeched, and two mini-cyclones at the edge of the compound changed directions and descended on the hapless guard. Before our eyes, his limbs were ripped loose, his body torn open like a pillow.

Sur shrieked. *"YOU HAVE SLAUGHTERED MY CHILD/YOUR SAVAGERY ENDS HERE!"* The fringes on her neck were glowing red with her anger.

But the Air dragon looked unstoppable. It curled the ends of its wings so the spikes were poised over Sur's head and hissed its reply.

Translator, his voice high and tense, interpreted. "And now, the first of the mewling dragon kits will fall!"

Sur's glowing fringes were brighter than ever, shifting from red to orange to white, dancing like an exotic octopus stripper. The Air dragon's right wing shot forward, but in that moment, Sur reared back and opened her mouth wide. It wasn't poetry that shot out, but a spray of fire so hot and terrible that even halfway across the compound, I had to cover my face. Squinting through my fingers, I watched the flame engulf the Air dragon's shoulder. Skin and sinew burned, bone charred. The dragon screamed and tried to pull away, but it was too late. The wing broke off and fell to the ground with a crash.

Still spitting sparks, Sur stomped the ground, making little earthquakes, chanting, *"NO MERCY/I CURSE THEE, DRAGON OF AIR/REALM OF NO BALANCE/YOUR PALACE WILL FALL/FORGIVING IS NOT IN MY VOCABULARY/BETTER BE WARY, MY FLAMING DOES THE BLAMING!"*

The Air dragon writhed on the ground, one wing gone, three legs charred and misshapen. I almost felt bad for it as the wind died and all life seemed to leave its skeletal body. A thick, scary silence descended on everything. Was that it? Were we safe? I looked back at Translator. I looked up at Davix and Stakrat on the ridge.

I was just about to officially exhale for the first time since the attack began when, in a shower of embers, Tiqokh burst from the fissure, rising high in the air.

"Crispin, now!"

I yelped and dug into my pocket for the stones, dropping one in the process. As I picked it up, I realized I couldn't bang them together with my left arm out of commission.

"Damn it!" I yelled, looking around desperately.

Translator called out, "Kras-pa-han, what are you doing?"

I spotted a flat rock and ran for it, placing the blue stone in the middle and raising the crimson one high in the air. I brought it down hard and missed, sending the blue stone shooting sideways off the rock. I retrieved and reset it, raising the stone again.

"Are those trigger stones?" the cat hissed in alarm. "No, wait! Don't!" But there was no time for different orders.

I slammed the crimson rock down with all my strength. A flash of light erupted from the fissure, and the ground rumbled beneath us. Everyone except Sur was knocked off their feet by the underground explosion. Fire and smoke belched high into the air, and the pit collapsed on itself.

I looked up at the strands that led to the Realm of Air. They were fading, blinking fainter and fainter, and finally failing. With no strands above and no firepit below, inky darkness engulfed us. Only the red and yellow glow of Sur's fringes remained, dancing in triumph like a hundred snakes at a club.

Behind me, Translator gave a heartbreaking howl. I turned and saw a glint off his black eyes. "My home…" he said. "My family…The strands are broken. I cannot return."

My stomach dropped in horror at what I had done to him.

"I-I'm sorry," I stammered. I had no words. I turned and walked away in shame.

Korda and the guards pulled out torchstones and scrambled down from the ridge in the dim glow. Now that I could see where I was going, I hurried over to Sur.

"Are you okay?" I asked as she licked a wound on her shoulder.

"POETRY IS ACTION / POETRY IS MUSCLE / POETRY BREAKS THE BACK OF THE WORLD / NEVER DOUBT THE POET HERO." She leaned down and sniffed me. *"YOU ARE INJURED, DRAGON GROOM."*

"It's not too bad," I said like a freaking war hero.

Up on the ridge, Davix shouted my name, and I waved my good arm at him.

Korda called, "Stakrat, Davix, remain on the ridge. The compound is not secure."

Sur sniffed me again. "*I BELIEVE YOU HAVE MINGLED BODIES WITH THE IMPUDENT YOUNG HUMAN/YOUR BLOOD MAKES FIRE WHEN IT FLOWS WITH HIS.*"

"Not that it's your business, Ms. Nosey. But yeah, he's my boyfriend."

"*CLIMB UP ON MY HAND,*" she commanded, "*AND I WILL REUNITE YOU.*" I did as I was told, and she lifted me up to the ridge.

Sur's head remained close, inspecting me and Davix as we hugged, which made Davix pretty nervous. He said, "Come, X'risp'hin. I'll make a sling for your arm. And give me those stones." I had forgotten I was still gripping the trigger stones. I felt the ache in my hand as I finally let them go.

When he was done with his nursing duties, we kissed. I knew Sur was checking us out again because I could feel her hot breath on my back. I turned and said, "Are you researching human love? Or are you just waiting for someone to scratch your head?"

Stakrat gasped. "X'risp'hin! We do not speak to the Five like that! Forgive him, Great Sur," she said, bowing. But a deep rumble was bubbling out of Sur's chest, and I recognized her dragon version of a laugh.

"*HUMAN AND DRAGON FOUGHT TOGETHER/PERHAPS IT IS TIME TO LOOSEN THE TETHER/FOR HUMANS TO SPEAK TO FIRE BEASTS/AS EQUALS, NOT AS MOSTS AND LEASTS.*"

Sur had recited this poem in the modern version of the Tongue of Fire. Stakrat and Davix looked stunned by her revolutionary pronouncement.

I said, "Ha! Grav'nan will shit his pants when he hears that." I reached out my good hand in their direction. "Come on! Sur's right. We won this war together." With surprised smiles spreading across their faces, Davix and Stakrat took my hand in theirs, and we lifted them together, whooping and cheering.

Sur spread her wings and, rising up high on her back legs, proclaimed, "*HEAR US, ANCIENT SPIRITS OF EARTH AND REALMSPACE! THE REALM OF FIRE IS NOT FOR THE TAKING!/IN BALANCE, NOT WAR DO WE...*" But her words collapsed into a strangled cry, and her yellow eyes went wide. We watched in uncomprehending horror as a glowing white spike emerged through her chest.

"No!" I screamed as the wounded dragon of Air, more skeleton than living beast, rose behind Sur and withdrew the spike of its remaining wing. Hot, yellow blood spurted from Sur's chest, and she fell, body smashing against the ridge, knocking us all off our feet. She crashed to the floor of the compound at the Air dragon's feet. The wind began to rise again, putting swirling flesh on the horrible bones. Below, Korda and her guards shot useless arrows and spears at it.

The dragon's voice was a long, deep, growl, and this time I couldn't find any meaning in it but *Death! Death! Death!* Unable to stop the howl coming out of my own throat, I reached to take Davix's hand…but he was gone. The world was ending, and the boy I loved was nowhere, sucked into the abyss, into *death, death!* I stumbled in circles, calling his name. Maybe he'd fallen from the ridge like I did before. Maybe he was lying unconscious, about to be trampled by the horror creature of Air. Dropping to my knees, I squinted into the darkness below. Then I heard his voice.

"Hail to the mighty ruler of the Realm of Air!" Davix called against the howl of the wind. He was down below in the compound, holding a lantern high above him. Just behind him, the tethered sky steeds stomped in panic and rose on their wings to escape, only to be pulled back down by the ropes that held them.

"Translator," Davix yelled, "I need you to relay my words."

Translator was as tough a soldier as Korda. Despite everything that had just happened—to us, to him and his family—his voice now called out clear and strong, translating Davix's greeting to the Dragon.

The Air dragon turned and looked down at Davix, who stood too close to the monster. Way too close.

The voice he used was one I had never heard before—authoritative, cold, and confident. "The earliest verses of our DragonLaw command the People to put their faith in their mighty dragon leaders. You, great dragon of Air, are the leader we have awaited for thousands of cycles. Bless us with your might and mercy, and in return, we offer our worship and obedience…and more!"

No one moved. No one breathed.

Then the Air dragon spoke, and Translator translated. "And what '*more*' can weak creatures like you offer to one such as I?"

"This, Great One." He put down the lantern and lifted something else into the air. At first I didn't realize what it was, but then, in an instant, I understood his risky, maybe suicidal plan. A cold chill went through me.

"This is the crown of our realm," Davix called. "Worn only by the mightiest of dragons. It would be a mockery for it to sit on the heads of the weak creatures hiding in Farad'hil. What kind of rulers are they, who sent their youngest and least experienced to fight you? No, this crown must go instead to the noble dragon of Air who now graces our land."

The dragon's question was the sound of cyclone and storm. "The one who wears this crown...That one is the mightiest?"

"Yes, Great Master. Please grant me the honour of placing it on your head as a token of our obedience."

I felt like I was going to scream. I wanted to run to him, pull him away to safety. But this had to happen. If death or life awaited us, Davix's plan was maybe our last chance.

"*Iiiiiisssssfffffffff*aHhaaaaNnnn-haaaaa," breathed the dragon.

"You may," the cat translated.

The dragon lowered its head. Even from where I stood, I could see Davix's hands shaking as he closed the end of the circle into the clasp. The red crystal lit up. Davix placed the hoop on a pointy bit of the Air dragon's bony head. Careful not to let the crown fall, the dragon raised its neck slowly, raised its chest up and up, towered as high as it could so we could all appreciate its newly crowned majesty.

"And thus is justice done in the Realm of Fire," Davix said, and I realized the voice he had been using was more than a little like Grav'nan-dahé's.

He held the trigger stones in his upraised hands.

"For the Realm of Fire," he said, bringing the stones together.

Light, force, a noise like the end of all things.

Then nothing.

When I finally struggled to my feet, I had no idea how much time had passed. Through the shifting dust, I could just make out pinpricks of light from the fallen torchstones.

"Davix!" I called, though it was hard to hear my own voice through the ringing in my ears. I staggered in what I hoped was the right direction, calling his name, coughing. I found him sitting up, dazed, hugging his knees. I wrapped my uninjured arm around him, but he didn't seem to notice.

"I killed a dragon," he said, his voice flat.

"Yeah! You were amazing!" I enthused, because I didn't understand yet what was going on with him. Korda appeared through the cloud of dust, holding a bright lantern. In its light, we saw the shattered Air dragon looming above us, its head and neck gone. And as we watched, it disintegrated, turning to mist and smoke that sailed away in little spinning eddies until all that was left was a pile of ash.

And then I saw Sur.

I ran to her, dropping to the ground beside her head.

"Sur? Are you alive?"

She wheezed, and finally managed to say, "*THERE ARE MANY STATIONS ON THE ROAD FROM LIFE TO DEATH.*"

I laughed through my tears. "You talk kind of cryptic sometimes, anyone ever tell you that?"

"*VIXTET OFTEN CLAIMS MY VERSE STEERS A POINTLESS-LY MEANDERING PATH. I OBVIOUSLY DISAGREE.*"

"Obviously."

"*BUT YES, KHARIS'PAR'IH'IN, I FEAR MY OWN DISSOLU-TION IS NEAR.*"

"No!" I cried. "Don't worry; we'll get help. And screw Vixtet, I understand you fine."

"*PERHAPS BECAUSE SHE IS OLD, AND YOU AND I ARE YOUNG.*"

"Yeah, you're not a day over a hundred and seventy-five." I leaned my head against her, my tears running down her cool scales. "Hey, Sur, you know that rhyme you couldn't find? *K'rizat-zhis?* I was thinking about it when I was in the cage. What about *d'niz'that-khis?*"

Sur was silent for a long time, and just when I thought maybe she'd died on me, she let out a long, shaky breath.

"*YESSSS,*" she whispered and recited a verse in the ancient dialect with faltering voice: "*Lok'lik khrav k'rizat-zhis/Nof'fethan karu dniz'that-khis...TO THE SOULS LOST AND SCATTERED WHEN CAME THE FLOOD/COME YOU TOGETHER AT THE CALL OF THE BLOOD.*"

"I like it," I said, stroking her fringes.

Her reply was almost inaudible. "*IT COULD STILL BE...MORE... CONCISE.*" And she died.

I pulled myself away as her body, like the Air dragon's, disintegrated. But unlike that beast of darkness and death, Sur decayed to a pile of embers, glowing low and red in the night. And in the embers were the coloured jewels from her breast. Davix and Stakrat joined me, kneeling on the ground as the embers slowly went dark. We were witnesses to all that life, all that history crumbling to ash.

PART VI

THE DRAGON GROOM AWAKENS

CHAPTER 46: *Rising Up*

"What will you do with Translator?" I asked Korda as she ate her breakfast. We wore matching slings.

"He will return to Cliffside with us. If he wants any kind of clemency, he'll have to tell us everything he knows about the cat soldiers. We must round them up before they can establish a stronghold."

I walked over to the cage. Translator sat inside, cross-legged. He hadn't said a word to anyone since the strands were broken.

"Are you okay?" I asked. "Can I get you anything?"

He didn't move, didn't even look up at me.

"Translator, I'm really sorry. I don't know what to say. I didn't have a choice." My words were pebbles thrown at a stone wall. Their inadequacy humiliated me, and I walked away. The cat didn't owe me forgiveness. I'd stolen his life from him.

Translator wasn't the only one silenced by grief. Since we'd woken up, Davix had been perched on a rock, staring out at the Badlands, crying quietly. We'd already spent half the night having variations of the same discussion:

"I killed a dragon. There is no greater crime."

"You saved us."

"I killed a dragon."

"Someone had to. It murdered Sur."

This time we said nothing; I just held him so he wouldn't fall into a pit of despair. Truth was, I needed the support as badly as he did.

One of the guards came over with two bowls of soup, and we drank in silence. When we were finished, I followed Davix over to Korda's tent, where she was staring into a grace book.

"I wrote a message to Great Renrit," Korda told us, "and I'm waiting for a reply."

Davix asked, "What did you tell him?"

"That we secured the enemy outpost and shut down the strands. That we're ready to return to Cliffside."

"What about…?"

"Yes, I told him all about the dragon of Air. And Sur."

"You told him what I did?"

"I had to file a complete report, Davix."

His shoulders slumped. I couldn't do anything to make him feel better, and it broke my heart.

Just outside, Sur's jewels were laid out on a piece of rough cloth. Through the door of the tent, I watched reflections of the early morning light dancing playfully inside them as if they didn't know everything was about death today.

"We have to take Sur's jewels with us," I said. "For her funeral or whatever."

Before Korda could reply, the page of the grace book went blank, and large, loopy writing appeared in its place.

"*YOU WILL BRING THE DRAGON GROOM TO FARAD'HIL IMMEDIATELY. <ref. Ceremony of Succession, copper blood, five must there be> TIQOKH WILL ALSO ACCOMPANY YOU.*"

"Excellent," I said. "Wait till you see Farad'hil, Korda. It's super swank."

"You will go to the dragon abode," Korda told us, "but I must take one of the steeds and return to Cliffside with the prisoner."

"But don't you want to see Farad'hil once in your life?" I asked her.

I'm sure she was tempted, but she shook her head. "I must return to the city so we may defeat the threat of the cat soldiers. Perhaps Davix should come with me."

"What?" I had to stop myself from shouting. "No, I need him with me."

Davix's voice was quiet. "X'risp'hin, I am not worthy to enter the holy mountain."

"No, shut up. I'm the Dragon Groom and I totally need you."

"Very well," Korda answered. "Stakrat and another of the guard will accompany you. They must assess the security of the dragon abode in case any of the cats make their way there."

We struck camp, and soon, three sky steeds headed off in two different directions. As we flew over the top of the world, I gasped at what I saw. The endless fog that had covered everything since the day I arrived in the Realm of Fire was burning away in the morning sun. For the first time, I saw huge, awesome views—mountains, forests, fields;

I even thought I could see Cliffside in the distance—the Atmospherics Tower and the Citadel shining in the sun. I turned around to look at Davix, who was sharing a sky steed with me, and saw he was crying again. But he smiled when he saw my excitement and squeezed me tighter.

"*Sarensikar* is finally over!" he yelled above the rushing wind.

Chapter 47: *The Groom of Etnep*

No one greeted us when we landed at the entrance to Farad'hil. Tiqokh had to hammer on the high gates with his big fist before someone opened up.

"Greetings, Lak'wyr," Stakrat said to the bedraggled, exhausted guy at the door. I seemed to recall him from Cliffside.

"Please hurry inside," he replied. "We have to serve the dragons their dinner shortly, and we are behind with cleaning their quarters. Do any of you know how to repair a fountain? Great Vixtet says she cannot concentrate on her tasks since the one in her workshop went out of service."

Without its little army of mixed beings doing all the work, Farad'hil was not the well-oiled utopia I remembered from my last visit. Nonetheless, it was fun to watch my friends freaking out with awe at actually visiting this sacred place. Even I had kind of forgotten how impressive the central core was, dropping down twenty stories below us, and rising ten above, the road spiralling around its edge.

Davix, his voice choked up, said, "I didn't think I would ever see the halls of the Dragon Lords."

"It is truly wondrous," Lak'wyr said. Was it my imagination, or was he giving Davix some creepy side-eye? "However, we have been so busy since we arrived, I've hardly had the chance to appreciate it. And now the news of Great Sur..." Everyone lowered their heads a bit.

Stakrat said, "I must speak to the Dragon Lords, Lak'wyr. I need to gather details for Korda on the defences of Farad'hil."

"Mostly we've been meeting with Great Vixtet. You can accompany us when we bring her dinner."

"May I be allowed to accompany you as well?" Davix said. "Vixtet is patron of my house, and...and I feel I must explain what happened in the Chend'th'nif."

Lak'wyr's mouth grew thin and hard. "Great Vixtet was most emphatic. She does not want you brought into her presence. I'm surprised you would ask."

"What?" I asked. "Why not?"

Davix walked away until he was standing at the edge of the road, looking down into the core. "I am a dragon killer, X'risp'hin. I am not fit to stand in the presence of our honoured lords."

I was furious. I told Lak'wyr, "What a load of crap! That Air dragon needed killing. Davix is a hero! Let me go talk to Vixtet about it." And to Davix, I said, "Don't stand so close to the edge."

"Dragon Groom, you are to be brought to your sleeping quarters where you will await instructions. If you don't mind, D'gada-vixtet-thon could accompany you there."

The guy was really getting on my last nerve. "Of course I don't mind! Wait…what instructions?" Then I realized what he meant. I had to go and wait for my, uh, *appointment* with Queen Etnep. Somehow, I had forgotten about that, and now that I remembered, I wanted to forget again. I grabbed Davix's hand, taking the opportunity to pull him back from the edge. "Yeah, come with me, please. Forget about Vixtet."

Gulga, a girl of maybe twelve in Earth years, was assigned to lead us. She was shy of me but held Davix's other hand as we walked up the road. I was glad to see her mind hadn't been poisoned against him.

"It's beautiful here, Davix. And it was so much fun riding the sky-steeds. When we arrived, all the dragons were waiting for us. Inby's my patron, and I got to touch his head!" She was practically dancing with excitement.

"I am surprised they sent children to Farad'hil, Gulga."

"The dragons asked them to send four kids. Maybe it's because we could all fit on one steed. Mostly we're running errands and helping the dragons get dressed and such."

That was when I realized where we were headed. "They're putting us up in Sur's abode?"

"The dragons said you stayed there before."

When we got to Sur's gates, we were startled by a sudden flash of black and red shooting out of the air.

"Flak!" Davix cried in delight, as the kingsolver landed on his shoulder.

Gulga clapped her hands. "Oh good, he flew off after delivering his message, and no one's been able to catch him."

The bird played with Davix's hair, and Davix reached up to scratch his head. "He knows me."

When we entered Sur's abode, we found everything was a mess— curtains pulled down, trunks upended, like she'd been turning the place upside down looking for her phone.

"What happened here?" Davix asked.

"It was like this when we arrived. We think Great Sur did it before she flew to the Chend'th'nif."

The sight really upset me. What had been going through the dragon's head? My vanity wanted to think she was crazy with worry about me. But then I thought of the prophecy. Maybe Sur went nuts because she knew she would die if she went to the Chend'th'nif. Maybe she was beating back at death itself. But if leaving Farad'hil meant death, why did she do it?

Because. Because she alone of the five dragons was brave enough to face the invaders. She flew to her death because she didn't believe she had a choice. *Ekdahi.* Shit, I would have trashed my room, too.

My thoughts were interrupted by the sound of yipping. Four foxes ran out from a little alcove and began jumping all over me, licking any piece of my flesh they could get to.

"Hey, guys!" I said, laughing, squatting to scratch their heads. Flak cawed in alarm and flew up to sit on a beam near the ceiling.

Gulga made a face of disgust. "Lak'wyr plans to shoot those pests when he has a minute."

I turned a serious eye on her. "You tell him—are you listening carefully? You tell him that the Dragon Groom forbids it. These were Sur's pets, and they will be treated with respect and taken care of. Is that clear?"

"Y-yes, Dragon Groom." Gulga made a fast head and heart gesture at me. "But watch out. Their scat is everywhere."

While Gulga filled the big bath for us, we wandered through Sur's abode. It felt haunted. We even climbed up the ladder to her sanctum. All of the flying words that had buzzed around my ears like talking mosquitoes were gone. The scraps of swirling paper lay lifeless on the floor and on her work table. Despite having been right in front of Sur when she died, despite having watched her disintegrate, I don't think I really believed she was gone until I stood in that dead room.

My voice came out hoarse. "We need to gather up all her poetry, make sure someone takes care of it."

"You must give it to Great Renrit for inclusion in the DragonLaw,"

Davix said. I supposed he was right. The DragonLaw was the best place for it, but somehow that sounded like a sad fate. Her work shouldn't just be an appendix, next to last year's corn crop yields and the number of cases of diarrhoea in Cliffside.

When we returned to the bedchamber, I couldn't wait to get into the bath. I washed off days of dust, sweat, and fear, and then just luxuriated in the heat and enjoyed the show of Davix stripping to join me in the big tub.

After Gulga served us dinner, a woman from Health and Healing examined my arm and told me it was only sprained. She rubbed a warm cream into it that smelled like mint and fitted me with a fresh sling.

When they all finally left, I climbed into bed, exhausted, but also wired and horny.

"The mattress is really comfortable, Davix," I said, hinting as broadly as I could, dropping onto it and rolling back and forth on the cushions and sheets. But I could tell he was still upset. He walked back and forth, muttering something too quietly for me to hear.

"Is that a prayer?"

"The Prayer of Balance. We recite it every morning as soon as we wake up. But I haven't said it in a long time. Not since I was arrested, probably."

"Why don't you come to bed?"

"I'm not sleepy, but you go ahead."

I was too shy to just ask him to have sex. Up till now, he had always been the one to start, and I didn't know if it was creepy for me to just ask like that. Davix, meanwhile, had approached a table with a huge book the size of the sandwich board in front of a trendy coffee house.

"What's that?" I asked, more out of a need to keep the conversation alive than real interest.

"Sur's book of the DragonLaw." It was a dragon-sized volume, and he needed both hands to open it. "Beautiful," he breathed.

"Hey, can you look up something for me?"

"What?"

"See if any dragon groom has ever died doing, um, his job."

"X'risp'hin, no! There is nothing in the Law about grooms dying. I'm sure you'll be all right."

"I wasn't last time." I reached under my shirt and felt the bone spur on my rib.

"Last time was not the appointed time. It was a terrible mistake."

"Or maybe an assassination attempt." Only when I'd said it did I realize it might be true. Maybe getting rid of the Dragon Groom was part of the mixed beings' plan for killing off the Fire dragons.

"Try not to worry," Davix said, returning to the big book.

"So, what are you looking for, then?"

He searched for another minute and then read me the passage. "'The death of every dragon diminishes the Realmverse. The dragon killer scars the beauty of all creation.'"

"It wasn't your fault! Why are you fucking torturing yourself?"

"I'm not."

"Liar. I want you, Davix. Come to bed and touch me." I was finally being direct, but it didn't help.

"Soon, X'risp'hin. I just want to read from the Law for a while. It will make me feel better."

I rolled over, sulking. A sleepy fox barked his objection as I pulled the blanket from under him. *But what about me feeling better?* I wanted to say. *I have another date with Etnep, and I'm scared!*

Tangled up as I was in all this emotion, I didn't think I'd ever be able to sleep. But in the end, my fatigue proved stronger than my fear, stronger even than my desire to stick parts of my body in Davix and parts of him in me.

I dreamed I was in an adventure-horror game set in my house. It started with me waking up in my bedroom on Earth. A big, red arrow blinked on the right side of the screen, so I navigated my avatar out into the hallway. There I found a girl Gulga's age sitting on a chair. She had big dark eyes and long, straight black hair that fell across the shoulders of her plain blue dress.

"You have to go downstairs," she told me.

"Have you already done this level?"

"Yes, twice. But every time is a little different."

We walked down and down the carpeted stairs—the game version of my house was, like, seven levels high. As we descended, I checked out the family portraits on the wall. There were my parents as a young couple, goofy and in love in the days before I existed. Then I appeared—first as a happy, careening little ball of destruction, then a serious kite-flyer on some sunburnt beach, and finally the sullen years, where I looked like someone had me in a secret half-nelson to keep me from running out of frame.

On level three, I caught a glimpse of my mom through a half-open door, but just as I was about to call out to her, she closed the door with a decisive bang.

We reached the ground floor at last, and I asked the girl, "What's your name?"

"I'm Ethel. Come on, there's a clue in the living room."

Consul Krasik-dahé was sitting in the easy chair just as she had when she visited our real house. Her back was straight, and her eyes closed. She held a long, red crystal. I waved a hand in front of her face, but she didn't wake up, so I took the crystal, and it appeared in my inventory at the top of the screen. An eight-bit trumpet fanfare sounded, and a set of glowing, gold clothes appeared, hung over the back of a chair.

"Put them on," said the girl. She looked different now, more like my age, with hips and breasts, sitting cosily on the sofa with her legs pulled up under her.

"Sorry, what's your name again?"

"Juliet."

I undressed down to my shorts with my back to her, because my dumb dick had chosen that moment to get hard. I tucked it to the side as best I could as I pulled on the gold pants and tunic. When I stood up to examine myself in the mirror, I realized Krasik-dahé's eyes were open. A blinking red arrow pointed down and to the left.

"You must go down," the octona told me, so I took the stairs to the basement. Instead of the cramped junk room with our washer and dryer in one corner, the basement was an enormous cavern, its ceiling thick with glowing stalactites in every colour of the rainbow. My dick was still super hard, and it was distracting me a lot. It might even have been the source of the barely audible whispers that were filling the air.

I had forgotten about the girl—the woman—but she was there, waiting for me, tall now, very tall, her long hair braided, with strips of leather woven in.

"You're making me question my homosexuality," my avatar told her.

"Give me the crystal," she replied.

My heart was pounding as I pulled it from my pants pocket and handed it over. "What did you say your name was?" I asked over the sound of the shouting whispers, over the singing and the drums.

"*I AM ETNEP!*" she replied, as she slipped the long red crystal up her dress. At the top of the screen, my score shot up into the stratosphere.

❖

So, that woke me up!

Davix and three of the foxes were in bed with me. Through the big window, a beam of moonlight lit the gold pants and tunic, which hung neatly over the back of a chair, just like in my dream game. I climbed out of bed and dressed in silence, leaving my left arm in its sling under the loose tunic. I knew what I had to do. I had been instructed.

I think I was only person awake in Farad'hil as I walked the long, spiral road down from Sur's abode to the very bottom of the core. The only sound was the waterfall. Maybe half an hour later, I stood before the jagged crack in the wall that marked the entrance to the Matrimonial Tunnels. Voices whispered in my ear, and other voices sang. When I concentrated, I could make out the words, mostly in the ancient dialect of Fire, but also some poetry in English. Roses and thorns and blood flowing black in the high-contrast moonlight. It was like watching a movie with the director's commentary on, the movie sound playing quietly underneath.

I climbed through the crack, and inside a wide foyer stood Tiqokh as well as the last person I wanted to see: Grav'nan-dahé. The floor was a mosaic featuring a huge dragon with her wings spread and a much smaller dragon flying her way. To my eyes, the little guy looked kind of intimidated. Tiqokh was standing near me at the entrance to the foyer and Grav'nan was deeper inside, in front of a second cave entrance, shaped with eye-rolling obviousness like an egg.

"The Dragon Groom approaches with joy and awe," Grav'nan chanted, waving me over. Despite the fact that this was the last thing I wanted to do, I obeyed.

"So, you're done with the 'Copper Guest' stuff?" I asked, but my heart wasn't really in the snark. Walking closer to the egg tunnel was making me woozy and unnaturally calm. I peered through the door. Torchstones were mounted on the wall down its length, disappearing deep into the roots of the mountain.

Grav'nan wasn't interested in chit-chat. This was obviously some ceremony he had stayed up late studying. "Hundreds of cycles ago did Great Rob'stel hide the copper blood in the Realm of Earth, safeguarding the dragon succession." He laid his bony hand on my shoulder, squeezing a bit too hard. "Now you stand here, Dragon Groom, ready to insert yourself into history. Why must this duty be fulfilled?"

"There must be Five?" I heard myself say. Was it a good guess, or was my copper blood offering up the answer, like cheat notes on the palm of my hand? Judging by the almost smile Grav'nan made, it was the right answer. Yay me. My mouth was dry, the voices in my head growing louder. As in the game, my dick was hard.

"Then go in joy and adoration. Queen Etnep awaits you."

My feet were already carrying me toward the threshold when Tiqokh spoke.

"Come back, Crispin."

Grav'nan made some noise of objection, but I turned right around. It seemed at that moment, I would obey anyone or anything. As I walked farther from the egg tunnel, my head cleared, and my fear returned.

"I would like to hear your unambiguous verbal consent before you go any farther," Tiqokh said.

Grav'nan's voice was icy. "That is not part of the ceremony, quadrana."

"Forgive me, Grav'nan-dahé. Perhaps the cycles I spent in the Realm of Earth have altered my perspective, but I will not allow this young man to proceed if he does not do so of his own free will. So, Crispin?"

I thought about it. I knew I would change when I passed through the egg door, but whatever I was going to become inside the Matrimonial Tunnel, I was still, at least for the moment, Crispin, and I still had free will. I looked up into Tiqokh's eyes, remembering how they had freaked me out when I first met him.

"Look, I won't deny I'm scared, but I also have a responsibility to the copper blood my father passed to me, a responsibility to this realm. People have taken care of me since I got here, saved my life—you included—and people gave their own lives in the war. In comparison, is this such a big deal? Most of all, I have a responsibility to Sur. She gave her life to save us, so the least I can do is, you know, give back some life. So, yeah, Tiqokh, I consent."

I turned from him and walked past Grav'nan, who gave me a head and heart bow, and through the egg door into the Matrimonial Tunnels. The mind fog and the voices returned, stronger than ever. The torchstones passed in my peripheral vision, slowly at first, then faster and faster, as if I was falling instead of walking. I couldn't understand the messages my body was sending my brain. Why did my feet feel so far away and the ceiling so close? I was stretching through space and time both, not sure where I ended and history began.

My vision was different, refracting through different eyes—eyes that saw colours humans had no name for. I looked down at my long clawed feet on the floor of the corridor, I snorted tones as deep as the earth, I shook my wings, and they slapped against the walls and ceiling. The songs in my head—for Farad'hil is always singing—grew louder, first a deafening, meaningless mess, and then coalescing into a beautiful unison, strong and clear: the voice of Etnep.

And the queen said to the dragon, "*COME TO ME, MY GROOM.*"

CHAPTER 48: *The Edge*

It was still dark when Davix awoke and found X'risp'hin gone. The panic overtook his whole body, as if he was back in the moment when the Air dragon had stolen away the Earth boy. His heart pounded, and sweat dampened his underarms and forehead. But he saw no signs of violence in the room, and the cat soldiers could not have gotten to Farad'hil so quickly. Davix calmed himself with slow, deep breaths. Would he ever again find the tranquility the war had stolen from him? He dressed and went looking for his fleshmate. *Boyfriend*, X'risp'hin had said with pride and overflowing happiness. Davix couldn't find him anywhere in Sur's abode, so he went out to the spiral road.

Dawn was just beginning to brighten the dragons' mountain home through the massive glass dome overhead. Davix moved to the inside edge of the road to look down into the core. There was no railing, and he should have kept well back from the drop-off, but a perverse impulse made him walk even closer. The terrible pit opened beneath him, and its precipitous depths seemed to call to him. He could do it—just lean forward and end his life. What was he now, after all? A heretic and a dragon killer.

He was no longer on the holy path that might have led him one day to the exalted post of Prime Magistrate. He wasn't even sure he still had a place in Atmospherics. And soon he would lose X'risp'hin. His *boyfriend* would return to the Realm of Earth, as he'd always known he must, and Davix would be left with a permanent hole in his heart. Another hole, alongside Grentz and Rinby, alongside his former tranquility. The solution was so easy. All he had to do was let himself fall forward into yet another hole.

His body began shaking violently. Even his teeth chattered. Head spinning, he dropped to the ground in terror. He didn't want to die. Not now, not like this. Davix crawled away from edge and sat on the ground beside the gate of Sur's abode, breathing hard. A pear tree was growing just up the road, and in it sat Flak, staring at him intently, head cocked to one side.

"All right, bird, you can spare me your disapproving glare," Davix told the kingsolver. "This life is the only one I have, and come joy or come sorrow, I won't discard it so lightly."

At that moment, Tiqokh rose up from the depths on his powerful new wings, carrying the unconscious X'risp'hin in his arms. He landed and walked to the gate. X'risp'hin was dressed in golden garments, finer than even Lok'lok-sur-nep-dahé could have sewn. Then Davix understood where X'risp'hin had been.

His head was still spinning, but now he had a purpose. Climbing to his feet, Davix asked, "Is he all right?"

"Yes, but he needs to rest."

"Of course. Follow me inside."

Tiqokh lay X'risp'hin in the bed and sat beside him, feeling his forehead with his scaly hand. "As predicted, the transformation was considerably less traumatic this time. All his life signs are healthy. But he will sleep for many hours."

X'risp'hin rolled over in his sleep. "His arm!" Davix said. "It's healed."

"It is the way of the transformation. When he came back to his human self, he was whole again. D'gada-vixtet-thon, if you have been assigned duties elsewhere, I can watch over him."

"No, I'll do that. No one wants to see me anyway."

Tiqokh rose to his feet. "The way you are being treated by the dragons is not just. I believe you to be brave and loyal."

Davix checked his impulse to reject the praise. "Thank you, Tiqokh. You are different from the mixed beings I have known."

"Yes, I remain loyal to the Five."

This made Davix smile. "Loyal you are, but not afraid to question their actions, nor those of Grav'nan-dahé."

"True. I am not the same as before my time on Earth. Perhaps that is why I was spared when the other mixed beings fell."

X'risp'hin moaned, and Davix bent to kiss his forehead. "I hope one day I can see the Realm of Earth," he said. The thought had not occurred to him before. And now the desire to follow his fleshmate home made his heart ache.

Tiqokh left, and Davix lay down beside X'risp'hin. He was careful not to disturb him, but he was anxious to have their bodies touching. He felt a strange power flowing in himself, like he would cure his *boyfriend* of all his troubles if only they stayed in contact. For the first time in days, he felt at peace.

He awakened many hours later to find X'risp'hin on top of him, kissing his face—cheeks, ears, forehead, and finally his responsive mouth. The boy was naked, the golden clothes tossed aside, his hands inside Davix's clothes, all but tearing them off in his desire.

"Where am I?" X'risp'hin asked, hands exploring, voice throaty with desire.

Davix could barely talk. "You are here...oh..." X'risp'hin's probing hands had found their mark. "Here in...Sur's bedchamber."

"And who am I?"

Davix tried to slow him down. "Do you not know? Are you delirious? We should stop if you don't—"

X'risp'hin would not be stopped. "Say it, tell me who I am!"

"You are X'risp'hin of the Realm of Earth. You are the Dragon Groom. You are my *boyfriend*, with whom I am tangled."

X'risp'hin made a noise from deep inside himself, a moan and a growl, ancient and primal, and quintessentially human. His hands and mouth ranged across Davix's body with no hint of shyness. He rolled them over and threw himself open to Davix's hunger, his breath broken like sobs.

And Davix found in X'risp'hin a set of doors, opening one onto the other for him, and opening still, until there was nothing left to reveal.

...and Davix opened me piece by piece—pieces of myself I didn't even know were in there—until I had nothing left to hide.

Chapter 49: *Pulling at Tethers*

The abode of Vixtet was about two-thirds of the way down the central core of Farad'hil. The spiral road widened out into a large outcropping, and Vixtet kept a small garden there, perfect and peaceful. That's where we gathered for Sur's memorial. In the middle of the garden was a flat-topped, polished stone of red shot through with green veins. On top were the jewels from Sur's breast. White flowers were strewn so thickly around the base of rock, it looked like it was floating on a cloud.

The small garden was filled with mourners. Tiqokh was there, as were the fifteen or so humans in Farad'hil, dressed in the best clothes they could find for the occasion. Vixtet and Inby were standing behind the flat-topped rock, and we were all waiting for Renrit, who was waddling slowly down the road in our direction. We could already see him rounding the last bend, but it would still be at least ten minutes before he reached us. Queen Etnep wouldn't be attending. She never left her caves except for her Cliffside flyover on *Sarensikar*. Not even for her daughter's funeral.

This was the fourth funeral of my life. A kid from my class died of leukaemia when we were ten, though we weren't really friends. Then there was my mom's best friend, who I used to call Aunt Sunny, and my grandpa two years back. That was the first one where the monumental cruelty of death really impressed me. I squeezed Davix's hand, and he kissed the top of my head.

We had hardly let go of each other since we'd woken up, but we also barely spoke a word. Neither of us wanted to state the obvious. Now that my groom duties were done, they'd be sending me back to Earth. And sure, I wanted to get home to my family and eat a really big plate of double-cheese nachos, but the idea of leaving Davix was a knife in my heart. So was Sur's funeral. The whole day was nothing but knives, one after the other. When I got back to school, I could tell my English teacher I finally got how Julius Caesar must have felt. *School.*

The idea of walking those corridors was as strange to me now as riding on Sur's back had been three weeks earlier.

Grav'nan had invited me to stand up front with him and the dragons, but it was clear Davix was not welcome to join me. I declined with a regally pissed-off look on my face. Hate on my boyfriend, hate on me.

Renrit was finally negotiating the narrow entrance to the garden when a kid called down to me from a nearby tree branch.

"Dragon Groom, do you recognize me?" I looked up at his smiling face and the unclouded freedom in his eyes. *Maybe the war hasn't killed everything good.*

"Oh yeah, you're the kid from the classroom, the one that stupid teacher was whaling on. Felix, right?"

"Fexil," the boy said. "I have something for you." He reached into his tunic and pulled out my wolf head necklace.

"Oh my God, thanks! Where did you find it?" The silver chain was broken, but other than that, it was none the worse for wear.

"After Great Sur flew away with you, a man from Stoneworks was showing it off to everyone. He said he found it lying in the square, but that's a lie. Everyone says he pulled it off your neck deliberately."

"So, how did you get it from him?"

With evident pride, Fexil said, "He put it in his pocket, and I, well, took it out."

I was about to say thanks again, when Fexil jumped down from the tree and gave me a big hug.

"Dragon Groom, I am grateful you came to the Realm of Fire. We will miss you."

I choked up. "Well, yeah, kid, I'll miss you, too. And tell that teacher of yours if he messes with you, I'm going to come back with all the dragons of Earth and give him a piece of my mind." The boy nodded with great seriousness, and I wondered for the first time whether there really were dragons on Earth. If so, what were they like? And where were they hiding?

The memorial service was spoken in the ancient tongue, with no eulogy or anything personal about Sur. Renrit did most of the reciting, but Grav'nan did a bit, too. His usual loud chanting voice got all messed up at one point, and I was shocked to realize he was crying, which set my own waterworks flowing.

When the chanting was over and everyone had sunk into silent contemplation, I called out from my place in the back. "Can I say something?"

Grav'nan, despite his red, teary eyes, managed to get bureaucratic. "There is no place for extemporizing at such a solemn occasion, Dragon Groom."

"*LET HIM SPEAK,*" said Vixtet.

I came forward, wiping my eyes on my sleeve, and handed Renrit a leather folder stuffed full of loose paper and tied with red ribbon.

"These are Sur's poems. I don't know if there's any other poetry in the DragonLaw, but I think these have to be there. They're important. They're part of her."

Renrit took the folder in his huge, dainty fingers and bowed his head to me, which felt kind of wrong, so I bowed even deeper.

I turned to look at the little congregation. "Sur was really amazing. She had a lot of personality. She could be friendly, or angry, or even funny, which is something I've never seen in another dragon." Behind me, the dragons grunted and shifted, making the ground wobble. "Uh, sorry, no offence," I said. "Maybe you're all hilarious at parties. And Sur was brave. She saved me, maybe saved the whole realm from the Air dragon. She was my friend. Please don't forget her."

Everyone was watching me as I walked back to the wall to stand with Davix, and I made a point of putting my arm around him. I had done my duty to Sur, making sure her poems would be remembered, but I also had a guilty little secret. I kept Sur's final poem for myself. Maybe this is total ego, but I think she meant me to have it as a token of our bond. And I also thought there was a message in it for me about the future: *To the souls lost and scattered when came the flood/Come you together at the call of the blood.*

At the end of the service, most of the humans headed off to get dinner ready or whatever the dragons needed them to do. Renrit, Inby, and Vixtet were deep in conversation with Tiqokh and Grav'nan, and I thought what a big day for dahé it must have been, like a full-access backstage pass with his favourite band.

I wandered over to eavesdrop.

Vixtet was asking Inby, "*IS IT POSSIBLE FOR THE CAT SOLDIERS OF AIR TO REPAIR THE STRANDS?*"

"*¿¿IF THE MIXED BEINGS HAD THAT KNOWLEDGE,*" Inby responded, "*WHY NOT THE CAT SOLDIERS??*"

Tiqokh said, "We cannot take that chance. The strands must never be restored."

"Nor the cats allowed to live," Grav'nan added, with a savagery that impressed me.

"*THE PRIME MAGISTRATE SPEAKS TRUTH,*" Vixtet said. "*BUT RIDDING OUR REALM OF THESE BEASTS WILL TAKE TIME. THE DRAGON GROOM MUST BE RETURNED TO THE REALM OF EARTH FOR THE PROTECTION OF THE BLOOD.*"

"I will take him across the strands to Earth immediately," Tiqokh said, staring my way. My heart began to pound. I turned to look at Davix, who was talking to Stakrat, oblivious. If I left now, how long would it be before we met again? What would happen to him here, now that the dragons were being such jerks to him? Something rose in me, fierce and protective.

"What about D'gada-vixtet-thon?" I said to Vixtet, marching forward into their meeting. "Will you give me your word that he'll be protected, too?"

Vixtet lowered her head until her face filled my whole field of vision. "*WHY DO YOU NOT UNDERSTAND, DRAGON GROOM? THE HUMAN SLAYED A DRAGON. WE CAN HAVE NO SYMPATHY IN OUR HEARTS FOR SUCH EVIL.*"

"Hypocrite," I snapped at her, and Grav'nan gasped. "If it wasn't for Davix, that Air dragon would still be around, maybe killing another one of you." Vixtet raised her head and looked away, like I wasn't worth listening to. So I shouted, "If you won't promise to protect him, then I won't leave. I refuse!"

Stakrat ran up to us, making a head and heart bow in Vixtet's direction, though the dragon was still having a big sulk and not looking our way.

"Dragon Groom, what's wrong?"

"They said I have to leave because of the stupid cats." My voice was getting all high, and I felt the tears coming back. "But I won't leave Davix alone if everyone here hates him."

Stakrat's voice was gentle. "We don't hate him. *I* don't hate him. X'risp'hin, there's no safety for you here in the Realm of Fire as long as the cats are still prowling. You are too important to die."

"So is Davix," I answered stubbornly. I looked over at him, and he was smiling at me, with one long tear running down his high cheek. I walked around Vixtet's body and back into her field of vision. "Davix is important to *me!*" For once in my life, I felt proud of myself.

Vixtet rose up on her hind legs, spread her wings wide, and roared so loud we all covered our ears. "*THEN YOU CAN HAVE HIM! SEND THE DRAGON-KILLER TO EARTH! GET HIM AWAY FROM ME, AWAY FROM OUR REALM. NOW, NOW! I WON'T LOOK AT HIM*

ANOTHER MINUTE." I wanted to freakin' slap her. But then I realized what she had said. Davix was coming to Earth. My heart started thumping with excitement.

While everyone else was backing away slowly from the ticked-off dragon, Tiqokh stood his ground. "Great one, I do not know if the strands to Earth, delicate as they are, can support the passage of three. Such a strain might shatter their integrity and—"

But she was not in a listening mood. "*I DON'T CARE. GO! GO! FIND A WAY TO MAKE IT VIABLE. DID WE NOT MAKE YOU MASTER OF STRAND MANIPULATION?*"

Tiqokh bowed low. "Yes, Great Vixtet. Your humblest word is my law absolute." Vixtet turned and jumped into the air, spiralling down into the core and out of sight. Without saying goodbye or thank you or anything, Inby and Renrit walked out of the garden together. If I had learned one thing in this adventure, it's that gods can be total dicks.

"D'gada-vixtet-thon, approach," Tiqokh called out. Davix stood next to me, and I took his hand. "Prepare yourself," Tiqokh told him. "We fly to the Realm of Earth."

"You mean me? You mean now?" Davix looked like he'd been hit with a brick.

"So has Great Vixtet decreed. We will climb the Stairwell of Lar'nak to the pinnacle of Farad'hil and there find the Garden at the Top of the World. From this holy site, we will launch ourselves across the strands when the realms are in alignment."

"But my friends, my fellow students, and my Master Tix-etnep-thon-dahé! He is sick, Tiqokh, I must stay and care for him."

"There is no time. We obey the orders of the great dragons."

Davix's hand was shaking in mine. I turned and hugged him hard. "Don't worry. This is fantastic. And you'll love Earth." I could barely process what was happening. There wouldn't be any heartbreaking separation. I was going home, and my wonderful boyfriend was going with me.

But he wasn't celebrating like I wished he was. "Tiqokh, please, no! Cliffside is the only home I've ever known. I don't want to leave." He pulled out of my arms and went to Stakrat.

She ran her hands through his hair and then held his face in both hands. "Trust that this is your path, my brave friend. Hold your head high and experience *Ekdahi*. This is how you will serve the balance."

"But what good can I be in a world where I can't read the DragonLaw? Where I don't understand the weather? In a world where I have no one?"

More hurt than I had a right to be, I said, "Well, you have *me*."
He looked my way, ashamed, and I put my little wounded ego aside.
"Davix, come to the Realm of Earth. I'll show you everything. I mean,
I don't know that much of the world yet—it's pretty big—but we can
discover it together. It'll be great, honest."

His eyes were wide and shiny, and in one big flash, I suddenly got
how hard this was for him. He was supposed to leave his world, his
religion, everything and everyone he had ever known, and just fly into
the unknown. There wasn't even time for a goodbye party and dorky,
sentimental gifts.

"D'gada-vixtet-thon," I said, heart pounding, "I'll take care
of you, I promise." I felt the promise settle on my shoulders, and its
weight frightened me. What would happen when he got to Earth? He
didn't know how we did things there. He didn't even speak English. I
didn't show Davix my fear. I held out my hand to him and smiled. But
it was Grav'nan-dahé he walked to.

"You were my mentor," he said. "But you banished me, reduced
me."

"You broke the law, D'gada-vixtet-thon. It was my job to correct
you."

"I know I did wrong, Grav'nan-dahé, but so did you. Your temper
clouded your reason, like the sheep fog lately passed."

With all the world-shaking stuff that had happened in the last few
days, this moment still seemed huge.

The old man straightened his spine, and I thought he was going
to tell Davix to get lost, but he said, "I fear you are right. I let childish
feelings cloud my judgement. I am old enough to know better than that.
I accept your rebuke, Apprentice."

A sob escaped from Davix, but he didn't look away. Tears running
down his cheeks, he said, "Grav'nan-dahé, Teacher, grant me your
blessing as I depart this realm."

Grav'nan got that broken look I had seen on his face after the cat's
first attack, like the extra hundred years he'd lived were all catching
up in an instant. He put a hand on Davix's shoulder, leaning on it for
support. But then he stood up tall and Davix dropped to one knee.

Grav'nan-dahé said, "D'gada-vixtet-thon, as you travel to the
Realm of Earth, remember the balance of our holy realm goes with
you, embodied in the teachings of the DragonLaw that live within your
heart."

"Teacher, I am scared."

"As anyone would be. But you are also clever and curious. You will meet the challenges with a clear and probing eye, and you will not flinch. And someday—may the day come soon—Reunification will be upon us, and we will all dance together in the One Realm."

It was a good blessing. I almost asked Grav'nan to give me one, too, but there's only so far you should push your luck. Davix returned to me. He took my hand. "Okay. I'm ready."

Stakrat insisted on walking with us as security detail, bow at the ready, but I don't think there was really any danger of a cat attack. She just wasn't ready to say goodbye yet. We walked the spiral road until Tiqokh led us up a narrow, winding side path that ended in front of a rough door cut in the wall of the rock.

"The Stairwell of Lar'nak," Tiqokh declared. I caught myself rolling my eyes. All of a sudden, I'd had enough of weird names with magical histories and the rest of the fantasy crap. I was done and ready to be back in the world of Wi-Fi.

Taking torchstones from the wall, we began the long climb up the stairs, which snaked up through the rocky guts of the mountain. My thighs were aching by the time we reached an ancient door, almost rusted shut. If it hadn't been for Tiqokh's super strong arms, we would never have been able to open it at all.

The dazzling sun was close to setting—a fierce, cold eye in a sky free of fog. It was called the garden at the top of the world, but if flowers were sleeping under all the mountain snow, we weren't going to be around to see them pop their heads out. Stakrat went out first and checked that it was secure before gesturing us to follow. It was killer cold, and Davix pulled me into his arms. Tiqokh kneeled and cleared the snow from a large wooden box. He took out a summoning stone and held it in the air, muttering words in the ancient tongue. I wasn't listening too close until he said something about "Uncloud our eyes." The realm sky appeared overhead.

We all stared up at that terrifying beauty. The Realm of Air was just going down to our left, and I thought about Translator. Were his wife and kits staring up into the sky, too, wondering when he would come home? Far to the right, the Realm of Water was rising, blue and peaceful. But above us, just climbing to the zenith of the sky, was Earth. And it was gorgeous. The clouds and continents, seas and rivers stretched across the globe, familiar and inviting. Well, familiar once I realized I was looking at things almost upside down from how a normal map looks.

"We are in luck," Tiqokh said. "The Realm of Earth will soon reach conjunction."

"It is not luck," Davix said. "It is destiny unfolding." I almost rolled my eyes again, but caught myself. Whatever he needed to tell himself today was just fine. We had to wait maybe twenty-five more minutes for the Earth to line up right, so me and Davix and Stakrat retreated back into the stairwell so we wouldn't freeze.

Stakrat was holding Davix's hand, and I was stroking his head, saying, "It's gonna be okay. I mean, you might puke a bit when we land, but other than that, the flight's pretty smooth." I even made a lame joke about getting complimentary peanuts from the cabin crew, but I was obviously just amusing myself.

Tiqokh finally called us, and we joined him in the centre of the garden. Stakrat and Davix held each other's eye. The tough soldier girl was crying quietly, but Davix was holding himself together now.

"We will meet again," he told her. "I know this."

"Dragon Groom," she called above the growing howl of realm space. "You have been a brave exemplar of *Ekdahi*. I am proud to call you friend."

I didn't know what to say to that, but before I could figure it out, Tiqokh shouted, "Prepare yourselves!"

CHAPTER 50: *The Realm Jumpers*

The trip along the strands wasn't exactly easy, but I was better prepared for it this time. On my last trip, I had spent the whole time gripping Tiqokh in panic and screaming into the void with my eyes closed. Oh, I didn't tell you that before, did I? Don't judge me. Anyway, this time I was able to keep my eyes open and experience the ride, like we were in the first car of the roller coaster. I stared up at shooting comets and clouds of mysterious gas that lit up the dark, and I watched the glimmering ribbons of the strands beneath us. But mostly, I looked backward at the craggy football that was the Realm of Fire. I watched it roll as it diminished, the whole Chend'th'nif turning slowly out of sight. I tried to catch a glimpse of Cliffside, but it was a small thing in this majestic expanse.

Before these three weeks of adventure, my life had felt like a small thing, too—a well-worn path between home and school, a tight orbit around my parents. Now I knew I was part of a great *muchness*. My life before had already seemed overwhelming, but now there was so much more. There was the copper in my blood and all the beauty and struggle it connected me to. And there was love. I wrapped my arms tightly around Davix. Unlike me, he wasn't looking at the home he had been forced to abandon. No, he was looking forward at the Earth as it grew. Looking into his future.

Suddenly, we began to shake. And then the shaking turned to quaking. Davix and I held each other tighter, and Tiqokh tightened his grip on both of us. There was a sound like a train derailing—shrieks, cracks, great *boom-boom-boom* pounding. I tried to scream over it to ask Tiqokh what was wrong, but apparently talking doesn't work when you're travelling the strands.

Something bright exploded in my peripheral vision, and I looked down to see the strands fracturing, great ribbons of energy shaking themselves across the sky like angry snakes. Davix and I locked eyes, like we were saying our final farewells. The shaking got so bad, we were almost torn out of Tiqokh's arms. Then, with a sickening sideways lurch, the shaking stopped, but now we were flashing through the void at impossible speeds. The Earth filled every inch of the sky, glutting our senses, pulling us toward some cataclysmic crash. I think I blacked out.

CHAPTER 51: *Where Credit Is Due*

I opened my eyes. I was breathing hard, and my skin was so hot in the cool air, steam was rising off me. I was lying on hard ground looking up into the sky. The setting sun glowed red in the gap between the clouds and the horizon.

I sat up and looked around. Davix was sitting on a low rock, head down between his knees. Tiqokh stood above him. I ran over and put my hands on Davix's shoulders.

"Are you okay?"

"Yes, just dizzy."

"Tiqokh, where are we?" It was only slightly warmer than it had been in the garden on top of Farad'hil. In fact, we were up another mountain, although nothing as high and impressive as the Chend'th'nif. But I knew we were on Earth because of the paved roads, electric streetlights, and fast food outlets, which all seemed to be closed. We were sitting on the patchy brown lawn of a picnic area shared by the restaurants. No one was around.

The quadrana put away the summoning stone into a pocket of his kilt. "We are in a resort town in the Laurentian Mountains, luckily not in season."

I gaped at him. "We're in Quebec?" That explained all the French signs. "Why didn't you bring us back to the roof of the Ambassador Hotel?"

"Our passage was precarious. Perhaps you noticed?" It's hard to tell when a quadrana is being sarcastic. "I had to aim for the highest and most accessible of my possible landing sites."

"The strands?" Davix asked, because he's on top of stuff and asks the right questions.

"Broken." We shut up and took that in.

"Damn…" I breathed. It was pretty cold out, and the last of the daylight was vanishing. "We need to get home. I don't suppose you have a phone in your kilt?"

"No, but this is Consul Krasik-dahé's telephone number." He pulled a scrap of paper out of the pocket. It had a ten-digit number printed on it in neat handwriting. He pointed to a small motel down the road with a sign that read Suites Sauveur. "You and Davix should proceed to that establishment and rent a room for the night. If you call the Consul, she will take care of the charges and make plans for us."

I took Davix's hand, and we walked down the hill. A pickup truck approaching from the down the hill caught us in its headlights, and I automatically let go of Davix's hand. We were back on Earth, and all my Earth fears were back.

The wood-panelled lobby of the Suites Sauveur was full of ski kitsch and French signage I could only semi-understand. Davix looked around admiringly, and I realized it takes experience to develop good taste. I rang the bell on the front desk. A woman with long, grey-streaked blonde hair and wearing a cheesy ski sweater emerged from a back room.

"*Oui, bonsoir,*" she said, then in unaccented English, "Can I help you?" She was staring at our Realm of Fire clothes suspiciously. We must have looked like we were coming from a slumber party or some Zen ashram.

"Yeah, we need a room for the night."

She blinked. "Sorry, I don't speak…whatever language—"

Shit. I closed my eyes and concentrated, and then repeated the request in what I hoped was English instead of the Tongue of Fire. Success.

"Okay." She tapped on her computer. "Just the two of you?"

I thought of Tiqokh, but I figured he was too hard to explain. "Yeah, just us."

"Where's your car?" She leaned over the counter and looked through the front window, apparently still trying to piece our story together.

"We, uh, hitchhiked."

This made her quirk an eyebrow. She turned to Davix, as if she wanted to hear his version of the story. He smiled back and ran a hand appreciatively down the back of a taxidermy weasel on the counter that was snarling at us in frozen fury.

"And you don't have any bags?"

"Not really, no."

I handed her the piece of paper Tiqokh had given me. "If you call this number and tell her Crispin is here, she'll give you a credit card number and everything."

"Your mom?"

"Our...foster mom, yeah." The lie had a weird core of truth to it. *Our dragon mom,* I wanted to say.

As she dialled, it occurred to me Krasik-dahé might be dead. Maybe she had gone down with the other mixed beings, creating a weird mystery for the police. But the desk clerk reached the octona right away, and I breathed a sigh of relief. After a brief exchange, she handed me the phone.

"Crispin, are you all right?" Krasik-dahé asked in English. She sounded concerned, which was nice, since she had been such a cool customer the last time we met. She sounded almost human.

"Yeah, we're fine. I mean, there was a war and everything, but we survived."

"Who is the other with you? Is it a human from the Realm of Fire?"

"Yeah, Davix. Uh, D'gada-vixtet-thon. He had to leave in a hurry."

"There is much for you and Tiqokh to brief me on. I will see you as soon as I can."

The desk clerk turned out to be the owner of the inn. I tried to make conversation as she led us to our room.

"I guess this place is hopping during ski season. When's that start? A few weeks?"

The woman gave me a look like I was demented. "Ski season just ended, obviously. Business'll pick up again in another six weeks when the hikers start coming through for the summer."

I was confused by this but said nothing. She opened the door of our room. Two beds, a trashy painting of a stag in a river, plastic bedside lamps shaped like big snowflakes. She showed us the bathroom and asked us to please use the bathmat when we showered.

"I don't have a lot in the kitchen, but there's some frozen pizzas. Or there's one restaurant open down the road."

"Pizza's good," I said. Even if we had cash to spend, I didn't want to go out dressed like we were, with Davix unable to say a word, just smiling weirdly at everyone. I realized I was embarrassed about him, and that made me feel like garbage.

As the owner headed for the door, I finally got up the nerve to ask, "Sorry, what month is this?"

She was so over us she didn't even hide the eye roll. "It's April twenty-third, kid. Shakespeare's birthday, according to my desk calendar." She closed the door, and I stood there, stunned. I had left Earth mid-November and spent around three weeks in the Realm of Fire, but five months had passed in my absence.

Davix was walking around the room, running his fingers along everything, experiencing plastic and polyester for the first time. I could have turned on the TV and really blown his mind, but I was busy freaking out. Five months. My parents must have been frantic. Was Krasik-dahé in touch with them? Reassuring them? How could she? She had no idea what was going on in the Realm of Fire. But I couldn't face calling them yet. I had too many difficult things to say. One more night wouldn't kill them.

As we ate our pizza, I tried to make small talk, but I was barely looking Davix in the eye.

"It's okay, X'risp'hin," he said. "So much has happened. Of course you feel discomfited." His maturity made me feel even worse about myself.

Speaking in Tongue of Fire was suddenly weird. I was aware of its "otherness" in a way I never had been when we were on the other side of the strands. And as I watched Davix trying out everything new— eating pizza, using a toothbrush, playing with the controls of the air conditioner—I was aware of his otherness, too. We went to bed just after nine and made out some, but it didn't go anywhere. We fell asleep in the same bed, but not curled around each other like we usually were.

I woke up at three in the morning and climbed out of bed. Wrapped in one of the fluffy bathrobes that came with the room, I walked the carpet in tight circles. I looked down at Davix and thought of the promise I had made to him. "I'll take care of you." What had I committed myself to? In the Realm of Fire, I had been the weird stranger and Davix had been the cool local kid who watched out for me. Could I be the same for him on Earth? I had no idea. I was supposed to be "tangled" with him. I had been broken-hearted at the thought of leaving him behind, but now I didn't know what to do with him.

What would happen at home when I was literally the only person he could talk to? What would he seem like to my family and friends? What kind of freak would he be at school, or at the mall, or anywhere? And what would be the blowback on me of having to explain this incomprehensible boy? I felt like the lowest person on Earth for even having these thoughts.

I almost screamed when I saw the glowing eyes on the balcony looking in at me. But of course, it was Tiqokh, standing guard over us through the night. I stepped out into the cool, clear night and slid the glass door closed behind me.

"You cannot sleep, Crispin," he said, stating the obvious. "Is there anything you wish to ask me?"

"I just don't know what's going to happen. Am I done with my part in all this? The realms? The dragons? Do I just go back to my old life now?"

"Such a peaceful turn of events seems unlikely, don't you think?"

"Yeah, I guess." I sighed. "But maybe that's good. Now that I know about everything, I'd hate to be out of the loop."

"And don't worry about D'gada-vixtet-thon."

"Who said anything about Davix?" You can't fool a quadrana, I guess.

"Krasik-dahé and I led you into the tide of events; we will not abandon either of you to drown." Tiqokh opened the balcony door. "Now go inside before your body temperature falls further."

I climbed back into bed with my back to Davix. It comforted me to know I wasn't alone. I had Tiqokh and Krasik-dahé, and there were my parents. And scared as I was to drop all of my truth in front of them, like a pet cat bringing in a bloody mouse, I believed deep down they would be there for me. Davix stirred and, without waking all the way, wrapped his arms around me. I was amazed and grateful all over again at the sheer joy of being held by someone I loved. It didn't take long until I was asleep again, finally at peace.

I checked the clock when we woke up, and it was nearly eleven. Sleeping that late always felt like an accomplishment, and I hoped it was a sign of a good day to come. I introduced Davix to the joys of showering, and then, for the first time in my semi-adult life, I climbed into the shower with someone. Fun was had, and by the time we got out, the bathroom was steamy as the second day of *Sarensikar*. We were starving, and I called down for some breakfast, only to be told we had visitors who were on their way up.

We scrambled into our clothes just as someone knocked on our door. When I saw Krasik-dahé standing outside, I was actually pretty delighted. The Consul was dressed to kill as usual, in a long, green cloak with padded shoulders and fur at the collar, and a big fur hat. Tiqokh followed her into the room, dressed in ski pants and a long nylon parka with the hood pulled up to obscure his less than human head. He was carrying a large suitcase which must have been Krasik-dahé's.

A third person was with them. Dressed in a cloak and hood that would have looked more normal in the Realm of Fire, he appeared to be about my height. He threw back his hood, and I saw he was a mixed being, similar to a quadrana, though much smaller than any I had seen before. He shuffled along in a crouched gait, like a chimpanzee.

"Hi," I said in the Tongue of Fire. "I'm Crispin."

"Srarkraw," he responded with a throaty bark and squatted down by the wall, where he remained for the next hour.

Krasik-dahé was busy introducing herself to Davix, who made respectful head and heart bows to her.

"Tiqokh," she said. "In my bag you will find the makings of a meal. Please move the desk to that open area by the door and lay out the food for us."

Over an impressive picnic of gourmet deli treats—I couldn't stop eating the herb-crusted smoked salmon—me, Davix, and Tiqokh spelled out all the terrible things that had gone down in the Realm of Fire. I was weirdly self-conscious as my lips and tongue wrapped themselves around the rumbling music of the Tongue of Fire. Back here on Earth, surrounded by cheap tourist kitsch, talking fluently about a war of dragons in this otherworldly language felt exotic and unsettling.

"So, the prophecy came true," Krasik-dahé said. "And you fulfilled your role as required, Crispin?"

I blushed. "Dragon stud, that's me."

Srarkraw, still seated in the corner like a well-behaved dog, finally spoke up. "We must convene a meeting of the full Council before week's end."

Krasik-dahé nodded. "I'll send out a group email tonight." Here in my new life, the worlds of fantasy and reality combined in an unexpected stew.

The meeting was making me curious. "Just how many mixed beings are there on Earth?" I asked.

"More than you'd expect," was as precise as she got. "And as far as I know, none were felled along with their counterparts across the strands. And in case you're concerned, humans are on the Council, too." Clearly, a lot more dragony stuff was happening on Earth than I figured. But my head was already full, so I decided to wait till later to ask the thousand new questions I had.

See, I thought I was Dorothy, coming back from Oz with no souvenirs but a bump on the head and a tall tale. Then I looked at Davix and realized it was more like if Dorothy had brought the Scarecrow home with her, and they were moving together to New York City to open a ruby slipper pop-up store. Munchkins were hawking T-shirts in Times Square, and the Wicked Witch had a condo overlooking the Park.

The owner of the inn looked even more suspicious when we checked out, surrounded as we were by three more weirdos. We all squeezed into Krasik-dahé's rented sedan and drove down the mountain into a small town. Srarkraw got out at some random corner, telling Krasik-dahé she'd hear from him the next day.

In an outlet mall at the edge of town, the Consul bought us new clothes. I helped Davix avoid major fashion errors—he almost picked up a clearance Christmas sweater that said "Who you calling a Ho Ho Ho?"—and soon we looked like we actually belonged on Earth. Was Davix devastatingly hot in skinny jeans? Hell, yeah.

We returned the rental car and walked across the road to the bus station, where Krasik-dahé purchased three tickets at the kiosk.

Tiqokh was waiting for us in the parking lot. He went down on one knee in front of me and said, "Dragon Groom, I will leave you now. I am anxious to try my new wings in the prevailing winds of Earth."

I felt a bit teary about his departure. "When will I see you again? Maybe I need you to keep guarding me."

"You are safe, at least for the time being. But I have no doubt we will meet again soon. Though such a concept is still somewhat foreign to me, I believe you and I have grown to be friends."

"You better believe it, lizard man," I said. I thought about moving in for a hug, but that would be pushing him a little too hard on his first day as a friendship intern.

Tiqokh stood and put a hand on Davix's shoulder. "D'gada-vixtet-thon, I remember how difficult it was to adjust to life on the Realm of Earth. But remember that with challenge comes discovery and growth. Trust in your curiosity."

Davix smiled and looked up at the clouds swirling around the mountain tops. "I'm already curious about the winds of Earth, now that you've mentioned them. Those cloud formations are spectacular, and unlike any we have back at home." His smile dropped. "Will we be able to repair the strands, Tiqokh?"

"I hope so."

Our journey was in two legs—bus and train—with a hotel stay in between. In the afternoon of the second day, the towers of Toronto came into view, and I got jumpy and excited as a Jack Russell terrier. I started pointing out everything to Davix, realizing only thirty seconds into my spiel that I was talking English. He wasn't listening anyway. He was staring up at the skyscrapers, taking in the sheer scale of everything. In the Realm of Fire, nothing human-made could compare, and I realized again just how much newness awaited him.

Two boys and an octona climbed into a taxi and headed toward the suburbs. I guess Krasik-dahé phoned ahead, because the taxi hadn't even turned into our driveway when the front door flew open and my mom ran out. She barrelled down the walk and into the driveway so fast, I was scared the taxi might knock her down. In the doorway, my dad was hopping up and down, trying to pull a shoe on.

My heart pounded; so much was about to happen. After today, I would be a different person in the eyes of the people I loved the most. I hoped they could love that new Crispin as much as they loved the old one.

CHAPTER 52: *Rumours of Reunification*

If you don't mind, I'm going to hurry through the sentimental reunion. There were hugs and tears, there were reproaches for having been away so long without calling. I explained that time works differently *there*, and besides, there wasn't any cell signal. Mom, true to form, shifted things pretty quickly to recriminations and blame, mostly aimed at Consul Krasik-dahé, but some at Dad, too. It pissed me off, because even after everything that happened before I left, she still acted like this was all being *done to me* instead of something I had chosen on my own. I was the one who chose to go to the Realm of Fire and fulfill my dragon destiny. No one forced me. So, I put a stop to the fight, basically by shouting louder than anyone else.

"Mom! Dad! I have to tell you something important." Mr. Kapetanos next door leaned back against his garage door, settling in for some entertainment. "Inside. I'll tell you inside."

"What about him?" Mom asked, pointing at Davix.

"He's coming in, too," I said, dragging Davix through the front door before Mom could raise an objection.

And there we were, back in the living room. Remember the living room? It's kind of where this story started—where Dad and Krasik-dahé told me about the copper in my blood, where Mom and the Consul each grabbed one of my arms and pulled in opposite directions. Amazingly, I had the whole scene stage-managed to my satisfaction, which was basically everybody sitting—Mom and Dad on the love seat in front of me, Davix and Krasik-dahé on the couch at my back—and me standing in the centre of the room.

"So," I said. "Here's the thing…here's what I have to say…what I maybe should have told you before, but I wasn't ready, and besides maybe you already…" I ran out of breath and gasped, then coughed. Dad was leaning back on the love seat, tensely casual, his eyes kind of scrambled and hard to look at. Mom, on the other hand, was pure alertness, back straight, eyes focussed on mine like we were the only two life forms in the universe.

My mom takes parenting very, very seriously. There's a section of her bookshelf with a volume corresponding to each stage of my development, from single-celled gamete right through to rolling ball of teenage hormones. For every situation, she always knew the drill. She would sit on the floor with me when I was having a tantrum at age five and encourage me to put my rage into words. When I was nine, she helped me untangle moral conundrums, also known as "Why Crispin shouldn't steal from Mommy's purse." At twelve, also twelve and a half, thirteen, 13.5, 13.6…I got horrifying talks about masturbation, sex, condoms, consent, internet predators and their tricked-out torture dungeons.

Sometimes she did the right thing only after she had a total meltdown, Jekyll-and-Hyding from screaming crazy lady to expert in child psychology over the course of one stressful hour. But whichever incarnation I got, I never doubted she loved me. If she was totally psycho about my dragon blood, it was just because she wanted me to be safe. *But, Mom, you can't protect me from who I am.*

"Dad, Mom," I said, catching a still trough between waves of panic, "I'm gay." What was it that made owning that word so hard? The panic wave caught up with me again, and I hurried to finish what I needed to say before the undertow dragged me down. "I know it's… it's not what you were expecting from your son, especially your only child. But…well, I've known, like, for a long time and…and…" My script eluded me. Tears were spilling down my face, and I couldn't look anywhere except at the floor.

Mom was on her feet in an instant, wrapping her arms around me and pulling my head to her shoulder. "Sweet boy, my little wolf, it's all right, it's all right. We love you. You know that." Dad, who was always tortoise to her hare, joined our huddle, although Mom hadn't left him much of me to hug.

I had to squeeze my words past a glob of emotion in my throat. "I just don't want you to be disappointed in me."

Maybe this situation wasn't as dramatic, but I felt the way I had in the Matrimonial Tunnels, like I was transforming into another creature before my parents' eyes. And like with that other transformation, I was scared I wouldn't survive. But my mom kept talking soothing words, and the sound of her calm voice anchored me.

Dad's voice, in contrast, was kind of choked up, but he told me, "It's okay, Crispin," before lapsing again into silence and taking a step back from the family hug.

Mom said, "I'm glad you felt ready to tell us, honey. Though, of course, I guessed a long time ago. And then your relationship with Altman blossomed..." My shoulders stiffened at that. "I tried to talk to you about it at the hotel, remember?"

I pulled back from her. "Wait a minute. There was no...It wasn't a *relationship* with him. Jesus Christ, Mom."

"Well, call it what you will, Crispin," she snapped back. "And then I ran into his mother at the mall, and I didn't know *what* to say. I had to spin *outrageous* stories to cover for you. I told her to send your love to Altman."

"What? Oh my God, I don't want to hear this." I turned my back on her and found myself facing Krasik-dahé and Davix, who were whispering to each other on the couch in the Tongue of Fire.

"What's wrong?" Davix said. "Why is X'risp'hin so upset?"

"He is telling his parents that he is sexually attracted exclusively to men. The mother is responding that they already knew."

"So, what is the problem?"

To be honest, I had forgotten they were there. And now, hearing that language was messing me up. The dissonance between that life and the one unfolding here with my parents was completely jarring. And I wasn't the only one who felt unnerved, because now my mom was staring daggers at them.

"Excuse me," she said in a tone as icy as a mountaintop in the Chend'th'nif, "but this is a very private family moment. Maybe the two of you could just leave?"

I ran over to Davix, pulling him to his feet. "No, listen. I have something to tell you. Mom, Dad, this is Davix. He's my boyfriend. He had to leave the Realm of Fire and come to Earth, but it's okay. He can stay with us, and we'll teach him English and everything."

This happy announcement didn't go down as well as I'd hoped.

Mom's voice was like glass shards on toast. "I don't think so. You," she hissed at Krasik-dahé. "I'd like you to leave now, and please take the young man with you."

My mouth dropped open, and I squeezed Davix's arm tighter.

"What is happening?" he asked, and I had to actively ignore him. Switching my mind back and forth between two worlds, two languages, was more than I could handle at the moment.

Mom was looking right past us at Krasik-dahé, determined to

make this an adult thing. "Listen to me, Dragon-lady, I am done with all this nonsense. You kept my son from me for five months. Five months! But now he's back, and we're going to have our lives back, too. Take this David person and please go."

I could hardly breathe. "Mom, his name is Davix. And you don't know what he's been through. He had to leave everything behind and run."

She finally looked at me. "Why? Is he a criminal?"

And that's when I got mad. Because, you see, I have the Jekyll-Hyde gene, too. I stepped forward until we were practically nose to nose. "Didn't you hear anything I said? I'm *gay*, you got that part, right? And Davix is my *boyfriend*. Boy. Friend. I love him and he's not leaving."

"Crispin, enough. I want every dragon person out of our house this instant."

"Oh yeah? Well, I got bad news then, Mom. Only two people in this room are one hundred percent human, and that's you and Davix. The rest of us are dragon people. Coppery dragon goodness from head to toe. So, why don't me and Dad and Krasik-dahé leave, and you can have Davix as your new, better son. Oh, sorry, he's gay, too, but you can't have everything!"

"Stop this," shouted my dad, stepping between us like it was a hockey brawl and he was the ref. (See? I can do sports metaphors when I'm all mad and testosterized.) "We do not speak to each other like this in our house. Crispin, Isabel, control yourselves."

I sputtered, "Tell *her* to control herself!"

"I just did."

Mom threw herself down on the couch, crossing her arms and glaring into the corner while Dad took charge. "Consul, is there anywhere else for the boy...for Davix to stay?"

"Dad, no!" I pleaded. He held up a hand, and I bit my lip, going back to Davix and pulling him into a hug.

"What's happening?" he asked again, and I just responded *shh*, and squeezed him harder.

Krasik-dahé, who hadn't moved from her seat nor betrayed the least emotion, said, "Arrangements could be made. I suppose I should have anticipated your mate's reaction. But I think it would be better for Davix if he could stay with the Dragon Groom." Mom snorted angrily at the term, and Krasik-dahé impressed me by saying, "My apologies. If Davix could stay with your son, Crispin."

I held my breath and looked back and forth between my parents.

Then Dad was looking at Mom, too, and we were all just waiting. Mom got to her feet with a groan that made her sound sixty years old and walked to us. I was reluctant to let go of Davix, but he gently shrugged me off and held out a hand, which, after a moment's hesitation, she took. In both hands.

"Please Mom," I said. "You'll like him. He's really smart. And way more mature than me. He won't be in the way. He can stay in my room."

"Like hell he will," Mom said, and I could see the thaw starting in the corners of her mouth. "He'll stay in the guest room until we find a better home for him. I do not trust that consul creature to even know what a human boy eats."

I happened to know that Krasik-dahé was more of a gourmet than my mom, but I answered, "Yeah, good point."

"Are you hungry?" Mom asked Davix, who just smiled. "Crispin, is he hungry?"

I exhaled. Figuring some snark would normalize the situation nicely, I said, "Oh great, Mom. Your own son is standing in front of you starving to death, but go ahead and feed the stranger first."

A week later, I was woken up in the middle of a dream by a strange feeling. The feeling is still hard to describe, so I'll tell you the dream first.

My mom comes home with this enormous bouquet of flowers, not so much enormous in number as in the size of the blood-red blooms, which are as big as human heads. They're in a butt-ugly vase on the dining room table—some rough, hand-crafted thing like you buy at a garage sale and immediately regret. Anyway, it's not long before I knock it over in a typical moment of inattention. Then Inby's there, filling the room with his long, skinny body, sniffing his big snout into the shattered remains.

"THAT'S NOT THE END OF THE STORY," he says, stirring the shards. I watch as they begin to vibrate and shift, drawn toward each other by some inevitable gravity. That's when I was woken by that, you know, *strange feeling.*

It was two in the morning and I was in Davix's guest bedroom, where I snuck into every night after eleven, and snuck out of again at six. Maybe the feeling had been a tiny earthquake—rare in Toronto but not unheard of. Or maybe something *else.* I lay there listening to nothing other than the occasional car on the street and a lingering impression that something had *shifted*. I knew I wouldn't be able to fall asleep again without reading for a while, so I figured I might as well head back to my room early.

Davix was lying with only his lower half covered, and the moonlight through the window made his smooth, firm chest glow silver blue, the dark nipples indigo. We planned to buy him some curtains soon, not that he was complaining. He said he liked being woken by the sun. I fished for my underwear under the covers, pulled them on, and got out of bed.

I navigated the moonlit room carefully, trying not to wake him. Davix's new clothes were folded on shelves in the bookcase. On his desk were sheets of lined paper on which he had written umpteen rows of abc's, like a grade one kid. Beside the sheets was a pile of beginner readers, and on his bedside table, a fat university text on meteorology. He would pore over the illustrations of clouds and diagrams of rain cycles for hours, begging me to translate bits of text into Tongue of Fire. But since I didn't know what half of it meant in English, the process was kind of hopeless. Plus, I hardly needed another subject to study. Mom had gathered a ridiculously huge pile of school material for me so I could write exams in August and hopefully get out of repeating a grade.

I opened the door silently—I was getting good at this—and slipped out into the hall. The guest bedroom was on the main floor, and my bedroom upstairs, but as I snuck through the dark living room, I caught sight of a silhouette at the window and almost cried out. Was it Tiqokh? No, too small…It was my dad. He was wearing a T-shirt and sweatpants and staring out the window into the front yard.

"Crispin? Is that you?" he said in a low voice, turning my way.

"I was just getting some milk in the kitchen," I said too quickly, but he turned and looked back out the window. "What are you doing up, Dad?"

"I thought I heard something. Felt something."

I should have just run upstairs before he decided to quiz me on my late night ramblings, but I was intrigued enough by his statement to go stand at his side.

"I hope nobody can see in," I said, and he put an arm over my bare shoulder.

"Nah, not with the lights out."

My dad was something of a mystery to me. I mean, I knew him pretty damn well, obviously. I knew his moods and when was the best time to ask him for money and stuff, but unlike Mom, he didn't feel the need to say every single thought that went through his head. So, he surprised me sometimes by saying something profound or sad or just kind of wonky out of the blue. And sometimes he surprised me with an on-the-nose comment about stuff happening in my life when I hadn't realized he was even paying attention.

I said, "So, what do you think you felt?"

He thought about it. "It was like something very far away turned and looked at us."

"Ha! Grandma would say it was Jesus and cross herself."

"What did it feel like to you?"

I shifted uncomfortably. "I didn't say I felt anything." But he kept waiting for my answer, so I tried to put the inexplicable into words. "I don't know. Like there was an invitation to a family reunion, and the first RSVPs were trickling in. Like a vase that was broken started to…" I closed my eyes and tried to remember the feeling. "I think maybe it was the other realms, Dad. Like they shifted. Do you think they might return? Is Reunification coming?" He just kind of grunted and looked back out the window. I felt sleep reaching up to reclaim me and leaned my head against his shoulder.

He said, "Your temporary driving permit runs out end of June. We should book you a road test."

I imagined Davix and me in a car, me at the wheel, showing him the world. "I better get some practice, then."

"I have time tomorrow."

"Perfect," I said. "Tomorrow's my favourite day."

About the Author

J. Marshall Freeman is a writer of fiction and poetry, a musician, and graphic designer. He is a two-time winner of the Saints+Sinners fiction contest (2017 and 2019). *Arthropoda*, a chapbook of recent poetry, was released in 2019. He lives in Toronto, Canada, with his husband and dog.